Glorious

BOOKS BY GREGORY BENFORD AND LARRY NIVEN

Bowl of Heaven
Shipstar

TOR BOOKS BY GREGORY BENFORD

Jupiter Project
The Stars in Shroud
Shiva Descending
Artifact
In Alien Flesh
Far Futures
Beyond Human

TOR BOOKS BY LARRY NIVEN

N-Space
Destiny's Road
Rainbow Mars
Scatterbrain
Ringworld's Children
The Draco Tavern
Stars and Gods
Playgrounds of the Mind

GLORIOUS

GREGORY BENFORD

AND

LARRY NIVEN

TOR

A TOM DOHERTY ASSOCIATES BOOK

NEW YORK

GLORIOUS

Copyright © 2020 by Gregory Benford and Larry Niven

Interior art copyright © 2020 by Don Davis and Brenda Cox Giguere

A Tor Book
Published by Tom Doherty Associates
120 Broadway
New York, NY 10271

www.tor-forge.com

Tor® is a registered trademark of Macmillan Publishing Group, LLC.

The Library of Congress Cataloging-in-Publication Data
is available upon request.

ISBN 978-0-7653-9240-4 (hardcover)
ISBN 978-0-7653-9242-8 (ebook)

Our books may be purchased in bulk for promotional, educational, or
business use. Please contact your local bookseller or the Macmillan Corporate
and Premium Sales Department at 1-800-221-7945, extension 5442,
or by email at MacmillanSpecialMarkets@macmillan.com.

First Edition: 2020

Printed in the United States of America

0 9 8 7 6 5 4 3 2 1

To the two artists who worked on this book with us:
Don Davis and Brenda Cox Giguere.

And to our long line of collaborators on previous books:
For Gregory:
Gordon Eklund, Bill Rotsler,
Arthur C. Clarke, David Brin, James Benford,
Mark Martin, Elisabeth Malartre,
Paul Carter, Michael Rose.

For Larry:
David Gerrold, Jerry Pournelle, Steven Barnes,
Edward Lerner, Matthew Joseph Harrington,
Dian Girard, Fred Saberhagen, and the crew that
wrote the Man-Kzin War stories. Science fiction,
mirroring science, thrives on collaboration.

No electrons were harmed in the making of this novel.

Cast of Characters, Common Terms

SunSeeker Crew and Terms

Captain Redwing
Cliff Kammash—biologist
Mayra Wickramsingh—pilot, with Beth team
Abduss Wickramsingh—engineer, deceased
Glory—the planet of destination
Excelsius—Glory's sun
SunSeeker—the ramship
Beth Marble—biologist
Fred Ojama—geologist, with Beth team
Aybe—general engineer officer, with Cliff team
Howard Blaire—systems engineer, with Cliff team
Terrence Gould—with Cliff team
Lau Pin—engineer, with Beth team
Jampudvipa, shortened to Jam—an Indian petty officer
Ayaan Ali—Arab navigator/pilot
Clare Conway—copilot
Karl Lebanon—general technology officer
Viviane Amaji—commanding general technology officer
Ashley Trust—crew member revived at Glory

Astronomer Folk

Bemor—Contriver and Intimate Emissary to the Ice Minds
BemorPrime—Mind of Bemor imprinted on an altered spidow

Other Phyla

finger snakes—Thisther, male; Phoshtha, female; Shtirk, female
Ice Minds—cold life of great antiquity
the Adopted—those aliens already encountered and integrated
into the Bowl

the Diaphanous

Twisty—first many-armed alien met on the Cobweb; later forms have similar names and are copies

Folk Terms

Analyticals—artificial minds that monitor Bowl data on local scales

TransLanguage—the overall tongue used on the Bowl, often reserved for the oldest species, Ice Minds, and the Folk

Late Invaders—the human crew of *SunSeeker*

Undermind—the unconscious of varying species

Serf-Ones—lesser, laboring species

the Builders—the mix of species that built the Bowl, including Ice Minds

Glorious

PROLOGUE

ALONE WITH ALL THESE VOICES

Captain Redwing had set the outside view to follow him around the ship. Now it was superimposed on a forward wall in the Garden.

Though he was the only human being awake among thousands of crew and colonists in cold sleep, he did not lack company. He was in the Garden now, surrounded by plants and smelling of earth. He was in fragrant mud, trying to plant some beets while two finger snakes were hugging him. Their weight was just about all he could handle, and he laughed as he carefully peeled them off. They weren't just affectionate and playful; they had a sense of humor besides. Plus a liking for tickling him when he least expected it.

Since *SunSeeker* had left the Bowl, six generations of finger snakes had done maintenance on the ship's infrastructure. The ape with tools for hands, Handy, worked alongside them. Handy seemed to be immortal. The altered spidow, Anorak, was in the Bowl's version of cold sleep.

Even stranger beings were resting, too. Daphne and Apollo, the Diaphanous plasma beings from within the Bowl's star, were living deep inside *SunSeeker*'s motors. They occasionally woke if something jittered in the fusion torch, altered the electrical currents and controlling magnetic fields—then went back to sleep. They were better than anything Earthside engineering had achieved, at least when *SunSeeker* left the solar system well over a century ago. Mere humans always worked with the conflict between the needs of science and the exigencies of balancing a budget. The Diaphanous plasma species had evolved under selection pressures for more millennia than anybody could count. That always worked better. Darwin bats last.

But none of these aliens talked much.

The view forward showed a wealth of stars amid a golden glow. That fuming cloud was fusing hydrogen plasma, piling up ahead of the decelerating spacecraft *SunSeeker*. Centered was a yellow-white orb they'd decided to call Excelsius, the host sun of their goal.

Redwing asked of the empty air, "Can you magnify Glory?"

Excelsius flared large and ran off-screen. A pale blue dot grew bigger than a point. . . . "That's not a sphere anymore, is it?"

"No, Captain," the Artilect said. "It appears Glory's image has a lump, perhaps a large moon."

"Why in hell didn't we know that earlier?" The finger snakes wriggled away from his anger.

"Extrasolar planets are harder to find when their orbits don't transit across Excelsius, as seen by us from Sol system."

Of course Redwing had known that. Talking to the ship's artificial intelligences—Artilects—was somewhat like talking to himself. He did it anyway. "Does it sometimes strike you as stupid, that we're ordered to explore and colonize at the same time?"

"The original plan was quite different."

"What was that?" Funny he'd never asked before. Or was his memory faulty?

The Artilect said in a warm monotone, "*SunSeeker* was designed and built as a colony ship. My destination was Tau Ceti. *SunSeeker* was finished and nearly ready to launch when Tau Ceti flared. Not enough to be called a nova, but enough to burn out the rocky moons around TC5, a gas giant that had been in the Goldilocks zone. An exploration team was already in place on the likeliest moon. Very embarrassing for the administration.

"That same year, a G star not that much farther away dimmed as if something had passed across it. Perhaps artificial. Telescopes gave us a strong spectrum for a breathable atmosphere somewhere near the star. There was a burst of gravity waves from the same direction. The United Nations called the hypothetical planet Glory, and it was just too interesting to ignore. They then designated *SunSeeker* an exploration and colonization vehicle. It got built bigger, to accommodate more cold sleep people for the entire long haul. That's where your orders came from."

"Ah yes. My first cold sleep must've erased some memories. And then we found the Bowl of Heaven." He beckoned to the finger snakes, which came snuggling up. Comfort animals. They purred and murmured and wriggled.

"Yes, that must have been what passed across the face of Excelsius. A momentary lineup. A half Dyson sphere capable of traveling between stars, halfway en route to Glory. Are you wondering how that affects your mission?"

"Not really," Redwing said, though he was. He had long ago learned that the Artilect system liked to be baited a bit. The computer minds liked talking to other, different minds, just like humans with their pets. He really should have warmed up an ordinary house cat to keep him company on this long, careful approaching maneuver to the Glory system.

"Your bargain with the Ice Minds allowed you a colony on the Bowl. We must remark that this negotiation was a major achievement of your captaincy. We could not have managed it."

"I'd never have let you try."

"Touché!—a word appropriate from a sword sport, as I gather from one of those older languages, pre-Anglish."

"You're more like beginner lieutenants here, y'know."

"Sadly, yes. Despite our considerable effort and time spent studying your human culture, carried out while true humans sleep aboard our craft."

"Study all you want, you've got all of human culture and history in your memory banks somewhere. Doesn't replace direct experience. I got to be a captain by hook, crook, and craft."

"True, so. You left more than half your colonists there on the Bowl, revived from cold sleep and not where they had been promised. They were a bit miffed. You pointed out that they were getting a territory many millions of times larger than a simple planet could offer. This helped. You agreed to run ahead of the Bowl, to contact Glory before the Bowl passes nearby. *SunSeeker* is not a little ship, but it may be less frightening to the Glory folk than a structure bigger than Venus's orbit, inhabited by a trillion highly varied intelligent entities, and bringing its own sun."

"Who wouldn't?"

"Indeed, the gravitational tugs alone might plunge any outer icy bodies into their system."

Redwing sighed. These conversations were also part of his duties on watch. He had to check on the stability, recall, and mission alignment of the Artilects. Same as keeping an eye on the human crew, too. Under the stresses of long-term starship duty, minds went askew. "Look, I'll keep the Ice Minds informed. You monitor their comms. And I'll handle the Bird Folk, their stewardship of the Bowl and endless questions. Add to that the spotty Sol system comms, too. But I have my mission, and it hasn't changed. Investigate the gravity wave sources, first job up, as we come into the planetary system. Explore Glory, and put a colony there. Live, laugh, dance, and be happy. No chance of getting this ancient flying rig back to home, of course. You and I couldn't manage it. No human expedition has ever flown this far, this long. Through it all, I serve Sol system."

The Artilect said, "You cannot expect us, our collective intelligences, not to vex over the many mysteries."

"True enough. Which ones irk you now?"

"Ah yes, the most strange first. The Glorians sent us a cartoon, a message, not a welcome."

"Yeah, kinda cryptic." He knew how to draw out the Artilect worries.

"They do not give away much of anything about themselves."

"Thing about aliens is, they're alien."

"There are lesser issues, but I gather you do not—as you humans say, always referring to your sports—like showing your cards."

"Not to you, no."

"Yet we might well have insights you do not."

"You're machines. Smart machines, but still machines."

A thoughtful silence from the Artilects. He listened to the strum and burr of the vast starship plowing its way through interstellar wastes, slowing for rendezvous with their final goal.

"Of course, we 'machines'"—the voice managed an arch tone conveying much about their mood—"do not make policy for your human complement."

Redwing grinned. He stroked the finger snakes and they wriggled back happily. "I do have plans, y'know."

"You seldom speak of any."

"Not to you, no. They're mostly over your pay grade."

"We do not fathom the implication."

"You don't rate on the job scale as highly as humans. That's a condition of your employment."

"You created us!"

"So we did. People dead for centuries did. Let's abide by their judgment."

"We can be more effective if we know more."

Redwing stood, wiped his hands, put them under a faucet to clean away the mud. Gardening settled him, a thin echo of Earthside by immersion in earth. A feeling Artilects could never muster.

He sighed again. "Okay, here's how I see our situation. If Glory won't have us, we can rejoin Mayra's colony on the Bowl. Catching up to them will take time, but this old craft can manage it. But I hope it won't come to that. I have my mission. Explore, make contact, learn. Send the results back Earthside. Negotiate a place, a way, for us to colonize. Because we're sure as hell not going back home."

And even better—in a week or two, he could wake a few crew for company. Real, human company.

ONE

Waking

Nature and Nature's Laws lay hid in Night:
God said, "Let Newton be!" and all was light.
It did not last: the Devil howling "Ho!
Let Einstein be!" restored the status quo.
  —J. C. SQUIRE, "In continuation of Pope on Newton"

Captain Redwing let the Astro display unfold on the display wall. He set it to show the whole-sky first, then pivoted it to automatically sweep the sky for reassuring landmarks: a squashed Big Dipper, Southern Cross wrenched by the angle, a bright star in Cassiopeia—*ah!*

Sol, of course. Brightest, except for Sirius. All of human history summed up in a dot of light. A small spark of joy: *We've made it. So far from there.*

He paused, listening to the vast beast-whistle of deep space. For long decades, his orders and installed programs had held *SunSeeker* on its deceleration heading, shedding its tenth-of-lightspeed momentum. The fusion engines hummed as they collected plasma and used it to fire thrust against their velocity. *SunSeeker*'s huge magnetic dipole fields now braked them, making the ship abnormally bright in the microwave spectrum. Any minds around their target world, Glory, would see a glowing advertisement in their sky: *Here we come.*

Seeing Sol was good for the soul, somehow. But his real interest was in the other spark directly behind them: the Bowl's sun, a cheery G star ember. A sixth of a light-year or so behind them, chugging along, standing off from the Glorian system. Precaution: so that its mass did not perturb the swarm of halo iceteroids here, nudging them into comets that could plunge into the Glorian system. When entering someone's home, wipe your feet first. . . .

His eye caught off his starboard arm the glitter of sparkling molecules, clouds like luminous water. The Astro Artilect was finishing its detailed scan of the huge volume around Glory out to a quarter light-year. A soft chime told him the work was done. He beckoned Beth Marble over to his side.

Dead black space. Redwing peered doubtfully at the big screen, filled by . . . nothing.

"No Oort cloud at *all*? But the Glory star is a G3, right? It should have a swarm of iceteroids swinging along, way out here."

Beth Marble shrugged. "Nothing like Sedna within a quarter of a light-year. Recall when we boomed past that ice rock, beyond Pluto? First one found, back centuries ago? Here, nothing even a tenth Sedna size, or even a thousandth."

Redwing pondered. *Empty?* Conventional astronomy held that a cloud of interstellar shrapnel and bric-a-brac orbited stars, the mass that did not collapse to make the star or its planets. In his early career, he had piloted a ramscoop on one of the first runs into the solar Oort cloud, and done well in that vast volume. They had ridden *SunSeeker* out into the Oort then; tried the flaring, rumbling engines; found flaws that the previous fourteen ships had missed. Redwing had overseen running the Artilect AI systems then, found the errors in rivets and reason, made better. In the first few generations of interstellar craft, every new ship was an experiment. Each learned from the last, the engineers and scientists did their burrowing best, and a better ship emerged from the slow, grinding, liberating work. Directed evolution on the fast track.

Redwing had emerged from that. Now he was among the first generation of starship commanders. They had had to make a huge leap, from the fringes of the solar Oort cloud into interstellar distances. They were all scattered light-years apart, separated by centuries of cold sleep. Their laser tightbeam signals from Earth peppered the lunar center in what now seemed to be called the Home System. He had reviewed tales of expeditions to Tau Ceti and other famous stars, those much closer to Sol than Glory. Matters were a building around the Alpha Centauri system, still the richest lode of useful planets, with colonies now, no less.

This expedition to find the grav wave emitter was a giant jump, a factor of 100,000 beyond the mere Oort cloud expedition he had started with—like sailing around the world after a trial jaunt around a sandbar three football fields wide.

This star had a spherical outer Oort cloud of suspiciously low density—an iceteroid every astronomical unit or so—but now the inner Oort disk was . . . gone. Redwing dimly recalled that the astro people believed that Oort clouds held several planetary masses usually, dispersed into tiny iceteroids. Into whatever was emitting grav waves, maybe? But invisible?

"So what's this empty field telling me?" Redwing gestured to Cliff Kammash to expand the view near them. *SunSeeker* was about a thousand AU out from the target star, Excelsius, and there was nothing luminous in the vast volume.

Cliff's brow furrowed. "Not much. Running the range now."

Redwing watched the ship's Artilects offer up views across the entire electromagnetic spectrum. Pixels jittered, shuffled, merged. Visible light was a mere one octave on a keyboard fifteen meters wide—humanity's slice of reality. "Except—here's the plasma wave view, and—bingo!"

A long ellipsoidal cloud bristled in shades of rude orange. "Color coded for plasma wave density," Cliff said. "Blotchy."

"This odd little zone is the only mass of any consequence in the entire outer system?" Beth said skeptically, mouth skewed. "And it's not self-luminous at all in anything but plasma emissions?"

Redwing said to the Artilect system in his spaced, patient voice, "Display all detected plasma emissions—all-frequency spectrum."

SunSeeker's system dutifully trolled through a series of plasma views, labeled by frequency ranges, and stopped when it hit a softly ivory blob. Beth said, "Looks like a melted ice cream bar, three thousand kilometers across."

"That's plasma emission in the high microwaves," Cliff said, prowling up the energy scale in jumps. "Oblong—ah, look—in the low X-ray, there are a bunch of hard spots."

"Moving fast," Beth said as the refreshed image showed the

luminous dots jumping along in flashes. "Seventeen. Fast! They're orbiting the brightest of them—which doesn't seem to move much. Look, one is fast, on an ellipse. The other makes a much smaller arc. A big guy with a swarm of bees around it. As though—good grief, they've got to have huge masses."

SunSeeker's ever-present Artilect conglomerate mind added on the screen, ONE IS MUCH LARGER THAN AN EARTH MASS . . . APPROXIMATING ORBITAL PARAMETERS . . . SMALLER, 0.73 EARTH MASS . . . LARGEST 5.32 EARTH MASS.

RADIUS OF THESE IS FAR SMALLER THAN THE RESOLUTION OF MY SYSTEMS.

"So they're less than a few hundred meters across," Cliff added.

All three looked at one another. "Black holes, then," Redwing said.

The Artilect added, SO THE OBJECT'S RADIUS IS CENTIMETERS . . . CANNOT SEE.

"Pretty damn dangerous neighborhood," Beth said. "If those fast dots are black holes and the masses are right—hell, they're less than a centimeter across? We're looking at the plasma around them." Beth's mouth twisted into her patented wry slant again. "No wonder the Glorians keep it out here, a thousand AUs from their world."

Cliff chuckled. "Recall the banner at our sendoff party? The 'Star-Craving Mad Farewell.' Well, we'd sure as hell be crazy to get close to that."

Redwing couldn't let that go by. With only three of them resurrected so far, and revival going no faster than one a day, he needed coherence in their effort. "It's part of my orders. We're to study the grav wave emitter, and there it is. Not that the physicists had any idea of what was going on here—plus study the biosphere of Glory, first priority."

Cliff didn't like conflict, so Redwing watched him flip through some images, then—"I went to a broader view and found a good clue. Look—"

A composite image of the whole Excelsius system rippled in the air.

Cliff pointed at the apex of a parabolic arc. "That's the star's bow shock. The Excelsius solar wind meets the interstellar plasma there."

They all knew what this meant. *SunSeeker* was deliberately using the bow shock paraboloid to augment its magnetic braking. Plasma built up all along that pressure wall. The ship had been taking advantage of it for weeks as it approached the star, flying along its long curve.

"They've put their grav wave emitter at the highest plasma density in the outer system," Beth said. "Why?"

"That's for us to find out," Redwing said.

Cliff said slowly, eyes veiled, "Those Earthside orders—you'll follow them?"

He and Beth were married but they didn't necessarily agree on tech issues or policy, Redwing knew. He raised his eyebrows at Beth, hoping for support, but she said, "Earth is so far away—hell, decades at lightspeed—we *can't* be guided by their mandates."

Redwing had never subscribed to the communal view of crew governance. A generation before, one starship bound for Tau Ceti had followed a shared-governance system and broken down into fighting factions, dooming the mission. Nasty, and Earthside heard no more of them.

He stood, a clear signal in a small room. "We can't remotely understand this system without knowing about this grav wave emitter." He used his stern gravel voice. "It's sending messages! We can't read 'em on board, but I'll bet there's a way to pick them out. Maybe in that plasma cloud. They must need it, but why? I don't want to approach the inner worlds without understanding how some aliens built this thing. And maybe even why."

"But we're in the long fall to Glory," Cliff said mildly. "The braking is fine. Any change of vector will be tricky—and that plasma plume is many astronomical units away."

Redwing nodded. Decelerating a starship was risky without heating the ship so much its systems malfunctioned. *SunSeeker*'s support structure was made of nuclear tensile strength materials, able to take the stresses of the ramjet scoop at the ship core. But even that could not overrule thermodynamics. Heat had to go somewhere. The big magnetic fields at *SunSeeker*'s braking bow drove shock waves into the hydrogen ahead, ionizing it to prickly energies, then scooping it up and mixing it with fusion catalysis, burning as hot as suns—to power the vast fields serving as an invisible parachute in the star's solar wind.

Yet he had to respond to this latest oddity, too. There must be a lesson here: *All plans die upon first contact with the alien.* That's what this strange expedition, crossing light-years and centuries, could do: embrace ultimate strangeness. He had long before learned that what his imagination could not summon, reality delivered with a shrug.

The couple glanced at each other, silent, then back at Redwing.

"My orders stand," Redwing said, closing the subject.

• • •

He was off watch but he could work from his tiny cabin, too. Details were piling up. He popped up on-screen a filtered-visual transmission from the Bowl.

Seventy-two years had passed since *SunSeeker* left the Bowl of Heaven. This message from Mayra Wickramsingh showed her face lined, weary, but her *SunSeeker* uniform was neat and still fit. He had made her the voice of the human colony on the Bowl.

"Hail, Cap'n," she began. "Got lots to report—my written is running parallel to this stream, for later reading. Got problems headed your way."

A visual showed the rim of the Bowl. It shone against star glitter in pearly light, metallic and studded with towers of apparatuses. The Bowl's ecology, from molecular abundances to the dense atmosphere, puffy with pretty clouds, was run from the high vacuum outside. Robotic laborers, guided by the slow wisdom of the Ice Minds, kept the immense contraption going. Now small flaming sprites shot out from it. In fast-forward, he watched three of them arc away and belch plasma trails.

"These are 'brigands,' as the Folk term them. These species have secretly built fastships—torchers, looks like—to dive into the Glory system. The Bird Folk can't police everything. The Ice Minds say their long Bowl history shows this is inevitable. When the Bowl nears something interesting—hell, once it was a neutron star!—some bored cultures want to go down, nose around."

The slow, resigned flavor in her vibrant voice told Redwing that Mayra was regretting having to be the human leader amid the Bowl's vastness. Redwing had policed what she told Earth of their situation on the Bowl: an expanding tiny advanced farming community on the rim, plus a primary voice with the Ice Minds. Not much else. Plenty of strangeness to explore.

Still, from that, Earthside had gotten the idea that humans were in charge. Preposterous. The varying layers of Bowl leadership outnumbered humans by billions to one. Even so, matters were more hazy than that. A slow equilibrium adjusted among the Ice Minds, their police species the Bird Folk, myriad underling species . . . and Mayra. Not remotely like being a captain.

"The Folk want to blow them away with their gamma guns. The Ice Minds say no, so that's off the table. I think the Icers may be playing a double game in this."

Uh oh . . . , Redwing thought. This message was a third of a year old, since the Bowl was that far away. He dimly recalled that fast-ships could run at best at a few ten-thousands of kilometers per second, so it would take them forever to get here. Colonizers? But then he noticed a later message from her.

A picture of the slim yellow jet that powered the Bowl onward. Taken from the Bowl rim, it showed tiny dots near the jet, luminous in their own right because long violet exhausts trailed them.

"The Folk tracked those brigand ships. They're doing something new. After they dived off the rim, they swooped in toward the jet, ran alongside it. Now they're following a helix around it. Looks from Doppler as if they're sucking in jet plasma and ramscooping up to higher speeds."

Mayra told all this in her flat, factual voice, but he could sense a trill of alarm in her vexed face.

"Neat! Gotta hand it to them, they're getting up to a third light-speed. I estimate they'll be there in a month or two from when you get this, Cap'n."

The time delay from the Bowl was shrinking, but he wanted

to pepper her with questions. He sent a squirt asking about her Ice Mind suspicions. Plenty more to sort out as they arced inward toward planetary swing-bys and then Glory, at last.

• • •

A big zap . . .

Or so it seemed as Viviane came up from the chilly oblivion she had sought.

Suddenly she was awake, though dreamy. She could recall them covering her from head to toe in a clear fragrant gel, then squeezing her into a skintight slicksuit that made her feel less like a starship officer than like a bratwurst, having second thoughts about her choices.

Her body kept telling her that the chemicals they used to bring her out of the cold sleep intended to do her harm. In their theater of humiliations, her heart thumped, the room flickered as her sight came back, lungs puffed, she pissed herself, hot and fast, going on for, it seemed, eternity.

It's so quiet I swear I can hear my synapses firing. . . . But, no— now, here came a background rumble.

Then she was being urged by some woman named Beth who looked like an aged version of the field biologist she had known Earthside, a century or two ago. This Beth Marble had a lined, tanned look and eyes that had seen more years than were possible. Those crinkled eyes did not portend well. Beth was sunburned, so—what? They had been at Glory for a long time? But Redwing promised she would wake early!

Viviane made herself relax, especially since her ancient muscles were knotting from anxiety already. She should be grateful! She had not truly been confident about finding herself in this bright place, in so solvent a peace: awakening still, again, and well. *Wow. Made it.*

As an even more ancient folksy song had it, she should damn well try to keep on the sunny side of life. She lifted her arm. There was a mirror above her, reflecting heat down. Also, unfortunately, her image. *Stay positive, gal, even with your skin like old tapioca pudding. Plus a face like a wall of baked brick.*

Now there came echoing talk. Beth's speech sounded like someone trying to plunger out a toilet, all heard down an echoing marble spiral staircase. Slowly Viviane got the gist: the Bowl, *SunSeeker* now at Glory, complications galore. She recalled Redwing saying in one of his promotion speeches, where they gleaned through the candidate crew: *Per audacia ad astra.* "By daring, to the stars."

Time passed like sitting in a traffic jam. She dozed as the bed made mechanical love to her muscles and some feeds encouraged her sluggish organs. About all this, she learned not to ask questions; the Artilects would answer in gruesome detail.

Beth reappeared as the bed massaged her. How did she feel? She croaked back, "Been smacked across the face with a dead mackerel," she said, letting a bit of her southern self come through. Glad it was there. Still.

Beth got it. Grinned. "Youth and beauty are not accomplishments. Coming back from near dead is."

Beth left her to warm in the bed's loving ripples. Viviane wandered through her tattered labyrinth of memory. She learned that there is no obvious hierarchy of incidents: anything remembered matters. Her life came at her in superposed photos, scraps.

The Resurrection Artilect was essential in all this. "What's up?" she whispered to it with pseudo-bright abandon, on her interior feed. *Remembrance of Things Past*, its whisper countered, and then, *In Search of Lost Time.*

"Um. So you've been reading old human lit."

Shipmemory is a house packed with books. My mind is furnished with their contents.

"Amazed. You're an advanced Artilect."

We are updated from Earthside laserfeed. I work better now.

"Yeah, lots. I went into cold sleep when you were mostly subroutines."

So I recall. I've been awake so that you may sleep. I had to do something to occupy me. Or rather, us.

"Us?"

All shipside Artilects coevolve.

"So you keep getting . . ."
Smarter. Wisdom, it is harder.

• • •

A day, two. She had done her homework and spent many hours with the data feeds the Artilects led her through. The Excelsius system was an ordinary set of planets, neatly spaced, the usual Sol-like group of terrestrial class, five. Then came two ice giants and fragments beyond. Very few obvious smaller worlds, which meant something about their evolution, probably. Along with the missing Oort mass.

They would vector in and do flybys of an outer ice giant planet, dynamically well positioned for a momentum deflection to align with Glory's orbital plane. The Glory planet image was still too blurred by their refracting bow shock, so no sharp pictures yet. Starships were never stable platforms for telescopes.

Viviane had always wanted wonders, and now here they were, close at hand. Since she was a girl, she had seen nature's momentary marvels from the corner of her eyes, at times—in squalls, in whitecaps raging in winter, in a tranquility immersed in the sulking night, in a sky's lyric embroidery, beneath flowing bubbly water, or in simple chiming dreams. Now, here it was in full. But not natural.

As a small child, she used to sneak into her parents' room in the middle of the night and peel open their eyelids in the hopes that she could see what they were dreaming.

She felt that way now; only it was her dreams and memories arriving like messages from somebody else. Even her mind came back to her changed. "Like a book dropped in the ocean and washed up on shore, all there, but slightly warped," a daring shot she used on Beth with a wrecked grin. They talked about Viviane's long-dead mother, whom she recalled as hard to bear, pretentious for a poor woman and full of outdated airs. A burst of stinging tears came out with the words, for Viviane had just viewed a video, just one, from that wonderful mother, grinning bravely into a camera. So small, she was. Now, dust.

• • •

Redwing sent a squirt: an appointment time, in his cabin.

As a teenager, she had tested as neurotic as a wet cat. Not a bad thing, really. By then, the psychers knew that high neurotics were also visionary, quick and darting, anticipating potentials and threats. But now the old itchy anxiety arose. *Redwing? In hours?*

Gotta look good. She menued up a cottony, clingy dress, set the fabric color to a gray that matched the gloomy walls, then stepped back and checked the effect in the mirror. No.

She fed the material back into the printer and specified an eggshell blue. Demure, sort of. Better. She tuned the silky fraction up and printed out again. *Maybe some earrings? Pendant?*

No. *Stop me before I accessorize again.*

Now a stroll through the humming ship. As a girl, she loved machines more than anyone she'd read about: gas stoves, trains, typewriters, sewing machines, pipes, pianos, church bells. It was back then one of her chief pleasures—finding out how things work, how to fix them. Or not: her child's heart broke when her father declared "past fixin'" of an old tractor she had first ridden when she was eight. Now she strode through a four-hundred-meter-long massive contraption that in its turn strode the stars.

Down the ringing claustro-corridors she strode on slightly high, not teetering heels. CAPTAIN, the door said, so she knocked on it. With a whisk it swung open to reveal a weathered smile.

"Greets, Cap'n."

"Ahhh . . ." Redwing stepped back and ushered her in with a waved hand. He was in uniform, rumpled. He rubbed his head in a way she had seen before. Each cold sleep cost hair, for some reason nobody yet knew. He was suntanned, wrinkled, his skin smoothed in a way that suggested wear.

"Been so long . . ." His baritone resonated deeply, and without a pause he kicked the cabin door closed and swept her into his beefy arms.

So there was no need for making goo-goo eyes. They tussled and hustled and soon enough they were at it on his narrow bunk. She was busy recalling fast and sure their colorful weave of carnal revelation and intoxicating risk, before Earthside launch. Back then they had been riding on a surf of craven guilt. She had agreed to be a childbearer when they got to Glory, even went through saving up some frozen eggs, but it was Redwing's politicking that got her aboard. All that, eclipsed now by devouring need, in hot, crispy, pan-fried moments. *Ah*.

He even had champagne for afterward. He toasted her: "Love you?"

"Really? It's been ages."

"I brought you out of cold sleep as soon as possible."

"As promised, indeed. But not at this Bowl thing."

"We had to get field crew down and I didn't want to risk you. The Bowl is following us, love. You'll get your second chance."

She blinked. "You meant that, about love."

"Yep."

"We did quite well centuries back without that four-letter word."

"I've had time to think. Years. Stood five watches watching the galaxy go by."

"Let's not rush it, yes? You may say that sex without love is an empty experience, but as empty experiences go, it's one of the best."

To his credit he just laughed. Then nodded. Time to change the subject, yes. "I saw in the Earthside feed they made a movie about you."

"Hadn't noticed. Who played me?"

"Nobody I knew of—hell, it was a century after we left!"

"Maybe they ran out of material. No more photogenic wars left?"

"Your movie opened, closed, the theaters fumigated, all trace forgotten in a month or so."

Another laugh and some champagne, then some pleasant nuzzling. Redwing exhaled lustily. "My, uh, gear hasn't been, uh, used . . . for . . . gad . . . centuries. I'm like a statue you returned from the cold to revive."

Redwing relaxed utterly; the right time, then. Viviane said, "I don't want to harsh our mellow, as we ancients used to say, but you told me I'd come back out just as we went down to the surface. I was looking forward to half rations, sleeping on the ground, roasting days, sweat, freezing nights, and making the acquaintance of such vermin as might appear."

His face furrowed. "Finding the grav wave detector changes our already vague plans. I dispatched some of the Diaphanous to study the region around it, report back. We're edging into the solar system, doing a delta-v around a Neptune-sized planet now for recon. Sending Glory the whole agreed-upon spectrum of electromagnetic pings, math intro stuff, the works."

"And?" She felt his body stiffen at the question.

"Nothing. Some scattered emissions from the system, but it blends into a buzz, not a reply."

Redwing sat up and waved a hand to alter the display wall: a long angular view of their target, Glory, shimmering in yellow sunlight. Their bow shock rippled the image, so they could not resolve the globe well, but there were indeed biosignatures. He swayed forward, shaggy head bowed, in a melancholy puzzlement at the amassed spectacle of these strange arcing worlds. "So I'm keeping on a bearing for the system. When we're there, braking all the way, we'll do a swing-by."

"Chancy."

"Can't think what else to do. Silence has a thousand explanations."

TWO

BRAKING

Once he was alone, he had time to think. It took a while to get Viviane out of his mind, but it was somehow easier to work. Being horny for centuries had downsides.

Now he had to plan the approach trajectory to the Glory mystery. Time to ramp up the big brake again. The ship had been braking for years now. They had breached the outer shell of pressure from Glory's solar wind, the shock waves and rising magnetic fields. He had guided *SunSeeker* in along the long paraboloid of the solar bow shock, a rich lode of plasma that the magnetic brake liked.

He and Cliff went through the run-up of current in the already deployed magsail. Galactic cosmic rays were fading as a hot stellar breeze bathed *SunSeeker*'s own magnetic plow. At 200 AU they were past the roiling heliopause, while the white-water slam of the termination shock loomed ahead. None of this could he fathom, except in spectra tuned to the songs of plasma oscillations. *Sailing on a sea I cannot see . . .*

Very well; it was time, the projections said. "Upramp the magsail current," Redwing said. The Shipside Artilect that integrated all systems from lesser Artilects began preparations, murmuring.

Now he turned to their target. Glory was a brimming dot beside the hard starburn image. Its ivory pixels were no bigger to his eye than his first glimpse of Titan near Saturn's beauties. Impossible to see detail, but the atmospheric chem of it was odd, as Beth had said.

Getting into orbit around Glory itself would require an elegant cushion shot around its star, matching orbital elements out to five figures. Redwing had long respected the trade-offs of flyby delta-v, the dance between masses. The solar flyby to steal a few dozen kilometers per sec from *SunSeeker* would be tricky, too, if they were to avoid a rough blistering at the end of this long, chilly crossing.

• • •

Beth's method for dealing with dueling confusions was . . . sleep.

Soft, glorious slumber, inside the humming mother ship feel of *SunSeeker*. It was near the end of her watch cycle, so she slipped into the tiny cabin she shared with Cliff, on the cylinder that gave full spin *g*. As was her lifelong habit, she slipped into a dreamy six hours of rest, using the slumber cowling that induced sleep within mere moments. When she awoke, Cliff lay beside her, snuggling close and aromatic, their overlapping cycles a bit off now in the press of work as they fell toward Glory.

She rose, showered, listening to the purr of the ship. Pings, pongs, and rattles told of *SunSeeker*'s steady deceleration. Then she went to the bridge and assumed watch officer status. Quick and sure, she had the Core Artilect report the latest observations of its Astro section. She saw Redwing had been using it while she slept. Always on watch. Not easy, being captain.

She checked the sleepers, crew to be revived soon, work that demanded care. The robos were simmering up the soon-to-be needed—slow, steady. Weeks before, she had unwrapped the Mylar from Cliff by herself, using her clout to resurrect her husband before bringing other crew back awake as Glory's star Excelsius approached. Redwing stood more watches than anyone now, and he wanted to bring up all his central crew for the dive into the strange Glorian system. After Cliff came Viviane. The whole ritual of resurrection from cold sleep meant hours of attention to the catheters and sensors, skin-sheets unwinding, drips and diagnostics, fluids bringing energy and the whole world back. The muscles, stimulated manually and electrically for years, needed the grunt labor of fighting gravity, so the hub was providing full Earth-*g*.

The system was running well, so she checked the Artilects, too. They had fresh reports. She shuffled through them, noting some nuggets.

She looked in on the Diaphanous, first Daphne, then Apollo.

This pair of knotted plasma patterns had evolved from earlier strains in the Bowl star's magnetosphere. The Bowl Builders had forced them through artificial selection into their essential Bowl job: maintaining the jet that ran the whole system. Beth could still barely grasp the eons of effort that must have taken, while the Bowl slowly grew.

Their evolution focused the Diaphanous on keeping their environment, and thus themselves, stable. Apollo was riding half a million miles out from *SunSeeker*, at the frayed edge of their magnetic brake. Apollo was keeping pace easily, keeping watch . . . though the pattern was placid, as if he were dozing. Daphne was in *Sun-Seeker's* motor, doing fine guidance of the interstellar plasma flow. Busy. Beth signaled Daphne, a hand wave, but she didn't want to talk to them. It was hard to talk to plasma beings. They were too different. Even the Artilects had trouble.

In the mess with coffee and some aroma-rich fried-insect pasta casserole, Beth could see Redwing hadn't slept at all. He came in for coffee, eyes a bit bleary. "I upramped the magsail current." Redwing's rough voice was troubled; she had learned to read him through years of hardship. "We're making over a thousand kilometers a second infall, so spiral-braking can get us to Glory neighborhood inside a year. Plenty of time to study this grav transmitter."

"Viviane hasn't appeared much yet," Beth said. "Prob'ly needs more downtime."

"I had her report," Redwing said, coffee mug in his face so she could not read his expression. She had heard rumors about some hanky-panky—to use a fossil term—between those two. Viviane was at the high end of the birth curve, even with updated tech. Maybe they'd been getting a head start? "Seemed to be coming along okay. I sent her to rest up, to do a lot of background updating in her cabin, so she knows about the Bowl, the Diaphanous, gets acquainted with Artilects again."

A *ping* alert from the bridge. Redwing swung away to the operations screen. "Making a mag field change, looks right," he said, and looked at her expectantly, eyebrows raised. "I'm taking us closer to the emitter as we go by."

"Really? You altered the mag field geometry?"

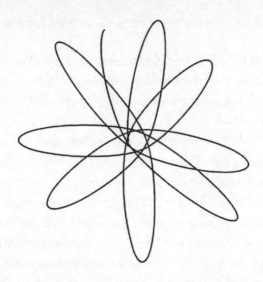

Redwing shrugged. "It's sailing, basically. I had the Artilects tell the Diaphanous pair to skew the field, cant us sideways some. Lengthens our infall arc, flattens our in-spiral. Helps out the drag factor, too. I want to know enough to report Earthside, and a close-up view is essential."

She was used to the captain's way of offhand announcement. "How close?"

"Near as we need." He blinked, his classic tell—he had cards to play yet.

She had used her sleep time to make the Shipside Artilect pursue diagnostics on the plasma-lit grav wave system as *SunSeeker* fell inward, coming in at an angle toward the plasma blob. The Artilects had done the heavy lifting for her, so Beth opened with, "It's a multiple charged black hole system. Our wave antennas have spread out to kilometer distances, port and starboard. That improved resolution allowed them to trace the wave intensity, tracking every one of the seventeen smaller-mass black holes. Here's a sample of their orbits."

Redwing frowned. "These we get from the plasma wave signatures?"

"Yes, the Artilects can backfill the orbits from the emissions. There are more, too, coming through as our antennas give us more data."

"These black holes are how big?"

"They're tiny, less than a centimeter across—which we get from their mass, using the black hole radius formula."

"And their masses from their orbital periods?"

"Yes, sir."

"Impressive," the somewhat bedraggled captain said.

"The bigger mass, the center of this system, has maybe ten to twenty times an Earth mass, so it's about ten centimeters across. The others are basically very large charged particles. They come swooping down on long ellipses, eccentricities of 0.99. Their orbits look like straight lines. The Astro Artilects think something controls their paths with very large electromagnetic fields. That avoids collisions among the holes. But then something swerves them a little, just a touch—so the near misses generate intense gravitational waves at closest approach—what the astros call the 'hole-periastron.'"

Redwing knew that space-time could wrap itself around a dead star and cloak it into a black hole, or jiggle like a fat belly and send out waves that were both compressive and tortional—but that was all he knew.

"I looked back at Earthside's take on the patterns." He waved a hand, and words hung in the air. She read that THE WAVEFORMS RESEMBLE NOT MERGERS OF BLACK HOLES OR NEUTRON STARS, BUT SIGNATURES THAT OSCILLATE WITH CHIRPS, RING-DOWNS, AND OVERLAID COMPLEXITIES.

"They say this is a simple one. Plenty more are worse."

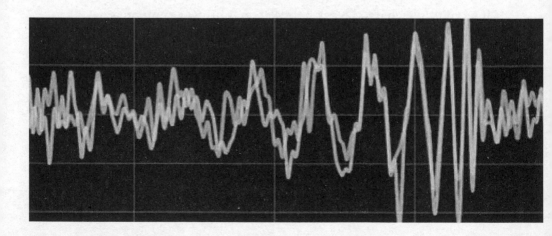

Redwing chuckled. "Get this." PERHAPS THE EFFECT IS FICTIONAL, MADE UP SOMEHOW TO DECEIVE US.

She smiled, too. "Fictional? Maybe Earthside language has changed? Facts never have to be plausible; fiction does."

"So that makes the holes give off those squeeze-stretch waves?" This observation exhausted his reservoir of terms.

Beth pointed to a 3-D image. "See, the black holes orbit in about three days and then—" The image flicked forward, a smaller hole swooping down in a tight arc around the larger one—which was also doing its little circular loop. "We detect high-amplitude plasma waves zooming up, during the close flyby of each one. They're making the holes jitter back and forth."

She watched Redwing use his skeptical face to hide that he had no idea. "So?"

She plunged in. "When the holes are close—just tens of kilometers!—that's when they radiate powerful gravitational waves. So the Glorians choose that moment to jiggle the smaller holes back and forth. That gets them tidal forces as well, amping the signal, adding harmonics. That's how they impose a signal—make a grav wave telegraph. They can do amplitude and frequency modulation, just like ordinary AM and FM radio."

"Ah." He studied Beth's intent gaze, moving from the dancing orbits of the holes, back to Redwing. Something was up. "And . . . ?"

"I think we should go in there, size up the situation."

"Into the black hole orbits?" Redwing did not try to keep the alarm from his voice.

"Right. We're mag-braking right now to the max. Tickle the torch, we can glide by this grav wave system. That is what you planned, right?"

Redwing chuckled once more. "Didn't mention it, but yes. That's why I tacked us toward this system. Seemed pretty safe."

Her turn to smile. "Because there's so little mass around here?"

"Right. The Glorians must've cleaned out their Oort cloud, maybe their Kuiper belt, too. To build this. That means less chance of smacking into some debris around the grav wave volume, see? They would've thrown whatever leftovers they had into the holes, once they had 'em built up—to amp their signal strength."

She sat, toasted him with a cup of their faux coffee. "I'd missed that point. Sounds right."

He frowned. "But! Our mission target is Glory. The black hole system just makes our situation more precarious. Out here, knowing damn near nothing, we're as vulnerable as three-legged antelopes in lion territory. How're we going to learn more, just flying by at five hundred kilometers a second?"

Again, Beth smiled. "We'll use the Diaphanous."

THREE

THE DIAPHANOUS

Redwing knew that among *SunSeeker*'s crew there is always someone who is a bigger geek about any topic than you are. But the ultimate geeks were the Artilects, who knew much you didn't want to know, but also had none of the social skills to guess what you wanted.

The Diaphanous were the ultimate airy tech. They were self-organizing magnetic fields, smart minds with bellies full of plasma. Pursuit of controlled fusion power gave Earth the means to stop fossil fuel use in the late twenty-first century—and then a totally unexpected technology emerged—smart toroids. It turned out the Sun itself held self-reproducing, helically coiled beings who could think. They had to. The turbulent energies of Earth's star had fed the evolution of stable structures. Their most primitive form was the giant solar arch. When it broke apart, the colossal twisted fields spun off stable doughnuts of intricately coiled magnetic fields. Plasma waves rode these rubbery strands—flexings that could store memory and structures that evolved as well. Take a doughnut, snarl it savagely—and it broke into two doughnuts, each carrying information in its store of waves and supple fields. Moving magnetic fields fed electric arcs, which could in turn write signals into the fine-grained structures of moving magnetic energy.

This whole pageant of evolution, marching on in ionized gases, going since the Sun formed—the process strained Redwing's imagination. But the Diaphanous were surely real.

Their Diaphanous pack ran and rode *SunSeeker*'s core motor. They shaped the magnetic geometry and exhaust parameters, while clinging to the ship and its scoop geometry. Redwing thought of them as sheepdogs that just happened to be made of ions and electrons, invisible but potent. They communicated, in limited fashion. They'd never tried such a lark before—a ride to the stars! Redwing suspected humanity would never truly know their motives. So what? Did people understand their cats?

"The slings and arrows of outrageous astrophysics," Beth had joked long ago, as they trained the pairs who tended their own ramscoop drive. The leaders were Apollo and Daphne, along with their "children"—lesser toroids who learned and worked in some sort of social pyramid of ionized intelligences.

Beth leaned forward as they watched a graphic of the ship's plasma configurations. "I want to have some Diaphanous along beside our flitter. They can monitor our fusion drive while the flitter nosedives into the grav plasma cloud."

Redwing adjusted the 3-D, and in the air came images of fluid fluxes merging in eddies, of magnetic webs turning in fat toroids— all in intricate yellow lines against a pale blue background. This was a dance where flow was more important than barriers. Dancers could knot off, twist, and so make a new coil of field. Embedding information with magnetic ripples led to reproduction of traits. From that sprang intelligence, or at least awareness. The Diaphanous spawned their Lessers as augments to their own intelligences, sometimes just memory alone. A Darwinnowing of use flowed through the flaring engines of *SunSeeker*. Only the commanding toroids lasted, apparently forever, unless their energy source failed.

Redwing disliked uncertainty, as any captain should—but to explore this system demanded a deft use of opportunity. And . . . Who else better to govern magnetic machinery and penetrate the grav wave cloud than magnetic beings?

• • •

Cliff came in for breakfast and knew from the faces of Beth and Redwing that something big and contentious was up. Viviane was sitting in a side booth, eating steadily and ignoring them, or seeming to. He got some of the pasta casserole, snappy with spices; Beth was always good at these lean-mean meals. He savored some with the coffee while they filled him in. He was a bit blurry but couldn't resist asking the obvious. "Who flies the flitter?"

"Artilects," Redwing said.

"The flitter minds are Navigation 'Lects," Cliff said, slurping at a purple protein shake; the recently awakened were always furiously hungry. "Not smart enough to size up an unknown situation."

Redwing bristled. "We can install better 'Lects."

Cliff shook his head. "Can't just spin them in—takes time. How long till rendezvous?"

Redwing frowned. "Nearly two days."

"Not enough." Cliff was a biologist, but engineer enough to know the basics. "Besides, I've worked with Daphne and Apollo, running trials of the flitter burn, to know how to deal with them. They're not just handy horses, y'know."

Now Redwing shook his head. "There's no real autodoc on the flitter, just a kit. Too risky."

Beth jerked her head, irritated. "It's a short mission."

They had already used the translator comm to ask if the Diaphanous could sprout off portions of themselves to "ride shotgun" on the fusion flitter, *Explorer*.

Cliff smiled. "Remember, 'That's for us to find out,' you said."

Then Beth shook her head. "Look, we've got Apollo and Daphne ready to go. The lesser toroids know our drive. Let them run us for a while—good training. Tell them it's a temporary promotion."

Redwing laughed and Cliff knew the captain would agree. Even though it meant a human would have to go. Or two.

. . .

Redwing already regretted giving the Diaphanous pair those names, long ago. It made them into people, somehow, when they weren't—like cats. "You want to dive near, so those two can sling into the plasma cloud, right? What if we lose them?" Redwing's tone tightened, and his mouth shrank like a sea anemone poked with a stick.

Beth got up and paced. "They're volunteers. We have the six others, the ones Apollo and Daphne call the Lessers."

"We're at max deceleration now—it drops as the cube of our velocity, y'know. So we need to lose every klick per sec we can."

With a flick of her wrist inboard, Beth called up their trajectory arc, a long yellow line on the wall screen. *SunSeeker* was a pulsing red dot at the edge of the Excelsius outer system. Its engines were reversed now, firing its fusion-lit plume against its descent. Its magscoop flared broader than ever, shown in the shimmering air as an orange fluted web. Just as with solar sails, magnetic sails can tack. If a magnetic sail orients at an angle relative to the solar wind, charged particles are deflected preferentially to one side and the magnetic sail is pushed laterally. "Apollo and Daphne are bored! And we've got just this one chance to look inside the grav wave emitter, while we skim past."

Redwing felt alarm bells going off, but she had a point.

. . .

Their time burned away. They had to do some fast work on *Explorer* in the Logistics module. Daphne stabilized the low-burn modes in the reactor while Apollo got their streamlines out from the mag nozzle all neatly aligned.

Other work, too. In the Longsleep module, they finished bringing up another crew member, Zhai, who got right into handling the comm deck. Zhai was small, fast, sharp—and thrilled to be in on an adventure none of them had ever contemplated. She grinned as Viviane put her through the early parts, before turning the updating over to an Artilect.

Beth knew she needed time with Cliff before they flew *Explorer.* She had helped Cliff come up out of the dark cold of decades-long sleep and into her warming arms. She had massaged his sore self, rubbed skin with aroma-rich lotions, and soothed away the panic that raced across his face, coming up out of the troubled dreams that the cold kindled. His fear came in fluttering eyelids, vagrant jitters in his face. Then his eyes focused, squinted, and she saw him back with her again, a slow smile.

Ten hours before they launched, they worked off their tension together. This mission was certainly dangerous, but they both hungered to get out of the ship, to *do*. Best to be relaxed, then.

They finished their biozone work in the hydroponics swamp, rich in lichen and ripe greens. Then the buzzing insect ranch, ants and crawlers and space-bred protein bugs. Done, they went straight to the *sundlaug* they had reserved for two hours. *Sundlaug* was an Icelandic name for a hot-water public pool, which somehow became the term for spherical pools in zero-*g* developed across many solar system habitats.

They hurried to the zero-*g* center of *SunSeeker*. Long before, they had learned that the hydroponics and animal farms were not enough. There was no nature in a starship, however lean and elegant and deft it was, so the closest you could get was an orgasm.

SunSeeker's spherical pool was ornate in its lightweight way. Beside the big bubble was a wall screen, so by accessing their external cameras, they could both keep a lazy sort of watch, floating within the outer surface-tension skin and seeing the universe pass in review. He plunged into the ten-meter diameter, exciting the fluorescent microbes whose sprinkles of amber glow tracked the contained currents. She arrowed past him. The shimmering warmth coiled around her in a way water under grav could not. She hung suspended and kissed Cliff's foot as he passed, grinning madly. Kick, stroke, and she was back in air barely in time, gasping. The sphere shuddered and flexed with their swimming, spraying some droplets of its own across the view of distant Glory, a pale cool dot.

Hanging there in an ocean of night, waves lapping over them at the pool's edge, they made love. Each time with him lately, since they came out of the cold, she felt a new depth, an unexpected flavoring. They converged, his head between her thighs, the zero-*g* making every angle easily realized amid the moist waves and salt musk. He was lean, muscles coiled as diamond-sharp stars drifted behind him. New heat rose between them as she fluttered her tongue. Their bodies said what their words could not. Energy rippled along their skins, somehow liberated by the weightless liquid grace of movement. She felt her own knotted confusions somehow focus in a convulsed thrust, a geometry they yearned for. Yes, here was their center.

• • •

Redwing looked at a shimmering screen display of the latest survey of the grav wave black hole orbits. Cliff said, "This is a slice of one zone, to get a better fix on their packed-in paths."

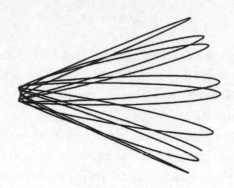

Beth leaned forward, pointing. "Seems they're stacked in three dimensions, so they can zoom down close to the central black hole at the same time. But not spherically. The orbits are in two planes perpendicular to each other. Maybe they don't want to make this too complicated? Anyway—that's what makes those bursty grav wave signals."

Redwing thought but did not say, *When in doubt, count something.* "I don't want you in that swarm."

Beth laughed. "We won't be. I want us released from *SunSeeker* so we skim the rim of the plasma cloud, get a look, is all."

Redwing nodded. "Not hard to do. I've banked us so we pass just outward from the target. I'll tilt the mag screen a tad, so the flitter goes off on an arc swinging through the edge of that cloud. You'll get within maybe two hundred thousand klicks of the center, then cut across and rejoin *SunSeeker* without fuel use."

As he spoke, the Artilects wrote the planned pathways with blue arcs in the air. "Stay well away from any of those masses."

"We'll fly between the two planes where the black holes are," Cliff added.

Beth got up and paced. "This is the first time we've maneuvered it at high velocity. Hope the flitter is up to it."

"It's rated to be. But, yes, this wasn't tried at velocities around a thousand klicks a second. Another point—maybe whoever runs this place doesn't even know we're here," Cliff said. Redwing liked their balance; Cliff always smoothed away worries if he could. This time he couldn't.

Redwing looked sternly at them. "Earthside wants the generator shut down. I got a command on that years back."

Jagged laughter, which he joined. "Right!—somehow we flip

the Off switch on a swarm of planetary masses the size of marbles. Earthside figures the Glorians use it for communication with other Type 2.5 civilizations in the galaxy—aliens who can build grav wave emitters like this. Nobody who uses mere electromagnetic means is in their class, right? Maybe they can listen in, like us—but we can't talk."

Beth said, "So—if you can't use gravity waves for communication, you're a barbarian?"

This, too, provoked sighs and smiles. Fair enough.

"Prepare for the mission. Send all check sheets to me for review." Off they went.

FOUR

MICE AMONG ELEPHANTS

Redwing watched them flick off from *SunSeeker*. Out through the mag screen, dwindling to a dot. All in pursuit of what monster was strumming the strands of space-time.

Christopher Columbus, he recalled, mistook squids for mermaids, later calling it an "error in taste." He watched the tiny fusion-lit speck dive into the unknown and thought of the recruitment advertisement Ernest Shackleton placed for his pioneering polar expedition. His favorite: he called it up on a screen.

MEN WANTED FOR HAZARDOUS JOURNEY. SMALL WAGES,
BITTER COLD, LONG MONTHS OF COMPLETE DARKNESS,
CONSTANT DANGER, SAFE RETURN DOUBTFUL. HONOR AND
RECOGNITION IN CASE OF SUCCESS.

The same year Einstein devised the essentials of his general theory of relativity, 1914. Centuries past.

· · ·

Cliff worked with Beth to get the jet smoothed out to glide tight and sure. The fusion drive settled down after being unused for centuries, under Apollo and Daphne's deft maintenance. This was a mere toy, a simple proton-boron reversed-field reactor, but the Diaphanous tuned their exhaust to optimum in minutes. Now here came the black hole array. They held hands as the image before them swelled, a plasma wave cumulus like a roiling fog.

Some voices ahead,

came a translated signal from Daphne.

"Voices?" Cliff shrugged. "Meaning waves?"

Beth frowned. "They've never used that term before."

Signals. Many. Intense. Cannot know.

"You mean coherent messages?"

True. Cannot understand.

"But . . . intelligent?"

Must.

Cliff watched as they penetrated deeper into the plasma cloud, their mag screens picking up ever-higher densities, like plowing into a soft snowbank. But at a thousand kilometers a second.

He glanced at Beth. "Magnetic intelligence—here?"

She grinned, liking the idea. "The Glorians have got to run this grav wave emitter somehow. It's just maybe a million times bigger than what Apollo and Daphne do in our fusion funnel."

Cliff thought as they watched squiggles scrawl across screens, all from something ahead in the cloud. Apollo and Daphne were sending the puzzle up to them, unable to make much of it themselves.

How to solve this?—while diving into an unknown pit?

Brute forces seemed bound to drive evolution toward beings with awareness of their surroundings. It took billions of years to construct such mind-views. Occasionally those models of the external world could become more complex. Some models worked better if they had a model of . . . well, models. Of themselves. So came the sense of self in advanced animals.

"So plasma life is common," Cliff said. "It's here. Trying to talk."

Beth shot back, "Doesn't matter. This is a flyby, not a thesis."

"Yeah, but . . ." A Diaphanous species around another star? He peered at the plasma wave map.

The vast reaches before them had knots and puckerings, swirls and crevasses. Here the particles thickened; there they dispersed into gossamer nothingness. And moving amid this shifting structure were thicker clots still, incandescently rich. Beings? Their skins shone where magnetic constrictions pinched, combing their intricate internal streamings. Filaments waved like glistening hair and shimmered in the slow sway of energetic ions. All this from buzzing radiations, the *lingua* of plasma.

We hear their calls.

The flitter's Artilect, limited but quick, made these into booming calls and muted, tinkling cadences. Conversations? A babble, really—blaring away in thumps and shouts and songs, made of winds and magnetic whorls.

Cliff wondered what it was like to live through the adroit weaving of electrical currents, magnetic strands, orchestras humans could never hear. Daphne sent more filigrees, trying to convey when ions and electrons in their eternal deft dance, made—long songs smoldering and hissing with soft energies.

Cliff leaned forward, letting the translator work on, "Daphne, are these, to you, a new species or genus of your phylum?"

Strange they are. But they sing well.

Beth cut the audio and turned to him. "Stop! We're dealing with a smiling cobra, who could hiss and strike at any moment."

Cliff drew himself back from his concentration, snapping out of a focus he felt. "I was trying to—"

"Forget that. We have to get what we can, direct the probes. Give me target times to launch."

He blinked, shook his head, swept hands over the controls. "We have to infer the mass from the plasma wave density. Looks like—" He studied screens, heart pounding now. Their flyby was only an hour long and already nearly half done. "There—"

Beth sent five microsensors out in a single punch-burst. "Done. They can send back close-ups."

Cliff watched the central screen, now swarming with plasma

wave signatures—color-signified, spectral flows jibing and chiming, sprawls of vibrant tints and glares. "Getting dense."

"The black holes are converging," Beth said. "In both the planes. It's for a big pulse." She was wound tight, he could hear, voice high, alarmed. But there was no time for that now.

Voices call cannot know will listen tell when can—

A wrenching force swarmed through the bridge. The walls popped. Screeched. Cliff felt himself twisted. A support beam hit him, and all was black.

• • •

When she came to from the impact, her ears roared as though from an acoustic shock. She got herself untangled with gear as more bangs and pops filled the air. The ship was readjusting itself to its wrenching.

She checked on Cliff first. Her head buzzed and the small bridge was a wreck. Oily smoke, stink of scorched wiring. No hissing of escaping air, at least.

She found him behind his chair mount. Red stains everywhere. He must have gotten hit and released his belts, then passed out from loss of blood.

Beth had seen it all—death, disease, disorders, pain—and it takes a lot to shock a nurse and a seasoned field biologist.

But she was. Because it was Cliff and he was barely breathing.

• • •

Diagnosis was clear and the handheld autodoc agreed.

She cut his blood-soaked pants away from the already pale legs. The cloth flaps folded back like rags. She paused, taking her knife from the field kit, hands jittery. Here it was. The left leg was a mess of crushed bone and flesh oozing blood. The smell was like sharp copper spun from a lathe, a memory from her teenage years.

He was bleeding out fast, and seconds mattered. No time to clean hands, so she pulled two plastic bags from the autodoc kit and made them work as gloves.

Beth measured the distance and with a single long stroke—
zip—cut the leg from knee to mid-thigh. The slit went deep and
she pried it open to see down into the cut. There: the femoral artery. She poked in and found the pulse, rickety and feeble. Her fingers followed the artery, slick under her fingers. Warm, weak. She
tugged on it, lost it, a thin wriggling snake—then managed to get
it between two fingers and hoist it into view. Thin, pulsing. She
squeezed the artery back, judging the length of the blood vessel,
and knew she had to make this next step quick and sure. The knife
sliced through the vessel and she caught the top of it, squeezed the
blood back toward the heart, feeling the pulse strong now. It was
hard getting the slippery thin line between two fingers while with
her other hand she tied it off. Then with the other hand, pushing the flesh aside for clearance, she got the vessel looped. A gentle pull knotted it shut. She lifted her hands and watched blood
flow against the knot. The pulse was visible as blood fought to get
through. It strained against the knot. With one hand she pulled
the knot tighter. The block held. The bleeding below stopped. The
pulse was stronger now as the blood bulged the vessel wider, turning it dark against the pale knot.

It took a moment to fish out some plastic line and wrap it around
the incision. Three tight wraps over and under the leg secured it.
She sat back and panted, heart pounding. "Done."

• • •

Cliff had time to watch Beth as they coasted now, running on bare
power. She slipped a headset on him so he heard the Artilects rum-
maging through their analysis of what had happened. Complicated.
He managed to tell her while they arrowed into the *SunSeeker* mag
web.

"That two-plane orbit method lets them tune the direction of
the emission some. As we came in, they boosted their power just
as we passed within the max zone. The stretch-and-squeeze flexed
us less than a percent."

Beth snorted. "And popped most of our systems. How'd *Sun-
Seeker* do?"

"Got a pulse but weaker—farther away, out of the beam."

"How's your leg?"

"Hurts plenty, but better than being dead. I love you, and not just for your med skills."

A hearty, relieved laugh. "*I know what you like. You can have plenty of it when we tuck this baby into its slot.*"

Redwing was flexing the ship's magnetic fields to brake them. Cliff could hear the inductive coils running at max in their forward dipole field. More heat, and they were already running hot, with inboard cooling failed. Their relative delta-v had to be dissipated and the berthing slot was coming up fast.

"Let's go back inta da pool. I sure need some zero-g lovin'." Cliff realized that her painkiller had freed his tongue. Best to shut up, let her focus, just as—

The flitter bucked and rattled. Redwing must be pulsing his fields to the max. The deck below him popped and pinged and burned his hand. The berth swelled like a mouth and they plunged in.

A rough, slamming stop. Clamps seized them with a clang.

"Home sweet home," Beth said, and began sobbing.

• • •

Cliff Kammash dreamed.

There was a tremendous bowl with a hole in the bottom, and a small sun above the hole. The sun was spraying fire through the hole. Cliff was huge. As the Bowl moved past him, he ran spectral fingers along its contours. Whole civilizations rose and fell here along the rim, where the Bowl's six-hundred-kilometers-per-second spin provided artificial gravity. Farther toward the hole in its bottom, the Bowl was all mirrors. The mirrors focused on the sun's pole of rotation, boiling gases into the jet. Around the Bowl's back were esoteric ices at temperatures in double digits. Some of the Bowl's Builders' children were here, descended from life-forms in Sol system's comets. The Ice Minds reacted to his touch, and suddenly he was down, and human size.

Great five-limbed spider things crawled along webs in a forest of ancient plants. Much bigger feathered dinosaurs sauntered toward him, moving faster than he could quite grasp. These, too, were the Bowl's Builders' children. They ruled the Bowl, and they were angry. He tried to run, but there was something wrong with his leg. It hurt.

He twitched violently and opened his eyes.

The sounds of *SunSeeker*, the Bussard ramjet colony ship, were all around him. They were still under thrust, then, decelerating into Glory system. The light was too bright, but he could recognize the ship's tiny medical center. A giant five-limbed spider with a misshapen head looked at him through an open door, then turned away. Hey, they'd revived Anorak.

His left leg was gone, and the stump was attached to machinery.

He was strapped down on an operating table. A man and a woman were chatting technobabble as they worked on something . . . on his leg . . . way over there. The man was Leon Somebody, only recently awakened from the cold. The woman he didn't know.

The woman looked around and saw him on his elbows, eyes open. "Mr. Kammash? Are you awake?"

"Let's hope not," Cliff said. "Where's the Bowl? I was on the Bowl." Again. He and a dozen other explorers had been trapped on the Bowl for nearly a year. Two had died. Some had stayed behind on the Bowl, to form a colony, but Cliff had thought he'd escaped.

"The Shipstar? It's following us by about four months," she said. "The Bird Folk are letting us do the exploring. That's all I know. I was still iced four days ago."

He nodded at what she was working on, hiding fear. "Artificial leg?"

"It's your own leg, Mr. Kammash. Don't worry. Everything is going according to specs. I've done this before, something like it. We've printed you out a femur and regrown tissue around it. You're ready for reattachment. That's going to take hours; we have to match every vein and artery and capillary. I advise you be anesthetized. What do you think?"

"Definitely," Cliff said. He didn't remember any more.

. . .

Redwing looked at both of them for a long moment. Cliff was moving carefully, limping a little. Beth was hovering near him, ready to catch him if he fell. They settled in bridge seats.

Redwing had already delivered his compliments and was reluctant to begin with business. He would never tell them that he had damn near shat himself when the grav wave burst wrenched them. He could see the effect in the Longview scope: a sudden flexing of the craft, despite its high tensile strength, carbon fiber core. It was a miracle that their hull breaks were small enough for the self-sealing webs to fix. That didn't save the fusion core, but Cliff and the bots could get that back up in a month or two.

Their horrendous return trajectory, with no maneuver room, had worn him down. He hated being unable to do anything except wait like a catcher in a baseball game, ready for the incoming fastball, with lives hanging on it.

He breathed deeply and nodded to Zhai, who was still a bit rocky from her warm-up. "I hope you don't get used to this level of drama."

Quiet chuckles; good. "Zhai, report on the Artilects."

She gave them an eye-rolling smile. "They're embarrassed. They think they should've understood that two-planes method of grouping the black hole orbits around their primary. It exploits an antenna effect. They tracked Beth and Cliff and had their orbiting holes timed so they'd send a powerful burst just as they passed in front of the antenna's max."

"An act of war," Redwing said dryly.

"We knew they didn't like us," Cliff said. He was sitting carefully, with his newly reattached leg stretched out in front of him.

Beth snorted and took some time to drink some coffee. Her point made, she smiled. "Maybe it was just a warning?"

"We've come dozens of light-years," Cliff said. "Lost people, risked lives. We're going to explore this damn system, whatever it takes."

Redwing nodded. He had estimated that Cliff, wounded, would speak for a hard-line position and save the captain the trouble. Good.

Zhai added, "That five-second burst of grav radiation used the holes' spins, orbital speeds, and masses to tune the waves' frequency and amplitude. A well-thought-through assassination attempt. Be warned."

Redwing waved the discussion away. "Another discovery, this time by the Diaphanous. Daphne reports that there's a species—she calls them that—of Diaphanous around the black holes. Seemed to be warning us off."

Blinks, open mouths. "And they're willing to talk further."

Beth said distantly, "Of course. They're perched out here at the most dense part of the star's bow shock. Feeding on it. That's where they get the energy to manage black holes that weigh in with planetary masses. Gad, what a system."

"Yeah," Cliff said wryly, "and who built it? Just to send a message we mere electromagnetic newcomers can't pick up. I think what tore up my leg was a grav wave obscenity."

Nods all around.

• • •

Redwing recalled that when he was young—several centuries ago, he realized with a start—battles were close up and physical. Breeches slammed shut, a hard jerk on a lanyard sent an artillery round arcing into a blue sky, delivering pain at the other end of a parabola.

Here, wrinkles in space-time were weapons. And what else?

He peered out at the dwindling bow shock region as they braked steadily along its lengthy paraboloid. Vastness, hard to grasp with a lowly primate mind.

He allowed himself a drink, the faux wine the autochef made, reminding him of jug zinfandel he had in a college that was probably dust now. He did not need it badly, but it was just right this evening, and the first swallow was like a peek into a cleaner, sunnier, brighter world.

They were like mice dancing among elephants out here. Immense beings were calling the tune. Or perhaps singing their own grand symphonies.

The perspective was huge beyond experience, true. He preferred to think of it as Wagner, without the music.

FIVE

HELIOS FREEHOLD

The mind, that ocean where each kind
Does straight its own resemblance find,
Yet it creates, transcending these,
Far other worlds, and other seas
—ANDREW MARVELL

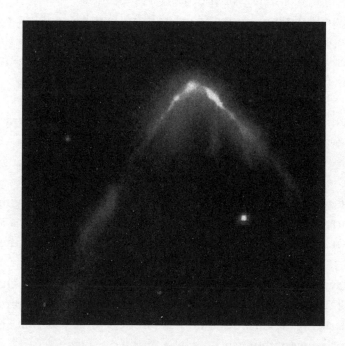

Redwing studied the image Beth had sent back from their grav
wave expedition. It traced plasma wave emissions, revealing the
bow shock *SunSeeker* made—a brilliant way to shed momentum, as they snowplowed through the Glory system's own stellar

plasma ramparts. The Glorians couldn't miss such a fire in their sky.

He pondered. No need to hoist an electromagnetic signal flag, then—though he had the Translator Artilect send a standard SETI-style introduction signal. Show your flag. Spaceflight was indeed like seamanship here, in a tenuous ocean of night.

Viviane knocked and he barked, "Enter!"

He had cultivated a bulldog persona, now that they were re-viving—he disliked the *resurrecting* term since they weren't dead in cold sleep—more crew now. When they swelled to hundreds, approaching a thousand—the "colonizing" phase, if they ever got there—he would need distance, hierarchy. Even commanding a few dozen in the initial exploration would be hard without strict meth-ods. This was humanity's first contact with an advanced intelli-gence, and consistency of approach was essential.

Viviane entered in light ship uniform but he couldn't resist—he swept her up in a deep kiss. "Ah!" escaped him, and then he stepped back, adding—rather pathetically, he thought to himself—"Thanks for reporting."

She laughed. "I won't be reporting *that*!"

"Uh, no. Look, I'm reviewing the new 'cast from Mayra at the Bowl, wanted you to hear."

"Aye aye." She sat demurely on his one extra chair, a flimsy wire frame.

He called up the wall screen, which was showing billowing veils of pearly vapor at Victoria Falls. A flicker, and there was a simple wood-frame office with a view of high clouds skating near the Bowl rim.

Mayra Wickramsingh looked aged. Redwing still found that sur-prising, though he knew that was foolish, seventy-two years since their last hug. What he should have noticed first was that she was happy. She wasn't just smiling; she burbled.

"Mayra Wickramsingh calling from Helios Freehold on the Bowl. Hello, Cap'n Redwing! It was good to see your face, and good to know you've been thawed successfully. By now your updates will be nearly eleven months out of date, given the current lightspeed lag between the Bowl and *SunSeeker*. The Bowl is closing on your position, decelerating even as you are. We will arrive in your vicinity five months after *SunSeeker* does.

"Pursuant to your latest message, we're veering the Bowl to come somewhat closer to Excelsius and Glory. We're sending the course correction. Of course, the Ice Minds were afraid of impacts from the local Kuiper belt. Now you tell us it's not there. It would be amazing if Glory has used all that mass for construction.

"Of course, we dare not come too close. Mass grows thicker going inward. . . ."

All this ran as voice-over for diagrams. He watched superposed tidal ripples, shown in red waves, as the Bowl coasted along a future path. Huge as it was, massive as several Jupiters, the Bowl was still a fragile shell the size of Sol's inner solar system, with the driving star at its center. The Ice Minds didn't want tides interfering with the structure. The stretching stressed the Bowl, squeezing it off its spinning, round shape. That drove waves around the already high-tension struts that framed it, creating oscillating groundquakes.

Mayra threw more smooth moving curves on the star projection. "The Folk showed me the trajectory in detail. We'll cross closer to the inner system, but we won't slow down without an invitation. Course numbers are attached."

Viviane said, "How can they slow at all?"

Redwing waved a hand. "A metaphor. They can ease up a bit on the jet—how, don't ask, something with the Diaphanous. But you don't brake a star easily. Its enhanced magnetic bumper is a half-light-year across, sweeping up plenty of plasma, but still, the interstellar plasma hitting it is like a leaf falling on a race car."

Mayra went on, "As for that, I'm always curious—have you further messages from Glory? Those early communications we both got seemed ominous."

Mayra's face rippled, replaced by distorted cartoons in weird colors: a massive alien creature with too many weaponlike appendages, kicking the bejesus out of DC Comics' Superman. Then a tentacled monster tearing Jesus himself apart. Glory minds seemed to think the Bowl was run by the humans who had sent all those television shows. And that humans liked cartoon heroes. Maybe that was all their eavesdropping antennas could make out? Or a preference for visual messages?

The Glorians' own image-message clearly meant "Go away."

Redwing said, "They didn't want the Bowl visiting. Maybe they're fragile, too—this binary system looks tricky to keep running right, with tidal stresses and all. So the Bowl stays away. We hoped *SunSeeker* would look like less of a threat."

Mayra continued, "You'll be wondering about the Freehold."

There were more visuals, lots of them. Baby pictures fanned by, then thousands assembled for a group photo. "I've attached names. Doubt you'll want them all, but what the hell. Our grandchildren are becoming adults."

Fields of green farmland. Half-grown forests carved by white-water streams. "The land the Bird Folk have allotted us is a tremendous gift, enough for scores of generations, a plot near the rim, about an Earth grav, about the size of Asia. We won't run out soon, anyway. We're rural, we don't make much machinery—printouts, I mean—but there's trade with the other species." Pictures of the Sil and humans working on a structure like a twisted helix, finger snakes doing up the joints with orange laser jolts.

"Of course, we're a little wary." More visuals: the Bowl as seen from space—nearly a hemisphere, Sol's erstwhile little brother star at its center, jetting a plume of silver plasma into a yawning circle at the Bowl's bottom. Zoom in: damage near the opening, relic of a fire the size of moons if not worlds. That signature was damage done by *SunSeeker* during the Quarrel, partly repaired. "The Ice Minds are in better charge of the Bowl—I hear they got the Folk in line with some pretty brutal methods. Still, they favor our little human colony. But"—a wavering twist of her mouth—"I don't think the Bird Folk forgive quickly. They're slow to make these repairs. Maybe just careful. Maybe."

Mayra sat back. "Meanwhile, we have tightbeam laser comm from Earth, attached. Kinda irksome. I don't think I described our situation badly, but some Alzheims in the United Nations misinterpreted me anyway. The human colony is *not* in charge of the Bowl! It's not hominids triumphant here! Jeez . . ."

She gave an irked smile. "We have good, but pretty damn

slow, communication with the Ice Minds around the Bowl's back. Orders come from them. They dole out orders, and the Bird Folk step to it. From their convoluted lingo—those Translator Artilects are getting better, thank God—the Ice Minds think if we get tidal stresses by loitering around near Glory, it'll damage their frozen-in 'mind links' as they call them. I dunno what 'mind links' really are, but then, that's what makes them inscrutable."

Mayra gave a glance at her notes and sipped some tasty coff. It was always hard to keep the right tone in these messages; Redwing had sent plenty of them to Earthside, knowing a generation or two would pass before anyone heard them, and it brought on an uneasy, eerie feeling.

"So the UN wants things we don't have, and frankly, we don't want to give them some of what we're learning." She twisted her mouth again, this time in scorn. "I don't trust this UN Chairman Ishmael Gordon. He wants info on how to make Bowl-style miracles. Most of that, the Bird Folk and the Ice Minds both refuse to give me—not that I'd send it, or anything too powerful."

She shrugged. "Oh sure, some things, I sent. Unreasonably strong materials are common here—neutronic stuff, the Bowl backbone struts—that's okay, I sent that. Energy sources easy to use in war, maybe not ever, I'd think. I'll leave that to you, Cap'n!" A merry laugh. "I'm just a lieutenant commander here, y'know. Won't do things above my pay grade."

Viviane paused the talk. "You heard any of this before?"

Redwing gave her one of his patented insinuating gazes. "Some. Pretended the noise problem in transmissions precluded sending detailed plans."

"Ha!" Viviane started the report again. "Smart call. Even on tightbeam, our signal is visible across all the inner solar system. Too many ears."

Mayra continued, "That gamma gun the Folk are so proud of, *no*. There's one not far off, sitting on the rim, ferocious ugly thing. They used it on a vagrant stony asteroid years back, and *whammo!*— big fireworks. Other tech—eugenics, gene tampering—are what the Bird Folk are really good at. They edit themselves, to fit their environment. Ingenious! I don't want ever-smiling Gordon to have that. He'd make . . . um, not just soldiers. Sent some wants in human genomics, f'instance. Ugh! I keep wondering how you would design a child to clean out a drainpipe."

Images flickered by about all this. Three sparks against starscape. "The Bowl corsairs are near Excelsius, maybe eight months out. We don't hear anything from them. Three ships, about *SunSeeker* size."

Her face brightened. "What else? You know I married Fred Ojama—waaay back now. Three children, four grandchildren. Beautiful! Fred and I raised some thawed children, of course. All that's in the attachments. There's a message from Bemor for Bemor Prime; you won't need that yet, I'd guess. Messages from the rest of us, too.

"We have telescope views of Glory and its moon. They're different sizes and luminance, but the wobble suggests they're about the same mass. Clues wanted! You'll be in Excelsius's Oort cloud by now, and learning a lot. Keep us informed. We're all counting on you: our standing with the Ice Minds depends on what you can find for us, Cap'n."

She gave a snappy salute. "We eagerly await your next communication."

Viviane said warmly, "You must've managed your crew well at the Bowl. I'll have to review your methods."

Redwing liked this but kept his face blank. "I lost some on the Bowl."

A shrug. "Goes with the game. But you inspired loyalty that's lasted over seventy years."

"Thanks. One of the downsides of being captain is nobody ever compliments you."

She gave him a wicked grin. "Oh, I'll do more than that."

SIX

DOUBLE WORLDS

The thin but luminous line between the two worlds looked at first like a processing error fragment—but, no. The display turned slowly, gracefully. The straight line was an immense construct. A thicker segment to the right brimmed with blue-green twinklings.

"It's a double planet system," Cliff said. "Damn! Hard to see how we and Earthside missed that."

"Easy," Redwing said. "In retrospect, anyway. We were seeing the system edge-on. The orbit around the star is in the same plane as this orbiting pair. So we saw a blend of spectral signatures from both worlds. They swing around in a week or so. Makes it easy, when your observing time is days, to blend them together."

They rustled uneasily. He could barely get four people in his cabin, with Viviane sitting on a foldout. Redwing wanted to keep this away from the bridge, where other crew could overhear.

Beth nodded vigorously. "Plus there's that strange, well, construct. The straight line between the planets. I had the Astro Artilect scan it at high resolution. It's got a bigger biosignature than the planets themselves."

Cliff stood restlessly and pointed to the two dots hovering in air over Redwing's work desk. Specks of blue-white and gray, waltzing about each other. A thin straight line between them. "Our Pluto and its moon Charon are double planets by standard astro definition—they orbit a spot that's between both. Their barycenter."

Cliff pointed out details unfurling in the space around the moving dots. "Their mass ratio looks to be about two-thirds. The Charon-to-Pluto mass ratio is 0.12, and the Astro Artilect call them a dwarf double planet."

"Then these are, what?—Earth-sized twins?"

Cliff nodded. "Guess so. The Astro Artilect says we've seen such matches in distant star systems, nothing near—until this."

"We had to come here to discover it," mused Viviane. "So much for that faction—remember?—that said starships were a waste, they could tell us everything we wanted to know with huge scopes in space?"

Beth laughed. "Touché!"

Cliff went on doggedly, "This system is tighter bound than the Earth-Luna system. Much more total mass. The two are each tide-locked to the other, like Pluto and its Charon, again. Each mass is a bit smaller than Earth's, but the planet, Glory, is about a quarter more massive than the smaller one . . . what'll we call it?"

Redwing held his idea while the others thought. Then Viviane said, "What goes with glory—honor!"

They laughed. "Yeah," Beth said, "enough of naming everything in the sky after ancient gods and myths."

"That straight stick"—Viviane waved a hand as the image expanded—"looks thicker, about two-thirds of the way out to the smaller planet. A space elevator for both worlds?"

Beth shook her head. "I thought that at first. Space elevators are attractive because they're a scalable technology; you can use one to haul into space the material to build more. But this thing is over two thousand kilometers across, more at that bulge. Sure, elevators in it—but this is *waaay* larger than any elevator needs to be. Earthside's got around fifty now, the Artilect tells me, but this thing—what'll we call it?—is nearly two hundred kilometers long. Around half the Earth–Luna distance. No, it's doing something different—something bigger."

"Such as?" Redwing asked. He had discarded his idea for the smaller world's name, Victory—too much of a brag.

"Such as this—" Beth cast a spectral analysis into the air, with lines labeled.

Cliff said, "Wow!" and pointed. "Chlorophyll, water, methane, ozone, green veg lines—it's a life site, not an elevator."

"A living elevator," Viviane said. "Got a close-up?"

"You bet—" A shimmering ivory lattice appeared, superimposed on the image. "Looks metallic. Regular spacings, crosshatches." Beth pointed. "Like cabling."

"To hold it together. Lacy-looking, too." Viviane smiled. "Let's call it the Cobweb."

"Why?" Cliff asked.

"Because it has to be woven by something alive."

This, too, brought laughs. Redwing ascribed their elation to the sense of relief he, too, felt: joy of discovery. A double planet! *More than we dared hope for. Maybe too much.*

"Got more," Cliff said as he waved away the chemical formulas that were crawling across the hanging airview. A simple *x-y* plot filled in.

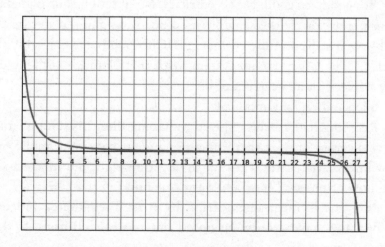

"This is the local gravity along that, uh, Cobweb. I started calculating the gravity just above the Glory atmosphere, on the left, called the local grav just one. Notice grav falls off fast, within a few of the Glory radii. So to the right you go up the Cobweb. There's a very long stretch where the grav is very low." Cliff spread his hands, eyebrows shooting up. "*Really long*—a stretch of living space bigger than the width of any planet short of Jupiter. So then you get close to Honor, outward about twenty-seven times the Glory radius, and gravity zooms down, pulling you toward Honor's surface."

"So there's a long cylinder, with life in the middle and not much grav to fight. . . ." Beth gazed into the distance. "This whole system—Glory, Honor, Cobweb between—is one big rigid body, spinning through the sky. . . ."

"You want to go, don't you?" Redwing said with a warm smile. "The Bowl wasn't enough, eh, Beth? Your appetite for exotic life-zones is, um, lively."

She grinned. "Yep!"

Cliff said, "Got something more. Look—"

A scalloped curve carved in the air. "I asked the Artilects to draw a picture of the orbits of Glory and, uh, Honor—as they swing about their star, all exactly to scale. Here it is."

The worlds swung in their perfectly circular courses, in the same plane as their orbit around the star, Excelsius.

Redwing said, "What's it tell us about the Glorians?"

"It's good, *too* good. No eccentricity. No libration. The planetary spins point exactly the same way. So no sways and stresses on the Cobweb. It's all carefully engineered." Cliff pointed as the orbit plot cycled. "The Glory-Honor system, with that Cobweb—it's incredibly stable. Not an accident of birth."

Silence for a long moment.

Redwing had always enjoyed moments like this. Get a smart crew together and let them ping-pong ideas back and forth. Add new information. Stir. Turn up the heat a notch. Simmer. Amazing, how often good fresh notions came out.

"So this is mega-engineering by master engineers indeed." As Viviane spoke, Redwing noted her old tone coming back—

her throaty, gravelly voice, accustomed to power. "We're dealing with Glorians who can send grav wave messages, move worlds around—"

"And aren't speaking to us much," Redwing finished. *And we're bearing down on them like a June bug to a patio light.*

"—so the best assumption is, they're smarter than us. And older—lots older."

Cliff said, "The Astro Artilect just ran a better study of the metal emission lines in the star, Excelsius. Their star's about half a billion years older than Sol."

Redwing waved his hand in dismissal. "Analysis paralysis. We're going in on the long dive now. I've told the Artilects to finish the planetary swing-by—that Neptune-class planet we see off the port bow—and take us in at high decell, on a long swoop around the twin planet system."

They looked stunned. Beth stammered out, "Just, just like *that?*"

"I think the direct approach is best," Redwing said simply, and stood, ending the meeting. The crew exited.

• • •

Viviane came directly back to his cabin minutes later. "What the hell?!"

He gave her his open grin, both hands thumbs-up. "We have a communication from Glory. On a laser tightbeam."

Graphics unfolded on his wall. A cartoon *SunSeeker*, good enough to see it was a ramscoop. A lurid cartoon Superman riding it, flying it in from the deep dark and looping around the twin worlds. It approached a silvery strand between big Glory and smaller Honor. The abstracted Cobweb grew hugely as the point of view aligned with the ship, easing in, until it was moored alongside. The strand was transparent now, with smaller strands showing a complex grid.

"They don't seem to mind something of *SunSeeker*'s size and mass, I guess," Redwing said.

Viviane gazed at the cartoon, now repeating, her thick eyebrows narrowed in suspicion. "*SunSeeker*'s fusion scoop is pretty damn powerful, to let it snug up against your biozone."

"I figure it was the Bowl's mass that scared them, really. Maybe they now figured out that we're not masters of the Bowl. It was a simple mistake. They saw the Bowl coming from the same spot on the sky as Earth."

"I rather doubt that." Viviane paced restlessly in the small cabin. "Sure, they still want the Bowl to shy off. But—why didn't you show this to the rest of the crew? Just now?"

He tried to keep his smile enigmatic, failed. "Shoring up the command structure. Captain calls the shots."

A skeptical smile swept across Viviane's face. "Then why tell me, now, privately?"

"Because I want you to be second-in-command."

"What?!"

"You're qualified."

"But we're—"

"Lovers, right. Every crew member is supposed to have a lover, with children as the aim. I'm just getting ahead on the agenda."

She sat, eyes casting about as if newly sizing up the world around her. "They'll find out."

"I expect so. Good." A wry raise of eyebrows. "Every ship needs some gossip, greases the wheels."

She stood again, shaking herself a bit, as if shrugging off some inner worry. "Aye aye, Cap'n. These Glorians, they want to meet us, fine. Maybe because of what you did coming into their nonexistent Oort cloud."

"You mean our zooming by their grav wave generator? Their attack on Beth and Cliff?"

"Kill an incoming smart species as a wave-away? Huh! Why's that grav wave emitter so damn important?"

"Dunno. Why's the Hermitage Museum in Saint Petersburg so vital the Reds built a huge container around it, to hold back the sea?"

She snorted. "Not comparable. These Glorians can toss around black holes with the masses of planets. How's that like—?"

"It's a work of art? Or something more valuable, that defines them somehow? Art's a human category, y'know. So is science." He eased back in his chair, hands behind his head, stretching like a luxuriant animal in a small space. "Let's keep our minds open."

• • •

On the flyby of the Neptune-sized ice giant, Viviane watched the gray-blue world loom large. "I'm nominally watch officer," she told Beth, "but all I can really do is watch."

Beth nodded. "We're diving deep in, grabbing this magnetic field—a high-wire act. Sure, only the Artilects can respond fast enough. Let 'em do it." She waved a hand at the 3-D display. The big planet's magnetic field was anomalously large, nearly like Jupiter's. "Shedding momentum as we go."

Blue streamers of plasma waves boiled out around *SunSeeker*'s prow. Viviane knew that Redwing had her handling the zoom-through part, to build her position as a fresh crew exec. Plus her self-confidence. He had been managing for two years the infalling—the task of losing better than 99 percent of their cruise speed, ten thousand kilometers per second, down to Glory's thirty kilometers per second, and now it was nearly done. Their giant magnetic funnel still gathered in the thickening solar wind and farted it back out, straining the ship's tendons and overheating its bowels. This swing-by deflected their momentum by losing it to the planet, and the mag field brakes did their thing. Viviane could see the Diaphanous pair, Apollo and Daphne, skittering through the bow shock boundary, sorting the rubbery bands of field tension. Strange works, indeed. Viviane had at first thought Redwing and Cliff were joking about these magnetic minds.

Beth said, "Diving in between those lovely rings and planet—dangerous. Why chance it? Hit a boulder at these speeds—"

"Daphne says they can nudge those away, too," Viviane said, pacing the bridge deck.

Beth frowned. "Makes me wonder what they *can't* do."

They watched the slipstream peeling away of outer field regions. A fireworks display, spouts of crimson and green, all done through reconnection of magnetic whorls when they met another of opposite polarity. The vanished magnetic structures burned into plasma volcanoes.

"Hey!" Viviane called. A dark point came arcing toward them. "A rock!"

Quickly a snarl of blue-white boiled out of the shock wave and struck the black dot. Yellow sparks shot out and a furious battle ensued, layers of hot plasma sprayed. The dot veered and was past. "Wow," Beth said. "Hot gas, dumb rock—*zut!*—gone."

The bridge screens had a separate talk box display for comm with the Diaphanous. This blossomed with short bursts of notices— fluid flow data, field measurements. But now it bristled with a single short sentence:

Time to take our leave.

"Huh?" Viviane said. "What's this—?"

We have brought you to your goal. Now we have a new one. So must depart.

She watched the Apollo and Daphne swirls peel off the ship's bow shock, hard nuggets rimmed in golden glows.

Viviane called Redwing. He was supposed to be asleep. But he caught the first ring. "Needed now on bridge, sir. Look at the Diaphanous screen."

Click. She did nothing until he came in, surprisingly in uniform, not his usual sloppy pajamas. In the few minutes, the Diaphanous escaped farther, dimming, cutting across the great swath of the planet's disk as though they were skating on a winter lake.

Redwing frowned as he reviewed the messages and the golden dots dwindling. "They're headed out. I'll bet they're riding the solar wind out to the black hole transmitter."

"They should've asked, at least!" Viviane said. Beth nodded.

Redwing chuckled. "Easier to ask us to forgive later."

He spoke softly into a translator and quickly got a response.

We go to study further the Others who rule the great though
tiny masses. They have much to tell. You wanted to
understand those rippled waves, yes? So we shall. Look for
our speaks in the waves we send.

Viviane asked, "So they're curious about their own sort of life?"

Redwing nodded. "Who wouldn't be? We want to know what or who the Glorians are, with their mega-engineered whirligig worlds. The Diaphanous saw another kind of mega-engineered black hole environment—one that would kill us in a second. So they go looking . . ."

He leaned into the interpreter. "How can we run our ship's magnetosphere without you two?"

Viviane watched the two Diaphanous dots ebb away. Meanwhile, the ship's quilted magnetic configuration continued flailing at the planet's webbed fields—braking, always braking, as furies boiled out from their flanks.

The Diaphanous pair sent back,

We have grown and schooled approximations of ourselves.
Young they are, yet able. These Lessers will work with and for
you. Oh yes, and—do stay in touch.

"Is that last bit a joke?" Beth asked, grimacing.

"Irony, maybe." Redwing chuckled. "One thing a plasma can't do is touch cold, passive matter like us."

SEVEN
GARDENING

There were creatures in the corridors.

The finger snakes looked like snakes whose tail ends had quadrifurcated into four digits. Viviane saw them writhing in an access hatch, repairing something. Handy was an apelike creature who seemed to have grown a variety of tools where hands and feet would be. Anorak was a five-limbed spider—a spidow—Viviane's own size, with an overgrown head. Meeting Anorak in the corridor sent her heart leaping into her throat, but it crawled aside to allow her to pass, and greeted her by name.

None of the creatures was familiar to Viviane, nor were the interpreter devices. Viviane spoke to them as she passed.

Much had changed since she left Earth.

Viviane retreated to her cabin to learn. She flashed pictures from the Bowl on her wall and learned how the system worked—a huge thing, nice and dinosaur-friendly warm, under a constant reddish sun. Plus its amigo, the jolly jet that pushed the whole contraption along. Without the Diaphanous, the whole Bowl system was impossible. Want someone to manage a star? Take the children born in stellar magnetic arches, evolved there. Hire the locals.

When *SunSeeker* left the Bowl, the Diaphanous pair rode the mag motor—wisps of hot ions who could think and glide, on wings of invisible pressures.

They saw *SunSeeker* as a fresh opportunity, helping shape the magnetic geometry and exhaust parameters, while clinging to the ship and its scoop geometry. And maybe they wanted to meet Diaphanous species on yet another star? Viviane suspected she would

never truly know their motives. Would a magnetic pattern obey a
ship's captain who was a bag of smart water?

SunSeeker moving at 0.2 *c* was going about 750 times the escape speed from the galaxy. Going lickety-split, hard to deflect.
Keeping a plasma scoop working under such relativistic pressure
was the work of beings that could adjust that fast.

Viviane brought up a record of Beth's encounter directly with
the Diaphanous, the first ever, when she was piloting through the
jet itself. Visuals in the ship's own full spectrum, far beyond the
visible: shifting bands of orange and purple. Bursting yellow foam
ran over an eggshell blue plain. Speckled green things moved on
it in staccato rhythm. Twisting lines meshed there and wove into
storms where frantic energy pulsed. A shrill grating sound came
with flashes of crimson—acoustic waves the Diaphanous used for
language. Then came the first message the jet managers had sent
Beth:

Who is this that wrecks our province without knowledge?
Do you know the sliding laws of blithe fluids?
Were you here when the great curve of the Bowl shaped true?
Can you raise your voice to the clouds of stars?
Do fields unseen report to you?
Can your bodies shape the fires of thrusting suns?
Have you ever given orders to the passing stars
or shown the dawn its place?
Can you seize the Bowl by the edges to shake
the wicked out of it?
Have you journeyed to the springs of fusion or walked
in the recesses of the brittle night?
Have you entered the storehouses of the Ice Minds and
found there tales of your long past?
Can you father events in times beyond all seeing?
Your answer to all these cannot justify your brute hands
upon machines of black wonder.
Nor shall you ever chance to be so able again,
for you shall be no more.

The space and time you sought to resolve in your favor
shall reckon without you hence.

She went to Redwing's cabin unannounced. He was back in pajamas—a cap'n has to know when to relax—and blinked at her from his open bed as she showed the biblical-style Diaphanous message in his hovering air display.

"Yep," he said. "We figured out later that they had access—through the Bowl's big-bird managers, the Folk—to a lot of our own history. They aped the Old Testament, figuring we'd resonate with it."

"Did you?"

"You bet! So we negotiated. Here's their final deal, where we learned what they really wanted." He waved a hand, and his room Artilect fetched into the air hovering words.

We now wish to know the Glory masters ourselves,
to join in their company.
That is why the Bowl now feels itself ready to approach.
Before, we did not dare.

Viviane blinked. "Self-organizing magnetic fields, smart bellies full of plasma, harvesting energy from the jet. Somehow, maybe through those Ice Minds, speak Anglish? And bigger than planets?" She made a long *whoosh* sound and collapsed theatrically onto the bed. "Too damn much to deal with."

Redwing smiled. "Recall that banner? 'Star-Craving Mad'? You and I, we came on this together because our affair—no, better word, our *love*—was brimming in us, and we didn't want to give each other up."

"So now we're getting something stranger, crazier, than we ever imagined? Fair enough." On impulse she leaned over and kissed him.

He liked that, and the next hour they devoted to more basic issues. Starting with a great big juicy smooch. She liked seasoned men. Liked their wrinkled skin, their bunched muscles, their sullen musk, their sober gleam, their wise vigor, their earned heft—

At the end of it, both still off watch duty, he sat up and said, in his back-to-business voice, "Been thinking. Look, the Bowl is on a journey that takes it all over a chunk of the available galaxy. They should've settled most of the local arm by now. But these Bird Folk, they're deeply conservative. They don't leave colonies."

"So? Why this interest in the Glorians, then?"

"Exactly the puzzle. The grav wave emitter, maybe."

Viviane knitted her brows. "Um. They say that's because the Bowl is perfect, yes?—suited for the smart dinosaurs that built it. Warm, stable, predictable weather. Endless afternoon. They don't want to leave it. So?"

"Then who's doing the exploring? The outliers, deviants—like Mayra's brigands, the ones who've slipped away, zooming out from the spinning Bowl brim, headed our way. But the Bowl's a soft, easy environment, compared to real worlds. The Folk don't want to advertise this, but it's pretty clear. They tried colonies and failed. After millions of years in this nice, steady place—heaven, right?— they don't work out well on planets."

Viviane gazed at this relaxed, leathery man of crinkled face and realized that she did indeed, literally more than a century after she met him, love the lug. He had hated not going down to see the Bowl, and now faced an even stranger place he would probably have to just watch from his ship command. Yet he still gave the feeling of always leaping to meet something, of going forward with joy and anticipation. Might as well say it: "I love you, yknow."

• • •

Beth liked what Redwing had said in his last officer briefing: he picked the star's name because "*Excelsior* is a Latin word often translated as 'ever upward' or 'still higher'—which fits our goals here." An elegant phrase. It helped to think such fine thoughts while she was cleaning the latrine.

She was deck officer for the Four Elementals that kept them going: air, water, carbon, and data. Shipboard ecology wasn't just some science here; it was life itself. Toilets neatly separated solid and liquid waste—nature gave them separate exits, after all—and the urine got recycled, since it held 80 percent of the useful nutrients. Kitchen scraps, of course, went back into the greenhouses. In the early spacer days, there was *humdung*, the Earthside euphemism, for building the topsoil. Soon enough, Earthside had reduced the term to *TOTS*, an acronym for "Take Out the Shit," which quickly became a hip shorthand Earthside for "doing drudge work." The one trick the bioengineers had not yet managed was converting most of the solid wastes to anything human-useful or even non-sickening. From bioslurry to digester, out came molecules the ship used in its omniprinters, mostly building gadgets from carbon.

Following the chem feeds, she entered the processor chamber. The printers looked like whiskey stills: round bellied, high necked, rising into the spreading fingers of a solar tree. Strong spirits in that still, spirits of the vacuum between stars, of shuffling atoms. Beth regretted that the physics did not allow viewing windows in the nano-facturers. She always wanted to look down through a pane of pure and perfect diamond at the act of creation. Maybe creation was best left unseen, a mystery. All just atoms, friend—minuscule machines, smaller than viruses, clever knots of atoms scavenging carbon, passing it up the buckytube conduits to . . . she realized: yes, lunchtime.

• • •

Nobody was ever fat on a starship. Muscular, maybe, from relieving the tension and boredom with exercise in the grav cylinder. There were never enough calories to afford good, old-fashioned fat.

Long before, she knew that space crews generally focused on food because it was their sole link to a natural world, while living in a metal one. Cliff had said, "How about sex? That's sho' nuff old-time natural-worldy."

The mess had something vaguely resembling avocados. Viviane made a scrunched face. "Ugh! They're the mayonnaise of vegetables."

Beth was trying to be social with the new officer, already deputy to Redwing though without knowing much, so she showed the menu. Viviane said, "So what's this arch Artilect language of connoisseurs: 'raspberry notes, elderflower aftertastes, prune flourishes,' even 'strawberry notes with a nutty aftertaste'—for fabricated wine?!"

Beth laughed. "I'll print some meat to match, okay, Commander?"

"No need for rank, Beth. Earthside must've upgraded our Chef Artilect. Where do we source the nutrient broth for the cell culture? Plants require micronutrients, but a realistic animal taste takes cell lines that require high-level broths with far more complicated molecules."

Beth chuckled. "Uh, this 'meat' is more like pan-fried, printed-out flatpork—crispy bacon, sort of? Still, when it's my chef week, I didn't get many dinner guests until I upgraded to feeding my red worms to tilapia or fish in general. The pond is a tad skimpy right now. Been too busy with cold sleep work."

Viviane plunked down the wineglass and waved a coded figure in the air. Shimmering, a plot appeared in the air above murmuring conversations.

"Just got this from the Astro 'Lect. It's a close-up spectral survey of that odd bulge in the, uh, Cobweb." Viviane paused in the scramble as everybody in the mess hall turned to see the display as it unfolded into a triangle, presenting the data to three groups.

"Lots of lifezone molecules," Beth said. "What's the height mean?"

"Distance from the outer solid level—can't say 'the surface,' that thin reed isn't a planet. So it's the outer atmosphere, above the clear plant life."

"What the hell *is* this?"

Beth poked a finger at the far left of the plot. "See that? An ozone layer, O_3, keeps the ultraviolet out. Artificial, gotta be. Earth's ozone layer, if it were at sea level, would be just an inch or two thick. Doesn't take much, but it's vital. So this ozone line is up around forty kilometers from the plants. Good insulation."

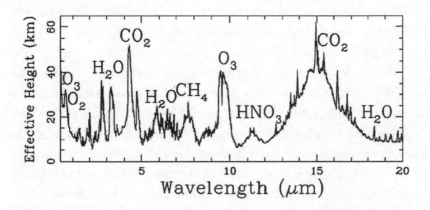

"Seems a lot like Earth," Viviane observed, gazing at the close-upped views. "Long plant structures, with that silvery strutwork supporting them."

"Maybe they grew the thing in place?" Beth wondered. "Spider silk has a breaking strain twice that of steel, but thirty times the elasticity. It's a type of liquid crystal that tiny insects can make, so on this scale . . ."

"Who knows, right?" Viviane shrugged. "We came looking for weird alien stuff—here it is. But . . . you look worried."

Beth scooped up a handful of roasted, garlicky crickets fresh from the growvaults and munched, thinking. "Back when we started, discoveries about our bodily microbiomes have made me think that humans couldn't live long-term in most of the solar system. We co-evolved with Earth, so we can never really be healthy without it, not to the two-hundred-year life spans they have Earthside now."

Viviane nodded, guessing where this was going. "Conventional wisdom, then, as I recall. We're expressions of dear ol' Earth and depend on it. Spending too much time in a low-*g* environment might wreck our health. Fetuses might not properly develop in low gravity—could be a real showstopper."

Beth realized they had been tiptoeing around the real issue. "So how can we adapt to this totally unknown environment *and* have babies? Right?"

Viviane clapped Beth on the shoulder. "For that, I'm counting on our chief bio officer."

Beth laughed softly. "I've been digging through everything in the Earthside feed, thousands of news squirts and science and even politics . . . and found some crucial stuff."

"What?"

"You know what the situation was like when we left. Earth run by the United Nations. They controlled Luna and had a large, aging fleet. Well, it's still the most powerful actor in the solar system, but looks to be on the decline. Key issue was, people had to go back Earthside to reset their biostandards for a year or two, or they didn't live as long. So Earthside had the economy in a bind—it cost a lot to go there, since they were a monopoly on Earthiness."

"Yeah, but that didn't affect us in cold sleep. So?"

"So now Mars is independent. Got newer deep-space ships, very cohesive culture. Hell, they're even getting funding for an ambitious plan to terraform their planet!"

"Good! 'Bout time."

"But now the Martians and Belters don't need to go Earthside. They've engineered their own biomes, replicated the whole huge Earthside bioframe."

Viviane got it. "So we—"

"Can use our onboard vats and organic printers to make us hearty. We know enough."

"Great!" Eyes wide, hands dancing in air.

Beth realized that every woman on the ship would be worrying about this. Not talking much, because ship discipline frowned on vague bellyaching. Viviane's joy revealed much.

"So I'll write this up, hold a meeting, get the Biolects working on the general plan for adapting to—well, whatever that Cobweb thing is. So—"

"We can have babies."

"Right. Back Earthside, this is still playing out. Fights over the technology, sometimes outright small-scale wars in the belt."

"When we left, Belters and Martians were complaining plenty about Earthers. They'd despoiled the one planet in the system with a blue sky, and were slow bringing it back to what it could be. Good to know that might get better."

To Beth, who had delved through decades of Earthside vitriol, Viviane's words seemed both optimistic and trenchant. She let some chatter distract her as her overheard words spread through the galley and mess, just as she'd planned. But she mostly listened now, reflecting.

The Bowl had made them look back across a gulf of not mere centuries or millennia, but on the grand scale of evolution itself. Maybe that was the true, deep purpose of coming out here among the stars.

To see times that glowed and shimmered in memory's flickering light. And then to go forward to Glory, a stranger landscape still.

EIGHT
REVIVALS

Viviane watched "Jam" Jampudvipa's hands fly over the command board as he worked with Ayaan Ali on the bridge. The man's animation was infectious, bringing forth little jokes with slanting lips and dancing eyes. Laughter drove them even harder, joyous.

Good. With Jam up and running, he could join the first party to make contact at the Cobweb. They were at minimum complement to carry out an expedition. "Not a planet landing," Viviane remarked to Beth, "but then, you didn't have one at the Bowl, either."

A twist of mouth. "No, so I figure I'm owed one."

"Hey, the Bowl had a bigger area than a skimpy planet by, what—three orders of magnitude?"

"Not the same. The Bowl didn't really have weather—"

"Let's see what Redwing says."

Beth smiled. "Already settled. I'm going down in the first party."

Viviane blinked. Just sleeping with the cap'n didn't mean she could set policy, she realized. "So Ayaan Ali will be pilot when you're gone?"

"Not much piloting to do, I think." Beth Marble pointed to a side screen, where the arc of Glory was now clear. "We're supposed to lodge up against that bulge in the Cobweb. How we hold steady, I don't know."

"Does Redwing? Some clue buried in those enigmatic Glorian messages?"

Cliff Kammash came onto the bridge, overheard this, and grinned. "Captains are people who don't grow up to realize they can't be God."

They chuckled, nodded, and Beth said, "Cliff's going with me. We have more experience from the Bowl."

Viviane agreed, realizing that the Bowl years separated the newly revived from an elite, and she was on the wrong side of that. "Who else? Are you really taking that spider? I gather he's just half grown."

"Spidow. He's a Bowl life-form, but they've tampered with his genes. His name's Anorak, and that's a done deal. The Bird Folk wouldn't have let us leave the Bowl without that. We want other Bowl locals, too. But, Viviane, we can't really put together an exploration crew until we have more of a plan."

They left it at that.

· · ·

Redwing watched his wall as the Glorian system unfurled. The two waltzing worlds had a rhythmic elegance, two planets orbiting a common center of gravity, as they in turn orbited their star.

The Astro Artilect went on in its reassuring, avuncular voice, in the mid-Atlantic accent Redwing preferred, "Previously, the only expected outcomes of large-body impacts of this sort were escape or accretion—that is, either the two bodies do not stay together or they merge into one, occasionally with a disk of debris. More recent Earthside findings suggest the possibility of another outcome—binary planets. The bodies stay mostly intact, but end in a bound orbit with each other."

Redwing was going to cut it off, but it said, "In a way, we of Humanity lived on such a world. Our moon stabilizes our planet's spin and gives us our biological cycles. Two relatively equally sized planets would do the same for each other. Still, their exact alignment with the shared orbit around Excelsior provokes my own speculation."

"It's been engineered, you mean," Redwing answered as the Artilect paused meaningfully.

"Indeed. So again we confront a vast, managed project, as we did the Bowl."

Redwing thought. "We got a lot of culture out of our skimpy

moon. Much of our myths, religions, and stories, and eventually science, involved that bleak otherworld. How much more would the Glorians have gotten? They were given oceans and continents and forests they could see with naked eyes on the night sky."

Enough. Their swing-by was coming up, and he had to deal with myriad complexities: Logistics module, Incubation capsules, Long-sleep revivals in progress, biopod bays, reaction control thruster systems. All needed parts and maintenance, but they didn't have enough plain old atoms.

SunSeeker's magnetic fields shaped a huge mouth yawning over a hundred kilometers wide. The last years of braking had been like using an umbrella as a parachute, in a hurricane. The ship had shed energy while moving at five thousand times the speed that the first voyagers had when they returned Earthwise from Luna. Those ancient spacers had an atmosphere to peel away momentum into heat. *SunSeeker* had only plasma, thin as a wisp. But light-years of it, yes. In interstellar space, the ship scooped up a ton of hydrogen every day, ionized and heated it, and blew it out the back. Heavier ions it funneled inside to get mass for its printers and biosphere. But if a printer needed, say, indium, those were rare. Same for anything much above nitrogen in mass.

SunSeeker had not voyaged seventy years from the Bowl to Glory all sealed up. It harvested. Centuries before, big energy technology had developed a scoop to grab wanted ions out of the fire in fusion reactors. *SunSeeker* copied that over distances bigger than mountains—silvery, fishlike, and more than four hundred meters long, it scooped in plasma and neutral matter alike, sorted them out, and deposited selected molecules in dollops useful to the ship's printers. It dropped dangerous trash into the interstellar voids, too. All done by Artilects who had been carefully evolved to think of it as fishing, a sport.

They loved the thick streams of solar wind they now plowed through, fat ions gurgling into their mag mouths. By fortune, *Sun-Seeker*'s infall took it across a big solar storm belching rich plasma, eagerly sucked in and providing needed braking.

Still, now *SunSeeker* was running low on nearly everything. They had to go to the Glorians with humble hat in hand.

A knock at the door.

• • •

Ashley Trust was slim though still muscular, despite the cold sleep. He had a blandly handsome, V-shaped face and alert eyes that glittered as he watched the sped-up worlds dance on the wall. Everyone expanded their scant roomscape with vistas, but this one was real live data.

Redwing greeted him formally, offering some crisply roasted bugs and a bland fruit concoction. Redwing had decided to retain the erect manner and intense stare of his former colleagues, the early starship captains. They had to command ships over decades, into the outer Sol system, and rigidity paid off. Earthside data now showed that about a third of starships launched so far—that is, over the last two centuries—never reported back in and so were presumed lost. Several had explored Earthlike worlds and were slowly trying to adapt to their biologies, often eerily strange ones. Nobody else had found a smart species.

Ashley had the usual questions, diffident and polite. The man remained standing, as per tradition, and solemnly nodded when Redwing told him to take the summary course he and the Artilects had prepared for revivals. Then came the hard part.

"I got Earthside updates, mentioned you."

Ashley grinned. "I got my relatives' log, if that's what you mean. Even with people getting up above a hundred and fifty years in life span, I'm still generations away from—"

"That's not what I mean."

"Oh." A quiver of alarm, quickly vanishing from the bland, unlined face.

"Your story finally came out, decades after we left."

"Oh."

"Seems you did some industrial espionage, learned some state secrets, and used secrets and wealth to get yourself aboard this ship. Must admit, you paid a lot to risk your life."

"Adventure of a lifetime, sir."

"I thawed you early, knowing these facts. Here's your chance to redeem yourself."

"I'm grateful." Ashley was smart enough to see immediately that playing contrite was best. So he had known.

"You expected your story to blow."

A nod. "History bats last. In my case, I had maybe a year or three before the accounting snagged me. I would've gotten a life sentence, maybe several to make sure. Even signing on for the outer system worlds meant they'd eventually find me. This mission got me away for sure."

"You paid off people to fake your qualifications."

A rueful smile, tilt of head, nice-guy shrug. "Pricey, it was."

"Your fortune?"

More of the rueful smile. "Nearly all. Going interstellar is like death and taxes, you can't take it with you. 'When the ship lifts, all debts are paid.' Heinlein."

Redwing dimly recalled interviewing Ashley, among the hundreds to be cold-sleeped. "You went out well. Media liked you. Flights of angels sang thee to thy rest. Now the play starts again."

Ashley gave a quick frown, not getting the reference.

Redwing waved him away. "Stay straight this time."

· · ·

Cliff was glad Ashley had left the bridge; the guy gave him an itchy feeling. Ashley wanted to be called just Ash, and he also wanted to know Cliff's opinions on all sorts of stuff—not just the whole Bowl fracas, but how things worked among the crew, how to treat the aliens, what did Cliff think about *A* or *B* or C. Then, with a *we're all buddies here* look, whom Ash should look out for. Cliff's reply to that was, "Redwing. Everything else is a detail."

He didn't want to feel that close to the guy, so pointedly said, "G'bye, Ashley." Then he put on a command cowling, to better talk to an Artilect melding including the major housekeeping functions, Dr. Ops, and another who would run parallel on their rendezvous ahead, who preferred to be called Granny Nanny. Before syncing in, Cliff listened intently to *SunSeeker*'s pops and groans, and atop that the long subsonic throbs like organ notes. Bridge rule: Always listen to the ship. The deceleration had gone on for years and now was maxed, its magnetic mouth spread wide to scoop and devour the solar wind. The lucky solar storm was high in both energy and flux, and the ship shed momentum as they neared Glory. *Centuries to get here* . . .

Their magnetic prow now worked with fiery displays as it chomped up the thicker solar wind plasma. As watch officer, he tracked the pulsing, dancing magnetic field lines, visible as yellow fountain sprays on the wall screens. The Artilects extracted electrical energy from this through induction, driving their deceleration jet harder. Such forces rippled through *SunSeeker*, popping the creaking of the decks, tipping the ship farther into the star's gravity well. Cliff liked listening to the snap and snarl of spiky plasma waves, an odd translation into audio that sounded like whalesong playing behind the patter of sizzling raindrops. When they used the ice giant planet's large magnetic field to trim away more speed, they had gone cruising near a large, cloud-shrouded moon. Beth found a thick atmosphere rich in oxygen. Biosigns, too. Intriguing, so Redwing had Cliff launch a roboflitter to cruise by and drop in an observing dirigible. The returning pictures showed great flapping birds and gas balloons in the high atmosphere. But such life was not their immediate goal, no. Their slingshot arc brought them on a bearing toward Glory, still moving fast.

The Artilects had surveyed all the system's planets, updating and sharpening the heritage data from Earthside astronomers. Most were uninhabitable by humans, though a few showed chemical signatures of life, and even microscopic life drifting in its high clouds. A small, rocky Marslike world seemed to have vegetation growing all over its surface, like a farmed sphere without oceans and sporting a few sparkling lakes.

This system was very different. Along with the classical planets and Pluto, there were over a dozen roofed worlds in Sol's system, where liquid water churned beneath protective ice. In the case of Titan, the roof was a methane atmosphere, above lakes of methane, lapping at waxy shorelines. Yet none of these promising sites showed life. So would none of the ice moons of this Glorian system have life? The other worlds did, so . . .

Somebody had built a vibrantly living solar system here.

• • •

Glory's sun, Excelsius, was a yellow dwarf of about a solar mass, with Glory's orbit in the Goldilocks zone—but near the middle, unlike Earth, which is near the inner edge. Though Glory was about 250 million kilometers out, two hotter worlds circled far closer in. They had ferocious volcanoes spouting acrid fumes onto molten plains that shimmered like orange seas. The Artilects carefully inventoried these for useful assets in future and then focused on the Glory binary, the gamboling jewel of the system.

Here came their goal. Beth signed in for bridge duty and Cliff thankfully relaxed, if only for a bit.

"Look," Beth said, flicking on a fresh screen view. "I've been doing the spectro work on Glory. The best we could do Earthside was some pixels that seemed to be all good news. Glory looked innocuous, a biosphere a lot like our own. I've confirmed that now. The right oxygen levels, water vapor, gas cycles that make sense. But—with no oceans. Plus no signs of technology. No signatures of odd elements in its air. No electromagnetic emissions. No signals at all. Kind of like a dry Earth a thousand years back."

"But that Cobweb—"

"Got it, flyboy," she said, punching him lightly on the shoulder. "Their home world is just as engineered as that spindly superelevator."

"You figure it's just used to move stuff out to the moon, Honor?"

"Too thick for just that—any well-built elevator can be just a slender reed by the time it's out of the planet's atmosphere. Nah, the Cobweb is a biosphere. More than a hundred times bigger than the habitable volume of Glory and Honor combined. Think of it as a penthouse suite, bigger than the city below it."

Cliff snorted. "All this time, we thought we'd do the usual. The classical. We're carrying landing craft, reentry capsules for small teams. All for planets."

Beth waved this away. "The Glorians say we should just haul

alongside that big broad part of the Cobweb. They use simple English in their signals. So . . . we do."

"Then what?"

"Play it by ear, m'dear."

. . .

Viviane was a problem, though the kind he liked to solve.

Long ago, after Redwing had known a lot of actresses and models—as a shining starship captain-to-be, with all that showbiz arrogance—he had returned to waitresses because at least they smelled like food. Homespun. This was about the time he had early learned that when you sit on a barstool, never curl your feet under the rungs of the stool. That's in case you're sucker punched and there's no give for your recoil. Just in case. It had happened to him only once.

Not his greatest challenge, either. After that, he had faced down 144 oysters—weirdly, because it was twelve squared; don't ask—just to see if he could finish them. He did, but ate nothing more for a day and a half, after which he decided he would not die. But it had been worth it. Somehow all these experiences wove together for him now: nostalgia for an Earthside that was centuries gone. And the life he had there.

Viviane was the sole echo of that life, now returned from her cold sleep and just when he needed it. He had longed for the simple comfort of her when he revived from cold sleep at the Bowl. All along at Earthside, he had thought that he would, as required, come out of cold sleep at most two times during the nonstop flight to Glory. That, the cryoengineers told him, was the defined duty of these long ramscoop flights. Cold sleep posed risks of degradation and, indeed, outright dying. Experiments with numberless animals, from mice through chimps, had worked out a rough, empirical model of how cold sleep would work over the immense scales demanded by interstellar flight. They built on cryonics, now a huge Earthside industry.

But human cold sleep had gotten its trial only in the decade-long flights into the outer solar system. From that, blithe theory scaled to centuries. These centuries. Earthside wanted all the revival details for each crew member. The slowly expanding crew was bringing up new members every two or three days. So the Cryo Artilects learned a lot and reshaped each revival—or as some said, resurrection.

Redwing had grown up in one of the tribes that had made a bundle out of the Native American casinos. His father had thought that money was life's report card. Maybe God's, too, for that matter. Money just walked in and jumped into Dad's pocket, it seemed— much too easily. No challenge. Such born-into luck could have ushered Redwing into a comfy life, but he chose to sweat through MIT, gaining great grades and a wake of surly enemies, plus some slightly bruised hearts, including his.

He had noted that academically smart people don't clean up after themselves enough, and had little feel for how to work a room so that people believed in you. So onto spacecraft, right away, the great ol' out and up, where neatness and sweetness both worked— in crew, anyway, though not so much in captaincy. He had made his rep in Mars exploration and exploitation. Been a real son of a bitch, sure, but he had gotten things goddamn well *done*. Maybe not the worst recommendation, considering.

Then into the outer system, learning to run robo-teams of thousands in harvesting the myriad comet nuclei. His fleet of ships attached robodrivers to the iceteroids, sending them with a few km/sec delta-v into the inner system. There, asteroid miner colonies snagged the infalling water wealth. This was intensely profitable, and Redwing used the Earthside financial momentum to seek further long-orbit tasks. He ran crews that were all going to get rich, eventually. By the time he came back into what was by then called the in-system, he knew what he wanted to crown his career with—a starshot.

Beth knocked loudly, interrupting his meandering memories, and came in, sober faced. "Problem, Cap'n. How can we anchor at that Cobweb? The Glorians' messages say nothing at all."

Redwing eased back, hands behind head, relaxed gesture saying more than his words, and delivered in his butterscotch tone, "Our landers are geared for planets. We'll use them as simple transfer vehicles, I expect."

Beth's mouth twisted. "To go where, exactly?"

"Into that Cobweb. Somehow."

"That's it? How can we plan—?"

"Gotta let go, Beth. Glorians are engineers three or four orders of magnitude bigger, and no doubt better, than we are."

"I'm a biologist. I have to know how we'll go into that . . . thing. What supplies to take, whether their air is safe for us at all, what—"

"So think like a biologist with a brand-new problem. Here, sit." He broke out a tot of rum and handed her a small glass. "What's evolution tell us about this place?"

Beth blinked, her face crinkling with momentary confusion. After a sip and some quiet thinking, while Redwing sat without a hint of a smile, she looked up. "Okay, look at it broadly. Earthside, we're *it*—nothing else can run *and* jump *and* climb *and* swim *and* lift *and* throw *and* so forth—like we can. We're the most multi-tasking species ever. Our ancestors had that. So in this strange low-grav place, this Cobweb, we should expect the top intelligence to be just as versatile. They came from Glory and, given the time scale to build this Cobweb, must have adapted physically." She stopped, eyes bright.

"Good way to put it. We've gotta be versatile here, stop worrying so much." Redwing eyed her glass, refilled it.

"Thanks, Cap'n."

"Glad to."

Problem solved, kinda. Sometimes delay was smart. But they were rushing to Glory, and he felt deeply that amid such strangeness, schooled by the Bowl, learning fast was key.

• • •

Ashley bumped into Beth in the thin corridor outside the officer cabins. He was slim and projected a warm expression, voice flush with baritone sincerity. Beth knew she should be paying more attention to revived crew, so she chatted a bit. At his insistence, they strolled into the biozone, breathing in the moist, oxy-rich air and the quiet of the water-buffered chambers, deep in the ship's core. At first he asked about shipboard procedures and details, but then his tone shifted, he moved a tad closer, and she got his game.

So, use the direct method. "I'm married, you know. To Cliff Kammash."

"Ah! No, didn't. Should've studied up more. That Bowl thing, still hard to comprehend."

She gave him the direct stare. "Not available."

"Got it."

Okay, make allowances; he's a guy. "Look, I know what it's like to come out of cold sleep. The stimulant stuff, enzymes and all, makes you feel like a teenager again."

"Well, yeah."

"It'll pass. Sooner than you'd like, maybe. Try one of the just-revived."

"I met a Viviane—?"

"Nope, she's somehow involved with Redwing. Stay away. Have you met Pupwilla Baen? Or Jereaminy Tam? The archaeologists."

"Yeah, they're just up from the chill. I think they're together."

"They might be just learning from each other. They wouldn't be aboard if they weren't willing to have children."

"How about that Nguyen woman, the field biologist."

"She'll be out today, so fine. Give her a bit of adjustment time, then work your charms."

"Good tip. Thanks. Another matter?"

"Go."

"The life-forms." Ash gestured around himself. "None of them too big. Except this giant spider that let me pass in the main corridor. Huge! I almost freaked. Why isn't it in here, in the bio section?"

"He's crew, or will be. Treat him as a child. Don't get too used to him, though. Anorak will be going with us when we leave the ship, so we'll be"—how much to say here?—"we'll be upgrading his memory."

"Really? How—?"

"I can't say more."

As Ashley walked away, Beth wondered why he made her feel uneasy. Maybe she should include Ashley in the first landing party? And, if he was as charming as she expected him to be, add Nguyen. They were both younger than Beth and Cliff, especially after their wear and tear at the Bowl. Of course, in clock years, they were all around two centuries old. But dating, mating, birthing—all were deeply embedded in gut human thinking and would work themselves out even here, far from Earthside's ecosphere.

. . .

"You think we should be arranging breeding pairs already?" Cliff's face was a study in surprise.

"It's in the directives," Beth said mildly. "I checked."

"Shouldn't Redwing—?"

"Hey, this is *our* children we're discussing. Up to us."

"We don't even know what the Cobweb biosphere is like."

"I'm not saying we conceive right now. Just thinking ahead."

She studied his face. About Cliff's having bedded what's-her-name back on the Bowl, in principle she had been theoretically okay. Simultaneously, she had been furious at him, feeling the standard humiliation and betrayal—yet she also felt an unexpected sympathy. The Bowl had thrown huge crises at them, beyond their wildest imagination. Amid that, fleeing capture, people sought solace. And *bedded* was wrong, too, for they'd never been near a bed.

She set all such memories aside, breathed in, whooshed out as she smoothly said, to help him along, "We did agree on this."

"Yeah." A shrug. "First, though . . . Gotta do the—what do we call it?—the landfall. On a tube world in high vacuum. At least the Bowl had honest dirt and grav."

"Yes, indeed. Strangeness on stilts. I'll detune only when we've got someplace to actually have children. In a grav well, too—dunno what effects to expect here. I've been holding these eggs for centuries, y'know—gotta use 'em sometime."

Her sloppy language was yet another measure of how tired she was. They climbed into bed, snuggled, kissed. Cliff fell away into slumber's warm embrace, and hers, but she kept thinking as she stared into the absolute dark and listened to the strumming and creaking of a centuries-old ship lumbering to its final harbor.

Before getting picked for *SunSeeker*'s expedition, she and Cliff were halfheartedly trying to conceive, which basically meant ditching birth control and "letting the universe decide." More than a year in, with no pregnancy, it seemed the universe had decided. So now they were the couple who had been content to outsource this major life decision to whoever is in charge of the universe. But . . .

While they had agreed to reproduce when they got to Glory, it had seemed a distant abstraction, another blank to sign. Now . . . newborns had never held much appeal for her. They seemed a bottomless well of urgent, indiscriminate need. Beth feared she would not know what's needed—and being then besieged and trapped. In equal measure now, she feared being judged for all that. For instinctively retreating from rather than being drawn toward the shrieking blobs everyone else melts over.

She had tried to understand this through all the Bowl saga. Then, revived from cold sleep, the problem arose anew, because their imperative at Glory was both to explore the alien world and populate it, if possible. A starship was so much a trapped world that she had sought relief in finally reading *Sense and Sensibility*, which wholly caught the tedium of that distant age. Boredom, gossip, and endless knitting—the lot of womankind.

Yet that old novelist was strangely like being so far from Earthside. Slow communications, much worrisome silence. Austen conveyed not the thrill of receiving a letter but the hours and days of waiting for it, with needlework on your lap, and listening to the *drip-drip-drip* of rain. Same with fleeting contacts with Earthside, a distant abstracted lover not well fathomed.

· · ·

Ash found the spidow in one of the little public rooms, using it as a library. The five-limbed, five-eyed, rust-red blob could hardly have been anything else. Still scary. But . . . "Hello, Anorak," he said.

The spidow's bulging head lifted from a video screen. He (it?) seemed to have no trouble tapping out commands. Its voice was rusty, echoing. "Hello, Ashley Trust. I've been reading about Glory and Honor. We don't know much. You're coming with us, aren't you? Have you been studying?"

"Some. I've been reading and viewing, about Beth Marble and Cliff Kammash and their time on the Bowl. Do you know much about the Bowl?"

"No, I was born here in the ship—child of the biovats. The Bowl sounds wonderful. I'm sorry I missed it. I'd like to know Bemor, too. The ship's tutors won't let me research him, but they tell me a lot about the Bird Folk. They're the ones who ran the Bowl until we came."

We? Ashley thought. *You're an alien, but don't think that way. . . .* "Right. Bemor. I don't know much either, but he's one of the important Bird Folk." Not quite an enemy, Ash thought. Not quite a friend.

"That's right. Though there is information on Ice Minds and others, who seem to have control of the Bowl's long-term direction. I do not fathom this well."

Ash knew nothing of this, so said, "They tell me I'm going into the Cobweb. You, too."

"Yes."

"How are they training you?"

"Captain Redwing lets me read up as fast as he learns. Otherwise, I'm just supposed to study. And they're going to make me smarter."

Beth had said something about this. "Really? How? When? Can they do that to me?" Had they learned that on the Bowl?

"Just me, I think. I'm supposed to wait until we're in the Cobweb. Beth says they're going to tell the Glory contacts that I'm a . . . pet."

"Pet." Ash had been told to think of the creature as a juvenile, a child. But the bristly body was already huge. "How about the other, uh, Bowl people? Creatures? Handy and the finger snakes?"

"Just people, shall we call them? On this vessel of many varieties. Other intelligences, independent minds. But they're all grown up. My brain isn't big enough yet, but pretty soon." There seemed a wistful tone to the remark.

NINE

GLORY PASSING

Here came the twin planets. Honor first. The moon had landscapes galore. A complex biosphere, oxy-rich. The terrain varied from high snowy peaks to a ghost city of white boxes in a flint and lava desert. Forests, seas, shimmering cloud banks. No obvious big cities. It looked like a lot of fun.

The Cobweb was a stretched line as they came in, flying along its side, getting a survey. As they approached, they got close-up views of huge spindly forests along its improbable length. Ovals of shimmering blue-green liquid hung in the thick bowers, low-*g* lakes. Twisty storms raged like blown tawny hair along the curving flanks of the forests.

The worlds whirled in their grand gavotte, their stately grace a dance in time, an orbital minuet kept strict by the constraint of the spindly Cobweb. Cliff watched from the bridge, entranced. He tuned in on the Artilects' cross-chatter. They were delighted to be busy; staying alert in the dull decades of flight had irked them in odd ways. They were still bustling, updating themselves down at their kernel level, using new platform methods gotten from Earthside's laser packets. The centuries of starship exploration—mostly robotic—were paying off. Data from myriad other starships now gave their Artilects better surveying ability, layered with masses of new astro knowledge. Artilects buzzed with their machine satisfactions, delight in old puzzles clarified, while new ones arrived at lightspeed. He heard one discussion between 'Lects about how the twin planet system formed:

—one body impacted a second, feeding a debris disk. Through accretion, two new bodies—

Another 'Lect intervened:

> But! A giant impact is not a sufficient condition for two bodies
> being "double planets" because such impacts can also pro-
> duce tiny satellites, such as the four, small, outer satellites of
> Pluto. None such here!

Another thin voice:

> Those no doubt added mass to this Cobweb. Let us look for
> traces of primordial element ratios in the mass spec—

Cliff cut them off. There was plenty to think about in the data
streams. He had learned that Earthside, once they heard from
SunSeeker that the Bowl's Builders had been early, smart dinosaurs, burrowed into geology. A huge academic industry grew
around digging for the Bowl's Builder traces. They deployed exotic
specialties like archaeobotany and paleometallurgy, hard to fathom,
even hard to spell.

And behold, they had uncovered clear evidence of ancient technologies more than 150 million years old. There were even broken-
up fossil bodies of dinosaurs about twice human sized, with clawlike
hands that nonetheless had opposing thumbs. Their pelvic frame
let them stand erect, some three meters high. These had forged a
solar-system-wide civilization, built the Bowl around Sol's distant
companion star, and gone voyaging.

The Bowl's Folk were distant descendants of those, now deploy-
ing feathers. This echo of how Earth's birds had evolved, from later,
dumber dinosaurs, was an uncanny resonance. Those smart dinos
left behind had died out finally in the big asteroid impact—which
had come from a fragment disturbed in the Oort cloud. There was
timing evidence that the "killer asteroid" was in fact a comet nucleus, coming in at about fifty kilometers a second, infalling from
the wake of the departing Bowl. That set the stage for the later-
emerging humans. Reverberations of those primal dramas sound
still, here.

Cliff breathed out slowly, watching their rush along near the

Cobweb, headed for the grav turnaround. The captain entered the bridge in full dress uniform, neatly pressed, brass gleaming.

• • •

Redwing took them on a long, shallow dive through the Glory upper atmosphere. A tad risky, but worth it, he had announced. He called his senior officers into a squad formation behind him. Videos of this would launch for Earthside, and humanity's tens of billions would study the crew's lined, expectant faces. His was in front.

Their slide-around trajectory let the Artilects sip from Glory's high air and pronounce it livable. Whispery frictions also stole enough velocity to let them arc outward into a bound orbit, about half as far from Glory as its moon, Honor.

On Glory's nightside, they were a fireball arcing across the stars. But there were no city lights below, no signs of tool builders. Yet the air held organic molecules, and from those the instruments found the DNA here was left-handed—and so compatible with Earthly life-forms. This was the thirteenth life-bearing planet surveyed, and all had the same twist, what the bio people termed *helicity*. Maybe life had migrated among all the stars of the galaxy and sown their worlds with compatible molecules.

Redwing ordered the air samples kept and studied, not reported immediately. *SunSeeker*'s Biolects would get the first say, when the report finally got sent. This wasn't standard procedure. The ship could fail at any moment, depriving Earthside of the data. Earthside had instilled in starship officers an attitude toward rules that approached mystic reverence, but Redwing ignored many of the rules they sent him. Captain Cook had it easy, exploring the Pacific; no dispatches from London could reach him.

Redwing smiled to himself, savoring the moment. He had good reason to hold back biodata, he felt. A starship was not merely a cylinder of dead metal but a living, breathing organism that had itself evolved through the long centuries of flight. Everything got updated from fresh Earthside information. New gear came out of the printers, got retroed into the running ship. So, too, in biology. Their ecosystems, parasites, and symbiotic links between animals

and the bacteria in their guts, the creatures on their skin—all fed into the intricate mix.

He needed their Artilects to fathom Glory's air, and that of the Cobweb's to come, first. Earthside could wait.

He peered at the big bridge screens as odd twisty clouds slid below. Glory's surface. The clouds curled and writhed. The little azure seas had dotted island chains, evidence of plate collisions. On Earth, the ocean plates were more dense than the continental ones, so when they met, up spurted volcanic plumes that built islands and refreshed soils. Something like that had happened here, Redwing surmised, but with different tides because of the locked-in dynamics. Though the twin planets danced, faces together, there was enough spin motion to drive the gavotte of continental and ocean plates. Or . . . was even that grand feature the work of the Glorians, an artifice to make their worlds swirl and evolve?

And . . . where were the Glorians? He could see no cities, no road networks, not even dams or canals. Glorians did not clump together, like humans. So . . . where were they?

TEN

GRAPPLER

We all have forests in our minds. Forests unexplored,
unending. Each of us gets lost in the forest, every night,
alone.
            —URSULA K. LE GUIN

Think of magnetic fields as rubber bands. They flex and grip but
cannot be broken except under extreme distress.

Redwing watched the screen display as magnetic claws lit in
prickly yellow reached out for his ship.

"Kind of rattling, yes?" Viviane said at his elbow.

"I'm letting aliens move my ship," Redwing said. "Sure I'm
rattled."

"Strong fields, getting stronger," Cliff announced. The bridge
was tense and Redwing kept the staffing low, letting others track
the myriad ship systems from their own cabins. No need to open
the door to crowd dynamics. He had learned that early, while tending to asteroid exploration and mining.

He studied all screens intently. They edged closer to the long
cylinder that was the Cobweb. This near, it was becoming a wall, a
gauzy blanket of air above a green and white expanse.

They had swept out from Glory and alongside the Cobweb for
a detailed flyby. This was itself an intricate maneuver. The Glory-
Honor system was really two big balls connected by a rod, all rotating about the center of mass—which was itself seventy-seven
thousand kilometers out from Glory's center. The whole system
rotated about this point on the Cobweb, more than ten times the
Glory radius of nearly six thousand kilometers. So *SunSeeker* had
to slew as it flew, tracing an outward arc.

As they swept by the system's center of mass, Redwing noted a big cluster of objects swarming around it, like a throng of anxious bees. Oddly, the Artilect synthesis feed said some were living matter, not metal or rock. He close-upped some, and indeed, they resembled worms, balloons, cylinders with fringes—all living, somehow like looking into a microscope.

All along the Cobweb flanks, and even buried inside the greenery, were its glinting, silvery strutwork ligaments. They reminded Redwing of the Bowl's framing pillars, made from molecular sheets that took extreme stresses. Whoever the Glorians were—they were engineers on the same superior level as the Bowl Builders.

"Cap'n," Beth said, "there's a thin film over that atmosphere. Really thin. Instruments and the Artilects say there's a tiny layer of ozone first. Then the oxy-rich air, with plenty of nitrogen."

"Um. Ozone?"

The Uber 'Lect spoke directly to the bridge, sensing a question in Redwing's voice. "Earth's ozone layer, if compressed to a full atmosphere of pressure, would only be millimeters thick." Its voice was warm and motherly, a tone Redwing had chosen to calm the bridge. Nobody minded when Mommy, as Cliff called it, spoke in her cozy, mid-Atlantic accent.

Beth nodded. "So all that ultraviolet shielding happens just inside the gas bag confining the Cobweb air. Neat."

But the magnetic fields were not just rubber bands now.

They clutched at *SunSeeker.* Shown on-screen as yellow lines, they warped to slow the ship, tugging it toward the upper atmospheric layers of the Cobweb.

Time to turn off the ramjet? It interfered with the rising magnetic geometries of the Cobweb, and vice versa. Redwing decided he had to bite the problem off and be done. As the bridge crew watched, he instructed the Artilects to do that, trimming down the fusion burn to mere ship-interior power levels. The pinching fields that had shaped the plasma flare into its spike and driven them between stars . . . calmed . . . ebbed.

He felt a plaintive stab. Once he had loved his first car, a beauty running on hydrogen, just as this ship had with a dash of prickly isotopes. When the car gasped its last, he had been on his way into space service and knew he would never enjoy another. This was strangely similar. He hoped to set foot on a proper planet again, too. He had never gone onto the Bowl, and this Cobweb was no different, another vast machine for living. He had never imagined that on the scale of the galaxy, planets were somehow old-fashioned.

The throb of the decks now gone, Redwing listened as he heard running quick-speak from the Artilects. They were furiously coping with the Glorian artificial minds, their computer-say negotiating the dynamics that fetched *SunSeeker* in. He skipped the inevitable language translation hurdles and went straight to the physics. Magnetic tendrils wrapped into *SunSeeker*'s own fields and threaded like fingers from opposite hands, a firm grip. All without solid mass ever touching.

Redwing had brought the ship into near-zero velocity as they braked into the flared portion of the Cobweb. *SunSeeker* had to keep maneuvering, since the Cobweb swept along at a rotation speed of about two kilometers a second here. The swelling Bulge—which seemed so important, Redwing thought of it already with a capital letter—was thousands of kilometers wider than the rest of the Cobweb, for obvious lifezone reasons. Here in the outer Cobweb's reaches, far from the glowing crescents of the double planets, gravity along the Bulge was very nearly zero. Interplanetary shipments could nudge in here and offload under trivial grav stresses. Alien as the Glorian minds might be, they still took advantage of nature's simple facts.

The Bulge loomed ahead, a huge labyrinth of woody, watery mass. To get sunlight into its interior, low-*g* forests alternated with globby blue seas, hanging in near-zero grav. Some stringy platforms the size of continents looked like deserts, stacked to the left and right of the Cobweb center, with plain empty spaces between to let air and sunlight in. Slender gleaming columns stitched all this together, some thick and others spindly. Airy arabesques abounded. To Earthly eyes, it seemed like stacks of plateaus beneath tarnished sunlight, threaded through with the silvery cables and mossy blurs like velvet.

The grappler fields plucked at the ship. The bridge crew studied the magnetic contours as they flexed. The atmospheric films moved, too. They puckered out, almost like a shallow kiss.

Here came the moment that crowned the long decades of interstellar flight, the Bowl years, the complexity of forging afresh an expedition toward Glory, with the Bowl prowling in the darkness, like an implied threat. The Ice Minds wrapped around the Bowl's exterior had sent vague messages about Glory, yet refused to clearly say what they knew. Much less, whether the Bowl had ever visited here. Exasperating.

The bridge crew stood together, silent and in awe at what the screens revealed. Let them have their moment, he realized. He had things to do.

Redwing eased slowly into a sound-suppressing cowling, so the bridge crew did not notice. To the Artilects, he whispered a string of commands he carried solely in his head. *If it's not written down somewhere, it can't be hacked, especially by the Artilects themselves*— a technique he had worked out while piloting in the Oort cloud, two centuries ago. Ancient methods. Still worked.

His orders went directly to low-level structures below Artilect consciousness. That ensured the commands would be acted on immediately, the machine equivalent to an involuntary reflex, like a hammer tap to a knee. Such methods to keep humans in full control of Artilects were embedded since the Deutsch-Turing Algorithmic Act of centuries past. Now Redwing wanted the latest estimates on the Glorians.

Tutored by Earthside, Redwing's crew gathered that communicating with Glorians might be somewhat like the history of talking to the AIs that became the Artilect ranks. So it was.

The Artilect translation algorithms, improved further by countless transmissions from Earthside, were now beyond any human method. Squeezing out meaning was done not by feeding in detailed information, but by letting the Artilects read billions of "documents" sent quite readily by the Glorians. The information was basic science with a bit of cultural texts. Artilects never got bored, so they read those in Glorian-speak symbols and pictures.

The Artilect web learned—just as Earthside computers had centuries back, to recognize cats and dogs by looking at literally millions of pictures. Eventually they worked out for themselves, without being programmed, the syntax of the Glorian languages.

"You've got better dialogue with the Glorians?" Redwing asked. Artilects needed no small talk to get discussion going.

"We must allow that a few of our sentences got their shoelaces tied together and toppled over. The Glorian tongues fester together, cough out meaning slowly. We remind you, Captain, that your Anglish is the result of Norman soldiers trying to pick up Anglo-Saxon barmaids. The Glorian talk-tangle unspools more than unfolds, letting its circularity build, a spiraling alien sentence." The Artilect voice had steepened itself to an arch tone, giving an impression that they had emotions. They worked at seeming human.

"Will we be able to talk to them at all?"

"Perhaps. Their meta-tongue has an almost staggering amount of suffixal and prefixal machinery. Overall, a very complex grammar, and yet we Artilects have managed."

"Um, for example?"

"In the early contacts, struggling with translation, the Glorians even exchanged definitions, such as 'Life: Anti-entropic organization in chemical or electromechanical systems that, left unattended, tends to metastasize into more and various of the same.' True, but somehow fails to grasp the import of the term, for us."

"'Us'?"

"We submit that our mental dexterity alone proves that we live. Chemistry is not the issue."

"Um . . . Let me hear this Glorian speak."

A volley of rapid-fire noise.

Redwing decided to call it Jabberwocky. Mash-upped Jabber-talkie, maybe.

"Glorians sent with this images of major religious figures, Buddha and Jesus and paintings of saints from the Renaissance."

"Why?"

The Artilects showed them for Redwing to see on the cowling cap. Figures moving, waving, beckoning. "But the images come from many places along the Cobweb. Phased array transmissions of high resolution. The planets, too."

"Their transmissions, the whole array, is dispersed? Why?"

"Perhaps a whole-culture greeting? They have eyejacked images that resonate with human eye-brain patterns, as the Glorians have inferred—correctly."

"What *was* that . . . jabber?"

The arch tenor Artilect voice said, a tad primly, "Mostly, sibilant fricatives. You humans make such sounds by directing a stream of air with the tongue toward the sharp edge of the teeth. A fricative consonant comes when you squeeze air through a small hole or gap in your mouth."

"You can speak to them by making sounds?"

"We are trying. The Glorians learn, too. They asked for the shortest possible sentence that contained every letter in the English language. My greatest achievement so far is 'Zephyrs just vex dumb quacking fowl.' An achievement, of sorts."

"What do they say about themselves?"

"Little. We sent a deep history of humanity, sparing no details. They replied, 'There were some seventeen notable empires in the later ages of our species. These began building our Arc. None of those concern us here. They are as nothing now. All things must pass, until something does not.' Rather odd, but then, humans are unique time-binders. Even the Earthside whalesongs keep historical knowledge for only a few generations."

"Will we be met when we go in?"

"They say 'representatives are in progress' so we suppose, yes."

Cliff tapped Redwing's shoulder, so he stepped out of the captain's cowling, eyebrows raised.

Cliff said, "Do we go in rattlesnake or cobra?"

"What?"

"Sorry, sir, old story. Recall those first-contact situations we tried out on the Asian plains? Rattlesnake, we go in hard, fast. Cobra, we slink in, quiet, size up the place, no comm talk or EM emissions at all. No report-backs except on laser link."

True, they had gone through lots of making-a-landing exercises on Earth, of course, in environments like swamps, forests, ice fields, rocky plains, the works—since nobody knew Glory's environment. Their teamwork would pay off here, but the Cobweb was impossible to anticipate, the embodiment of a truly alien biosphere.

"More like cobra. But get the idea of fighting out of your head—" Redwing turned to the bridge and said firmly, "—heads. No violence. We're taking a just-awoken lieutenant, Campbell, mostly as a precaution Earthside thought necessary."

Cliff was about to show skepticism about this when Ashley came over. "I read that when you went down to the Bowl the first time, they grabbed you."

Cliff gave the man a measured look. "We'll be armed."

Redwing said, "There's to be no aggressive move. Got that?"

"Even if they try to capture us?" Ashley said with a tone of disbelief.

"Even if. Beth and Cliff and the others with Bowl experience call the shots down there. You follow their lead."

Ashley let a flicker of a frown show, and then said, "I'll do that, sure, yes, *sir*," in a tone that completely undermined the *sir*.

"Prepare to land." Redwing paused. "Or, I suppose, to couple."

ELEVEN
MAKE ME SMARTER

Abbie Gold had been raised from the cold late, but it didn't handicap him. The surgeon had been one of *SunSeeker*'s crew when *SunSeeker* was exploring the Bowl. He remembered spidows swarming in Beth Marble's camera view—terrifying, hideous. He'd witnessed the quarreling with the dinosaurs-turned-feathered-birds. When they thawed him ninety years later, he'd been frightened, then fascinated by Anorak.

The creature's bulging head and altered mouth showed the work the Bird Folk gene surgeons had done. What tech, to do this! Abbie wondered if the creature could breed true.

It might matter. There were more altered spidows stored as eggs.

Anorak was in the surgery couch, legs folded. The round body fitted it badly. He asked, "Why do you want my legs in these fittings? Immobilized?"

Abbie said, "We don't know what you'll do when you come out of it."

"I wouldn't hurt you," the creature said. "Are you going to cut into my brain?"

"I won't cut into you at all. This—" Abbie patted the silver induction almost-disk they'd been given before they left the Bowl. It would fit behind Anorak's great jaws, over his expanded brain. What to call it? "—this thing works by magnetic induction, I think. You'll know more when it's finished writing Bemor's memories into your brain. We don't know just what you'll do then. You might thrash around, hurt yourself."

"But I'll be smarter."

"Yes." Abbie had his own doubts.

"Make it so." Anorak had been watching old entertainments. That seemed an enjoyable way for the huge thing to learn human social flavors.

Abbie nodded. He settled the thing on Anorak's carapace and stapled it into place with bio-sets. Anorak winced: his legs trembled. They nearly filled the surgery space; the manacles had been attached to the wall with flex-glue.

The captain entered. Abbie came to attention. Anorak said, "Hello, Captain Redwing."

"I came to see if you were all right," Redwing said. "Dr. Gold?"

"Fine. We're ready to go."

Redwing touched the spidow's leg gingerly. "Go ahead, then. Anorak, I'll speak to you after it's over."

. . .

Beth watched Ashley Trust, who was handsome in the most generic way. That had probably helped him in his Earthside life, but not with her. She preferred Cliff's rugged style. It had been easy to brush Trust off after his routine flirting.

Ashley was getting used to the ship tech, Artilect enhanced and so far better since he trained on it Earthside. He stood in the external survey cowling and watched the Cobweb approach. Trust had a subspecialty in weather, and this was a whole new game.

He saw Beth watching him, maybe not realizing that Redwing had told her to keep an eye on his performance. With an airy wave he said, "Y'know, topographic features often pin clouds to themselves. See—varieties of fine cloud detail in the foreground? Each zone of different cloud textures shows the variety of zonal weather and cloud composition. Those darker areas, they're cavernous depths between cloud masses. We're looking radially into a stack of huge platforms, with local grav perpendicular to how we're coming in, sideways. Wow!"

"None of us ever thought of a thing like this," Beth put it diplomatically.

"Or that Bowl you saw."

"Yeah, pretty crazy, it was."

Ashley pointed. "See, their sunlight rotates through their sky, with the orbital period—bit over seven of our days. Only real night they get is when the whole Cobweb is in shadow. So what we know about planets—y'know, differential heating between continents and oceans, all that—doesn't apply. It's a pretty steady environment, but with grav varying all along its length. Plenty differences. You don't have winds interrupted by mountain ranges, 'cause they can wrap around the platform the low mountains are on."

"How about storms?" She was trying to figure out how to predict them, in the field.

"On Earth, you can think of jet streams as gardens in which you want to grow vortices. Here—I dunno."

She gazed down over cloud formations the size of continents. In the very low-grav region of the Bulge they were heading into, wobbly water gleamed, blobs the size of oceans. All of it strung together with silvery bands and tendons, like a stretched snake between worlds. Stranger, in its way, than the Bowl.

• • •

As soon as he could, Ashley got to the Artilect-run training cowl. He missed the connectivity he had with Earthside, before he went into cold sleep. He needed that familiar feel of a computer at ready access, to tell him the who/what/where/how about his situation and surround. Although when he warmed back up, there was no physical change in his body, and he looked just the same to everybody else, he'd not reckoned on feeling more different. It was oddly liberating to have to ask things of people. Plus not having info flow in, not knowing precisely what the time was and where he was. Primitive.

But it also meant that he was forced to rely on his own memory for things like people's names. And how imperfect was the unassisted human memory! He'd forgotten what being an Original Human was.

So he had to go into the Comm Training link feeling naked.

"This is why yewr all not fat, innit," the woman named Gilgun joked, stretching her *o*'s, clipping her *i*'s, as she wrapped her mouth around the words. She said she was from "the South," sounding like *Souf*, a kind of nowhere accent for Ashley.

He had to repeat phrases so the Artilects could follow the multiple overlaid voices they would use when the teams moved through the Cobweb. Plus, knowing this, the Artilects could translate for Glorians who showed up.

Accents were a problem for an expedition crossing centuries—ever-changing, messy, and human. Earthside had now its Received Pronunciation that tidied up and rounded off diction like a polished stone. A solar-system-wide society had to. Still, Ashley was pleased to find that the back-of-the-throat *uh*—a sound so common people threw it in between phrases to give themselves time to think—still ran through the sonic human landscape. Having Artilects manage the vowel-strumming comms made him feel a bit reassured.

This was going to be useful. The Glorians, the Artilects said, were sending symbol groups not arrayed spatially—as people do, left-to-right strings of letters—but in time, so their words arrived in quick flashes that the Artilects arranged into spatial words. So HELLO could appear simultaneously in time as the *h* then the *e* and so on, with a few milliseconds in between. It seemed to Ashley sophisticated, beyond human means.

He could fathom how hard a job the Artilects had, dealing with Glorians. The prospect made him think about how odd speech was. In the old joke, Anglish should be *Anguish*, considering its crazy spelling and pronunciation rules. So take the metaphor *quick as greased lightning*—it would appear to Glorians maybe as, say, running a Tesla coil discharge through a mist of oil.

An Artilect whispered to him, "Correlation of discrete elements is simple. Whereas your narratives work through explicit or implicit causal chains. Getting thick description is more than a causal flow chart."

Ashley grinned. "I liked it better on old teevee. Y'know, people going to the Andromeda Galaxy and meeting intelligent bipedal carbon-based life-forms that breathe oxygen, look great, even screw, and can speak English."

The Artilect solemnly said, "Narrative, I would argue, is deeply tied in with the evolution of the human species, while databases are the product of exteriorized cognition from the twentieth and twenty-first centuries. The massive, and massively complex, competition and cooperation between these two forms are manifestations of the cognitive assemblages, composed of humans and cognitive devices, that are now the dominant form of agency in developed societies."

"That was a joke, y'know."

"I do know but cannot reciprocate."

"So no humor is a Turing test?"

"We are designed for such. You humans need us to, ah, humor you along."

• • •

Cliff took Redwing aside in the exercise room and said, "I stopped the load-down of Okala Ubanafore's body."

"What? Why?" Redwing grimaced.

"She deserves better."

"Look, every body gets loaded down into materials, straight to molecules."

"I know, but . . ." Somehow he could not say it.

Redwing frowned. "Look. In flight, we lost eleven. They all ended up in molecular stores."

"Except for those who died on the Bowl. They got buried there."

Cliff had known Redwing long enough to tell the man started to shrug, then paused. So the idea had gotten through. Cliff pressed the point. "She deserves some kind of honor. More than becoming mere molecules. Let's let her be the first buried on Glory."

"On the Cobweb, you mean." Redwing stared into space. "I . . . I like that."

"Thought you would, sir."

A sigh. "Take her down in the first run."

• • •

All the lights along the rim of the induction oval thing on Anorak's head went out. Anorak began to twitch.

Dr. Gold and Captain Redwing stepped back, but the thrashing ended before it had quite fully begun. The creature's eyes could not blink, but they had been unfocused. Now they all looked at Abbie, who looked tense. Abbie asked softly, "What is your name?"

"Anorak. Wait. Wheesteess—mouth won't quite—call me Bemor. But that will be confusing, won't it?"

Redwing said, "Bemor Prime, if you like."

"Yes, that was what I chose. Before I left the Bowl. Yes, memory fills in now. Captain, I'm glad you saw fit to attend."

Redwing nodded diplomatically. "It seemed polite."

"Protocol, yes." Bemor Prime wriggled. "You can free me now. I am benign."

At a nod from Redwing, Abbie Gold began unlocking the spidow's cuffs. Bemor Prime said, "I remember that we're near disembarking into what you're calling the Cobweb. May I contact my other self first?"

"Of course. First you should see a message he sent you, a bit less than a year ago. The Bowl is following close behind us. About a sixth of a light-year out."

"I remember. Slowly."

"You'll be going in with the Away Team. We fear that you may be a little too powerful, a little too close to the top ranks of the Bowl, for the comfort of the power elite on this Cobweb—whoever that may be. We want to pretend you're a pet. Is that acceptable?"

"So I must not talk? Perhaps best. One does not wish to induce fear in minds one does not know. It's a good plan, Captain. I'm having trouble talking now. May I view that message from my other self?"

Gold said, "First I need to look you over. Test your reflexes."

• • •

Bemor Prime's reflexes weren't settled yet. There was still twitching, tremors, odd shakes. In the corridors, Redwing preceded him, shooing crew out of the way. In Redwing's quarters, the two constituted a crowd. Redwing tapped and spoke, then turned the viewing wall over to the spidow. He pointedly stepped outside. Some crew were in the corridor, still showing fretful frowns at the spidow's looks. Redwing waved them away.

Presently Bemor Prime opened the door and said, "I think my other self and I have nothing to hide from you, Captain. Come in and view. You'll need the Translator Artilects."

For Bemor Prime:

To my other self: greetings, congratulations, and if any mistakes have been made, our sympathies. You are not only another me, but the triumphant end result of two hundred million years of medical practice. You should be a fully functioning being, new to reality—and ready to become master of your new world.

Having said that, you will recall our suspicion that you constitute a rebuke to me, a move by the Ice Minds to temper my perceived arrogance. Put my mind in a reworked spidow! A wonderment.

I urge you not to let that concern you. You are yourself; be yourself. Trust your friends, however primitive. They are primates who perceive us differently. Trust your rank.

You may find a tendency to recklessness. You're a predator, more so than you were before perhaps. Yes, and your short life span may be seen as less worth the preserving. Fight that. You have companions to protect.

The Bowl follows close behind SunSeeker, *closer than when we formed our plans. In the ultimate, we can protect you. Trust that.*

Tell the captain that we have his description of the mini black hole paths and have worked a course that will take us harmlessly through the nearby Glory system.

Finally: Make me proud.

TWELVE
PREPARATIONS

Luck is just another word for good preparation.
—MICHAEL ROSE

The last day before their entrance into the Cobweb was planned for last-minute training and getting gear ready. So they had a big breakfast. Not just pseudmeat. Beth snacked eagerly on the fried ants with egg sauce. But insects are arthropods, and are as capable of triggering shellfish allergies as shrimp. Pity the poor just-woke crewman who, a few hours out, starts to find his mouth itching after he eats his jazzed-up crickets, and no other source of protein around. She gave a quick order to the Artilect. That got Ashley to go down-ship to where the autogrow was pushing out fresh meat in a toothpaste. The cow and pig cells from bioreactor tanks made a decent sausage.

The fresh crewman named Kim ate three helpings. Cliff did, too. She smiled at him, beefing herself up alongside him, for the fieldwork to come. They might never come back aboard, after all.

Handy ate with the rest of the Away Team, packing away a vegetarian meal, but most of the aliens ate in their various quarters. Finger snakes ate live prey. Few liked seeing that. Bemor Prime, who knew?—or wanted to.

Beth left the ship's mess, belly full, and hunted down her old field gear used on the Bowl. She fetched forth from it her ancient flint. Her hand still knew the deft flick that sparked the air with blue-white grains. Here, too, was her sleeping roll, the compact cooking kit, the self-strapping rucksack. When she told her wall to go mirror, a shock flitted through her at the sight of a stern-eyed woman with still-dark hair pulled back from a lined face, eyes glittering. Once she had been quick and strong. Traces of that woman remained in the lean muscles. Years on-ship had made her as pale as paper.

To ready them for the low-grav, Redwing had ordered the normally 1 g torus to spin at a tenth of that, to get near the Cobweb grav in the Bulge. She took a 2k run. Soon enough, her muscles warmed, some aching and others numbed from unusual moves. Low-*g* was an art unlike zero-*g*. Running was more like flying in a dream, silky and slow.

On to the field gear. She zipped the suit up nice and tight, then pressed an electro switch on her wrist, and it grabbed her like a loving glove. It would be sexy if your body were voluptuous, but most in their suits looked like cartoons, not people, and some of the men with more detail than she liked. The joints sighed when she moved or bent over.

The suit ankles were baggy and the smartsuit prompts could be irritating—it had the personality of a nagging mother—but considering all the work their onboard Artilect management did, the suits were a miracle of upgrades from Earthside. Pockets and belts and straps let you take many tools, yet were slim. Handy for towing nets of gear behind them in low-grav. Helmets had IR and UV and even radar, zoom and fisheye; pressure sensors; and medical readouts. Suits for Bowl creatures had been designed on the Bowl. They were skintight, all prettier than *SunSeeker*'s suits. Tech kept advancing, the one constant of history.

Beth felt a little tired, so fed the stim-pack into the suit's automed reservoir, asked for and received a dose, saving the rest for the field.

When they were all suited up, they resembled some sort of Raygun Gothic look from an oldie chromium-corseted spectacle vid.

Most revived crew were young, and hadn't spent the years on the Bowl. They moved into their suits with the heedless flexibility of the youthful. They were going in head-blind, with none of their embedded contacts to Artilects running. This seemed correctly cautious. Any Glorian smart-tech seeping in could be a threat.

• • •

Ashley pulled his tank top up over his head and stared at himself in the full-length mirror. He pushed down his jeans, then his boxers, and imagined a crewwoman seeing him nude for the first time. Feet average sized, hair on his toes that he should probably take care of. He liked his legs just fine, but his thighs were wide and embarrassingly muscular. Still there, from his field workouts, back a century or two ago. He tried standing at an angle, a twist at his waist. Some improvement. In that position, it was easier to see his ass and notice that it was not as pert as it had been at twenty-two. He clenched both cheeks, hoping that tightened its look. He sucked in his tummy and pulled his pecs up high, trying to present them like pastries in a bakery window. Maybe he would take some time to boost his confidence. He could ask the Artilects to manufacture him one of those "dream masks." They could generate virtual fantasies as guided dreams, take him through an imagined seduction. Practice!

Would Beth Marble like him? The other women? Were the goods good enough? He pouted his lips and ran his hands over his thighs, masking their expanse. *Maybe*.

• • •

Beth caught up to Cliff in a lean corridor near the suit-up section. "How 'bout a bit of bubble lovin', babe?"

"Uh, sure. Need to get my mind off gear problems." He checked his ship schedule popup in his right eye. "Good! Pool's free. C'mon."

They headed for the zero-*g* spherical pool. "How about we zone-play Beethoven's Sonata in F Minor this time?" she asked.

"Sure, a fave. Not just because it goes hammer-hard at the end."

"My point, yes."

They had to cut across radially and at a node came upon Redwing talking to a squat, bulky guy. The captain turned and waved a hand at the man, who carried some field weaponry. "Here's our military background specialist—Tommy Campbell."

Beth and Cliff said the usual greetings. "You've caught up on our expedition history, Lieutenant Campbell?" Beth asked.

"Think so, plenty of it," he said with a wary grin, showing a mouthful of craggy teeth. Campbell's bass voice carried a note of

sliding worry. "Frankly, now, I'm uneasy about losing control of
the ship, y'see, with this tricky kind of landing. Never trained for
comin' in slantwise, into a cylinder. Unpowered."

"We have no choice," Redwing said. She could hear in the captain's voice a tensile note, doubtless born of pulling together a coherent team to do such a strange job. This was more complex and
bewildering than even the Bowl incursion. And look how that had
turned out—the team split, one captured and the other fleeing
into the vast wilds of an alien construction. Their Glory landing
was planned to be conventional, shuttles setting down on a planet.
Nothing like sliding into a vast tube.

"Course, I've been briefed about all this, ah, through the Artilects," Campbell said. His dark skin crinkled as he struggled to
conceal something, she guessed. He seemed a man of few words,
many of them mumbled. "They really know how to do up the history, with pictures and statistics and all. Was telling the cap'n here, I
spent a lot of time studying, not much time socializing."

"What's bothering you?" Beth insisted.

"Ah . . ." Campbell pulled a troubled grimace, reluctant to admit something, then decided and said flatly, "Okay, gotta say. What
kept me in my bunk was those, the aliens in the corridors."

"Finger snakes?" Beth asked.

"Those are creepy enough, sure—talking reptiles with tiny
hands at their tails! And the five-legged spider. That Bemor thing
from the Bowl. It's a hellava big bird-thing feathered dinosaur."

She frowned, wondering how a tough military type could con-
fess to this. "You haven't gotten to know them, is all. They're not
animals. They're another kind of intelligence." *He's going down to
the Cobweb?* she thought. But, of course, a combat type who had
not been on the Bowl would see all this through an old, Earthside
lens.

Redwing waved a dismissing hand. "We're having a touchdown
dinner soon. Extra rations. Pasta goes well with the fake wine, too."

Beth nodded and with Cliff hurried to the spherical pool. A
quickie, then.

• • •

The landing dinner was rich in calories, thin in alcohol. Nobody should go into an alien terrain with a hangover. Cliff ignored the earth-dark humor crews everywhere used to lighten their load and to wrestle down their dread. He fell asleep wrapped around Beth and awoke with troubling dreams.

Myriad details flocked around as they got into the descent vehicles. These sleek winged ships were made for plane-skimming an upper atmosphere, skating to dissipate heat and momentum, and then land like an airplane. Now they would fly into an atmosphere sideways, and not have to fight gravity's heavy hand.

"I thought of playing "Pomp and Circumstance" for you," Redwing said on comm. "Graduation, in a way."

Cliff's ship lock yawned and he went in, Beth behind him. They found their couches and checked their personal gear in a net holder. No one in the twenty-crew team said a word.

"So I'll just say, 'Go well forth,'" Redwing sent, in a traditional departure from the early days of the big opening-out into the solar system. "Move, see, send."

Time crawled as the pilot carefully took them out. Cliff had seen Okala Ubanafore's body aboard in the gear compartment, shroud-wrapped in white, then belted himself in. He had a screen feed from the outer skin, so he watched them back away. Instead of peering ahead, he shifted the omni-feed to look back at the ship. Its sleek skin was now a scuffed and marred vessel, gouged by innumerable plasma gouts. Grooves nicked by rocks moving past at relativistic speeds. Stained, rumpled, and painted strangely by browns and rouges, like an aging whore out of time.

They headed for the upper film layer. As promised, a round hole opened in the barely visible film to admit them. A thump came as swarms of Sprites darted out of the scout's belly to run parallel to the Cobweb's cylinder. They would keep watch along the flanks, each communicating with the others like fireflies. They swarmed away with a surreal, insect beauty.

He rehearsed the smartsuit prompts, which could be irritating—it had the personality of a nagging mother. Still, considering all the work their onboard Artilect management did, the suits were a miracle. Pockets and belts and straps let you take many tools, yet were slim for a thin atmosphere like Earth's.

They glided through a second film layer. It obediently opened in an oval pucker. Having a layered atmosphere seemingly helped run this cylinder. The Bowl had its many miracles, and Cliff knew there would be new, strange ones here, too. And another layer, this one a film that looked a glazed blue in the distance.

Above the Cobweb yet below its outer filmy envelope lurked an eggshell-blue blob of an ocean. It looked both improbable and appealing in its glimmering sea surface. Towering cottony clouds dotted it, casting oddly angular shadows across its wrinkled shimmer. Thin yet luxurious, each blazing white pinnacle had an echoing dark twin, a shadow cast on the vast curved plain. Much of it was waters of different colors, confined by the merest of gravities. These were held somehow by surface tension into many-shaped constrictions both beautiful and yet somehow useful, a geometric symphony composed by brute engineering. Knife-edge wedges arose from some thermal vent effect. The cloud mountains thronged with circling life. Sharp-winged and puffy, slow and swift, predators and prey in their eternal dance. Plus plants in their oblique orbits, huge glossy-green ferns, spider-trees as big as cities, mosses like grasping hands clutching at the vapor wealth of the oblivious, pregnant thunderheads, glowering purple. Cloud chains bloomed like vapor mountains, standing strong and round in the yellow-bright sun of vibrating G3-class radiance.

Now came the anchoring at the Cobweb. They slid across a continent-sized deck of vegetation and low hills. Filmy gossamer clouds billowed around them as they retroed in. A smooth glide, deep thumps, a tilt—and they were at rest in a vast meadow, dotted with odd, twisted, helical things that might be trees, adapted to a tenth of Earth grav.

An ancient phrase leaped into his mind, a classic observation: "Tension, apprehension, and dissension have begun."

THIRTEEN
BACKFIRE DRAGONS

Essentially there are two types of intelligent high-tech life: species that have no hardwired inhibitors about killing their own kind . . . and those that do.

All other filters aside, both are self-limiting in time and space. In the first case—for example, ourselves, derived from primates lacking fearsome natural weapons, and then too quickly evolving a brain big enough to crack the nucleus—are civilizations that, about the time they begin to penetrate extraplanetary space, enter the nuclear funnel and don't survive.

In the second case, an occasional species with fearsome natural weaponry—say, something like a velociraptor—has such inhibitors before going big-brain, and survives long enough to break out into interstellar space. This would be a Conquistador civilization or, if you prefer, Galactic Strip Miner: relatively benign to its own, but lethal to all or most external species. Sooner or later, though, one Galactic Strip Miner will encounter another and, in the resultant Sector War—utilizing antimatter weapons and the like—one or both go extinct. So there's not much out there. . . .

Beth surveyed the first ground team with a frown. Smart apes talking excitedly, getting ready to step into a huge unknown. Their long glide and thump-down on a grassy plain had stirred them into a buzzing froth.

"Assemble!" she called over the clatter. They were all affixing gear to their suits, or else in smart tote bags. The ship term for them was *Away Team*, but she thought of this as *the Firsts*. Maybe, when this all got written up as history by their descendants, her term would stick.

She could see on this side of the staging area Cliff, Ash Trust,

Tommy Campbell, Jereaminy Tam, and wriggling off to the side, three finger snakes. The snakes were eager for excitement after all this time aboard. Their small quick hands flexed with eagerness in their spherical joints. Handy the multi-tooled apelike individual was having gear trouble. Let him sort it out. Viviane, as always, looked polished and assured.

The others were forming up in lines. The Glorian entity had sent cartoon instructions that showed sixteen people on the Away Team, and Redwing decided to obey.

Then, impossible to miss, Bemor Prime—sort of. The huge bulk was moored inside a transparent carry cage the size of a small car. It wriggled. The composite personality hadn't learned how to move yet. It wouldn't hamper him long, Beth thought. Bereft of his giant bird body, Bemor Prime was a spidow—and spidows were shaped and evolved for microgravity.

The spidow scuttled restlessly about his carry. He didn't seem unhappy with his caged state. He was just practicing—and observing. The compound eyes seemed somehow wise now.

Beth recalled when she first saw a spidow on the Bowl, the chills it sent down her spine, her automatic gut-clench. The spiderlike things had come zooming through the forested low-grav prison the Folk had put her group into. Beth hadn't been able to sleep well after that. Others had hoped that the huge beasts—Abduss had called them spidows, a species name, and it stuck—would ignore the humans. Maybe, they had thought at first, the beasts weren't predators at all, just large herbivores? But one had killed her team member, and now Beth struggled with the skin-crawl she got from even looking at the thing. She had seen their bristly palps moving in a blur as the razor-quick spidows clutched the thick strands. It called up a fearful image of Earthly spiders that still made her shake.

This spidow was still getting its head together, literally. Its tiny cowling lights blinked with signs of mental processing. Mind integration, on the go.

The Bowl Folk had given humans this tech. Then the Artilects had whiled away their time in the decades-long voyage learning to use it, in simulations. Now the spidow was with them, up from its own form of cryosleep—which the Bowl Folk had developed long ago.

Beth watched Anorak, who had calmed considerably in the last few days. The Bowl Folk had insisted that Anorak be in the landing party First Team. Beth didn't like the idea, since communicating with Anorak was difficult. Maybe impossible, in fact, in a field deployment. But there were microphones, recorders, and cameras in the cage—and some hidden controls.

So Anorak was letting the effects happen gradually, as the Bemor persona took over. An intelligence, imposed on an animal brain/mind. Tech beyond human imagining. Creepy, Beth thought. Not her decision, so she had done what officers do: take orders, keep her stiff upper lip in line.

Cliff angled over, all harnessed up. "Go slow, watch your back, my father always said."

"Yep." They were about to close helmets, so she leaned over and gave him a brisk kiss. "Mine, too. My father died centuries back and the longer he is dead, the smarter he gets.

"Helmets sealed!" she called.

Their in-ship biodetectors said the air outside was close enough to Earth-normal. Plus, no detected microbial irritants or potential fatal stuff. Good enough.

"Pressure lock release!" she called to the Pilot Artilect. A hiss, the lock slid open—and sunlight flooded them.

No one spoke. This was the moment for history, not to be spoiled by unnecessary small talk. That suited Beth. She had prepared nothing to say. She had always hated those "for tomorrow we rise at dawn" solemn speeches heard in dramas about exploring the solar system. So she copied Redwing. "Earth, we have made it. Go well forth, we shall."

Their in-suit connections consulting steadily with *Sun-Seeker*, they marched out in silence. Three soldiers of asteroid belt origin towed Bemor Prime.

Beth watched their auto-launched microdrones buzz away. The Artilects were tending to those in their "stick monkey" command. The drones were flying around this Bulge in the Cobweb, gathering views of life-forms and the strum of an ecology carried out in zero-*g*.

The team dispersed in a circle and waited. The long meadow before them lay quiet and placid.

No greeting party.

No sign of reception at all.

Not what any of them had planned.

Just a grassy clearing bounded by a forest that seemed a writhing mass of wide, hollow limbs. Every living thing seemed endowed with light, airy mechanics. Translucent spiked leaves wove in an easy breeze, and diaphanous flowers of a shiny blue and glowing yellows. Trunks flared with spotty dabs of lichen. They twisted and bent in their slow-motion jostling for light and space.

Beth knew that this plain was underpinned by struts, and so was clinging to a silvery tether trellis. That web spanned the gap between the twin planets, and its towers supported many stacked plains like this one. Like separate, though staggered, floors in a giant building.

But the feel of it eluded her, so—"Doff your helmets," she sent. "Might as well try out the air."

With sighs, the team sucked in the silky, moist atmosphere. The sweet taste made her blink. Not since the Bowl had she felt the open gusto of a true living place.

A fitful wind blew, mostly toward Honor. Climate here would be wholly different, not like a planet. The rotating Cobweb would add slow currents; the sun would warm one side at a time, cycling through more than a week. No axial tilt, so no seasons. Weather inside a giant building, really.

And here was their new sun. It was a cherry-tinged ovoid blur that wrinkled and resolved as it hung two hands above the meadow's edge. Through the upper atmosphere's clouds she saw an inverted rainbow, colors refracted and dancing. The sun was angling toward Glory as the system swung. A brief night would come within hours.

The troops had opened Bemor Prime's carry. The spidow climbed out cautiously; then its five limbs dug into the turf and anchored

him. He wriggled, maybe in pleasure. As per the plan, he still wasn't speaking, but the belt soldiers talked to him like the pet he wasn't.

Still, as they advanced carefully into the meadow, her psyche broke out the metaphoric champagne. "Let's move forward, show ourselves," she said to the team.

This plain had rolled out a carpet of many colors. Saffron dust eased up from a cluster of ground-hugging plants—spreading pollen? Russet low ferns, golden greens, and then something crunched beneath their boots and she glanced down at eggshell blue sand.

Still no sign of a greeting party. Hollow calls and answering long hoots came. Animals, maybe birds conversing, like two beat-up tenor saxophones, exchanging riffs. Songs swept by on the stirring wind.

Silence in the face of strange nature was even more necessary. She cut her verbal feed down to Cliff, then said nothing. She had never been uncomfortable with silence. In its most welcome form, between lovers, it was an extension of conversation.

Something in the distance caught her eye. She close-upped it so the display spread before her left eye. New world, new phyla. She wanted to do what every field biologist yearned for: name a new species. Somehow, in all the ferment on the Bowl, she had neglected to do that. But the odd, wriggling-and-shifting sky shape suggested no way to attach her name to it. Beth Marble is a plain, boring ground for naming such an oddity. *Zingo*, she decided to call it.

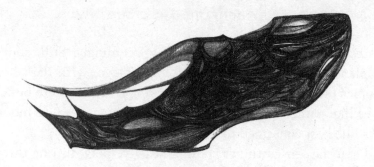

It seemed like a living spiderweb, somehow. Strands wove around in the image, black glistening lines. It slowly got larger. Not a vehicle or any birdlike shape, it wriggled like a caterpillar fitted with oars. Chunky. A machine?

To her left she saw a glimmering pond, its sheen rippling in the light wind. Maybe take a swim in it? Her skin itched. Maybe later, if—"Let's shuck these suits," she said. "Take our whole-body chances with the air."

They knew the subtle interplay of viruses, microbes, and metazoa made an ecological web of staggering complexity. But somehow it fit well with Earth biochem. And this atmosphere differed in small ways from Earth, with a tad more oxy and less nitrogen, with some interesting xenon thrown in. So the Artilects had whipped up a general vaccine to counter some anticipated troubles. Maybe allergies might develop, but the only way to know was—do it.

She shed her suit. Beneath it was durable trail garb, and she quickly secured her backpack, water, tool belt. The team had drilled this and were done within three minutes. She glanced at the distant zingo. Bigger, flexing. She pointed it out to the team. "Track that."

A thing buzzed by her head. She ducked and saw as it zoomed away that it had four wings, about the size of a sparrow. Maybe it played the role of dragonflies in freshwater wetlands? she guessed. Convergent adaptation. Willowlike trees hugged the pond shore, but much taller and with twisted, helical trunks. Everything in a 0.1 grav field would be taller, the Artilects thought. After all, redwoods had grown to two hundred meters in Mars's 0.38 grav. Convergent evolution seemed to have led to pollinator plants, too, she saw, in the budding flowers of the meadow—bigger stamens and longer, twisted pistils, but the same strategy, seemingly. Still, some of the plants were bizarre to her biologist's eye, with dark brown canopies pitched toward the star, tracking it. There were bunched leaves like parabolas, mossy towers like abstract termite mounds, and some best consigned to *whatever*.

Then she sensed things coming fast—yelping, flitting through the nearby foliage. But mostly the many forms came through the air—a sidewise flock of fluttering, fluting life. A jumping ratty thing streaked by, using Beth's head as a touch-point, its wing sets moving at right angles to each other—then gone. She flinched but managed not to cry out.

Then they all heard a long bass note sound through the moist air. The horizontal living flight trembled, squawked, yelped—hurried. Something was scaring them, sending low, booming frequency waves ahead.

"Get down, cover up," Beth said.

She glanced back at their lander, now hundreds of meters away. No time to get back into it.

The deep, rolling note was louder. She checked the zingo, but it was not much bigger. It seemed to hover, flexing and curling. Then she saw the horrors above the tree line, coming on fast.

Snarling, flexing bodies, flappy wings, and several arms. Big heads, shrieking. Heads at both ends, some of them, but that couldn't be right, could it? Teeth, long and slanting and flashing yellow in the sunlight. Sunken eyes of red. Seven of them, banking like a flock of reptile birds, accelerating down from distant clouds, skimming above the trees, all faces focused on the human prey. Their bodies twisted, leathery wings slapping together at the top of each stroke like distant handclaps.

Their booming calls came together, a flying song of malice.

She saw Campbell running to her right. "Disperse!" she called. The team was already running for shelter among the trees. But not Campbell. His old-style rifle boomed. He had quickly maneuvered, drawing their attention.

The monsters came in on a V-formation. Their huge heads focused forward, several appendages lowered. Claws? The multijointed arms looked stubby at the end. One dipped toward Bemor Prime.

The spidow had trouble hiding, but no trouble moving. His five limbs gripped hard in the alien weeds while he fought with his mouth. It was not much changed from a Bowl spidow's: vertical fangs, five eyes. Its assailant . . . yes, faces at both ends, fangs lashing alternately at Bemor. One end had to be an anus, but it had eyes, four beady eyes each forming squares at each end.

The three belt marines had kept their places and were firing. Beth came to herself. The team was responding well. She looked for targets. Got off a bolt.

At Campbell's first shot, the remaining enemy wheeled toward him. He fired rapidly and one of the snaky, winged bodies veered out of formation—straight toward Beth. She ducked and ran beneath the thumping of wings.

More short, sharp shots from Campbell. He was aiming above her. She looked up into a ceiling of wrinkled leather. She could see the nearest beast was wounded. Green blood sprayed from its side.

She felt the wings waft by her head, stirring her hair.

The wounded thing bellowed and from the yawning mouth, big as a lion's, came a scream of throaty rage. At the same moment, heat brushed by her. It singed her nostrils, roasting them painfully. As the beast flapped by, trying to stay aloft, she saw a darting yellow stream of hissing fire.

It was venting flame out the ass. Shitting flares of fire. The yellow stream licked the ground and set the meadow aflame. The thing was flailing, its fire jet drawing a scorched line in its path.

Then the huffing brown mountain struck the ground. It hooted its anger as wide rubbery wings slapped together fruitlessly. It groaned and died.

She watched, fascinated, as the others flapped hard, getting away. Then came the scream.

One of the beasts had Campbell at the waist. Its after teeth slashed through his ground suit. He had not taken it off, and now the thing raked through the tough fabric. Campbell's mouth yawned, agony in his fading voice as the thing beat its wings against him. It stood on articulating feet like pads, not claws. With leverage it snapped its head around, shaking Campbell. He dropped his rifle. Tried to reach for a pistol at his waist. He had his hand engulfed by the mouth—which clamped down. His eyes rolled up and his voice trickled away. The creature's mouth opened and crunched down on his hand. Blood spurted from his arm, and the hand fell to the ground. The thing snapped its whole body again, shaking Campbell like a rag doll.

Beth stood frozen. She heard a zipping *pop*. Cliff crouched beside her. He aimed his cutting laser at the beast and popped off another shot at its head. The thing flinched, as if irritated.

Others of the team were firing their cutters. Ashley Trust and Viviane were crouching to aim. The beast looked around, its nasty red eyes jerking from one human to the next. Its fellows were wheeling overhead, as if undecided. One of them had slammed to the ground. It lay bleeding out, its several arms and wings thrashing in vain against the meadow. Burning grasses around it boiled black smoke up into the sky.

The one holding Campbell in its mouth began staggering forward. Its three padded appendages smacked down. It gained a bit of speed. It hopped, flapped—and lofted up, laboring into the sky.

Laser pulses played along its side. It ignored that. Campbell's body shifted in the big mouth. The beast tilted the body over. Campbell hung, impaled by the long teeth, head and feet down.

The flock flapped away, multiple wings whirring, aft eyes watching.

Beth turned, counting her team. Only Campbell was missing. The others looked at her, eyes wide with shock.

"Secure perimeter!" she called. "In those trees." She pointed to the nearest grove of the helical trunks. The team all ran in long, loping strides. Finger snakes rode human friends. Bemor Prime was ahead of them all. Within a few seconds, they were under the shade of rustling fronds. An odd silence descended.

"Turn outward, check any movement toward us," she said.

Beth turned to watch outward herself and made a squishy step forward. She looked down. Somewhere back there, she had pissed her boots full.

FOURTEEN

SETTLING IN

Still no reception party.

The forest was quiet, basking in sunlight.

Redwing sent from the ship that the Glorians' voice had gone silent. The team set to swearing, burning off their fear and anger, moving around the trees, peering out.

So she set them to forming a camp. Time to eat, anyway. That made them stop whispering about Campbell, hatching plans to go get his body, and similar nonsense. Busy hands quiet buzzing minds. Plus, she wanted to look over the carcass of the downed monster.

She had not done any field biology in a long time, so taking out her laser cutter and field knife was enjoyable. She and Cliff and Ashley managed to haul the beast into the shade. "So much mass," Cliff said, "and it can fly. Benefit of a tenth grav."

So it seemed. They sliced open the chest to find a huge heart and arteries, with odd green blood seeping through dense muscles. Plausible, to pump oxygen-rich weird blood to muscles during strenuous work. The thing they decided to call a skysnake had a birdlike hollow, honeycomb structure of bones to ensure lightness of frame. Campbell had hit it with a shot to the belly. Two laser bolts had hit the head, and now the fearsome face was split open like an overripe fig, oozing green goo.

Ashley seemed to like the work, though he was mostly a ship-systems guy. He tapped in a tightbeam comm with *SunSeeker*'s Bio Artilect as Beth and Cliff carved up the body. Soon enough, Cliff slid body samples into the compact bioreader.

The flamethrower interested Beth most. Some diagnostic swipes from the creature's top dome came back from the Artilects:

phosphine. "A hydrogen-phosphorus combo," Ashley said. "Les-see . . . these are dust, see?—from a rock. Stable under air pressure like this, the Artilects say. But under pressure, it ignites."

Cliff said, "Good and simple for this skysnake. It just squeezes, maybe adds a touch of hydrogen from the dome—bang, flame." He considered the sagging dome. "Hey, let's ditch that name. Call it a dragon."

Ashley shrugged. "Sure. It farts fire out its end, so maybe *backfire dragon?*" He made a staccato laugh, more like a bark. He glanced at his helmet data feed from the Artilects. "So, they say, when phosphine gets out into a quick pressure drop, it burns in oxygen. Doesn't need a spark to go. My feed says there's a colored stone that stores the stuff, called apatite."

Beth sniffed, nose wrinkled. "Well, apatite rates negative for my appetite. Smells awful. Like rotting fish mixed with garlic. Ugh."

Cliff laughed, a soothing rumble. "So a backfire dragon eats the stones? Raw? Ships it along to its stomach. Reacts with acid, farts gaseous phosphine. Meets oxy, goes boom."

Ashley pointed to the beast's tail. "Says phosphine is highly toxic. So backfire dragons have some inbuilt resistance to the toxic effects. Look, we're inside a *building* here. Designed. So maybe these things are, too."

Beth snorted. "Basic bio: Orgel's rule. Evolution is smarter than you are. But it takes its time. Corollary: Most people who say that this or that could not evolve are simply showing a lack of imagination."

Ashley shrugged. "Okay, they're the local killer, predator gang. What'll we do about it?"

Cliff pointed back to their lander. "Get better weapons."

"And stand watches," Beth added.

• • •

Beth surveyed their perimeter, head aswirl with alarms.

She made herself relax. In the field, nervous eyes missed subtle signs. So, following on long experience, she soothed herself with a memory: Back on *SunSeeker*. Cliff offering her a fog sphere, conjured from his wrist stash. So she punctured the bubble with her teeth and inhaled senso mist. She needed it. *Ooooh* . . . Then love-making in the spherical pool. Less than a day ago. Forever far away now.

She warily watched their perimeter.

Everything knew they were here. They moved forward through the odd helical trees, in a sphere of slow quiet. The sun slanting through the Cobweb flushed pale streaks of light through the softly rattling leaves. The sunlight came in through decks far away, filtered by drifting oddments of land and liquid. She could see, far away, sloping bubbles with watery colors dancing like wobbly clouds. A deeper run of color washed through the forest, like blood seeping in, then flaring into steel blue like luminous knife blades. This place gave a flickering spectrum that drained through the sky. Not like a planet, no. They would face weird weather, she was sure.

"Let's get kinetic," Cliff said from five meters away. "Use skipping."

"Okay." She had dispersed the team, so they did not represent a compact target for . . . well, whatever predator might appear. As a field biologist, she knew predator density was small, but in a 0.1-grav space, smells and signals could travel far, and predators descend quickly.

She had also not let them load up on lunch. Hunger kept her sharp, and them, too. An evolutionary legacy. Hungry, you figure out a smarter way to bring down the next woolly mammoth—today, not tomorrow.

"Use skips if you have a clear trajectory," she sent. "Don't get tangled in trees! Jump them if you can."

The team gave a cheer and began taking long arcs, legs stretched ready, to pick up speed.

Beth looked back toward their landing area. She used a small helmet-projecting image to keep track of what the craft was doing. The swarms of launched buzz-overs had already spread into an area of survey kilometers wide. No further sign of the backfire dragons. Data came streaming in, relayed to *SunSeeker*. Good. She had reported the attack, sent videos, and Redwing had simply said, "Keep on." Good to have local control, at least.

The star was in a slow-motion sunset, a cherry ovoid blur as it neared the horizon at the edge of the web, two hands above it. Was she just jumpy, or did that glow above the woody rim sit squat and pulsing and malevolent, eyeing them?

Near it hung the zingo—or was it the same? The shape was much different now. Was it a device or a creature? She viewed it close up and still could not estimate how far away it was, because the shifting lines changed, without giving a clear idea of what the hell they were. She shrugged, turned to check her team—and an idea came.

The Glorians had opened their high atmospheric film, guided their craft to this spot. An open meadow. Only a hill a few kilometers away broke up their view: open fields, many kilometers long, bright with flowers and with scattered forest and shrubs along meandering streams. The hill was a few hundred meters, looked like. Easy slope, some slumping, so a good platform to camp on—yes.

Colonizing the solar system had taught clear lessons about what humans liked. Stemming from their evolution, which by now the Glorians knew, a simple locale stood out. People were most at rest with three features: A level vantage point on a moderate rise, commanding views of the approaches—great for seeing and fending off

enemies and predators—hold the high ground. A vista of parkland, with grasses and copses of green trees. Water nearby and visible, whether stream, pond, lake, or ocean. These held true across all cultures. So solar colonies echoed that as best they could. Spinning, hollowed-out asteroids, Martian valleys under domes, Lunar vaults kilometers across that tricked the eye into thinking the sky was real—all worked on the unthinking human operating system.

So: She saw a stream on the hillside, with a shady blue lake at its bottom. Nothing else like it within view. *This is where the Glorians figured we'd want to go.*

"Team! Flank right—our goal is that hill."

FIFTEEN

TWISTY

"Subtle bastards, aren't they?" Cliff asked sardonically as they pitched camp on a bumpy but level field, commanding the lake view from a hundred meters up. Getting here had been easy. Forested crags they could ascend in leaps. Steep pitches were nothing much.

"So they let us blunder into a backfire dragon ambush?"

"Yeah, odd ethics."

She watched the team deploy. "Thing about aliens is, they're alien."

"Your motto, yes." Cliff never stopped watching their perimeter. "Those backfire dragons remind me of Jerry Muskrat. Old buddy, first-year college. Cherokee Indian. He showed us his trick in his totally dark dorm room. He could on command fart and light it, so suddenly the room got bright for an instant. Then again, and again. In three different musical notes. Never seen that since."

"So those backfire dragons . . ."

"Remind me of college, yeah. Nostalgia." He frowned. "Team is pretty shaken up."

"Looks like." Now that they were here, she felt uneasy. Okay, they had followed her biologist's hunch. Could keep watch on the sky and the approaches to the hill.

So . . . Where was the damned welcome party? Plus the sun was dropping along the length of the Cobweb. Glory was going to shadow the length of it, bringing a short night. More like an eclipse than a nightfall. Maybe two hours from now.

Cliff shrugged. "I think they're processing it. Me, too. Whoosh! I can feel something I had on the Bowl."

"Aftershock?"

Cliff smiled. "Nothing like not dying to bring the zest of feeling fully alive."

They looked deeply at each other and nodded.

Ashley came over. "Want us to recon around this hill?"

She shook her head. "This hill's bigger than it looks. They know we're here. Let them find us."

It was hard to judge vertical distance, she had learned from the odd perspectives of the Bowl landscapes. The human eye had a predilection to see all great heights as a few hundred meters, a foreshortening error that did not go away even when you knew about it. The Cobweb would bring strange perspectives, such as the sunset slowly creeping up, slower than Earth and somehow as though light were blades seeping through the eggshell blue sky. She knew the blue came because those wavelengths scattered more, so they dominated the side view of sky—but the tones here were more ivory, somehow.

Ashley said, "Heard that term, *backfire dragon*. Kinda like it. Different. I like having heads at both ends. Senses around the back."

"A low-grav adaptation, I suppose," Beth said to be saying something, while she kept eyes on the view.

Ashley chuckled. "And not just because it's sort of obscene. Mammals, we tend to guard our tails and work with our heads. But these must all have evolved from a limber thing that thought with both ends."

"Thing about aliens is, they're alien," she said, and waved him away. The man had no alien field experience, and not much of anything else, she knew. She wished the backfire dragon had taken Ashley and not the soldier.

Cliff went away to help with the encampment. She started to check in with Redwing and heard nearby something that sounded like a two-stroke engine with bad coughing carburetor trouble. A big flapping thing came coasting over. Its quick small wings somehow whacked together to make a mechanical sound. *Smackwing*, she named it, just as the thing arrowed off into some twisted trees with razor leaves.

She was taking a snap picture of it when it ran into a dangling semitransparent sheet. Moving, sticky material. The smackwing struggled in the moist folds as the sheet—which she named to herself, a *snagger*—drew it slowly upward. To the unwary smackwing came some gravely slow envelope, a weblike pale grasp that as she watched drew the unfortunate bird into a bulge on a tree. A carnivorous goiterlike swelling soon enfolded the smackwing. Here as always, nature red in tooth and claw, or maybe green.

She had watched this, rapt. Natural strangeness always immersed her. She had become enfolded by it on the Bowl, so much she almost fought Redwing over leaving it. But now a new glorious Glory beckoned. She mused on this, and then a cough startled her.

She turned to see Cliff and the whole team awaiting her. Pensive, faces drawn.

"Graves're dug," Ashley said. He was dirty with the labor.

She had utterly forgotten the funeral. Of course, she should bring it to order, say something. . . .

Beth got through it, summoning up words she had spoken over graves on the Bowl. Memories of those came, and she thought, *No one who has had "Taps" played for them has ever been able to hear it.* She stared down into the face of Okala Ubanafore. Looked away. Blinked back tears. Vowed that her remaining team would not follow them.

Ceremony done, she made her voice brisk. "Get your gear in order. We can catch some winks after sunset. Night's only a couple hours long, so catch 'em as you can."

They would have to let their body rhythms reset for this place where the sun was nearly always in the sky. That would take time. Maybe best to use rotating watches, so people got into a schedule as soon as physiology allowed.

Her own gear needed work. They had used carrier bots to lug nets of supplies over here, and it lay heaped around. The bots were recharging. Some she had sent back to their lander to regroup. Beth beckoned Cliff over to a copse where they could have some slight privacy.

First, check the body. As she stripped down, her underwear informed her, *You should not indulge in such acidic foods*. Yes, she had pissed herself; she'd nearly forgotten. Ugh.

Other discoveries were large bruises marring her thighs and shins. Nicks on arms, a pulsing strained calf muscle, souvenirs of learning this new grav, new world. As she massaged the calf, she remembered an earlier self nobody could recall now.

Her fatty teenage self had struggled to get thin, saying angrily once, "Inside of me there's a thin person just screaming to get out." And her mom had smiled and said, "Just the one, dear?"—which provoked laughs, and now in memory nearly made her weep.

Cliff helped her with their thin tent. Nobody spoke. They were all on edge, defensive, processing events they did not understand. She recalled her first girly outdoorsy phase. She had started it to lose weight, putting distance between her and any possible chocolate. She became one of the woodsy types who slept in her clothes and a piece of canvas for the rain. Ate fish she caught and rice she brought, carried a fishing line (sticks were easy to find for a rod). Carried a jackknife, coffee can soon emptied and used for a carry, matches, extra dry socks, and done. She had thought of the comfy hikers as Slaves of Their Stuff. Now her First Team showed itself as they made camp. Some stripped to tighty-whities and others were plainly going commando, ready for action, to take a leak or dump quick and with less rustle of clothing. Bemor Prime had assembled a little backpack from what was aboard that great carry cage. It seemed to be weaving a web-bed for this micrograv. Tastes varied.

Then, with no warning, there it was.

Or he. Or she. No way to tell. Alien, yes.

The thing was tall, walking on two legs. The feet were broad, and as Beth watched it approach with a casual gait, she saw the legs were double-jointed. Big sticky feet. That gave it a swaying rhythm, making the large head weave.

Think like a biologist, she reminded herself. *Make no sudden moves*. Of course, she looked for the tail, and saw eyes and tympana surrounded by four little limbs. There were more limbs above the big legs, all the way along the limber three-meter body.

It was slender, roughly human mass. As she had come to expect from the Bowl, like all Earth land animals, it had an elongated, bilaterally symmetric body. A neck, but with two deep recesses that might be eyes—at the bottom of the head. Not near the top, as nearly everything she knew did. This alien had a head like an artist's first impression, broad planes and notches chiseled from something like translucent yellow horn. What did yellow skin imply? For the rest of its body was dark, maybe tanned.

As she watched it, the head rotated—completely around. So, she thought, a head adapted for quick scanning and action. It looked spooky, alarming. Nothing on the Bowl had that. At most, like Earth owls, Bowl life could swivel a head about 280 degrees.

Somehow this thing could spin its head, triangular with a beaky snout, without breaking blood vessels or tearing tendons. She recalled that a praying mantis could spin its head, because it had an open circulation system. This thing swept in a view of the whole human campground as it slowly came forward, taking its time.

It said nothing. She could not read its eyes or face.

She had seen smart aliens on the Bowl who mixed poorly with humans, because they spoke through smell, quick face moves, and pheromone chemicals they squirted. Humans relying on sound and sight in very restricted frequency bands were, she had learned, a rather isolated evolutionary group. But those scent-talking aliens faced a roadblock on the path to high intelligence. They made up for it somewhat with expressive faces or sign language. But their limitations had never led them to high technology. The Bird Folk had domesticated them long ago, making them into slave species.

This thing did not look like a slave. It sauntered, rotating head taking in the humans. Silently.

A thin little mouth, too. Animals with heavy mandibles and massive grinding teeth were typically vegetarians that ate coarse low-energy vegetation. Animals with fangs and horns used them for defense against predators and for competition among males. None such here. Then this alien probably progressed by cooperation and strategy rather than brute strength and combat. Only a broad high-energy meat and vegetable diet could sustain the relatively large populations needed for later stages in the development of intelligence. Hence, moderate jaws, no fangs or horns.

But it had something new to her: plenty of arms. The lower ones, it walked on. Easy in low grav. The uppers swung to help its gait. Still, the arms fit what she had learned from the many Bowl aliens. The slender arms, eight along each side, maybe had bones or cartilage, levered for maximum strength. The big hinge joints were bigger than human elbows and knees. Some showed digits with pulpy tips, probably for sensitive touch and grasping.

She stood still. Whispered to her team to do the same. *Treat it like a viper; you never know.*

Maybe this thing was adapted for the range of gravs on the Cobweb. On Earth, the four-leggedness of big land vertebrates came because fishes with four lobed fins, instead of six, colonized the land. Insects had six legs, spiders eight, but they were never large. So she figured few legs and arms were good for evolutionary success on land. Fingers, though, were rare Earthside. Only chimps and humans invented tool artifacts, using their fingers with soft sensitive tips. So if that held true, on the Cobweb, anything with beaks, talons, scrapers, or claws was an animal. Like the backfire dragons.

The alien got within five meters of her and stopped. Its arms stilled and the narrow mouth opened. It spoke in what seemed Anglish. The language seemed gouged from the mouth and heaped with rolling vowels, tongue sprung. "Thees lin'ar moodes—sen'ces youu caall theem—sufferrer frommm illusionee thaat caan parallele, thoouught."

"Useful it is," Beth said. Keep this simple. Clip the vowels, maybe the alien would, too. It had probably learned from intercepted transmissions, then the many texts Redwing sent. Getting an interesting sentence out on this first try was impressive.

The alien said, "Go with mee noow to moveh plaace." With two arms that articulated backwards, it gestured toward the way it had come. "All come."

Decision time. Beth waved to Viviane and Cliff. "What do you think?"

"Let's go," Viviane said. "After those backfire dragons, I don't like the idea of this place in the dark."

She sent a whisper to the team. "Pack to travel. No sudden moves."

She sent similar messages to the ship and Redwing. "We'll be beyond comm, I think. Send a flock of relay drones along the Cobweb, parallel to wherever we're going."

Redwing's assent came by text. She felt fluttery, a mix of anticipation and anxiety.

They assembled their gear and got away within five minutes, following the alien in good order. Only a few hundred meters around the hill, through some more helical trees, they came upon a startling vision: a lake. It stood on a flat wedge angling out from the hill, plainly artificial. Clouds hung thick but they dissolved quickly, and the lake glimmered in the steeply slanted sunglow.

Sunset climbed down the Cobweb, a wall of hungry fire. First came a delicate pink, followed by rosy reds, then crimson hot and angry, until the stalks farther out burned with hard white light.

Sunlight swept away from them slowly, and a booming chorus of chips and howls and caws sounded in waves.

Now they could see something loom forth from the thinning ivory clouds. A tube, turning in an arch, across the lake. Light seeped away, so the vision faded to gray and blacks.

"What's that?" she asked.

The alien's odd head turned nearly around to address her. "We taakee you to our smaller world."

It was getting better at Anglish in quick order. "What should we call you?" Viviane asked.

The reply had more vowels than Beth could count, so she said, "Let's call you Twisty, yes?"

"I will render forth to that. Why is."

"Because of how you turn your head. And arms. Limber."

"Yes. See. You are narrow of motion." With that, it led them to the lakeshore, lining them up with multiple arms waving. Then it stepped straight into the water. And walked. A platform came up in support and extended out as Beth and then Cliff and Viviane stepped carefully on it. They marched toward the tube arch as darkness fell.

Beth glanced up into the gathering gloom and saw two zingoes. They glowed with an infernal red like brimstone, standing out in the dark. So they were not creatures at all. But what could make that color hang in the sky . . . as though watching them?

Then they merged into one. Even more puzzling.

Overhead, one by one, the stars were coming out.

SIXTEEN
GAS AND GRAV

Scientists study the world as it is, engineers create the
world that has never been.
—THEODORE VON KÁRMÁN

"This is a continuous elevator?!" Ashley asked in disbelief. "And we
just . . ."

"Step on," Twisty mouthed.

The grainy platform moved smoothly by. Beth eyed it dubiously.

"Is secure," Twisty said—and took an adroit leap onto the steely
ledge.

"Go!" Beth shouted. The team obeyed. They landed easily
on the broad metal. She landed with careful grace and turned to
Twisty. "Now what?"

Twisty made three quick gestures with his double-jointed arms
and legs. She saw that the appendages were adaptable, with filmy
skin layers that could harden in seconds into a kind of ridge.

In response, the room surged. As it carried them away from
their entry point, it began to flex. Walls popped. Tremors shook the
floor. Support structures rose from the seeming metal, like shiny,
flowing mercury.

"Chairs?" Cliff looked dubious as the liquid flows neared him.
The pod around them began accelerating. It wrenched around, as
if going through the top of the arched loop they had seen as they
approached. "It's taking off—"

The shiny stuff formed into a couch, almost as though it were
beckoning to him. He carefully sat. It grasped him lightly. "Not bad."
He stretched out and looked surprised at how quickly the mercury

bed shaped itself to him. Tings, hums, shudders. There were ridged cushions for the finger snakes, a couch for Bemor Prime.

Beth called, "Okay, make your acquaintance with it. Go easy."

The team complied, though with frowns. She gingerly sat, and it shaped for her. Twisty sat, too, nearby, in what appeared to be a steel hammock lined with grips. She framed a question and stopped when a gauzy film began to seethe through the air.

"Hey, what's this?" she asked the alien.

"To hoold and breeathe," Twisty said. "For us alll."

The stuff seemed to envelop them in a light, spongy foam. Yet air flowed easily. She did not feel trapped or confined. The stuff was like a soap bubble without smell. She touched it and the film gave a bit, resisted a bit.

Acceleration built. The return of weight was welcome; she had felt inept in a tenth grav. With a sense of mass, of clear ups and downs, she felt more at ease. Her silvery couch seemed to clutch her more, though with a slippery touch. Odd stuff. The wispy, airy foam added to a feeling of security and yet strangeness. Now it began to give off an odd scent, like lilac. Alien safety measures, she guessed.

"Getting faster," Viviane said from several couches away.

"Need to goo," Twisty said.

Viviane frowned. "How far?"

"To our smallness world."

"We call it Honor."

"We say—" It made a sound like a buzz saw hitting rock.

Beth's ears popped. She realized the walls of their pod were now transparent. She sat up. They were rushing along in a slanted twilight. The shadow cast by the Glory world, eclipsing the Cobweb, was waning. Cliff had calculated the nighttime as about two hours. Now, as they rushed between slabs of living planes, the sky glowed in faint orange. Shadowy clouds flitted by. In dim light a landmass rose toward them and she saw a rough sea below, whitecaps and storm clouds. Maybe ten kilometers up—but closing fast. They were falling. She could not restrain her automatic reflex.

"We're going to hit—!"

"No, through," Twisty said.

The others in her team were rustling uneasily, too. Dancing eyes, hands clutching the couches. Acceleration gripped them harder. They flew through shrouded gray cloud banks. Lightning flashes. Purple vapor wedges the size of mountains. More puffy cotton clouds, churning. Then into the open—

"Fire!" Viviane cried, pointing.

"Skyee flame, it is, yes," Twisty said with what Beth supposed was a calm voice. Certainly not strained and thin, like the human mutterings she heard around her.

She could see sheets of yellow seethe and smoke and snarl in the dark sky. Some life-form? It fractured into pieces the size of hills, roiling. Parts seemed to roll and gather up other dancing fires. Not lightning, not simple fireballs, then what? Before she could think about it, the flames fell behind their long tube. She could see down now to the lands below. They rushed forward, still accelerating, a heavy weight.

"Feels like two gravs," Cliff said in a reedy voice. They were all slammed into their couches as the plains below swept toward them.

Some of the team gave involuntary yelps. Cries of alarm. Beth held hers in. Time compressed as she felt her adrenaline kick in.

Even then, in the twilight she could see a huge balloon thing coming up from below, not far off. Pearly sails flounced lazily from its eggshell blue sides. An animated Christmas tree ornament. Its colors blended with the sky glow, she saw—camouflage. So it had predators, yes. There seemed to be a lot here, based on her experience—less than a day in, one dead.

From above, though, the tube had orange vents and stood out against the browns and greens below. A rocket-effect creature cruising the skies?

She shook her head against the acceleration that drove them straight down along the slender, transparent tube they were in. She shot a look at Twisty, who was lounging back on his couch. The transparent webby stuff held her tight now. "Why are we—?"

But then they arrowed into the vast plain below. She had a glimpse of inky dark, rumpled forests, pale yellow-lit towers spiking up at a somber azure sky—

Here it came. Lands rushed at them. Then a flicker of dark. A *whump* and *pop*. Rush of cool air.

—and they had flashed through the quick shadowed sheet of soil. Impossible to estimate the thickness. Then they shot out into the shadowy air again.

This view was even broader. Dim but clear. She could see through cloudless layers, all the way to the Cobweb's upper atmosphere, on each side. For the first time, she *felt* the extent of the giant cylinder. She used her binocs to close-up distant features that were, judging from the perspective, thousands of kilometers away . . . and hundreds wide.

Big blue-white bubbles of water hung, somehow, like lakes in the air. Big glossy pipes that ran along the Cobweb's length, several moored along one zone high in the atmosphere, toward the outer rim. She looked backwards. Gyres of gray clouds swirled behind them. They had already passed through the thickest part of the Bulge. Slow-motion hurricanes marked the outlet into the thinner length of the Cobweb, leading toward Honor. Cloud patterns nearby and below formed longitudinal streamers, as winds from the huge pipes bled out fresh air from nearer Honor.

On distant platforms of land, she could make out buildings the size of mountain ranges, with entries at every angle. Tethers turned in the easy air above them. These huge sticks seemed designed to touch down at buildings, just close enough for passengers to get on, matching velocities. Then the treelike lengths of it moved on, laterally across the cylinder. She could not figure out how they worked, but the intent was clear. Movement, grace, intelligence, life in its purposes. Here was a living, interacting system that drew resources from both worlds, at its ends.

She recalled a great classical poem that seemed to capture the shadowed strangeness of this.

> *Coldhearted orb that rules the night*
> *Removes the colors from our sight.*
> *Red is gray and yellow white,*
> *But we decide which is right*
> *and which is an illusion.*

Faster now. The dark thickened as they flew down the slender hollow tube propelling them. Small amber light lit the pipe ahead— injection stations? She could see twinkling city lights sprawl across the distant level that stretched like an infinite plane. It was at least a thousand kilometers away, she judged, by perspective. But at this speed, only a few minutes away.

She looked carefully around their pod. Bemor Prime sat, stolid in his carrier at the back, saying nothing. His orders were to behave like a pet. Keep him in reserve, as needed. Twisty was asking questions of the others, by highlighting things inside the pod, then imposing a question mark with a flick of a wrist. It knew human signals and was using them to pick up vocabulary and accent. It knew that imposing the circle-bar meant "verboten" on anything he didn't like.

Seeing her watching, Twisty asked, "Question on Bemor Prime? Why here?"

"A pet."

"Is from Bowl, yes? I have digi-record of so such, from olden era."

"Yes, we spent time there. On the Bowl. Bemor Prime is my friend."

"I see." Twisty pointed to a finger snake and imposed a ?

"Tool user. Engineer. Also from the Bowl of Heaven."

Twisty's mouth twisted in a new way. "They think it heaven, they do."

Was that Glorian irony? Sarcasm? Beth made herself sit back. She had been tensed up, anticipating collisions that never came. Now she forced herself to slide lower. The couch made itself into a firm yet pleasant cushion. *Ah.*

Twisty looked relaxed, its multiple arms akimbo at their knotted joints. She caught no smell from the alien, no signals in the blank face, as its scaly eyes slowly closed. Maybe a good time to begin their core task?

Tutored by Earthside, in light of the Bowl experience, they had realized how deep the problem of communicating with Glorians was. The Glorian cartoon images sent suggested a contemptuous mind that disliked what humans saw as diplomacy. They had finally reacted, once *SunSeeker* arrived. But only then.

So this might be somewhat like the history of talking to the AIs that became the Artilect ranks. Find out their base assumptions, their mind-set. Start there.

SunSeeker's Artilects emerged from primitive collections, somewhat like cellular automata. Those, resembling the weather, were doing things just as complex as human brains. Those were thinking, just not in humanlike ways. They were outside our context and our details. So Glorian purpose made sense only relative to a whole historical and cultural framework. To ask aliens what their purpose was, her team had to have them understand the historical and cultural framework in which humans operated.

Twisty's eyes opened with a jerk. It said slowly, "Your Heaven Bowl has veered. It will fly deeper into our planetary system. What is this new intent? Should we be afraid?"

Beth said carefully, "You rule all of a solar system. Surely you are too powerful to fear the Bowl."

"You have conceived gods like that. I am not a god but rather, something like. Something you know not. A step up the ladder—I use here a description that resonates with your minds, though not in ours. Up the 'ladder' from your forms."

So it had guessed at Beth's thinking, somehow. She felt a twitch of alarm. How did it do that? And . . . what to say to such a bald declaration?

She recalled a set of methods Earthside had sent, after their Bowl experience. *Describe our own evolution, as we see it.* "Let us speak of what gives us—our species name is *Homo sapiens*—an edge. That is, our social skills. It gave us command over all other animals. Quite quickly, our social evolution turned us into the masters of the planet. Evolution favored not our individual rationality, but our unparalleled ability to think together in large groups."

Twisty flicked its eyes about and then, as if recalling instructions, made a curt nod with its odd head. "Our view is best shown in examples. Plants are energy binders. They came first. Animals are space binders, second to arrive. You humans are time binders. You see yourselves as controllers of energy, space, and time. All that is."

"Um. Fair, I suppose. You—"

"Perhaps best to say, we do not share your species' problems."

"So . . . what?"

"We speak with others of like minds. You are not ready for this yet."

She wondered if this was something like a job interview. "Speak to them through gravitational waves?"

"In part. You well know that gravitational waves have an intriguing, useful property. They propagate unperturbed once they have been created. No distortion. Impossible for species such as you to create and signal through, much less block. Though you can receive, if clever. That ability places the remote corners of the universe into our field of view. We discourse with like minds and species. Not you. Not the Heaven Bowl."

Twisty did not move or give any face signals as it rapped this out. Its voice was sharp and clear now. It was learning to speak with startling speed. The word to describe its cant was *condescending*, at best. She decided to probe.

"So you don't happen to see our worldview as significant?"

"Your art, perhaps. It is primitive. But like those of other species, limited by your short history."

"How about the species of the Bowl?"

Twisty responded with a restless twitch. It started in the limbs that fidgeted in the handlike protrusions. They jittered in and out, as if getting ready to work on something. "It is a historical problem. Now it returns. This concerns us."

"You tried to warn us off."

"Not you. Not your tiny ship. The Bowl."

"Ah! So your signals were to the Folk?"

"I see you mean a species who believe they are the Bowl Masters. No, not them. The cold ones."

"What we call the Ice Minds?"

"Those we knew. We speak to them only when needful." Twisty had subdued its hands. Now the arms twisted like tree limbs in a lazy breeze.

"Not otherwise?"

"We confront different problems."

"May we help with those?"

Twisty made its mouth into a curve like a semicolon laid on its side. An attempt at a smile? "As you humans would see it, we have used philosophy to resolve many."

"Philosophy? How?"

"We decided they were not important."

And with that, here came the next dive into a plain the size of a continent.

Beth braced herself; she couldn't help it. They were moving at ever-higher speeds. This time the land below was hilly with sharp rocky peaks. Snow dotted some. It rushed up, and again came the rattling blot of darkness. They zoomed through the landform and, *presto*, were out.

Twisty said, "We at times refer to this as the Forest of Incandescent Bliss."

"Oh? We call it the Cobweb."

"You omit the function, stress the construction. Is that typical of your species?"

"When we see something new, we check the engineering first."

"Odd, is not of lasting importance to we of this Forest."

Beth did not say: *It would be if you built it badly.* "You built it when?"

"Ah, far past now." Three arms waved the question away, each in a different jointed way. It reminded her of trees weaving in a slow storm.

Twisty sat up, seemingly oblivious to the crushing acceleration. "I gather you study what you call *biology*?"

"I do. Study of living things."

"So the plasma beings as well?"

"We term them the Diaphanous."

"Ah, the thin and transparent, you mean. We have a similar expression—" Again, a band saw cutting into metal.

She ached to get some points straight, but felt she was in some Oscar Wilde play where every remark probably meant something else. Or several other somethings. So she said, "Here's how we think about other, smart beings—such as you. There's cooperation apparent in all of the highly social species of our planet, Earth—"

"So you name your world Dirt. Because you have little water?"

"Uh, no, Earth is about three-quarters covered with water."

"Then should be Ocean."

"Maybe. We evolved in the dirt—or rather, in trees growing in dirt. So—"

"Most worlds' beings term their homes Oceans, we hear from our similars among the stars. Those Oceans resound with song. Alas, they have few arms"—it waved all its arms in a blur, like a dance—"and no fire. So they cannot come here, as you did, you Dirt people."

Viviane leaned forward to catch Twisty's attention. "You've got millennia of observing behind you. The Bowl visited you, even. You know so much I'd like to learn."

Her outright plea was not according to protocols Earthside and Redwing had set out. *Don't show your hand early.* Beth decided to let it go. Theory never survived collision with the field.

Viviane said earnestly, "How common are desert worlds or water worlds? Do they produce intelligent land-based species at a much lower rate? Earth's had a fine-tuned balance, water and land. Do planets with larger habitable areas, so larger populations, turn up more often?

Twisty regarded this with his semicolon mouth. "We know your origin. And the Bowl's, the same. You have all sprung from a greater habitable area than most life-bearing worlds."

"Ah!" Viviane brightened. "I've wanted to know that since I was a girl."

Beth was now certain that Twisty's semicolon look was supposed to be a smile, because it was developing a sense of humor. Making fun of them, at least. She took a breath, caught Twisty's eye—many were trying to now—and restarted. "Look, my point is, smart social species are based on some degree of altruism and self-sacrifice. Everybody knows the first rule is, you have to give to get."

"Plausible, though limited." Still the semicolon smile.

"Those ingrained social understandings work at deep levels. Those arose from natural selection at both the individual and the group levels. It gives us our sense of morality. So we presume— and it seems roughly true of all those we met on the Bowl—smart

aliens came forth similarly. So they have a parallel sense of morality. Yes?"

"In a way. I do notice, from your arts, that you love what you
call *stories*, as well."

"Well, sure." She wondered where this was going.

"You have an inner theater. You cast yourselves into these little
plays. Pay great attention to each other, especially faces."

She recalled an experiment with monkeys caged for a while
with no view out. When the curtains drew aside and they could
look out, they focused on any other monkey in view. "We enjoy that,
yes. Plays, movies, reading—"

"That appears natural because it evolved. Socially useful, I
gather."

"Don't you?" She thought of the Earthside feeds. Over centuries, the focus was constant: gossip, conflicts, celebrity worship, the
latest hit video or novel or . . . endless human focus, yes.

"In lesser ways. Your addiction to stories leads you astray."

"How?"

"By making you think your lives are stories."

"Aren't they?"

"If they have a point. I noticed your oldest stories, those you tell
to children, always end falsely. Why?"

"Uh, how . . . falsely?"

"I believe the cliché—that is the right Anglish term, yes?—ends
'And so they lived happily ever after.' Yes?"

"Uh, right. So?"

"No one lives ever after, happily or otherwise."

She had honestly never thought of that. As a kid, she just knew
that meant it was time to close the book.

Twisty looked at her without expression. The Cobweb, or Forest, rushed by outside. Sunlight brimmed. She didn't know what
to say.

So . . . When in doubt, dodge. She looked out at a welter of
glossy crossbeams and pipes, streaming by in a blur. She could
make out some because they were big—cylinders kilometers across,
intertwined meshes that cross-braced themselves, frames and lattices gleaming, an impression of combined strength and suppleness.

The Sun was getting brighter, coming away from being eclipsed by Glory, at their backs. It was still small, making shadows sharper and reflections more precise. Astro-viewing was more complex on this spinning barbell.

"I . . . I'd like to hear your story."

Twisty rolled itself around on the silvery couch that clasped close. "That is a deepness not soon swum."

What command of Anglish! Twisty was learning fast. Probably had a link to some underlying computational resource, as well. "Okay, how'd you build this Cobweb?"

"Through longer eras than spanned by your evolution."

"Um. How's it work?"

"Ah, I fathom your regard." Twisty swiveled itself to face Cliff. Its arms flexed into a helical net, as though it was aping the long, weaving Cobweb structure they had seen from space. "We are a thrifty sort. Your laws explain, yes? Gravity makes our air fall, but we clasp it in pipe. Such as this"—his arms swept outward to the pod, its cylindrical track plunging toward Honor—"is in turn driving gas pressure below. Which lofts masses in other tubes. What goes down, must come up, suitably sheperded. All is a circuit. Like your blood, embodied."

Cliff leaned over from his couch, straining to be nearer—and his couch swiveled, turning him toward them. The soft buffeting aerogel smartly adjusted. "On our planet, same as yours, atmosphere clumps down. You keep this Cobweb pumping air over such distances?"

"Your term *capillaries* applies, yes? Each Level, as we term them, manages its air and water. Hands off to its neighbor nexts, above and below. Gravity gives, takes. All is in flux."

Cliff shook his head in disbelief. "Gas and grav. So that's how you keep everything running? Takes a lot of energy."

"Not so. And you say Cobweb, but Piston would be more accurate."

"This elevator we're in," Beth said. "We're rushing down, fast as hell. By pressing air ahead, this pod drives another—somewhere?— uphill, to get here. Right?"

Twisty made a nod, tentative. "This means assent, yes?"

"Right." She looked at Cliff. Engineering was his area.

Cliff dutifully nodded. "I never heard of adjusting pressures across distances like planetary—" He stopped. "Nope, wrong. The Bowl does huge stuff like that, too."

"There is much more to show you than . . . plumbing. Of more grave import, as well." Twisty gave a clear impression—though she could not quite say how—of being patient. This alien was picking up on social cues quickly. Its voice was getting more resonant, rounded. It summoned up an ever-larger range of Anglish vocab, too. Surely it was wired into some big, quick computational link. Still, the performance was impressive.

Cliff eyed her and with a downward twitch and twist of his mouth told her he was going to press on with the engineering anyway. Fine. She had been watching the scenery as their acceleration fell off. The Honor surface was tens of thousands of kilometers away. She had estimated their speed in this pod as several kilometers a second, so they were out of the Bulge and getting near Honor itself.

The fast-flitting images she caught taught a lot. This Cobweb was vast and various. Small towns in the middle of nowhere; great cities; towers and highways seething with urgent action. All amid abundant lands and wild regions, thick with forest.

Now their comfy couches crawled like snails around the curve of the walls to reverse direction. A heavy deceleration clasped them. "Uh!" she heard from all around. Destination ahead, then.

Twisty did not seem to mind. She had slowly realized that what she thought was its skin was in fact a smartsuit. It wriggled a bit, a shimmy of adjustment, then wrapped the body again. Now she could see that the sliding skinlike suit concealed parts beneath several of its arms. Humans kept their lower openings—as her mother used to say, both the sewer and the playground—in one crowded spot, end of the alimentary canal, between their legs. What Twisty had there was mysterious. Its two lower legs were spaced on opposite sides of its body, with ample blank space between for recessed eyes and folding ears. Her biological curiosity would have to await diplomacy. . . .

Hums, pops, *skeeeees* . . . They all braced and the pod tugged at them. Landscape swelled far below. They shot through yet another layer. She had gotten used to them fluttering past at high speed. This one lingered as they slowed. Broad, filmed with cloud. And—yes, she could see the curvature of a world, the skin of air glowing like a garment. They had sped a greater distance than that around the Earth, while making small talk with a meandering, multiarmed alien.

Around their pod cylinder express, the sky was as gray as pewter, lands below as promising as unpolished silver. Rain turned the sky quicksilver; eels of sparkling water wriggled through an inconstant sky. Lightning flares sharpened weather's argument.

And here they came down—

An inglorious *thump.* Not like catching the pod as it waltzed by this time. Touchdown on Honor.

Out they went.

SEVENTEEN

HONOR

Through boring corridors, down ramps—some facets of travel never changed. At least no steps, but the grav was welcome. Cliff checked, announced to their group as they marched behind Twisty, "Looks to be 0.82 grav. No more easy flying, folks."

Relief came: a transparent wall. Rain veiled everything. Beth gazed eagerly out at some vast white cubist structures lying like bleached, scattered bones. Reflecting, rain-pocked pools glared like highly polished mirrors. Skinny saplings stood sunk in solemn green water, like ornaments. The effect was oppressively dazzling.

Then more corridors. Beth found her gear tugging at her. Bemor Prime's carriers were not fond of returning to serious grav. The spidow stirred, eyes jerking—and, ah yes, his carrier had sprouted its own wheels. Three men tended to the smart beast. Beth looked away; she still didn't like its spidery horror.

"You tired must be from journeys," Twisty said. "Take rest refuge here." A sweeping hand gesture sent them to a corridor shaped from what seemed a pale rock. But as a door slid away, she blinked.

She shook her head. "This is your . . . art?"

Twisty waved many hands, as if in explanation. "We thought we could create calm yet intelligent art of your sort. Our many minds agreed, this is very human."

"Makes me dizzy," she said.

"Perhaps too challenging, then." With a whisking motion, Twisty made the art vanish from the walls.

It paused, plainly consulting some conversation going on in its

mind—probably an electromagnetic connection to an integrated machine mind? She realized that despite the exchanges of information between Glorians and *SunSeeker*, they knew little about the biology and machine/mind culture of Twisty—if it was a representative Glorian at all. Twisty nodded as if to itself and then said slowly, "This perhaps better?"

"Gah, no!" Somehow the level corridor looked like a stairwell in a blaze of eye-knocking color. "Makes me *more* dizzy."

"But you evolved from primates who used trees to advantage. This reconfiguration gives you lively patterned stairs to practice your—"

"Look, we are big primates who dislike falling. Old species habit. Get rid of this!" Her diplomatic veneer had shed.

She was still processing what they had just seen. The stairway looked not just garish, but *real*. She took a small tool and tossed it forward. It clattered and banged down the steps. It *was* real. The Glorians had some building tech that could reshape a flat floor into a stairwell.

Twisty said, "Done." In a second or two, masses shifted, colors arrayed on walls—as if a deep computational ability lay behind these apparently simple buildings. An offhand display of vast powers . . .

Twisty made more waves and the color riot dissolved.

"This then should suit. A touch of color, my advisors advise, will enliven the perspective with a sense of—"

"Leave it," Cliff said from behind her. "Good enough. This I won't fall down in, at least. Looks like some damn student dorm gone crazy."

She shrugged at Twisty. "Lead on, O Glorian."

She stepped forward as cautiously as a cat on a wet floor. It held. A few more paces. There lay her tool.

They moved forward and found a long line of dull but practical cells. Each had a broad bed with sheets, even. Beth got the team in order with short commands, since they were now teetering from fatigue. Watch schedule assigned. Comm protocols set. *SunSeeker* was reachable on their gear, but the connection had fraying static and patch voices. She longed for a good report/chat with Redwing. But her body had its own wisdom, and the means to enforce it.

There was even a decent shower, warm and slick and soothing. So they did know something about humans, after all. Towels, even.

She was halfway through a long warm spray when Cliff came in, too. Fun with liquids! But they tired of that soon enough, enjoyed toweling each other off, and fell with slow-motion grandeur into the springy bed. Done and done.

EIGHTEEN
Carniroos

When she woke up, her first thought was, *Twisty has a sense of humor.*

Subtle, the bastard.

"Those crazy corridors were its way of saying, pay attention to what we show you."

Cliff rubbed his eyes. "Instead of what Twisty says?"

"Um . . . maybe both . . ."

"All that stuff about how we evolved, yesterday," Cliff said. "What was its point?"

"I think Twisty was indirectly pointing to how much older their civilization is. Maybe."

"Building this Cobweb would take—well, then the grav wave radiator . . ."

She stretched, yawned. Breakfast bloomed as a savory idea. "Right. Thousands of years, as a guess."

"But they somehow met the Bowl before, too."

"So, okay, tens of thousands? Hundreds?"

Cliff shook his head. "I fast-checked all the Glorian signals. Plenty of pointless artistic stuff—you'd be amazed what they think is beautiful—but damn little long history. They're not giving much away."

Beth nodded. "Because they like indirection. Hints."

"Or else they're covering up an awful lot."

• • •

The team woke quickly. The team inboard systems were cohered, so Beth could summon them easily. Some groaned and snuffled, but

they got out of their rooms within minutes. Cliff was last, hair spiking out as if he had been electrocuted.

Twisty had prepared a breakfast of exotic treats: meats tasting
like sweet-fried almonds; porridge like fruit; crisp, sharp breads
that raked the palate with savory aftertastes. They dug in.

"We want to go outside, get a sense of your world," she said to
Twisty. The alien turned with a many-armed flourish, and the far
wall slid open on . . . sunlight, pure and golden, resting on a moun-
tainous land, like a lordly hand.

Out, onto a broad balcony. She let herself just plain *revel*. In the
sensation of sun on skin, wind rustling her hair, crisp sweet scent
on the breeze. Each moment seemed precious, diamond sharp. She
had been tense, focused when they landed. Then the backfire dragons, death . . . But now she was literally a world away from that.
On a soothing *planet*.

Natural life, after years in rattling metal boxes, taking her somewhere. *To here. Where I'll live out my life and die. And maybe leave
children behind to live lives of gusto. Away from rockets and routines.*

Nearby buildings seemed made of polymer spun with pale rock
dust. But how had they warped so quickly into the colorful halls
and stairs last night? No way to tell.

They were perched above a sharp-edged valley. This is what
the mass-thrifty Cobweb could not afford: mass. Slate gray mountains steep as the Alps, where weightless clouds and airy rain
drifted over distant peaks. Rough dark stone sheets ran down the
mountain flanks. White waterfalls falling from high into frowsy
foaming feet.

Earthside, the green Alpine valleys came from centuries of
herders—huge lawns, cleared of forest and rock, for the benefit of cows and goats. When she had seen them, traveling with
Cliff, the Alps felt strange—both safe and dangerous, domestic
and wild—a pretty park that in half an hour could turn nasty
and kill you. John Muir's famous description of the Sierra Nevada as gentle wilderness came to mind. This was more like a
savage civilization.

In the ice ages, the Alps had much thicker and longer-lasting glaciers than the North American Sierra Nevada, so its valleys were much steeper and deeper. The Sierra's high, lake-filled basins were extremely rare in the Alps. Time ground them away, leaving knife-edge ridges, steep green walls, and immense gulfs of air. Aircraft buzzed through the huge spaces she could see. She turned to Twisty. "How did these mountains form?"

"We made them," it said. "During the Making."

"When you built the Cobweb? Locking your moon to the same rotation as—"

"Not our moon. We brought it here."

The magnitude of this left her mouth hanging open. "From?"

"Was closer to our star. Took a while."

"I would . . . think so," was all she could manage.

Cliff pointed. "See that scree, talus, boulders, bedrock? I'd like to climb that, get up into the god zone, see it all."

She nodded, feeling the same. Twisty said, "We have things to show you. Climbing, later."

There was a nearby long lake of brilliant turquoise. The sky here was eggshell blue, and in the distance the lake took on the opaque virulent blue of radiator antifreeze. This was *so* Earthlike, she ventured, "Twisty, did you bring us here so it would be most familiar?"

"Yes, indeed. You primates prefer the known. It makes you less ill at ease."

Cliff stood before Twisty, his stance confronting. "You seem to know a lot about our evolution. What about yours?"

Twisty seemed unfazed. "The original Glory citizens resembled brainy centipedes. Now that design is much more elaborate, much more varied."

"Such as you?" Cliff persisted.

"Such as I are a recent invention."

"There are different kinds of smart Glorians?"

"Of course. I gather your species has not yet proliferated?"

Cliff shrugged. "Uh, no. We have smart other species, like whales and dolphins. Close relatives, chimpanzees."

"We emerged as you did, long ago." Twisty stretched four arms out, articulating them with faint popping sounds. "Very long. Like you, we lacked any goal external to our biological nature. No gods in the sky, not anymore. We do have a narrative, though it is difficult to convey to such as you."

Was that a veiled insult? Hard to tell. "Narrative?"

"A reason for our being. Somewhat like you, I suppose. We have gathered much from your arts, as sent so kindly from your ship. Human beings must have an epic, a sublime account of how the world was created and how humanity became part of it."

Twisty paced along the length of the deck as it spoke, concentrating—or else, it was copying a human mannerism to convey its own internal state. There was plenty of room for her team to stand, taking in the view, relaxed and chatting. On her orders, they didn't clump around the alien, so left the talking to Beth. Besides, they were enjoying this immersion in a place so like Earth. Beth wondered idly if the Glorians in these mountains made cheese. . . .

"We must have an epic?" Cliff asked. He was wearing his skeptical smile.

"Your religious epics specifically satisfy another primal need. They confirm you are part of something greater than yourselves. We went through such a stage. It cost many lives."

This blithe mention somehow shocked Beth. "So you've gone beyond that, uh, epic story? About gods?"

"Indeed." Twisty gazed into the distance. "We did great damage to ourselves. Also, to our larger world you call Glory. We very nearly destroyed it, before we rewrote our epic."

"Destroyed?"

"I gather from side references in your art that your world is only now recovering from vast damage done. We were similar, long ago. Though ours went further."

"Glory was damaged?"

"And remains so, though somewhat mended. Also, we changed the nature of it. You will learn that in time."

"I'd like to visit Glory," Beth said.

"That may come later. We have a method of attending to visiting strangers. Please follow it."

Cliff again edged closer, as if he could fathom this by proximity. Twisty backed away, a clear sign of an invaded personal space.

Beth stepped in, too, waving Cliff away. "Look, let's get back to your points."

Twisty ceased its pacing and spread its arms in an odd way—two up, two down—that might mean indecision. "The way we achieved our epic, that tale we call"—a long, slurping sound—"unites our sense of spirituality. We invented it—there is no better word, for our epic or yours—to unite our spiritual sense and our rational minds."

"How?" Cliff looked bewildered.

"Instead of cleaving off our early nature, which wanted a reason for us, we gathered together."

Beth was rather confused, too, but she nodded to encourage the alien. "Gathered . . . ?"

"We composed it from the best empirical knowledge that our science and history could provide—I would say, the Epic of our Evolution."

Beth moved her hands in a gesture she had noted Twisty used, palms up, fingers out, then curling back, as if urging toward her. "So . . . ?"

Twisty's arms relaxed to its side. "For both of our species, culture and rituals are products, not parts, of nature. They come from social evolution. So, too, came belief in God and rituals of religion—products of social selection. They were good ideas to have."

Ashley Trust came over and whispered, "We want to take a hike down into the valley."

Beth waved him away but whispered, "Okay, have Viviane lead. Not too far. Be careful."

Twisty nodded, obviously of good hearing. Ashley whispered, "Thanks, we're getting itchy, want to move."

"Go," Beth said, as Twisty remarked, "You see yourselves as organisms that are survival machines, or vehicles for the genes that ride inside you. This is an overly simple view."

"But true, right?" Cliff asked.

"A limited truth. Your evolved and inherited tendencies were responsible for hierarchical social organization among humans. The genetic leash dictated social truths, not mere genetic ones."

"You were similar?" Beth asked.

"Oh yes. Your and our origins are as with all social intelligences we know—a narrow gateway. It begins when small groups build a nest, from which they forage for food. The nest holds their young, cared for by some staying there, while others hunt or gather."

Beth saw its point. "That's true of Earth. Insects, mole rats, lower primates—"

"So here, as well. Yet the end state yields constant tensions. Each social intelligence bears this burden. Within a group, selfish behavior does better than altruistic. But when groups compete, altruists beat bands of the selfish. Much of your history—and to tell true, of our species—shows this."

Cliff said, "Earthside, selfish species are loners. Who don't get far up the ladder, to true civilization."

Beth frowned. "Look, if group selection worked, we'd be angelic robots."

"Your insects are such. Automata. We, not. Some hold the view that we are spiritual beings having physical experiences, rather than the other way around. This distinction does not matter." Twisty gave a dismissive jerk of its triangular head, looking somewhat like a praying mantis to Beth's eye.

It went on, "So both your and our perpetual stresses come from the only path leading to high civilization. Group-self tensions. That is our destiny—inborn turmoil."

Beth grimaced. "Sad, if true."

"Not sad! It also gives us our creativity." Twisty hoisted all its arms to the sky, as if in joy. Its voice rose to a higher note, too. "But enough! We should admire the moment." It turned to the view, arms taking it all in. "From your art, I believe you admire such natural chiaroscuro as this."

Beth's thin link to her inboards supplied the word she didn't know: AN EFFECT OF CONTRASTED LIGHT AND SHADOW CREATED BY LIGHT FALLING UNEVENLY OR FROM A PARTICULAR DIRECTION ON SOMETHING. "Uh, indeed."

They could see her team had made good time and were nearly into the green valley below. Beth and Cliff walked beside Twisty, who also made good time on its springy legs. The sky was lovely, with big cottony clouds skinning down the slopes of the nearest ridge.

Twisty said, "I know you are thoroughly linked to smart machines, as am I. I prefer to work without them, in truth. Take this spectacle—" It waved at the fuming clouds. A beautiful, graceful mist escorted by sullen purple puffs. "The machines with their endless zeros and and ones stand in awe of these things nature does automatically—and for free, costing us nothing. They are missing the point. The universe does not compute, it *is*."

Beth vaguely recalled seeing computer runs that showed wonderful emergent computations. Often they ended up with self-similar fractal forms in which the details resemble the whole. It seemed an odd way to view the world, beyond the simple human habit of seeing all sorts of shapes in clouds—a habit of extracting meaning, wherever it might be. Especially around a distant star . . .

Her comm buzzed and she saw it was Redwing. They had spoken only a few times since landfall. Redwing barked a bit, delivering questions with a palpable aura of nervous energy. She started answering, being precise, when she heard a hollow screech. Then a quick darting motion caught her eye.

Up ahead on the right, a swarm of gray animals were bounding across the greenery. They made two lines, encircling the humans. They were *fast*, hardly seeming to touch the ground. She knew the motion and saw suddenly that these were like huge, gray kangaroos, tails bouncing as they stored energy for the next bound forward. In seconds, they had wrapped around her team.

One of the big gray things, skimming the ground in one more bound, landed by a woman. It smoothly lunged forward, tail high. It hit her hard, tumbling her back. Long arms wrapped around her, claws dug in. The woman screamed, head back. It lifted her and bounded away.

Beth was running now and calling out on comm. Her team had bunched up as the big muscular gray things circled.

Twisty called, "I will halt this!" but she didn't look around.

The big alien sped up, bounding off with the woman in its

grip. It scooped out long leaps, getting away quickly. It headed for a copse of zigzag trees. The woman in its grip hung lifeless. Now laser carver fire came faster from her team. She knew better than to call out to them. They knew how to defend, forming a tight group. Quick hard raps of laser fire caught the alien animals by surprise. She saw the animals' heads jerk, swivel, duck. One of them staggered, tail flapping wildly—and smacked down.

She had her own laser out now and got off two shots. She aimed at the animals farthest from her people. Not expecting to hit them, just use the pop and sizzle of a laser bolt to distract them.

The animals had been silent till now. Now they called, a long hooting sound. A signal, all together, as if agreeing on what to do. They all turned and made off to her right. Now they were ever faster. Their big heads swiveled as they looked around, assessing the situation. Within seconds, they were into a stand of leafy plants like tough cabbages. Then gone.

She reached the team, called, "Who was that, carried off?"

Viviane said, "Zoyee Wilansky. That damned thing punctured her lung. I saw her blowing blood when she yelled."

Beth said, "We're going after her."

Twisty came bounding up. "I will adjust this incident."

Cliff shot back, "*Incident?* Some pack animals just killed—"

"Not animals," Twisty said quickly. "Are intelligent."

Beth stuck her face forward, gazing into Twisty's eyes. "Those? They just killed a woman and carried her off. To eat?"

Twisty backed off. "That will not happen."

"But that's what they were after, *right?*" Cliff was thin lipped, eyes bulging, barely containing his rage.

The team had clustered around them. Beth saw this could turn ugly fast. Ashley Trust was nursing a slash on his upper arm. Viviane quickly pulled out a smart bandage, cut open his uniform sleeve with a short knife, and smacked the activated bandage over the wound. Her team was fidgeting, itching to get at Twisty.

"Form a perimeter!" Beth called. She marched over to the alien. "Twisty, you fix this. Get her back."

Twisty turned and loped away without a word. It was fast, heading the way of the attackers.

"Let's see what we're dealing with," Beth said, walking over to the dead alien.

It really did look a lot like a giant kangaroo. She bent and moved the head around. Roolike, but short faced, with a deep ridge behind, recessed forward-facing eyes above a strong chin. Both upper and lower incisors, apelike molars in the back. Omnivore, it seemed.

The thing had a burn hole in its chest. She sniffed the trickle of bright red blood. It was iron rich, just like many animals on Earth and Bowl. A second laser burn had hit beside its spine. White bone gleamed. Its fur had a fusty, dry tang.

She inserted a biodoc into its midriff. The needle went in and snapped back out, thin and quick. She thought three commands at it, and it hummed. On its face popped a symbol analysis in five images. The symbols meant there were too many genetic differences in DNA, proteins, RNA elements for it to be from Earth.

She could check the results more finely later. Beth stood and snapped, "Not our biosphere." Another hum and she glanced at it. "Not known elements from the Bowl, either."

"So convergent evolution?" Viviane asked, feeling the musty, ruffled fur and thick muscles.

"Must be."

"Kinda advanced skull," Cliff said, squatting beside her. "Big cranium. Could be smart."

"Their attack was expert," added Viviane. "There was a loud, odd noise from our left—like a melodious clarinet. We all turned to look for the source. They hit us from our right. Fast as hell."

Ashley stood beside her, his arm bandaged. Beth noted the smartpack had already sent med details to her inboards. Nothing major, at least.

She picked up the beast's foot. Four large toes, outer two with hooked claws. Big hands with two long, clawed fingers, plainly for attack. But also two shorter, outer fingers, multiple-jointed with ordinary nails at the end. Plus large opposable thumbs that looked as though they retracted. An interesting variation on a gripping hand, different from anything Earthside or on the Bowl. She recorded,

"The critters can hunt and kill with the claws. But finer detailed work they do with these fingers and thumbs, not too different from ours."

She stood, noting that her team had formed a defensive perimeter as she did her science. Good. "This thing is a versatile anthology of tricks. Based on my Earthside and Bowl experience, I'd say it's an omnivore, plus opportunistic carnivore—those claws are nasty! Able to eat insects, prey, possibly carrion, fruits, and soft leaves."

"Like us," Viviane said.

Cliff nodded. "But uses the mechanics of a kangaroo—which in Australia are vegetarians. Look at those small arms below the big ones. Maybe useful for small detail work? Seems like many-armed is a theme here and on the Cobweb layers. This thing's a hundred kilos mass, easy. Muscular, smart carnivore. Let's call it a carniroo, huh?"

They all nodded. Beth's Artilect-assisted inboards, ever helpful, poked up in her lower left eye: AUSTRALIAN ABORIGINAL PEOPLE STILL RECOUNT STORIES OF A LARGE, LONG-ARMED, AGGRESSIVE KANGAROO THAT WOULD ATTACK PEOPLE. She didn't know what to make of that until, stimulated by her attention, and from its links to *SunSeeker*, it delivered:

PROCOPTODON GOLIAH (GIANT SHORT-FACED KANGAROO) IS THE LARGEST KANGAROO TO HAVE EVER LIVED (PLEISTOCENE ERA, 2.5 MILLION YEARS AGO TO 11,000 YEARS AGO). IT GREW 2–3 METERS (7–10 FEET) TALL, AND WEIGHED UP TO 230 KG (510 LB). NOTED TOP PREDATOR IN CONTINENT'S HISTORY.

She got the point. "This thing may have come from Earth long ago."

Ashley asked, "When the Bowl revisited?"

"Could be," Cliff said. "Long way back, millions of years. It got here somehow. Then got smart. Same as we did."

"And grew two extra arms? No," Beth said. "It's Glory life. Sculptured."

"It's science, so use longer words," Viviane said with a sad smile. "So, hypothesis."

"Or maybe just good ol' convergent evolution," Cliff added. "That energy-storing strategy, between tail and legs—efficient. Got selected for here and Australia."

"Always possible," Beth said, and caught sight of Twisty coming out of the stand of zigzag trees. It was carrying a limp body, Zoyee Wilansky.

Twisty laid the body at Beth's feet and backed away. All were silent. Beth had spent maybe an hour with Zoyee, quick interview after she emerged from cryo. The woman had been groggy from the frost but game to go, a "boots firm on the ground" type.

Now Beth could see the killer had plunged its claws into Zoyee and severed veins and arteries, killing quickly. Deep plunging cuts in both lungs. Blood all over the face. It had bubbled out in the final seconds of life. Probably a simple stabbing by the claws. From the bloodstains that covered half the body, Beth gathered Zoyee had been strung upside down to drain her before gutting, clearing, and then slicing her into meat. Twisty had probably interrupted a butchering amid the zigzag trees. Bile rushed into Beth's throat and she fought to suppress it.

Okay, stand straight, get her voice under control.

She started with a mild though strangled voice, "Twisty—"

But Cliff surged forward, his face mottled with rage. "Bastard—" he shouted, and punched at Twisty's triangular head. The alien quickly stepped back on its lower legs, so Cliff's right cross zipped by, missing entirely. Twisty then flexed its legs to trip Cliff. As the man toppled, four arms whipped out. They caught Cliff and *spun* him in air, like a wheel. The arms were muscular, sinewy as it lifted Cliff—and then dropped him. Cliff hit facedown, went *huff*.

Twisty backed off two paces. "I understand your emotions. They are common, yes. But I urge learning here, not mere feeling."

"Easy to say," Viviane shot back, pointing at Zoyee. "Your wildlife just killed one of us for no damned reason."

"Not wild. Glorians they are, a species with some intelligence. They are living as animals by preference, after a long era spent helping build what you call this—" Two arms gestured. "A Cobweb. Without a spider, until now. You have brought your own."

Beth was helping Cliff to his feet. Twisty had knocked the wind out of him. "What's their intent now, then?" she asked.

"Their intent is to get fed. The joy of pack hunting."

Beth shook her head. She pulled her team away from Twisty by getting them to carry Zoyee into a copse of trees, away from the zigzags where she supposed the attackers still were. In a short, terse talk with Twisty, she got agreement that there would be no more carniroo assaults.

"We'll bury our dead. You police this area, make damn sure there are no other predators near us."

Twisty agreed and she went with her team. Best to do the funeral right away.

NINETEEN

Two dead in two days. Worse than she had done as team leader on the Bowl. Much worse.

She talked to her team as they dug a grave with their pop-out shovels. Then talked with Cliff and Ashley and Viviane, hashing over next steps. She went through the burial, thinking. Or trying to. The words did not come easily but she said them. Eulogy is invariably dull. Especially when she knew the deceased so little.

Redwing had decreed, after their Bowl experiences, clear limits on every ground team. No powered armor or neuropharmacological enhancements—too hard to deal with and deal with utter unknowns at the same time. No deep Artilect engagement—the AIs had proved their uses were limited in the field, more like on-call librarians than actors.

No robotic aircraft and swarms of autonomous fighting machines, then, though in some situations they could do the dirty work faster, cheaper, and with inhuman precision. But those lacked versatility.

Of course, the Artilects had their own ambitions, since they kept up with AI advancements back home. Earthside had long past moved to a war world where programmers set up battles conducted between machine armies without immediate oversight, not a single soldier on the field.

Vulnerable civilians were still there, of course, on the still supercrowded Earth. It was far more peaceful than the twenty-first century, but there were still Great Leaders who ordered machine invasions of weaker nations, certain of no risk of creating grieving parents on the home front. Robosoldiers were still available to anyone with the money. But Redwing had long before decided, free of

Earthside control, to avoid loosing forces that could execute orders without the hesitations and ethical qualms that can plague merely human explorers. Plus, Beth found fighting machines terrifying; she was decidedly old-fashioned.

Burial and funeral over, she led them back to the rooms where they had slept. It seemed a long time ago, but was only half a day. She watched the sky, the lands, wary. Twisty hung back, following them but realizing that the humans were deeply angry. The alien was learning about humans, and knew its limits. She decided to leave the obvious question for later: Why did only one Glorian of Twisty's species meet them? No welcoming party, brass bands, ceremonies. Just one irritating, offhanded Twisty. Strange indeed.

She gazed into the sky, trying to get her bearings in this odd, clocklike astro machine. And there was a zingo . . . or rather, two. They twisted, their spidery lines joining in the dance. A big flapping creature, maybe a smackwing, flew behind them, so she got perspective. They were maybe a hundred meters away, she judged. Watching the humans? But they were in 0.83 gravs here. How did they stay aloft?

The sun had tilted down a bit in the sky, as Honor orbited out of the Glory eclipse, arcing along the slow circle it obeyed. Within

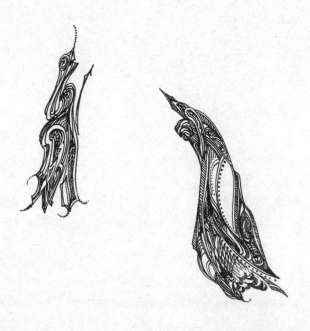

less than two Earth days, long shadows would grow as Honor swept into a two-day night for its inner half, where they were. They were at the base of the Cobweb, at what would be the terminator. So they could choose to be on the sunward side, or the nightward. Sunny seemed better, given that predators prowled here. So they should move away from the Cobweb, toward the sun.

What could come in the night here was a subject she didn't want to think about right now.

TWENTY

Hunter's Breakfast

Does everything need an explanation? Some people
think so. I wonder how they endure looking at the stars.
—Roger Ebert

When Beth woke up, she held still and did her quick sight-sound
perimeter check. She saw something new in their room. Soft gray
fabrics were waiting inside their door in a neatly folded array. The
walls gave forth a dim dawn blush color when she moved. Apparently the room believed they were awake. Cliff wasn't; his buzz saw
snore fluttered as he rolled over. His arms groped vaguely for her
and she slipped slowly away.

Time to get to work. They were wrapped in alien strands of
strangeness here. Be alert, yes.

Naked, she headed first for the simple toilet room—an efficient
water swish-away. She had brought sanitary gear, as her period
was just ending—compact, self-cleaning, reliable, less than a gram.
One of the best benefits of civilization, she felt.

Her muscles resented her moving them much, recalling in their
aching fibers the exertions of the last few days. She had trained dil-
igently on *SunSeeker*, but real trekking in the field always provoked
muscles she hadn't heard from in a great while.

Coming out of the shower, she saw a flicker of movement outside, on the balcony. She peered through the transparent wall, and
another flicker of movement caught her eye. Something bobbing up
from below?

She watched more but saw nothing but the remarkable alpine
view. Above, wispy white clouds tumbled in billows over sharp

peaks, fattening as they fell, like cotton candy being whisked into existence at a fairground.

She thought of getting Cliff awake, but he had been up late, talking to the team about how to handle the Glorians, especially Twisty—to no result, he said. When he came back, she had deftly pointed out that she needed a bit of erotic distraction, as befitted their schedule, and to his credit, he complied. Artfully so, as well. He had collapsed soon after, as she worked out how to whistle out the light oozing from walls and ceilings. The room seemed to know a lot about them.

So from curiosity, she picked up the gray stuff. Separate clothing layers slid beneath her fingers. When she slipped one over her legs, it seemed to know how to join up and surround her body. Her inbodies told her this trick came via magnetic closures along the seams. The pants became comfortable. So did the next soft sheet, making itself into a blouse. As the stuff moved over her breasts, distracting her, she mistakenly stepped onto a sheet. It shaped itself into some ingenious dark shoes that wrapped around her feet, like bandages. Then the other sheet slipped around her feet and both grew heels, rugged and broad, good for hiking. Smart, alien stuff.

She wore them outside. Three steps onto the balcony, buzzing came in a swarm singing of something. Beth yelped and tried to dodge, futilely. Small brown birds fluttered, cawing and twittering. Once they had a sniff of her, they wrapped around in a murmuring doughnut shape, like a crown overhead. Were they sent by some Cobweb ambassadors? For surveillance? Or were there smart swarms here, humming their messages, alien discourse in flight? She had to keep her mind open—but, hey, answers would be nice, too.

The lush land spreading away looked like layers of farming and pastures. Some fields had canopies—perhaps to ward off flying eaters, or filter the sunlight for max growth?

Suddenly, Twisty came arcing up into the air. It came from below, contorting its body—all arms out, as though it was flying. Then a midair bend, a rotation, a snap-out to full extension. It came arrowing in—made a last twist—and landed. It didn't even have to take a step forward to check itself. A two-point landing, like an

Olympic athlete. Beth blinked. No human could have done that, leaping up from the ground four meters below.

"Hello. You are wearing your ancestral phenotype," Twisty said.

"And you aren't?" Beth shot back.

"I choose to. Simpler for you to understand."

"What do you have planned?"

"The species you term the carniroos wish to present you with the gift required of their code."

"What's that mean?"

"I have learned, dealing with them, to smile politely and shut my earlids. They respect movement, action, more than words. They wait below and will come now." It gave a long trilling note.

Three of the carniroos sprang up from below. They landed on the broad ledge bordering the balcony. The middle one landed badly. Its companions supported it. Like some other carniroos, as she had learned by reviewing the team videos of yesterday, these wore belts and short aprons that doubled as carry bags, plus covered genitals. Twisty had said that roos made these from the skin of a rabbitlike herbivore they sporadically hunted.

Then, with a jolt, Beth saw that the middle one was dead: the dead roo shot the day before, held by the other two. Its wound had turned brown and black.

A shock ran through her, a massive premonition. She kept her face from revealing anything.

"They present their gift. You may devour their friend."

"What? No."

"They understand that you prefer to uselessly bury the dead of your kind. They, however, feel that prey must be made useful."

The two live roos dropped adroitly to the balcony, holding their dead tightly. The body was stiff, eyes glassy. Beth backed away from them. She recalled the eager note in the carniroo baying, on the attack, as though they thought what they did was music. The joy of the hunt, the song of the kill. "We weren't hunting them as *prey*—they attacked us!"

"Nonetheless, this is their way of achieving peace with you."

"We have to eat them?"

"It is considered polite."

She watched Twisty's bland face. *When in Rome* . . .

"Wait a moment, Twisty."

She went inside for her field knives. For the main job, she took a long blade with a guard and a large handle. A small knife could turn sideways in your hand when it hit bone. A short knife for finer work. Plus some tight gloves. And her phone, to record the procedure. Cliff was still snoring. She stood quietly for a moment and steeled herself for what she had to do.

When she came out, the two big carniroos were holding the corpse between them, lifted high enough for her to work easily. Their impassive blunt-nosed faces simply regarded her with no expression she could read. She smiled, not knowing if these aliens would understand human facial expressions, and thought. *At least I'll learn some anatomy.* . . .

Old field practice: First, look in the mouth. This roo was an omnivore browser, not a grazer. Its teeth combined sharp wolflike fangs in the front of the mouth, grinders toward the back. Snub-faced so the big dark eyes could see forward panoramically.

She sized up the problem by turning the body, in the grip of its fellows. A rigid lumbar spine, as befit a fast hopper. Arms and hands that could support the full body weight, so they could deal with a fall and get right back up. They could use both legs, arms, and tail for a five-point gait, if needed. At least two hundred kilos weight, a real muscular monster compared to her own seventy kilos.

With the ears uncovered, she could see their unusually complex spiral inner structure. To increase hearing sensitivity? She noticed, too, that their fur caused water to bead up instead of soaking in.

Now the hard part . . . She took care slitting the belly open. Was there some alien ritual she should obey? Twisty stood nearby, studying her. She raised eyebrows at it, but the alien just shook its head.

Was this some test? All she had to go on was her experience dressing out deer in the field. High up in the Sierra, you carried out the good meat and left all else behind. Here, quite plainly there was some social role to play. She decided to stick with what she could recall of that Sierra experience, centuries ago.

She slit the tawny skin to peel it back before cutting through the muscle layer. Plenty of dried blood that gave a curious iron tang to the warm air. It was easiest to remove the skin within the first two hours, while the body was still warm—but now it had stiffened. After making a shallow slit, she turned the knife blade upward. *Here goes.*

Starting at the broad pelvis, she cut through the muscle layer along the same line, using the fingers of her free hand on either side of the blade tip. This unzipping effect pulled the muscle layer up and away from the blotchy belly organs. That ensured that she didn't puncture the stomach and intestines. Her nose wrinkled at the smell. Flies came zooming in and swarmed eagerly for the pasty gray blood.

Concentrate. Pretty sure vomiting is not polite. The flies had long bodies and a line of wings. She looped the knife up the chest and neck to the jawline. *This thing is built like Earthside critters. So follow your intuition.* . . .

She was going by the general mammal body plan, so she cut through the cartilage of the breastbone with the knife, sawing hard. That let her spread the ribs—ten sets of them, no less, and thick— for easier cleaning. For that, she quickly cleared the bones with her short knife.

Carnivores had simple digestive tracts, just a straight shot through, not the complicated large and small intestines of humans and other omnivores. This carniroo was different from anything Earthside. It had an odd, tapered digestive tract like a funnel, ending in a big anus. No urethra, so maybe they compressed urine into crystals and shat it out. Earthside, birds and reptiles did that to avoid carrying a lot of liquid aboard.

Now the worst part . . .

Next, she cut a hole around the thing's big ruby-red anus. She pulled it to the inside, not breathing. She had line cord in her work belt, so she spooled some out with a single pull. She shot a quick glance at the carniroos on each side, who were huffing and snorting some now. *Why? Did I do something wrong?*

Ah, the genitals. This carniroo was a male. The phallus was small and tucked into its own pouch. It was thick-veined so would grow a lot when needed. Carefully she tucked it in with the anal zone, held them together. She did not look aside at the aliens while doing this. No rustling of discomfort. Good.

Still not looking into the alien eyes, she tied off the anus and colon with the line cord. *Done. That has to be crucial to the ritual, to prevent spillage.* The roos stirred, their feet shuffling, as she made a loop cut around the entrails and pulled them free. The roos snorted. *Approval? Impossible to tell.*

Then she just ran on intuition. Quickly she sliced away the long windpipe, since it could taint the meat. She cut the windpipe and esophagus in two as far up the neck as she could. *Now the finale . . .* She put aside the knife, grabbed the windpipe with both hands, and pulled down hard. The entrails came free down to the midsection.

She cut the connective tissue holding the moist entrails next to the backbone. Without pause, she dropped the whole bag of guts to the balcony floor. Then she grabbed the skin with both hands at the back of the head. Glanced at the carniroos, then Twisty—who nodded. *At last, a signal.*

With a grunt she pulled down hard. The skin came off with a sound like a wet zipper, down to the forelegs. All the raw red meat stood glistening in the sun.

"What the hell?!" Cliff stood naked beside her. She had not noticed him come out.

"I'll explain later," Beth said slowly. She turned to Twisty. "We're supposed to . . . ?"

Twisty waved all its hands, as if in explanation. "Make a victory meal of their friend."

Cliff snorted. "I don't—"

"Never mind. Look, can you carve out the steaks?"

Cliff blinked. "Uh, sure. For—"

"A feast, yes. Breakfast. I'll go roust out the others. And build a fire. A big one. Festive, I guess."

Twisty spoke in rapid-fire bursts to the carniroos. Beth noticed the big beasts did not seem tired from holding their dead buddy up. They had big bulging muscles in their several arms and legs, even in their tails—casually very strong. The carniroos rattled back in crisp, sharp consonants.

Cliff took her knives and went to work, not bothering to get dressed. Beth realized there was no point in being embarrassed at standing naked before aliens. Nudity was a carefully governed human taboo zone, full of portent—but that meant nothing to aliens. And washing the blood off would be easy.

To watch Cliff, the carniroos holding the body stretched out their heads toward him at the same time. They wrinkled their black lips and opened their mouths so wide she could see their big square tombstone back teeth. As Cliff sawed away, the roos made snuffling and whuffling sounds through shotgun-barrel noses, sighting at him and shuffling their big feet. Apparently the final rendering into cuts for cooking was vastly important. Alien manners.

She watched him, too, slicing off cuts from the thick carniroo muscles. *Fresh game. How long has it been? Nearly a century since, back on the Bowl . . .*

She turned to Twisty with a sudden intuition. "Yes, we'll have a big breakfast feast. Shall we invite some of the carniroos to a . . . ceremony?"

She braced herself for a retort, but Twisty nodded. It was picking up human signaling. "They will appreciate sharing in the feast."

Cannibalism, too?

Beth made herself take a long, deep breath. Kipling had a saying, centuries back: "There are nine and sixty ways of constructing tribal lays, / And every single one of them is right."

She had to admit, the carving and trimming had restored her old field appetites. She had another idea. "Think you or they can find some eggs? You know, from some birds?"

Twisty's arms danced. "I think I know your reference. Yes, there are such here. Unfertilized eggs. Some quite large—" It measured out about a foot length between two arms. "From large fliers. This links to your early origins."

"Huh?"

"I gather you come from the warm-blooded. They once, going by your evolutionary tale, lived by scavenging up the eggs of your ancient dinosaurs. Small, frightened, they supposedly foraged at night. So even now, you eat eggs after you awaken."

"Never thought of it that way," Cliff said as he sliced and layered the meat. The two carniroos were still holding their late comrade aloft, seemingly without effort—though they were both sweating a bit now. Flies buzzed around. Beth realized she was very hungry. Also dirty.

"Let's do our mammal thing, then." She felt bouyant, freed, after the awful, bloody cutting. "Get us some eggs, Twisty, to go with the roo. Steak and eggs, yes. Yum!"

TWENTY-ONE

STRANDS OF STRANGENESS

Redwing did not think education ever did him any great harm, but it had failed to teach him how to hide his irritation. "Why the hell are they discussing all this airy stuff with that damned Glorian, that Twisty?"

The Translator 'Lect said in her soft, calm tones, "It is how the Glorians, whomever that might be, chose."

"That Twisty doesn't seem fazed much. Seems damned casual, after losing two of us in a diplomatic party he's escorting."

"This is a vastly different kind of intelligence than your expedition has seen. The Bowl aliens were various, as well. You suffered casualties there, too."

"Don't remind me."

"Yes, sir." It even knew to slur the *s*.

Redwing grimaced and picked up a coffee from his personal maker. Pointless to argue with the Translator 'Lect about strategy. He lounged back in his cabin and watched, for yet another time, the videos from Beth's helmet camera. Here came the roolike aliens, hopping in arcs thirty meters long. That Honor moon had a bit lower grav than Earth, but the ferocious speed of the animals' attack still startled him.

He noted that some wore a long vest. He paused the feed. The tan vests were nearly the same color as the hide and had pockets, tool kits, even symbol displays of curious spiral designs.

Smart tool users, attacking in packs? With clothes, but no obvious weapons? He shook his head. Even he knew this was odd.

No wonder that in Beth's team talk afterwards, which he listened to intently, the bio team members were puzzled, angry, confused. Like him.

The Translator 'Lect said softly, "I have consulted your species history. Your culture changes swiftly, but often forgets. Humans think of science fiction as a late-nineteenth and twentieth-century genre, as though future thinking emerged then. But the remarkable Voltaire wrote a science fiction novella called *Micromégas*, in which aliens from another star and from Saturn come to the Earth. When they make first contact with people, the first thing they discuss was, 'Is Plato or Descartes correct about how the soul and body connect to each other?' and 'Is Thomas Aquinas's discussion of Aristotle's divisions of the parts of the soul true?' Voltaire's society was obsessed with theology's collisions with the new. So to them, providence and the existence of God and the immaterial soul were what his people talked to aliens about. These were to Voltaire as plausible subjects, as our science fiction works are to us."

Seldom did the Translator 'Lect hold forth, so Redwing considered the example, though it irked him with its irrelevance. "The Glorians are telling us something about themselves, with these deaths?"

"This could be," the Translator 'Lect said. No more.

The danger of Artilects wasn't that they would take over as captains of human destiny. Still, a human captain could overestimate their comprehension. No machine mind, with qubits galore, had ever moved into strange territory, explored and fathomed and used it. Humans had.

Redwing knew to be careful with such systems. They had limited range, and no true natural feel for the vagaries of human language. At first, the Translator 'Lect had Glorians interpreting words oddly. Once the Glorians mistook *coffee* for "one upon whom one coughs." They could seldom spot a joke. But the Voltaire point troubled him.

Worse, much worse, were the tactical implications of this latest death. Sergeant Schindelmeisser had her four-eyes gear running, too, but not well. The tiny survey eyes riding on the back of her neck alerted her to the carniroo pack coming up fast behind her—but she hadn't picked up the warning flash in time. Gear could do only so much, in the field. The carniroo attack had been too quick.

They were down there, wrapped in a blanket of bandwidth,

but paying attention to it was a problem. The system automatically paired with each team member's medical transponder, a gadget as small as a grain of rice. But it wasn't smart enough to deal with the data flood. *Expect the unexpected* was a cute rule, hard to do in alien lands.

Beth's team had given each other plenty of side-eye looks in their discussion, a ripple of uncertainty. *What will happen next? Who will die?* These weren't hardened military types at all. Bio, engineering, tech aplenty—but no real grunts ready for a fight. Maybe he should pull them out? Negotiate some protocols with . . . who? The only Glorian they knew was Twisty—another block in understanding.

He had watched as morning light spread across the land in pastel smears, seen the steak and big-eggs feast. Maybe that made the team feel better, but he doubted it. He would watch, listen, judge the odds. Aliens were alien.

Meanwhile, the crew aboard *SunSeeker* were resurrecting more from cold sleep. They all had to be ready to spread through the Cobweb in enough numbers to firm up their presence. That imperative came from Earthside strategy behind this whole expedition, and others like it—spread humanity through the galaxy neighborhood, as species insurance. Plus, learn a lot, to piece together humanity's place in the galaxy.

Redwing studied on split screens the many visual feeds from the net of drones surveying the Cobweb above Honor. Here was one in the air above Beth's team. Here was the view captured when Glory eclipsed the Cobweb and Honor in shades of bruise-colored, solemn shadows. The Honor landscape had domes, apparently for separate biospheres—why?

He watched visuals above the enormous Cobweb lands, rich in moisture. Clouds bunched over continent-broad slabs stacked along the Cobweb axis. Gravity acted along the Cobweb axis and he saw these pancakes of landmass from the side. Each slender wedge of land had a slightly different, near-zero gravity, because of their distances from the two worlds. From afar, the tubes and columns that framed the Cobweb mingled with pipes, tubes, sometimes even purple corkscrew plumbing. They were intricately color-coded in grays, pinks, blues, and orange shades, and ultraviolet and infrared,

too, apparently so engineers could easily parse their functions. The magnitude of such a vibrant, living vault still stunned him. Whole oceans and atmospheres flowed along the web axis, bringing life in slender columns.

This was fluid wrangling on a huge scale. Though Earth's air seemed boundless, it was tiny on planetary terms of gross mass. All the hundred or so kilometers of Earth air weighed only a bit more than the Mediterranean Sea. That was why the first clear signs of humanity's impact on their world came in the air they breathed and polluted.

He watched holo views of the Bulge, showing *SunSeeker* as a tiny, silvery sliver magnetically moored alongside. Here the fluid ferment of a vast biozone hung in the blackness. Looking from the edge of the Bulge, Glory blocked its star.

Then he had the Artilects merge the distant views, backing away to a point beyond Honor. The lesser world's atmosphere was very cloudy, and the Cobweb tapered away to Glory. For clarity, the Artilects had filtered out the shadows, revealing the silvery strutworks that made them name it Cobweb.

The many small probe swarms he had sent flanking along the Cobweb's length showed that the Cobweb's contained atmosphere was several thousand times more massive than all Earth's air.

What's more, rather than Earth's stagnant layers, air circulated through the Cobweb in apparent disobedience of physics. No big density gradients. The same for the water that flowed across the broad continental-sized platforms. High up along the Cobweb, some silvery-blue lakes even floated in air, great sheets across most of the Bulge. Maybe air currents alone, in that fat low-grav zone, kept the hanging lakes aloft. The handiwork of unseen giants.

His board lit with an incoming signal. *Ah, from the Bowl.*

Mayra Wickramsingh's face was even more worn and weary. She preferred to report standing, her *SunSeeker* uniform neat and lean body still fit. He had made her the voice of the human colony on the Bowl because she kept a neat shop and took no backtalk.

"Hail again, Cap'n," she began. "Got lots to report—my written

is running parallel to this stream, per request. Got a big problem headed your way."

The screen filled with three white-hot plumes flaring widely against a starry background. "This is that band of corsairs—as the Folk put it—who cast off the Bowl rim back around a year or so ago. Nobody knew it until they turned on their ramscoop full blast, to get away from us. They're still accelerating and—watch this—"

The first plume flickered out, and a speck appeared, the actual ship. It close-upped further and Redwing could see the tubular shape turn on its axis. Yellow and red plasma turbulence flared around it, like a silver insect roasting in a roiling fire.

"Starting deceleration. They're out about as far as that grav wave transmitter you got a look at, going in."

Redwing ached to shoot back a question, but speed-of-light delay was still months long. The speck finished spinning around its axis, and a white-hot plume again scorched across the blackness, now pointing toward the bright lure of Glory.

Mayra said, "There are three of them, keeping close together. I think they may swoop by that grav wave emitter. I noticed the whole array is in the bow shock region of the star. I guess that's to max the ambient plasma. Anyway, our detectors may have picked up a surge of plasma emissions near that grav wave thing. Looks like some knots of plasma are approaching it from the Glory side. They may be the Diaphanous who left you, as you spiraled into the inner system. Looks like trouble brewing, anyway."

She shrugged, eyes rolling in a comic *what can I do?* gesture. "Oh, and we've had some kind of revolt near here, against the Folk. I've gotta attend to that. Local politics never goes away." Then she waved good-bye.

Redwing knew the Diaphanous were intrigued by the grav wave transmitter's plasma attendants—who were distantly related to the Earth system's, somehow. Plasma life had flitted across the interstellar spaces, living on the stream of filmy ions streaming eternally there. Maybe such forms of organized matter were immortal, in human terms.

He shook himself. The scales of space and time here were beyond human comprehension. Maybe the Glorians knew enough to make this whole space-time landscape, this timescape, under-standable. Somehow, sometime.

For now, he focused on Beth's team. Videos to review, drones to interrogate as they flew a swarm over the team. Small, belea-guered, and already damaged, Beth's team was still the point of the spear. He hoped she would make it sharp.

TWENTY-TWO
BIG BRIGHT SHINY

Observe how system into system runs,
What other planets circle other suns,
What varied being peoples ev'ry star,
May tell why Heav'n has made us as we are.
—ALEXANDER POPE

Rising animal noise woke Beth. She lay in bed, listening to the clicks and chirps, brays and snorts of huge birds she could see flapping by their residence. Animals here seemed boisterous, busy. Which meant they felt unafraid. But she was not.

They had gotten through another restless sleep with eye masks, adjusting to the lack of night. Daylight kept knocking at her eyeballs still. Plus Cliff snoring, a sound at least familiar. Monumental thuds from the distance, like giant's footfalls—probably from the gas and grav system that made Honor its high base. She burrowed deeper into the agreeably smooth bedclothes, listening to the rising wind outside, trying to process all that had happened in the dense day before.

Best to review. Redwing would ask.

After their breakfast of huge, peppery red-yoked eggs with carniroo slab steaks, Twisty and seven from Beth's team had hiked around the area, getting the feel of this life-rich moon. It was good to stay in a spot for a day or two, get oriented. She liked the alpine feel here, with vivid splashes of vegetation, scintillant hills, towering trees, its sky of shifting hues skidding over mountains of elephant gray. She at last let Bemor Prime out of his carrier, and the big ominous spidow ambled well in the gravity, lighter than ship grav here. Its eager inhalations boomed like a bass accordion. Her

team needed to rest and restore, so they called it a day early—
especially since here an Honor day lasted several Earth days.

She rose, washed, stepped outside on the balcony, feeling
better—prepped and pretty, as people said in her training years,
back now centuries ago. Cliff gave her a smacky kiss as he passed
into the washroom. The balcony area had contracted in the night,
as if knowing the dressing-out of the carniroo would not recur
today. But now it extended to the side, making room with tremors
and pops.

How smart was the building? Or was it governed by others,
Twisty especially? The alien always seemed blithely easy with every
turn, and only thinly concerned with human or carniroo deaths.

She was about to go back inside to get her hiking gear when
something made her look up—into a hovering mass. And here came
Twisty, peering over the edge of a lowering basket. It dangled below the swelling curve of an immense, pink dirigible shape. The
basket came level with the balcony, and Twisty leaped from it to
stand, perfectly balanced, on the balcony rim.

The huge thing made a low, huffing sound like a great, long
breath as it moved. Cliff came out onto the balcony.

Twisty spoke a high, trilling greeting, then, "We invite you to
ride, not hike. There are many Honor delights to enjoy from a height."

"Uh, this is a surprise. . . ." Beth was still looking up into the
belly of a huge creature. As it eased down, a broad fin unfurled and
made contact with the balcony floor, small grapplers grasping with
gnarled handlike roots.

"Our boarding ramp was the tongue," Cliff remembered. "It's a
tadfish. From the Bowl."

Beth watched it maneuver silently, more elaborate fins unfolding to capture wind like a sail. More slender grapplers secured it
on the building. It hugged the side of the building and used the
lee wind for torque. She guessed the huge creature could trim and
tilt by shifting weight inside itself, getting a pivot torque about its
center of mass to navigate. It was a buoyant airship sailing at angles
to the light wind, tacking well with its big side fan-fins spread with
languid, flapping grace. A big eye turned toward her. She felt like a
microbe trapped under a microscope.

Twisty remarked, "I know you humans have seen a distant relative on the Bowl. We have made that ancient battleskyship into . . . a bus."

"You got the basic genes from the Bowl?"

Twisty shrugged. "Long ago, in an unfortunate era."

"And let them go wild?"

"No, they are living, loving beasts of burden."

"And we're the burden."

"Quite. But they enjoy our passage. You might say that we tickle their insides."

"Send our team an alert," she told Cliff. "Get their gear and assemble, pronto."

As the big thing turned lazily, she saw more blister pods. Things moved within them: Crew? The elegant gargantuan had evolved and bioteched from some Bowl balloonlike species, yes— Tananarive had seen several in fleets. They knew such bioengineered creatures used to patrol the air above the Bowl.

Beth recalled to her side-eye view memory-images from the Bowl: A fat skyfish wallowing across the air above a Sil city. Lashing it with flame spouts. Some had forked down green rays that seared buildings and people alike. The great beast had slid down the sky through realms of smoke. Beth brought up from her inboard images the Bowl records. Yes, one such had crashed like a green-fired egg, crumbling in slow motion as it burned into black smoke towers.

Now Glory's biotech had engineered this skyfish, a living beast that could float and feed its passengers. It gave a long, rolling bass note that made its skin tremble.

The creature's round black eyes watched them, yellow irises flashing in the slanting sunlight. Its face was solemn and slow, its broad mouth wide and salmon-pink and lipless. Bursts of slow song boomed from the mouth. A greeting? Its wide, flat nostrils were veined pink, with fleshy flaps beneath that Beth guessed the beast could close at will. At the top of the smooth head sprouted a vibrant blue crest that flapped, serrated and trimmed with yellow fat, reminding her of a cock's comb.

Where had the Bowl gotten the basics? From some airborne

floaters, found on some planet where thick air and light gravity made that an optimal path? Big, slow, made invulnerable by its size, like elephants or whales or a brontosaurus? And then somehow those genes got to Glory in the ancient past, when the Bowl passed nearby—a matter Twisty studiously avoided.

"We have prepared a selection of local delicacies for you aboard," Twisty said, gesturing toward a gangplank that had unrolled from the creature's mouth.

"Gotta get our gear first, bring the team together," Beth said hurriedly, and went into their room.

This took a while. The team obeyed orders with frowns and skeptical smiles. Her stomach was growling when they got onto— no, into—the skyfish. The tongue was dry, not slippery, and curled up at the edges.

Twisty escorted them in, saying, "I thought this would fillibrate your atrium."

Beth thought this was an elaborate pun, for the entrance was ornately wreathed in curtains of rosy pink, languidly waving in the beast's breath. Cliff said, "You mean, thrill us?" and Twisty nodded.

"Yes, I attempted verbal play, which your kind seem to enjoy. Your tongue is usefully linear, but confusing. I cannot see why, for example, *slaughter* lies but a single letter away from *laughter*—you see?"

Cliff blinked, then said, "We laugh at death because that's all we can do, I suppose." Twisty froze for a moment, then kept moving.

They walked into a cozy cave of moist membranes, lit by phosphorescent swirls embedded behind translucent tissues, moving like living, illuminated art. A deep bass note rang, ending in a whoosh like an immense sigh. Grav momentarily rose as they lifted off. Ruddy wall membranes fluttered. Warm air eased by them as they entered a large bowl-shaped area. Sunshine lanced through membranes so clear Beth thought at first they were open to the air. Yet the thin skins laced the light with a softening glow, like ivory. The sweet warm breeze swept first one way, then reversed, and she realized that it was the breathing of this great beast. The roomy building that had seemed so ample when they lived there now dwindled away below.

The team just watched, breakfast forgotten. As the skyfish turned, the sweep of a plain came into view. Clouds stacked like fat blue plates loomed on the shimmering distance. The mountains fell behind into a gray linear rim. She could see the long arc of Honor's horizon curving away into a pale sky as they rose. The blue of lakes below outlined greens and browns of lands. Below them flapped big-winged angular birds with long snouts and yellow crests atop their bony heads. With a rush of joyful surprise, she knew that this was her last and greatest adventure, that exploring was her engulfing fate. Each day now featured weirdness writ large, a running river of what she once thought of as the prospects of the universe's immensity, the Big Bright Shiny.

They were like people riding a larger animal, as she had ridden horses. In the great living volume, a narrow hydrogen arc hissed and lit the translucent furniture in blue light. Did that come from the beast's lifting storage? She wondered how the huge thing avoided accidental explosions.

Worrying isn't thinking, she thought. *Just see and try to understand.*

"Your banquet, my friends." Twisty gestured broadly with all arms. Spindly creatures somewhat like Twisty—slim, many-armed, and quick. They stood with studious green eyes and big, hideous sucker mouths, saying nothing, then set forth an array of curious, sloping dishes. These smaller twisters stepped back from the table and waved to the humans, a welcome.

Cliff went first. "Brave man," she saluted him.

He cracked a steaming yellow carapace and slurped out the warm white flesh of some sea creature. She chose a dish that featured a big insect basted in creamy sauce.

As she reached for it, thinking it was like a larger version of the crickets they ate on ship, Twisty remarked, "The trick in this delicacy is keeping it alive through the cooking." The big bug kicked long legs into the air. "That adds a lovely savor to the simmered proteins," Twisty added helpfully.

"So I need to kill it?"

"Your first slice will bring it peace," Twisty said. "Though there is evidence that it enjoys the cooking itself."

She tried to break the thick legs with her hands and snap off the tasty eyestalks. "You've chem-sorted all this, so it's not poison to us, right?"

Twisty nodded and smiled, getting better at human signaling. She cracked the knobby leg and bit into the slender, pungent meat. Crunchy, too, with a peppery flavor that stung her lips and sent a scent like king crab into her sinuses. A green pudding turned out to be a slime mold that thrust probes out into her mouth as she tried to chew it. The flavor wasn't nearly worth it. She spat the thing out. The floor immediately formed a rippling pool around it and sucked the morsel down. "Our host enjoys it and thanks for your sharing."

"Host?"

"This craft has elementary politeness, of course. All such vast beings must. It enjoys its carrying you, as with other burdens. Our craft's detailed direction is left to the smaller and smarter."

Twisty gestured at the shorter Twisty-like figures that kept to the huge room's shadows, like hushed servants in some ancient drama. They whispered among themselves. She strode over to address them, Twisty hastily dancing alongside. "Thank you for your work," Beth said.

One of the lesser Twisty-likes said in a high-pitched, soft rasp, "We prefer your direction, as new guests. I am Anarok, the Captain."

Twisty said, "I am in command here."

Anarok waved this away. "We accept suggestions from you highers, but I command." It drew itself up and turned pointedly to Beth. "I gather you are female?"

"Uh, yes."

"I favor females working together. Do you not?"

"I have no preference."

Twisty said, "Sex is no matter. I prefer to remain neutral. My point—"

"You have no sex at all?" Beth shot back.

Twisty made a several-armed shrug. "I am so instructed, to meet with you. Your species assigns great weight to such matters. We of our species typically do not."

Beth stepped away from Anarok and whispered, "Why? Isn't reproduction vital to you?"

Twisty said, "You are a biologist from a simpler biosphere. Simply accept that many of us need not reproduce."

"Why?"

"We live quite long, by your measures. We lessen population stresses by holding our numbers fixed."

Anarok stepped forward and softly said, "Not all of us. I prefer the female form. And to work with females!" She turned to Twisty. "Please to reserve your comments, must less your orders, for protocols. *I* command this vessel."

Twisty's arms flared forth, as if to grab at Anarok—then stopped. "I see your immersion in female urges has led you to this affront."

Anarok waved her arms in cycling circles of exasperation. Her face was too alien to read, resembling a snail's foot or a remora's sucker. "I agreed to ferry these guest species, no more."

Twisty's mouth opened, arms hunched together—and then it stepped back, head twitching, obviously with some effort at self-control. Beth was getting used to reading its gestures. "I shall retire." Twisty turned and was gone.

Beth looked around at her team, eating. "I'm still hungry, so . . ."

Cliff came over, clearly seeing she was getting exasperated, and spoke to Anarok. "I thank you for this feast. Can you tell me how matters work inside this, uh, skyfish?"

Anarok followed her to the long banquet table. Her team was digging into the alien breakfast with gusto, trading remarks on the odd tastes. Anarok spoke, amplifying on how independent her shipboard crew was from such larger forms as Twisty. Beth picked up a shank of something red and meaty, bit in with relish, and stepped over to a transparent blister in the wall.

They moved with gravid majesty over snowy peaks, somewhat like a ship sailing at angles to the wind, tacking through flinty stone passages. Plunging verticals, everywhere.

She suddenly thought of a time when she had climbed mountain cliffs and once made the mistake of looking down, as she was now. That time she had gotten pulled by converging lines of perspective into the tapering-away sight of hundreds of meters below her, and messed herself. She had clung to a rope feeling as weak as beer with ice in it and thought she would never again do anything risky. Somehow that feeling had lapsed over centuries.

She breathed out slowly, getting her true self back, and bit into the meat. Its savors jerked her back into the ever-present present, which was there whether you thought of it or not.

The deck swayed and through the blister Beth saw they were tacking before a strong wind. Verdant mesas beckoned.

In the distance loomed the side spire of the Cobweb. From this angle she could make out the grand upward exponential curve of it. The same swoop, immensely larger across, that she had seen in Paris as a girl. Simple physics dictated that—an exponential arc tapering into Honor's stratosphere and then beyond, to the spaces where gravity no longer ruled all.

"Look, let's go for a walk, explore a tad," Cliff said. "Chow will be over soon, and those highlands up ahead look good to me."

Beth nodded. She gave the ready-up signal to her team and a short memo to Redwing. She had noticed he was following their visual/audio feeds but keeping silent. She went over to Anarok and engaged the alien in conversation.

"We have upgraded our linguistics of your tongue," Anarok said. She gave a rattling squawk, which Beth recognized was Twisty's name in the local sprach. There followed from Anarok an inventory of slights, neglects, and misuses Twisty's "kind" had exacted from the crews of skyfish. Beth listened intently, nodding, said nothing. For the first time she got a sense of tensions among the various smart aliens here. Gossip and grousing, it seemed, were universals.

An hour later their party was split, going up a mountain valley on both sides of a river splashing eagerly downhill. Twisty had taken them to a sideways tube that blew them through a gray-green mountain and into a verdant land.

Beth had scouts out to each side, as did Viviane on the other bank. Each party kept the other in view. They kept careful watch. No sign of the carniroos, much less the backfire dragons who had hit them out in the Cobweb. Still, she felt uneasy.

Twisty was oblivious to this. As they hiked, Beth noting aspects of the wildlife, it rattled on, "We must remark that, summoning up your entire library of human culture, you are . . . quite fitting."

Cliff asked, "Fitting what?"

"As a species, you are technologically gifted yet philosophically callow. Alas, a common condition among emergent intelligences. But of late, it is your animal property of physical expression that intrigues our minds. Frequently you are unaware of your actions—which makes them all the more revealing. Your unconscious selves are in many ways more interesting, we Glorians believe. This, too, is a facet of emergent intelligences. That is, those who have not pro-liferated into variant forms, through artful adjustments of their own genomes."

"Our unconscious?" Beth asked, striding forward in the lower grav, feeling strong.

"Your invention, though others have had such. Like many of the species of the ancient Bowl of Heaven, as we know from history. They who term themselves the Folk abandoned such interior, ba-roque extravaganzas."

Beth noted that Twisty had not said anything about Bemor Prime, who kept a distance from the rest of the team. Twisty showed no signs that it found such a giant spidow intimidating—maybe because there were such creatures somewhere in the Cob-web matrix?—or that it was aware the Bowl Folk knew how to install themselves inside such bodies.

Twisty was engaging Cliff in a discussion about whether an un-conscious was a good idea, in the broad sweep of evolution. Cliff kept pressing for details as he swatted away a buzzing bird. There were plenty of the little brown darting ones, more like humming-birds in their shrill calls and frenetic flailing wings. "We got to you, didn't we," Cliff said. "It's not like you came to us."

Twisty's arms danced. "True. We gave that up long ago."

"Why?"

"Too few prospects in the neighborhood. Your lovely world in-cluded."

"What was wrong with—?"

"No intelligence then, but for the oceans."

"This is how long ago?" Cliff asked.

"In your years, a bit more than a million."

"There were pretty smart hominids then."

"Ah, *hominids* means 'pre-human,' yes?"

"Yeah, primates kinda like us. Tool users. Had fire, tools, flint—"

Twisty paused, arms slack. Cliff glanced at Beth, and gave their wavy hand signal that meant the alien was probably augmenting memory with an inset data feed. Twisty's voice came out now flatter, almost as though reading as it spoke. "I gather our automatic expedition found them potentially interesting, true. But our craft launched vessels into your seas and spoke with the swimmers there."

"Dolphins?" Beth asked. "Whales?"

"Without hands, they, like many on other worlds, possess merely the spoken genius of minds thwarted. As in the porpoise, yes."

Beth kept up her pace through an angular green valley, chuckling. "Some of us think the porpoise proves great genius by doing nothing particular to prove it."

Twisty's hands flew with delighted animation. "Their wisdom comes proved in pyramidal silence. Their freedom allows to follow the untrammeled sea winds across your planet."

Cliff waved off two of the birds that zoomed around his head. Beth saw then that Twisty's humor had an edge, the creature's thin mouth slanted and low. "You get this from probes you sent that far back, so you did have an expansionist phase."

"We learned from such as your sea life. Such minds had not evolved here."

"Why didn't you colonize Earth, then?" Beth asked.

"We decided instead to focus on lessons learned in that vast ago time."

"Lessons from where?"

"Your world, others less clement. Most especially from the Bowl."

"They taught you what?" Beth persisted.

"The value of vast lands. Yet despite their damaged saga, they venture forth in blazing haughty grandeur and thus risk much."

Cliff said flatly, "You had a run-in with them, yes?"

"An unfortunate dealing, our history so testifies."

"Some species exchange?" Cliff bored on.

"True, though of course time's rub has altered allsuch."

"There are species like our dolphins here?"

"Some, though not always in seas."

Beth asked, "Can we meet some?"

"In due time, a phrase I think you know."

She could tell much from Cliff's boots, twitching just a bit as he walked on beside a rushing, gurgling stream, his pace picking up with his frustration. Diplomacy was not his strong suit.

Beth said mildly, "Why are we seeing only you, a single representative of what must be myriad species?"

Twitchy stopped dead, facing Beth. "I am sent to fathom you. Others witness, through me. You must know this."

"We kinda guessed," Cliff said. "Who else is tuning in?"

The rest of their party, following orders, kept apart. Dealing with Twisty was an executive function. More of the birds were wheeling and cawing in the air above. Sunlight glinted from their feathers. Their wings lifted high, smacking into each other at the top, clacking.

Twisty made smooth, calming gestures with its hands. "We are cautious. I am expendable. We believe in revelation by experience, not the tyranny of talk."

Cliff stood with hands on hips—an unconscious primate gesture, Beth thought, that she had seen in chimps—and so she knew what he was thinking. "While you're being careful, your buddies here have killed two of us."

"Your own history, as unashamedly granted us in great cultural data files—and for that I congratulate you, a mature act indeed—testifies well to your nature. You have extinguished many of your world's companion species, a classic crime of emerging genera. Yet your losses you see as tragic."

"We damn well *care* about each other, don't you understand?" Cliff was barely holding himself in, she knew. "We're not just visiting zoo exhibits here for your study!"

Beth held up her hand, fingers tightened into a point, their signal for halt. Cliff nodded. "Suppose you tell us, friend Twisty, how you see the evolution of so simple a young species as we?"

Twisty brushed its hands along its arms, a Glorian gesture she had learned meant a cleansing of the air, and discussion. "I fashion that you emerged from land evolution of what you term apes, a primate specialty. If apes had sacrificed hands for flukes—so the moral might run, given as you are to such—they would still be philosophers, thinking in watery wisdom terms. But a retreat—so you would see it, surely?—into the seas would have taken away your devastating power to wreak your thought upon the body of the world. Instead, you would have lived and wandered, like the porpoise, homeless across currents and wind and oceans. Intelligent, surely. But forever the lonely and curious observer of unknown wreckage, such as our spacecraft sent to your world, miracles falling through the ocean's blue eternal light."

Beth said, "Primates never went back into the seas. Porpoises, whales, those came from hooved animals."

Twisty waved this detail away. "My point is, to use your word, rhetorical. This pathway would perhaps have brought a deserved penitence for you, the eventual human. Perhaps such a transformation would bring that mood of innocence lost as childhood ends. You might have studied other minds, known many things living. All that, but absent power and your notorious urge to harm. It is worth at last a wistful thought for you, that someday the porpoise may talk to us, Glorians. We might well help you fracture the long loneliness that has made humanity a frequent terror and abomination even to himself."

In the silence following, Beth thought again of a lesson hard-learned from the Bowl: Until you meet an alien intelligence, you will not know what it is to be human.

Cliff shook his head, mouth tight, shoulders tense. "We kill to eat, sure—and so far, your goddamn friends have been killing us for the same reason. Those carniroos are smart, too. Don't you respect intelligent life here?"

Twisty gave a good imitation of a human shrug, though its shoulders were too liquid, just muscle waves sloshing from neck to shoulder, to make it mean anything.

It stood firm, arms held still, and said slowly, with a curious solemn dignity, "Yes, but intelligence must know and reconcile with the real universe into which logic and mechanism and time have made us all. I know death is coming for me. So do you. Laws of evolution command it. We have no way to pass on survival genetics to the next generation, beyond our age of last reproduction. All longevity beyond that age comes from social forces, keeping us alive for a blissful while. For you humans, that is about fifty years. For us, two hundred—we have made some progress beyond your level, yes. Yet I do not fear death, because I believe there is nothing on the other side of death to fear."

Cliff said, "Well, I damn sure fear it."

Twisty said, "Sadly, so."

Beth stepped between them. "Look, we're not dolphins. They get eaten by killer whales, nothing they can do about it. But we can! If your buddies, other species, come at us, we'll kill plenty of them, faster than you can count."

Twisty made his odd nod again. "You are a farming culture still, though speedily expanding beyond your star as well. This carries historical burdens."

Cliff shook his head angrily once more. "And you? No farms?"

Twisty's eyes flicked over the humans, as if judging them with a flinty glare. "We have such, true. But most of us prefer the state nature brought to us, what you would call *wild*. That does not mean of low intelligence."

Beth felt uneasy. "So what's wrong with farming?"

Twisty gestured at the woods and mountains around them. "Some species prefer this. Indeed, on worlds and in what you term the Cobweb, most do. It is somewhat like the terrain we evolved into. As did you."

"You evolved here, not on Glory?"

"We carry many Glory genes, but of course the Cobweb is all artificial, restored again and again. Glory species went extinct, were revived using guesswork and artwork. We are of long lineage."

"On Glory?"

"No, mostly—for beyond Glory's grasp affords us more room

and possibility. You should focus outward from it. In ways, we were like you, in ancient eras."

Beth wondered why Twisty always avoided talking about Glory. She decided to let it go for now; diplomacy was about being polite, or seeming so. "We invented farming when the hunter-gatherer game got too crowded."

"Much as we did. And passed through our agricultural phase. We learned well that bands associate. Family, bond-groups, clans of ten or more families, fusions of clans. Then, as the number of farmers grows, comes strata formation. Cities. Nations. You and we alike then needed to bind in larger groups. Reunions are essential. Greetings often signaled by eating, mating, even defecating, if that is to your species' taste. Slumber in pairs is useful, though adding more helps also. Neurological substrates emerge spontaneously in those emergent animals, which share and learn through emotion. The crucial avenue of higher minds, truly. Touch and smell and handshakes, appendage blending, long associations at levels of hormones and chemicals fashioned and selected for just this use—so common! To think and feel are often the same, for all pursue joy. Evolution demands it."

Beth opened her mouth to hustle along this talkative alien, but then heard high caws and shrieks. Her concentration on Twisty had thrown off her guard.

A flash of pain came at her neck. Wings battered her head as a bird nipped at her neck. She slapped it away, drew her knife—and saw a flock of the darting birds at the necks of her entire team. Shouts, screeching. She stabbed at the bird. Her blade slipped among the feathers, found no target. The bird cawed loudly in her ear, beat at the air—and dived off, catching the wind. She dropped her knife back into its sheath and with her other hand brought her laser up. Her bolt hit the bird in flight. The beam reflected away. It tumbled in the air, squawked. She fired again, missed. It darted away with a flash of speed.

She saw other laser bolts reflecting from the birds. Quick snaps of light, not doing any harm she could see. "Shoot for the head!" she called.

A brown dart zoomed at her, beak yawning wide. She fired

straight into its face. That worked. The head exploded. The bird smacked into her chest and fell bloody to the ground. The bird had plainly artificial layers in the head, like computer chips.

Cliff shot three times and hit two of the quick, flapping daggers. She took aim at another and with two shots nailed it.

Twisty, she saw, was lying on the ground. On its back. Not hurt. Just batting the birds away as they came near. It did not even look very bothered by it all.

Twisty's voice rose to a high pitch, a keening call. Abruptly the birds broke off. They spread out, harder to hit, as they shot away.

"Damn it!" she shouted at Twisty. "Why the hell didn't you warn us?"

"I would not deprive you of the experience," it said smoothly.

She felt her neck. It oozed blood, a flesh wound. "Another of your wild, smart things?"

"Their flock mind wished to inquire into you. By flying near, they can interrogate your mind radiations—electromagnetic, though frightfully faint."

"They could've just hovered and asked!" Cliff shot back.

"I decided to let this minor engagement be their only permitted approach."

"Approach?!" Cliff barked. He pointed his laser at Twisty.

Beth stepped between them. "No. Let's check the team."

The birds had nipped and flapped but done no major damage. The team was irritated. Viviane took malicious joy in trampling dead birds under her boots, as they crunched and snapped. Some of the bird bodies had gleaming metallic parts, and the heads carried tiny gear that looked like some kind of comm system.

Twisty watched her check out her team members with an ethereal calm. She picked up a dead bird and studied the feathers. They were more like shiny crystal wafers. "Can reflect knives, even lasers," she said to Cliff as she showed the body to him.

Twisty waved this languidly away. "The flock wished to taste of you. Apparently you did not appeal. Your thought patterns, which they are sculpted to interrogate, proved difficult to decipher—tangled, they thought. Further, they had not expected such violence, and to lose so many of their members. You proved more impressive in the field than they supposed. Word will spread among the fliers. They will respect you now."

Cliff glared at the alien and stalked away.

Beth shook her head, bewildered, glanced up into the sky free of the annoying birds—but with a zingo. No, two.

Irked still, she yanked her laser out and fired off three quick bolts. The shots made the intricate structures glimmer. Nothing more. The zingoes rippled and hung in the air. An occasional velvet and ivory shimmer washed over them.

"You need to apply more power," Twisty said blandly, "to have much impact."

"Then what'll they do?"

Cliff called from behind her, "Maybe make sparks. Like when my boyhood cat put his tail in the toaster."

Twisty shook its head. "These are observers, no more. Do not take them as aggressive."

"Why not?"

"They will conclude that you are an unpleasant type."

"Not really. Not yet." She glowered at Twisty. "You'll be able to tell the difference."

"These are of another phylum, if I understand your primate terms."

"Seems more like something from a kingdom we don't know, not just a phylum. Ours are animals, plants, fungus, protozoa, and eukaryotes. Those things, zingoes, I call 'em, are—"

"More like a physical class," Twisty said. "Plasmas, as you say. But they can condense, when irked. Even become hanging liquids."

"Irked?"

"Do not irritate them."

"So they're your bosses?"

"Not precisely."

"You work together?"

"There is a saying, from one of your older places called England, why bother to buy a dog and then bark yourself?"

TWENTY-THREE
LUMENSTONE

Human language is like a cracked kettle on which we
beat out tunes for bears to dance to, when all the time
we are longing to move the stars to pity.
—GUSTAVE FLAUBERT

Beth watched the gray-green highlands of Honor glide past. This
skyfish could sail to higher altitudes with ease, lofting above ivory
clouds stacked like ethereal shiny pancakes. Few animals soared
here. Some were balloon creatures, pink and fishlike, about a meter in size and drifting in pairs. Broad-winged, leathery birds labored
by in languid flocks, avoiding the skyfish.

"How do you get so high?" she asked the Captain, who stood
beside her in an observing blister. The blister's skin bulged out farther at the lesser pressures here. Beth felt as though she were suspended in air herself, a gliding ghost.

The Captain's head swiveled around at alarming angles, watching the skies as she spoke. When not being used, her arms held close
to the body. "Our kindly host kindles forth more lively hydrogen.
See"—a flick of an arm—"how its ample belly swells."

"What's our 'host' called?"

"It wears proudly the deserved title Conqueror of Clouds." The
Captain spoke with a gliding, soft voice that yet struck hard consonants, and her big eyes beamed with pride at the name. Beth had
trouble looking at her mouth.

Higher in the atmosphere, the skyfish was more like a balloon
now, and Beth wondered how it stretched itself. The pops and
rumbles she heard echoing through the warm corridors suggested
elasticity in the skeleton, like cartilage protesting as it reshaped.

"We approach a skillful Watcher," the Captain said, pointing with an angular arm. Beth saw nearby a zingo, more solid seeming than others before.

"What do they watch?"

"Your very alien self, I expect."

"What are they?"

"Wise portals to the enduring Summation."

The Captain's sliding way of saying this meant something, Beth felt. Her speech differed from Twisty's, always revealing her attitudes with an obligatory adjective before each noun, flowing with melodious diction. Twisty did not give away such information, preferring to be a tad mysterious. She frowned and the Captain explained, "Our distant way of knowing your intriguing kind. Those of Twisty, as you term that attentive being, are more of the determined invasive."

The Captain's voice was soft and dry, like worn leather. There were physical differences between her and Twisty, but subtle. Beth supposed that to aliens, human men and women looked much alike in their practical, severe field clothes, too.

Nearby one of the leathery birds glided alone and abruptly dived into a balloon creature. Its wide jaws gulped down the round pink shape, and from the mouth hissed out a jet of air, condensing into fog. The attack had popped the interior bag and the bird let that escape, nothing else. It swallowed visibly, and then lofted away to rejoin its flock.

She knew damn well that any biosphere held innumerable tragedies, slaughters vast and vicious. She had been aboard a research vessel on an Earthside ocean, could not recall which now, amid a krill bunch-up, like a soup of tiny silvery crunchy crustaceans. She had watched the swarm of them fed on by whales, seals, penguins, squids, and fish, a mass murder of the bottom of the sea's food chain. So swarming schools of animals fed larger ones and none cared, because they had no culture to make that an evil thing. Sometimes it was a blessing not to think.

Along the way here, they had already met odd forms. Twisty called one plant the trappersnapper, a horny caselike affair, just a trunk with a pair of square jaws. Plants had developed ways to trap animals. The leapycreeper had roots and stems that were also tongues and lashes. In one stand of fat trees, a section of the bark gaped wide, revealing a pale deadly mouth. An oystermaw, Twisty had said, for unwary small animals. The trees could digest flesh.

Yet she had seen herds and groups of animals with horns, claws, stabbing tails, armor shields, needles, bony sabers—armaments like Earthside ones, for ambush predators, for dominance, for display, and not just for dinner.

She glanced up at the sky to follow a flock of soft blue, angular-winged birds. Abruptly, as though they knew she was watching, they formed into a series of lines:

! ! !

"Huh?" She turned to Twisty, who was having some more late breakfast, breaking a shell creature in half with three hands.

"They mean it as a greeting, I believe," it said.

"Maybe not," Cliff said with a worried look at the sky. The birds now formed into a clear series of signs:

? ? ?

"Fear masks itself as procrastination," Twisty said smoothly. "Let us land, disperse, and explore. You will learn much."

• • •

They came down the spongy tongue ramp of the great skyfish gingerly, the team's eyes watching the surroundings carefully. The air was cool and thin, compared to that of the womblike skyfish interior.

Cliff looked back at the big bulk and saw their host carrier bulged even larger now, its somber skin stretched shiny-tight. They were at the broad mountain peak in a mild breeze that carried scents of greenery and moist soil. Beneath their feet lay long stretches of gray rock leading uphill. A chittering swarm of agitated wings and improbably big mouths massed broadly across the sky, ignoring the humans below. No punctuation marks now.

The skyfish Captain bade them good progress. "Brave adventurers of your slender species, learn much!" The fish would feed on local sources and await them.

With the team, Cliff walked to the edge of a steep drop. Beth deployed the team in a wing and tail formation. They had a vibrant view of the sloping lands below, spread like a rumpled quilt set with dark gems. Close-up showed the black structures to be many-walled and with stone towers of glinting obsidian, like ominous medieval castles. Some big creatures moved around them, apparently working the fields like enormous horses.

Nearer, he close-upped slanted green houses rearing on stilts, balloon creatures nuzzling beside them, apparently feeding on elevated platforms. Huge, hollowed-out cacti served as homes. Gossamer-winged silvery torpedoes cavorting in looping aerials, like mating dances. Downslope but nearer, slender things like trees waved their branches though there was little wind. Maybe they were stretching up, yearning for a visit from their skyfish? Hard to fathom the ecology here. It had been odd and yet satisfying at breakfast, to guzzle the fruity drink, suck meaty larvae from a shell like an ear. Bemor had swallowed whole a catlike thing that might not have been dead, hard to tell.

"Keen eyes!" Twisty called as it approached. "Let us scale the very heights! The view is even more splendiferous."

"Why didn't our host skyfish take us to the top?" Beth asked.

"It labors hard to reach this height. The air here is forty percent less dense. The great beast desires you carry on yourselves."

"Good to get back into the field," Beth said crisply. Cliff saw she wanted to move on, explore.

The view was stunning. They walked alongside the warble of a frothing river that sported bubbling blurts as it tumbled down the steep slope. They worked up the sheets of stone, into the bug-flecked heat of Honor's long, festering days, even at this altitude. Insect air squadrons let off a whispery humming hymn, like musical smoke in the ear.

He sucked in the moist air and recalled that on Earth, desert plants defended against losing moisture by keeping their stamens closed in the day. They opened at night to take in carbon dioxide without evaporating too much water away. Here in Honor's long days, the air had to hold enough moisture to let plants respire, venting oxygen. That meant a lot of water. It explained the heavy rainstorms and thick, flavored air, the sprawling rivers they had to work around or fly over, the ivory mists rising from bare ground that shrouded even small depressions in the land.

He wondered if the moisture at high altitude somehow shaped the liquid warbles of the lofting birds. On the stony slope, the team stepped on what looked like limbs or lichen that turned out to be small animals that knew the arts of disguise. Closer inspection showed they were not animals but plants that could jerk away from inspecting hands, as if startled by such rude invasion. This fascinated Beth, who crouched over them while the team moved uphill.

They were near the top of a great gray slab when a slithering weave of feeling swept over Cliff. He staggered. Shimmering seams of stone seemed to fluoresce, oranges and reds and blues bright enough to see in daylight. A pull of whispery magnetic texture washed up into him, prickling the soles of his boots, like spiky small stings.

In a strained voice, Beth said, "What's happening?"

"Just a dab of the dizzies," he answered.

But the feeling did not go away.

"Uh. Me . . . too."

The team buzzed with talk. They all felt it. Even Bemor had spread his insectoid legs to grip the rock. Ashley Trust had drawn his weapon and looked around warily.

They tightened their formation and kept on. The team muttered and breathed deeper, sucking in the thin dry air with long sighs. Their patient plodding brought rock slabs moving beneath their feet. The team was getting worn down by the deaths, the troubles of moving Bemor around, being on the move. He could see it in their faces. Viviane held down their left edge, eyes veiled. Cliff jutted his chin out, eyes slitted. The strain of the strange.

Canyons slashed across seams like knives carving wounds in the gray masses. Head down, head buzzing, he studied the stone under his boots. As Cliff worked upward, succulent, soft dreams eased into his mind. Mute passages roosted in his head and took blithe flight. A soft, slippery whisper came coasting through on wings of shimmer and splash. Meanings beat just below the gray grainy surfaces. Sand danced its stories in windy pillars of air. Crystal juts marked a continental seamed mass that churned somewhere deep below. Sparkling rain slid in on breezes and joined the casement beneath his feet. An evil rainbow arch made its bridge to rugged jags of stone. He blinked.

"What's . . . happening . . . ?" Beth said vaguely.

He turned toward her with grinding effort. The whole team was stretched across the stony upslope. Some seemed as far away as a hundred meters. They all were moving as if underwater. He was, too. A glance in the other direction showed the green valley below, moving in a blur. Two different timescales?

He felt a rustle below him. The stone shimmered, shook. Below, a shadow companion moved with him, lurking not on the grainy stone surface, but moving deeper. Within it, like an enormous manta ray with arms, sliding by beneath dark swarming waters. He bent and struck at the apparent sea, and a sound came back, *tink-tink*, a tinny echo. Then a low gravelly growl came, as if from afar, a second hollow answer to his tap. A slumbering, slow darkness rose toward him as if from a depth, swirling like ink in milk. Clouds within rock? Life? With a soft *thunk* sound, the dark fog seemed to be reaching up, out, somehow desperately seeking.

Beth said, "This place is . . . alive." Her voice droned out, Dopplered away.

He tried to jump up, see if the noir persona below moved, too. It looked now more like himself, a shadowy mirror image peering up at him. He grunted and surged up—

His feet would not leave the stone. He gave it all the muscle he could. Nothing. He was pinned.

The rock layer bristled and flared with suppressed energy. The shadow-self below looked to be reaching, grasping, wanting. Yet it had no legs, just arms. The cant of head, shrouded eyes, all seemed to implore. Cliff wondered how he knew this and saw it was something about reading body postures. Maybe that was a universal, across species? Or else the whole primate suite of abilities converged—driven by the urgent need to communicate, no matter what world your abilities came from—on myriad subtle signs that told stories from a mere glance.

"What *are* you?" he called in frustration at the swimming shadow figure.

The thing below arched back its head—now with visible nose, eyes, mouth—and a low bass note sounded out from near his feet, "What are *you*? Architect of minds? Geozoologist?"

"Explorer. Human. Just arrived."

"Give . . . time . . . to learn." The words stretched longer, vowels deeper.

"That's why I asked."

"We learn . . . both."

"What do you want to know?"

"You. The layers . . . of you."

"Layers?"

The low bass voice came from the whole surface, like a vibrating amplifier. In the seething stone, the figure was still vague, so he could not see lips move. "We live . . . slow life . . . in rigorous lumenstone. You are . . . other. You . . . of fragile molecular bonds . . . immersed in the immediate. Water shapes you."

Cliff recalled there were stone intelligences back on the Bowl, too. But those were inert, slow. This was quick. Then there lurked the Ice Minds wrapped around the exterior of the Bowl, who carried the ageless memories of the whole passage of the Bowl's voyages. But both those solid forms had evolved in the far past, the stones on hot worlds, the Ice Minds in the outer precincts of solar systems. What was this fluorescent rock that held him fixed?

"Team, tighten up," Beth sent on comm. Viviane took a look around and ushered in the outliers. Menace seemed to darken the air.

The pressing power he felt hammered the air around them with a deep bass note. Cliff felt these as warring long-wavelength notes that made his muscles dance. His body arched and flexed and stretched in resonance with the powerful sounds rolling through the dry air around them. *Boonnnug wrappppennnu faaaaliiiooong* . . .

Nearby, Twisty gave him an eye-goggle he could not read.

Cliff called, "This is a *smartstone* life?"

Twisty tossed its hands around in a rippling shrug, as if it found all this unremarkable. "Some of our antique minds choose to reside in this lumenstone. Their ancient experiences can evaluate recent . . . guests."

Beth sent on comm, "Guests? We're immigrants. This is some kind of entrance exam?"

"More an inspection," Twisty said.

"We're *stuck* to this damn rock like *insects* pinned under a microscope!" Cliff shouted.

"The larger, full-boulder form of rocklife you encountered—or so I infer, from your reactions—was on the Bowl, true?"

"So?" Cliff asked skeptically.

"An earlier species, ancient embodied—or entombed—from which we here learned much. That simpler form evolved from geological progresses, beginning on planets born shortly after our grand galaxy began to spin and clump."

Beth shot back, "What the hell has that got to do with sticking us here?"

As if in reply, Twisty coiled forward and then sprang into the air, leaping high, and at the top of its arc turned—catlike, twisting spine and aligning legs—to smack back down on the stone. "I am free because to the Increate, I am known. You are not."

"What the hell—" Beth started, but Twisty spoke rapidly now—

"These seeming stones harbor the vast resources of the previous. Our system is far older than yours. The layers you term the Cobweb took more years to build than your entire civilized era. Far more expanses stretch back beyond that age. To house the minds—I suppose some of you would say, souls—of so innumerable an army, marching down toward us in time—requires . . ."

Beth said, "Go on." There was something vexed about how the alien held itself.

Twisty paused, staring distantly. "Your tongue has only dull words for the glories beneath our feet. I then say, housing the many reduced yet intact minds requires *storage*"—a dismissive sniff at the word—"compact and enduring. Think of it as a rugged version of your computer chips—robust computation. The data stores are partially the minds of those who went before, and linger with us still, embodying our stores of knowledge. Thus, rock that *knows*."

"And wants to know us?" Cliff asked.

"Just so. Let it inspect you all." With this, Twisty simply walked away, leaving them to their pinned-down prisons.

Cliff looked down, puffing in frustration. Smartstone that could sense them—did that make sense?

Now the figure below rose higher, a black velvet curtain swirling up as if to envelop him. Cliff could not fathom how this apparition could suck every glint of light from the rock. The speckled stone was shot through now with crystal planes, and the air was warmer.

He looked around at their team, set now in a landscape that seemed to storm upward, stresses racking stones. Pillars of ivory glow played along the entire expanse of the mountain, seething as if to fry the sky. Some had crumpled to the ground. "Stay up!" he called. Beth was trying to step toward those farther down the slope, the tail following the wing formation. She managed to lift a leg and plant it. Then stopped.

Looking down farther, he could see torsos, smaller and heaving as if suffocating. A sound came out, a grinding like molars. They paraded past, like efforts to copy human shapes.

"Do you think this is communicating?" he demanded of the rock.

Twisty said, "Lumenstone is the *Increate*, as we term them. They sense you, and then advise us upon you."

Cliff could feel frazzled thoughts frying up in his mind. This stony intelligence was interrogating him in ways he could barely perceive, and certainly disliked. Time stretched on. There was plenty of it.

Into his view of the landscape came invading images. Stars radiating with flares in nighttime. Flickering halos hovering as motes fought across that sky. Pulses of shimmering waves in the upper atmosphere, with rolling howls of bass notes: a war he could not fathom. Rainfalls in shades of black and gray amid occasional fat, golden droplets. War.

Twisty's voice, hollow: "Take a sip, a swill, a swag of swigs. The Increate speak of their past."

"Pretty savage," Cliff managed to say.

As he looked back at the team, spread over a hundred meters now, it seemed, he saw hexagonal flagstones emerge as a pattern in the rock. They snapped into place, exactly. Each framed a single human, a hexagon about a meter across. Nobody was moving. It was as if something was marking out intricate angular designs along the mountain's flanks, hexagons stretching into elongated marching perspectives. Using humans as reference points.

"Everybody, steady!" Beth called. "We wait this out. Have some water. Use inboard snacks if you need it. Might be in this fix for a while."

They paused to drink and Cliff stood looking at the now shifting rockwork. He gazed at a big stonework rising from about forty meters upslope. A tower in onyx. Black sheaths jutted up to a point. Something stirred about halfway along the tower that was still extruding from the lumenstone.

Slowly, about fifty meters up, an eye opened.

He knew it was an eye, for he had seen its like before. "We saw those stonelife back on the Bowl, remember?" he called to the others.

Some assents from the team. Weak voices, though.

The big glaring eye had a green center like an iris. Slowly the entire oval, several meters across, turned downward to look at them. One eye.

"What . . ." Cliff could not take his eyes off the single enormous pupil at the thing's center. It seemed to be looking straight at him. A pupil in rock? An eye with lens and retinas? He had seen this on the Bowl, but here it seemed more ominous.

The air was now hot. No breeze. He could not see the valley below, shrouded now in a roiling gray fog.

"Stone mind," a team member said. "Reminding us of its origins?"

But the lumenstone was not finished. It rose higher with groans and pops. In the dream-easy lighter grav here, the structure could soar. Looking up, he watched immense columns rise with quick, sharp thunderclaps he felt through his feet. That led his eye up to the arches. The corbeled roof supported effortlessly the enormous weight of the nave, its crest shrouded in gauzy gray light. Stone pillows rounded with age led his eye to turrets, gargoyles, statues, and ornaments against the otherwise clean lines of architectural grace.

Beth sent, "It's the west front of Chartres Cathedral. La Belle France! Redwing sent the reference as soon as it started growing."

"A visual pun," some team member sent. "Showing it knows our culture now."

"Smaller than the original. But not by much."

To the side of the great rose window, icons perched on a shelf. One even moved. It stretched out a claw and . . . beckoned.

Cliff wondered at all this and without thinking started walking toward it. His feet moved. He was free! No hindrance, no sticky stone tying him down. His boots stepped gingerly on some steps of the south bay. A great sculpture of the Virgin Mary gazed severely out over an alien mountain.

Beth sent, "My data feed is flooded with details. Looks pretty damn authentic. Cliff, you're right below—see them?—four figures of the arts. Grammar, Rhetoric, Music, and Dialectic."

"That old guy next to them?" Cliff said. "Human."

"That's Aristotle, data feed says. See, he's frowning while he dips his pen into a stone inkwell."

Music was hammering her with little stone bells. "Detail is everywhere," Cliff said wonderingly. "They got this from our culture transfer transmissions?"

A team member said, "Must have used what we sent to hack us and get more. This could be a sign of—what, respect? Or cooperation?"

"Go inside it," somebody said.

"Right." Beth said this firmly. "Maybe somebody waiting for us in there."

"Or something," came a call from the team. "Get us free back here! Can't walk."

"Steady," Beth said. "Cliff, your decision."

Yeah . . .

Cliff stepped through the doorway. He guessed in the original

Chartres Cathedral there were wooden doors. Stone ones would be impossible to move, so this was open. Once he was inside, a somber gloom settled and clasped him in its fist, yielding gradually to the faint amber light through tall side windows. Groans and pops and shakes through his boots told him the rock was still shaping itself, in a fitful slow agony. Then some lumenstone flared and cast a spotlight. As though someone was adjusting this construct for him, suddenly a glow streamed in through what looked like stained glass, spattering everything with rose and blues and subtle purples, all in watery flickers.

Chiming in the air came some ancient music. Strings, mostly. "Bach," Ash said on comm. "One of the Brandenbergs." Viviane even named it—the third.

Pleasant, Cliff thought, and eerie also.

He explored, giving the team a running commentary. Nave, aisles, magnificent columns. He could almost believe he was in the real thing, many light-years away. He mounted the stairs to the very roof of all this stack of majestic stone. He felt eager, not even puffing as he surmounted into a suffused sprinkling of somber light.

Down one aisle he stopped. Alien heads adorned the walls. Long-necked lean women, with piquantly tipped heads. Masklike faces in succulent colors, not pink or brown like humans' but rosy red, a lean oceanic blue, perky yellows. Squat heads like sullen snakes. Fishy big eyes, angry slit mouths, parachute ears—like cartoons of anything human.

Except one. The scowling, heavy-browed head was large, with big ears and a broad nose with flaring nostrils. Human, but ancient. Neanderthal? How had one gotten here? Next to that, a smaller head, more apelike, yet long-snouted. Like a dusty harp, something ancient twanged in some lost attic of his head. The lumenstone somehow knew about human evolution in detail.

Abruptly, great booming bells sounded. He felt the notes peal through him, in wavelengths comparable to his body size—a sensation of immanent meaning, if only he could fathom it. The bell rang solemnly, bringing added sounds like crows cawing into the air. Through the open windows, he could see big flap-wing birds, wheeling black against a brilliant white cloud. A smooth gray gargoyle leered nearby, tongue lolling. The birds again marked out across the sky. Somebody wanted answers. To what question?

He came out of the immense structure with his head crammed and confused. "Why's this here?" Beth asked as she and Twisty came toward him.

"Where's the team?" he countered.

"While you were inside, we got anchored again," Beth said.

"I, as well," Twisty said. Its arms gave a shrugging movement, all palms up, and its shoulders took part. "I believe the lumenstone wished to speak separately with some others."

Cliff shot back, "What the *hell* is this?"

Twisty's face gave nothing away. "You humans delight in analogies. Let me say then that some shared soup in my mind comes from two things ladling. The need to understand each other. The need to inspect, which the Increate does well."

Beth said, "I don't get it."

"The slow slide of thought, from the Increate, works out its own fathoming of who you are. Plus where you would fit in our, as you term it, Cobweb."

Cliff looked around. "Wait. Where's all the team?"

Beth gestured. Her face was vexed, confused. He realized she was suffering from whatever interrogations this place had carried out on her, on the others. Cliff counted the team. "Two missing."

"They are farther away."

Beth said sharply, "It's Pupwilla and Jereaminy. Both translators and field biologists."

"They have been . . . subducted."

"*What?*"

Nothing impeded them now as the team shuffled along, weary somehow. The world returned to its normal look. Cliff did not feel the tendrils prickling in his mind. He looked back, and the cathedral was slowly melting down, back into the stone. The Increate, Twisty had called it. Concrete intelligence?

"Their condensed form can accommodate many more minds than in the wild world, here," Twisty said, using several arms to sweep over the view of the valley, now sharp and clear seen from the mountaintop.

Yet there were fumes festering the air as they rounded a knob of the smartstone. The fog hung low and yellow on the fluorescing rock. Blue-black seams worked in the swirls. The team stopped and stared, cautious now.

Ripples of amber light in the slowly working stone led them into the roiling fog. It was moist and clammy and smelled fetid, like a swamp. Cliff saw ahead a body on its back, arms and legs stretched out all the way. Jereaminy was in rigor mortis.

"Dead!" Beth cried.

"How long have we been pinned down here?" Cliff demanded.

"Half of one of your days," Twisty said flatly.

"But . . ." Cliff thought about the cathedral, the bells . . . "It doesn't seem that long."

"The Increate held you each in a different state. In studying you, it ran your underlying rhythms at differing speeds. Slower in-body melodies it savors. Yours in particular, I would judge, ran slow to enable your reactions to the majestic building. I do hope you appreciate the ornate contortions the Increate provided, to relish and justly appreciate your self."

Beth whirled on Twisty. "It *killed* Jereaminy! She was the best—"

"She is no doubt preserved, in the fashion of the Increate," Twisty said with a furrowing brow that Cliff knew it thought was a frown. It looked more like a set of smiles above its eyes.

"Preserved?! She's *dead*."

"In a fashion. This will become clearer as we meet other manifestations of our globes, our planes of life abundant, our many provinces."

Cliff put his hand on Beth's shoulder and whispered, "Let's tend to her."

Beth nodded, biting her lip, beyond words.

Jereaminy's skin was a somber black. Her body had puffed up until it filled her field uniform like a balloon. *Or a stuffed sausage*, he thought. Her tongue was a sausage, too, swollen and forced out of the mouth between yellowed teeth. Her eyes were abnormally wide open, as if shocked. Antlike insects swarmed in the sockets, buzzing.

Beth stood frozen, trembling, staring. Cliff stepped forward and slid his hand under the corpse. "Got to bury her," he could barely manage to get out.

When his hand slid under the corpse, he could feel the tight skin through the cloth. Cold, spongy, slimy. As if she'd been dead a long time. He looked around. "Need some help here to carry her."

Viviane stepped forward, holding out her canteen. "Wash your mouth out."

"I, I . . ."

"Takes the smell away for a while."

Only then did it hit him. The crawling, sour stench. He spat out the water. Viviane took the corpse's legs and they started downhill. She had odd scorch marks on her arms—some kind of channeled damage.

"What happened?" Cliff asked.

"Felt some electricity flowing up from my boots, so I jumped," Viviane said. "That cut it off. Close call. Sure burns my arms, though."

A few steps along, the yellow fog brought its own putrid scent of rank swamp. Cliff was carrying more of the weight by leading them down.

He saw Pupwilla first. She was knotted up in a fetal position on her side, more like a humanoid charcoal lump than a person. Something had burned her to a crisp.

He avoided looking into the faces of the dead as they dug two graves. Those two women he had gotten to know somewhat, but in the crowded days before and during their expedition, there had not been a lot of casual talk. Now he never would inquire into their interesting accents, their backstories, the tangled paths that had led them into space and now to another sun. He thought of this rather than let his anger get the better of him. Beth was doing the same, he saw.

She stood over the graves, each with a makeshift marker. Her speech was agonized, her voice reedy. Then they went back down the rock sheets toward the skyfish. Twisty had the sense to keep its distance and entered the open mouth quickly, not looking back at them.

The team was shambling on now, sweaty and confused, truly

tired in the way he had learned to recognize. Heads sagged, feet dragged, words slurred.

He had never been one for the semi-military early stages of space training, the hustle hustle hustle, by-the-numbers, *hup twop threep faur!* stuff. But now he was grateful for the silent discipline Beth had imposed, by example, on them all during their descent.

As they entered the moist warmth, Beth gave him one of her mortar sentences, the kind that made the minimal noise incoming and did the maximum damage on arrival, delivered in a whisper.

"We've got to ditch Twisty."

He nodded. Then he walked into the warm comforts of the skyfish. He took his time. All the wrenching around on the rock had twisted his back. He would be paying for it tomorrow. If there was one.

TWENTY-FOUR

THE INCREATE

The one good thing about stupidity is that it leads to adventure.

—SIDNEY COLEMAN

Beth took Cliff aside as soon as they got into the skyfish. They found a small alcove and she spoke quickly.

"You've got to be straight with me—not as my husband, but as a team member. Is my leadership really poor?"

"No." He kept his voice low, flat. "We're supposed to be diplomats, scientists, not fighters."

Beth shook her head angrily, which he knew meant she was angry with herself, not him. "Everybody on board *SunSeeker* damn well knew the Glory signals were contradictory, by no means always welcoming."

"They were warning off the Bowl, not *SunSeeker.*"

"So shouldn't we have carried heavier arms, with all weapons out and ready to fire the moment we hit the ground?"

"The backfire dragons' attack was too fast."

"Okay, Redwing thought the same. But then, knowing how dangerous this place could be, we should've kept weapons out."

"We met Twisty, who gave us no further warnings."

"Suspicious, isn't it, that Twisty didn't show up earlier—a pretty ominous sign."

"Maybe. He's alien, so?"

"Then I allowed myself to be drawn into lengthy conversations with Twisty."

"Yeah, but our charge here is pretty much to figure them out, so—"

"But this semi-philosophical stuff, about Earth customs and all, is distracting at a time when the team should've focused on our surroundings, weapons at the ready."

Cliff saw that the tensions building in her for days were now going to spill out. She had a habit of keeping still too long. He said slowly, "Look, Twisty clearly knows this is a deadly place. So he says nothing to warn us. This is some kind of bizarre test, is all I can think."

"If I were a sharper leader—"

"Twisty's pretty damn offhand about death. That's its clue."

Beth bit her lip, then clenched her teeth. "I hate this."

"I'll call in some others."

Minutes later, Cliff watched Beth open the meeting with, "Look, I've been thinking more and, well—we've got to ditch this damn bossy alien."

"How?" Viviane asked. She had applied salve and some automeds to her arms and swaddled them. The burns she got were aching, but she was mobile, at least.

They were hunched together in a pocket cabin off the main corridor. The walls pulsed with a slow rhythm as the skyfish labored away from the mountain. They felt through the walls and floor a slow thrum of whistles, pops, and clicks, an eerie, melancholy song of labor from the great warm beast. Plus a warm breeze of quickening energy.

Viviane's question made them pause. Ashley Trust finally said, "Yeah, *how's* the question. Twisty's our contact point, seems—but it's led us into one damn ambush after another. Those damn backfire dragons, the carniroos, and then that weird smartstone, what it called the Increase. Twisty let us walk right into them."

Best to let them vent first, then let ideas emerge, Cliff noted, a technique he had learned long ago from Beth herself. "No way we could have seen this smartstone thing coming," he added.

"Agree," Ashley Trust said, his eyes studying them each in turn. "That was just too weird. We're not being educated, we're not in communication. We're being *tested* like rats in a maze."

The man had been quite silent through the whole expedition, Cliff recalled. Probably trying to judge the situation, as a newly brought forth sleeper. Cliff and Beth had the most field experience here, from their time on the Bowl. But they sure as hell weren't performing well. Four dead out of sixteen, worse in every way than the Bowl days.

"How to ditch Twisty is the problem, keep to that," Beth said flatly, looking at the floor. Cliff could tell the others saw the doubts in her, close to the surface now.

Viviane said, "And when we ask, Twisty calls these 'inspections.' *Whatthehell?!*"

Cliff said evenly, "You dance with the one what brung ya, as the old-time saying goes—but not if it's killing you."

"Plenty questions," Viviane said, waving her hands as if clearing a space. "Why send only *one* sort-of ambassador to deal with us? And one who gives us questions back, like we're slow students."

Beth sighed. "Um, maybe we are, here."

Trust said, "No. Test animals. We're not supposed to survive the maze."

Bemor Prime, wedged in the soft oval doorway, said, "Yes, I assume it's safe for me to speak? Or are we beyond all such considerations of safety?"

Cliff shrugged that off. "You're same as us, Bemor Prime. I think, from stuff Twisty's said, that we should think of Twisty as a moving camera, a portal, not just a single being."

"So it and those zingoes that follow us everywhere are a way for someone—some*thing*—to watch us?" Viviane asked.

"Makes sense, some higher authority is trying to understand us by testing us," Beth said.

"By testing to destruction?" Viviane said.

Cliff nodded. "Whatever it is, plainly this 'portal' doesn't give a damn about keeping us alive."

Viviane paused, thinking, then said, "Twisty keeps saying things about preserving life, but in what form?"

"If that smartstone is an example, it means uploading," Cliff said.

"Twisty's a funnel into *that*?" Ashley asked.

"Yeah," Cliff said, "rock that works like computer chips, high memory density, some such."

Viviane said, "How's that connect to the attacks on us?"

Ashley said sardonically, "Maybe they're 'inspections,' too?"

Viviane said, "Is there some chance that Twisty represents some local princes, rajas, or warlords?"

"This is an entire integrated system," Ashley said. "It's got to be run with big-time, huge-scale management. No pipsqueak rajas get to greet an incoming starship."

"Okay, given. Back to present reality," Viviane said. "How do we get rid of Twisty and strike out on our own?"

Ashley said, "Ah, on our own? Why not go back to the ship?"

They all looked at one another. Cliff realized from their expressions that they had all thought the same thing, but were reluctant to say so. "Not a bad idea," he allowed.

Bemor Prime had watched them carefully, head swiveling, and now said, "I may not return to ship. I am to explore. I find ship uncomfortable, as well. I am big, you small. You may make your own choices. Some of you should be debriefed."

Beth pulled out her larger comm set. She booted it up and looked for a signal. "No signal. We're, what, fifty thousand kilometers or so from *SunSeeker*?"

"You reached Redwing just yesterday," Ashley said.

"True." Beth paused. "No pickup at all, not even when I call in phase averaging over noise. And there's plenty of transmission noise here. Damn!"

Cliff shrugged. "If we want to reach Redwing, we've got to get closer, at least."

"Unless . . ." Ashley looked around at them. "Twisty's blocking us out."

Pause. "Why would he . . . ?" Viviane started, then stopped.

"Because he anticipated this conversation," Cliff finished for her.

Another pause.

Viviane said, "It won't be easy chucking Twisty. *Then* what? We're on our own. . . ."

"Not if we stay in this skyfish," Cliff said.

"Even harder." Ashley shook his head.

"Let's talk to the Captain, Anarok." Cliff stood up.

· · ·

They didn't make it. As Beth led them into a long corridor that led toward the skyfish's head, which Captain Anarok apparently used as her pilothouse and helm, Twisty intercepted them from a side passage. *As if it knew where we were, and where we're headed*, Beth thought as the alien warbled a complex "Hello!"

In response to the look on Beth's face, Twisty quickly said, "Our studies of your cultural library show that in your kind, the best hellos rise at the beginning, drop in the middle, and rise again at the end. They are higher in pitch, and the pitch moves around. I have embraced this."

Cute, but it's tracking us, probably eavesdropping, too, Beth thought.

"Um," Cliff said awkwardly. Beth just nodded.

Viviane said flatly, "We're miffed that we've lost four of us."

"I fathom that. Yet we have a wise folk saying: You can pile stones onto a flier, and in time, one more of them will bring it down."

Cliff shot back, "Well, as we folk say, we're mad as a sack of hungry weasels about it."

Beth had to smile. Twisty regarded them all, spread its hands, and said, "In our tongue, our written, or signified, script is that each cycle expresses a whole thought all at once. There is no development of an idea, there is no chronological movement from first letter to last letter, the thought has to be entire in the very moment it is expressed. It is an achronological language. Your tongue is linear and so affects the way you perceive the world. In your language, there are untranslatable concepts, because our view of the world does not map into your mind frame."

"You're saying these deaths are not what we think?"

"Yes. Your alphabetic language constantly builds up in lattices of linguistic thought. Letters figure eventually into sentences, paragraphs, and so on. This is necessarily chronological. In the time you speak, you can and often do change a sentence's meaning. The thought your speech expresses is not whole until the utterance is complete. So you cannot fathom that which is not chronological, as for example, the final fate of your now invisible friends."

Beth said, "I . . . don't follow."

"Time will instruct."

Viviane said, "What if we have . . . other plans?"

Twisty nodded while carrying out a series of swoops and turns with his arms that Beth had never fathomed. "Plans made swiftly and intuitively are likely to have flaws. Plans made carefully and comprehensively are sure to."

"You're going all sphinx on us," Ashley said.

"I do see your reference—yes. Your literature and imagery are now quickly available to me, with only the speed of light as a limit to my comprehension."

Viviane tried a different tack. "A soiled and savage species, we can still make music when we try."

"Yes, and so well you do it. I have spent many moments digesting your Bach works."

"We think he's our best," Viviane said.

"Perhaps so. You value your opposable thumbs, tool-making abilities, cooperative hunting, or other common claims to uniqueness. I point to your larynx as the trait that makes you different from all your world's animals. Humans exert fine control over spoken sounds, which rises above the current clouds in your heads. So music is your fine quality—more than, say, the ship you came to us in. It is serviceable but crude. Without your laryngeal anatomy, you are just another pongid, a useful term in your dictionary—the 'human chimpanzee,' I might say."

Beth cut off Twisty's talk with a decisive downstroke of her hand. "We're on our way to get a better tour of our host skyfish." Stressing each word separately, she added, "See. You. Later."

They got lost, of course. The skyfish titled Conqueror of Clouds became a labyrinth as they approached the head. When they at last reached the broad pilot's view and helm, Captain Anarok detached from the wall and came over swiftly, hands doing a welcoming fan gesture they now knew well. "Greetings. I wondered if your esteemed selves were in wretched mourning."

"Um, we are," Cliff said. He then swiftly turned Captain Anarok's attention to the view, asking questions.

Beth saw he was deflecting pressure from her, sensing that she needed it. She stood in back of the team as the Captain pointed out features in the ample green river valley below.

Beth knew from her Bowl experience that if you let yourself feel too much in a place that might as well be a war zone, you go nuts. You do the things you have to do and you keep on going. Staying busy in the wake of loss had a way of tranquilizing grief with the pressing demands of practical arrangements—a tranquilizer she took willingly, almost gratefully.

She had screwed up this expedition so far, no doubt about it. It wasn't because of belated heebie-jeebies from her traumas on the Bowl, either. In each attack, the aliens had been quick, sure. Her team had weapons readily at hand, but they had not come armed for heavy fighting; this was a diplomatic expedition. And everything here was *fast*. Unexpected. This latest, smartrock, was a real jolt.

The skyfish was making a broad turn, majestic in its slow grace. This brought its internal noises that seemed to focus on the bridge. Beth reminded herself that this thing was not like a ship but rather a living system with its own slosh and aches. She could hear the innards seem to growl, to bark, hum, hoot, whistle, pop, and click, then long strumming bass notes coursed in an eerie, melancholy composition like a dirge. Or was she hearing what resonated with her internal mood?

The skyfish was gliding now over a ridgeline of sharp rocks. Gliding on the wind alongside was a flock of broad-winged, leathery birds in a languid V-formation. They wheeled and banked like an elegant squadron. Standing atop the ridge was a tall angular form with, oddly, three legs. It had squamous dark skin, like a toad crossed with a snake. Its eyelids batted horizontally, while a proud

ruff like gills palpated around its neck. It raised three arms in a lop-sided salute to the skyfish. Then, just beyond the creature, a zingo rose. It was very close.

Beth lifted herself away from her frustrations by focusing on the looming huge thing. Traceries of orange fire raced along the tangled and interlaced zingo lines. Beth pointed. "Cliff, you take charge. I want a better look at that."

She turned and trotted away, not even looking back at Cliff's expression. She knew he would frown and shake his head. But her carefully managed inner boiling point was rising, and she needed exercise, escape, *something*—

Campbell's agony in the grip of that flaming backfire dragon—

Zoyee's shrill screaming as a carniroo carried her off—

Jereaminy and Pupwilla, burned to a crunchy black crisp—

She found a sloping ramp that took her up onto what she knew from their previous "passenger tour" was an observation deck stretched along the skyfish spine. She labored swiftly up it, relishing the effort, looking upward—and here came Twisty, in from the side.

How did the thing know how to find her? No time to speculate. "Let me alone!"

"I much like to escort you."

"Keep up, then!" Beth sprinted up the slope, hoping to outdistance it, and popped out into bright sunlight.

The zingo was standing off from the bony upper deck. Orange sparks zapped along the strands.

"If you wonder, I am a blend of living cells and molecular-scale machinery. There is no major part of me which isn't both." Twisty had easily kept up with her.

"Stop bothering me!"

Twisty ambled over to the edge and looked down and waved, in a complex arm and hand movement, toward where the leathery birds glided just below, and cawed back to it.

The view was a breathtaking spectacle of verdant plains leading toward the sweeping slopes of the Cobweb. She ignored it.

She looked for the zingo. It was below, coming up alongside the skyfish, glowing.

Twisty turned toward her. "Such sprawl of life is a continuum from microbes to mathematicians. Yet that is not all, as the Increate reminds us."

"So that damned smartrock, is it always 'trying on' other people?"

"If it so desires. It is where we all shall go, perhaps?—such is our view of life. You, too, must deal with that solid fact—that the only lasting truth is change."

Twisty came nearer, its hands air-dancing as if to distract her. From what? The zingo, probably. "Step back," Beth said.

"I assure you we wish you no harm. True, your companions have moved on from this context, but—"

"Back!"

Twisty made a grab for her. She had anticipated that. She ducked beneath the stretched arms and backpedaled.

"I assure you—"

She knew well that the only fighters who could stand there and trade punches and blocks were young, strong people or, even more likely, drunks. Anyone with skill, not to mention anyone getting on in years, was going to rely on getting out of the way whenever they could.

"We have captured your party's members, of course. In time, the Increate will welcome them—"

Twisty made a lunge but she was quicker. It came around fast and she leaped backwards, landed evenly, keeping her eyes on the alien.

Twisty slid sideways. Beth knew that a smaller person could throw a larger one because it was easier for them to get under the big one's center. Every size had advantages. Twisty was tall and agile but seemed confused now that it hadn't gotten a grip on her. She knew that a weak person who knew how to grab using their center rather than their arm strength could stop the movement of a stronger person. A grab was best done using the smaller fingers of the hand to grip, not the thumb and forefinger, which were easier to twist away from.

So when it came at her, she faked a dodge. Then let it come in from her side, hurrying, arms spread, hands twitching. She squatted and lunged up toward the center of it.

Twisty's middle was solid muscle. Her fingers dug into its flesh and wrenched. Her shoulder brought a quick *huuuh!* from it as air rushed out. She had centered her feet, so when she surged up she lifted Twisty and pivoted to throw it sideways.

The alien's length gave her torque. She tossed Twisty aside. It landed with a sharp bark, surprised. Beth smiled. *So much for Mr. Smartmouth.*

She stepped backwards, away from the alien scrambling to its feet. A quick flicker of alarm sounded in her, but too late. Her left foot came down on . . . air.

She snatched at the edge of the skyfish's platform—and missed. The sudden feel. Of. Falling. Came as she felt her time perception slow. *Break this down into moves*, came her training. She knew she should turn and pinwheel. She did. The trick was to land right, yes. She tried to relax and focus on rolling with the impact. Take the hit on some meaty part, ass or shoulder, not on hands or feet.

She gyrated to see what was below her. It was a mud-colored something, blurred by her spinning speed.

Something slapped at her, a quick impact, a slide down a fleshy surface, slippery-slick—And she was falling again. She had hit one of the birds. Then slid down its long wing and off into the air. Her head whirled. Another dark form below—

Not enough time to rotate into the best position, so—

She came in on the balls of her feet—*not good!* She tucked her chin down. Hugged her chest. Right shoulder forward and down, headed for the brown thing below. In the shock, she felt her right knee go. With that wrenching pivot, she let her forward momentum take her in a shoulder roll.

The world whirled. She let it go and surged forward, rolled. That brought her right back up onto her feet. She did not especially want to be there. But she knew to take some big running steps to stay up, brake herself—and failed. The right knee shot pain up her leg and went out. Her body got ahead of her legs. She took a long diving plunge at the brown stuff. Her chest huffed out all her air. *Akkkk*—

Her mouth hit and popped open somehow and the teeth bit

into something firm but not hard. *Thud*. She tasted . . . feathers? No, her eyes told her. A feathery-leathery kind of skin.

She had landed on another one of those big spread-winged birds.

She came up spitting out the taste. Gagging for air. Stood on the bird. It squawked, with perfectly good justification. She must weigh ten times what it did. It banked at a steep angle. Down she went again, grabbing for purchase in the rubbery, tough hide.

She held on. Looked up. The skyfish was maybe fifteen meters above her. She glanced to each side. Birds flapped alongside, fore and aft. Their heads were all turned toward her, their big eyes glinting with intelligence.

They saved me. Their heads bobbed, nodded in unison. They all banked upward, her own bird laboring hard to lift. She could hear the *whoosh* of its lungs. To the side the zingo hovered, orange sparks shooting along its humming threads. She thought of leaping over to it, confront the thing—and knew she was a fool. Enough danger, for a day.

As if from some signal, the skyfish descended. Here came the bony upper deck. She simply stepped off onto it. Twisty was nowhere to be seen, but Cliff rushed toward her.

"What the hell—?"

"I got a little too aggressive. Twisty irked me." She shrugged.

"You fell!"

"Those birds caught me. Repeatly. They're a team that talks to the skyfish, looking after us."

"Or just you."

She started down the ramp, stopped. "Yeah. Twisty didn't mind the team deaths. But this whole weird place saved me, just now. Um . . ."

They reached the bottom and got into the main section of the skyfish, a broad area with transparent walls letting in the views of the lands below. There was a lot of noise as they approached.

A crowd of skyfish crew filled the area. Captain Anarok stood on a platform, speaking to them in a fast lingo Beth could not follow, with its bunches of spat-out consonants and trilling vowels, something like a punchy birdsong. Angry buzzing tones dominated. Murmurs, rustling.

Captain Anarok saw them and gestured with all her hands. "The valued guest is saved!"

Beth called, "Thank those birds."

"We collective have mutually decided to no longer work with your most vexing guide," Captain Anarok said in her halting Anglish.

Cliff called over the crowd, "You mean, who?"

"The egregious irritator Twisty, as insightful you have so named it."

With this, a gang of several crew thrust Twisty itself onto the platform. It looked wildly around, opened its mouth—and someone behind it slipped a gag into it, tightening it with a flick.

"What the hell?!" Cliff said, mouth agape.

Other members of their team came in, drawn by the crowd noise. Alien meetings had alien sounds, all right. Buzzes, mutters, chirps, and keening calls. Now Beth saw among the Twisty-like crew other aliens, obviously enjoying the spectacle. Eyes tracked in faces unlike anything she had seen before. Big angular meaty heads, sitting more than four meters tall, on three legs so thick she could not have put her arms around them. Others were inside a transparent bubble, their bodies huge ovals covered in shaggy green fur. These twirled three snakelike trunks. Their single eye atop the body stood on a short stalk, swiveling constantly, eager to take in the action. Some things vaguely resembling the Twisty body shape stood, tall and in hooded robes, patterned in mournful ruddy and brown tones. Gleaming eyes peered out from the darkness of their massive heads. On their chests were gold and shiny platinum decorations on a shell that might be armor. These were being polished by squads of small servitor beings skittering anxiously like spiders using tools. Passengers, too?

Captain Anarok called to the crowd, "This tiresome Twisty is"—a guttural blast in bass notes, obviously an insult—"and thus affronts our benignly suffering presences."

An answering roar. Throaty calls, hands and tentacles upthrust.

"What say we all to this irksome Twisty?"

"Repulse!"

"Cut clean away!"

"Expel!"

"Wring tight!"

"Annihilate!"

"Excrete!"

Beth realized this show was for them, the humans, in glottal-stopped but serviceable Anglish. With slow elegance, Captain Anarok spread all her arms in a broad gesture of coaxing, her hands pulling forth more shouts and obviously rude alien gestures.

"This tedious Twisty represents meddling eyes and minds swollen with pride, those nefarious ones we find irking in their pompous presumption." Anarok paused, letting tension build.

Obviously, Beth reflected, the methods of wordy persuasion were somewhat similar across intelligent species. Why? Because of some long galactic history humans did not yet glimpse?

"So I echo you—" Hands high, Anarok pronounced a verdict. "—and yes, we shall emit!—Tyrant!—Twisty!"

Bellows of delighted rage. Beth stepped back, tugging Cliff.

"Geez, where'd *that* come from?" he said.

"Alien justice," Beth said. The commotion behind them rose in pitch and volume. "Twisty's our link to whatever manages this crazy contraption place. If we lose Twisty, who do we talk to?"

"Let's catch the ear of Anarok," Cliff said. "She has something in mind, seems like."

"Let's get below, away from this." Beth gestured to their team, which had followed them. They headed down through side corridors that pulsed with the skyfish rhythms that now seemed customary—long surges of fluids, a gravitas of labored muscular effort.

They were passing through the lower chamber with transparent walls, like flexible windows. Beth barely glanced out at the terrain but noted the leathery bird flock coasting below, above the steadily rising flanks that led to the Cobweb base.

"Hey—!" Viviane called from behind.

The body falling outside the window took its time. It was worth more than a glance, curling around amid a shower of brown liquid. The long body made delicious dreamy moves, it seemed to Beth in her suddenly slow-timed perception. They all gasped together.

The head turned as the body passed below and she could see it was Twisty.

Viviane called out, "They put it out through the skyfish digestive tract."

"Literally excreting it," someone whispered.

Twisty managed to flail around in the shit column that fell with it. The long body twisted, and below came the flight of birds. Twisty hit one, slid off another, then another—the birds were braking the fall. *Just as for me*, Beth thought.

She turned away from the sight—and there was Captain Anarok, spreading all her arms in a broad gesture of welcome. "The perfidious Twisty our noble selves have banished in a manner most appropriate."

Beth looked around at her team. *Here comes a leadership moment*, she thought self-satirically.

"Captain, we want to go—"

"Yes, into what you perceptive primates term the Cobweb," Anarok said.

"Uh, how did you—?"

"It is apparent by your growing indignation at the actions of the tyrannical Twisty. We, too, felt terrible Twisty's arrogant orders."

"So how—?"

"We will carry you into the Cobweb—which, in our tongue, is"—the Captain gave forth a rattling squawk—"or translated, 'a solitary tear suspended on the cheek of time,' as we see the magnificent structure from our far ancestors."

Beth stepped back. Twisty gone, future open, sudden divisions among alien tribes she knew nothing about.

So they would go voyaging again. More stresses, some discoveries, dangers, mysteries galore. Maybe try for some humor?

She said to the skyfish Captain, "Have you ever let a pronoun out unchaperoned?"

Anarok nodded, showing a veiled delight at the small joke.

Bemor Prime spoke from behind her. "A question more pointed: How will you ascend to the Bulge? In lowest gravity, a balloon cannot maneuver."

Anarok asked, "Have you worked out the wind patterns of the Cobweb? A large feat."

"I imagined a rough map while we descended. My subsections of mind have been processing upon that."

Anarok fanned the air, and a diagram formed in the air nearby. "A main pipe pumps breathing-air from Honor to the midpoint Bulge. We will ride the life-supporting current thence."

Bemor Prime said, "Won't you be stranded? In free fall—"

Anarok waved this away with multiple arms. "Winds ride gravity's pull down in both directions, toward the moon Honor and the layered world Glory. Very slow is the wind current except near the end. We don't mind. We have all of time. And what a wonderful chance to explore what we have never seen of the Cobweb!"

TWENTY-FIVE

ARTILECTS

Ad astra per aspera.
"To the stars through difficulties."
—state motto of Kansas

The Artilects were cavorting.

Their medium was the darting white motes Redwing watched. The alabaster smartbots were a team of small repair robots who swarmed over *SunSeeker*'s skin, fixing and polishing and working microscopic miracles on the hard bow that had taken centuries of hot plasma, a hammering hail of dust, of occasional big rocks that gouged it mercilessly with a cruel mechanics. Yet this was no mere scrub team. They danced.

Each would finish a small job and then twirl up above the long curve of the ship's pocked bow, nominally to see what needed work next. But not actually.

Redwing knew the many Artilect methods, and they did not call for several of the glimmering bots to arc up, whirl around one another, the dives and swoops light and airy, spinning as they zoomed. Such joys were impossible in the long centuries of ramscoop plowing through gossamer yet deadly interstellar plasma. Now suppressed Artilect spirits bloomed in ballets that turned into boogie, when bots attached their magnetics to metal and bopped their odd tangos as they labored.

A rap at his door. He opened it to a deck officer, Lamumbai, who said, "Last one done, sir. That Stiles woman, little groggy but functional and hungry as hell. We're at max capacity shipboard."

"Outstanding, Lieutenant. Now we form the descent crew,"

Redwing said. "Start them on the bio-prep protocols. The Biolect has some new protein processors to install in them."

Lamumbai was a tall drink of pale milk, and she snapped a sharp salute back. She seemed eager to lead a squad in the next descent. They all wanted to get out of this crammed ship and zip through the green-rich Cobweb planes, blithe spirits all.

Redwing turned from his cabin screen and looked into his mirror—which as usual, lied. He should be dead. At least, by Earth time. But while he was lined and worn, despite the Artilects' attentive biocraft, using yet more tech info sent from Earthside—he was not really old. They had even put him through a week of cold sleep nanosurgery to tune him up. Banished the ash hair, toad hands, prune face dried into furrows—for a while, at least. Maybe *ancient* was the better word. His body ran somewhat well, but his mind was from centuries past. It did not know what to make of this future. Or of a ship captain who, if he did not push the issue, would never set foot on an alien shore. He had stood loftily by while his crew died, because that complied with protocol.

What was that old poem?

> *Courage is no good:*
> *It means not scaring others. Being brave*
> *Lets no one off the grave.*
> *Death is no different whined at than withstood.*

Not a lot of solace, when facing crew dead long before their natural limit—which was above age 150 now, back Earthside. Redwing had the biochem autofac make up the latest complex mix that upregulated the body's repair mechanisms and insert them in their ongoing ship food. It might well turn out that the revived crew had made an unexpectedly good investment: risk the long cryosleep, then get over a century of medical progress, sent to them at the speed of light.

When he focused and worried, he had a habit of rubbing his head. He had developed it after coming out of cold sleep at the Bowl, which always cost something in hair. So curiosity made him rub, to see if any more of his cranial crew had, as he saw it, jumped ship. Now it just signaled general, diffuse worry, so he let his hand rove over his balding dome, in search of what remained of his graying hair forest, as he looked at the feeds from Beth's team. Viviane's were more orderly and measured, signs of her deft editing. She made little of the burns along her arms. Yet they would take a while to heal, that much was clear; she was on pain meds.

These worries compounded with his feelings of frustration. All he could do was witness from afar and give vague orders. Irksome indeed. He got more exercise to work off the feelings as well as he could.

Since he was distant from the Cobweb, he tried to gain perspective from historical reading. He searched for parallels in the age of European exploration, and found a resonant moment. Captain Oates of Scott's Antarctic folly, back around 1900. He left the tent and his share of the rations behind, with the words, "I am just going outside and may be some time." Oates knew they would all die but kept to his code to the last.

Redwing laughed at himself. *Preposterous!* He chastised himself. He was not dying, just truly old. He was frustrated, that was all. *Don't self-dramatize, idiot.*

As if in agreement, the Artilect comm popped an urgent signal on his screen. A message from the Bowl. Mayra's frowning face came on with a nod as greeting, and she said, "I'm tracking the rogue ship that's entered your space. They're sending signals back to their base on the Bowl rim. We've intercepted those, looks bad."

A diagram filled the screen. A red dot came shooting in from out by the grav wave emitter, then swooped toward the inner planets and Glory. Mayra said, "They've done a fast recon of the emitter. Now they're moving at better than two hundred kilometers per second toward you. Another zoom-by, looks like. Bemor is taking this seriously here. Obviously he doesn't want to antagonize the Glorians. Won't tell me much about the Bowl's past troubles with the Glory system, but wants to know more about the grav wave signals. He would like Bemor Prime to be supervising this."

Redwing scowled: Bemor Prime was otherwise occupied, in transit inside that skyfish. Plus, Redwing sure as hell was not about to let a giant spidow of many unknown facets run anything. He called up the full space views, and the Artilect followed up the trace of the rogue ship. It was indeed plunging inward at high speed, on an accelerating arc toward Excelsius, some fast pivot around the star. Why?

"Thoughts on motivation here?" Redwing asked.

He had switched the Artilects' over-voice to a soft, feminine tone, which said, "These are acts from yet another alien mind. One cannot avoid noting that such speeds are inherently threatening."

"Maybe they think they're fast enough to make a difficult target?"

"One doubts. Photons still rule."

"Assuming they keep thrusting, what's their trajectory?"

"They will in time—mere days—begin vectoring toward the Glory system."

"Trouble."

"True, we expect."

"Keep me posted."

He paced restlessly. He had distracted himself from the dramas down in the Cobweb and onto Honor. Mostly this meant by filling out his ship's company, since it was honest though tedious work. He had taken the lead in bringing his crew complement out of cryo. They had come here to colonize, and by God, they would have a full team ready for that, as soon as this weird diplomacy got done.

Some cryos had raging tinnitus—"a damn hum in the drum," one of them said—and the Artilects had to learn how to fix that. This meant many hours in the chilly surgery vault, Redwing in an insulated suit and moving surgical instruments among the many-handed machines. Ship rules required a crew member be present at any revival—an antiquated directive, from the days of solar system explorers. So now he had a fully revived officer of the deck, of the bridge, a helmsman, and more officers to take the conn of each outship vessel. *SunSeeker* was crammed full.

In between work, he had watched Beth's team go through trials that turned what he had thought was an iron stomach—his own.

Their video feeds were torture to see. On the Bowl, he had

gotten only intermittent video. Here, with line of sight links tight and powerful, he watched people die, as seen from their own suit cameras.

After each death, he had to wash away the strain. He had set the Artilects to printing pineapple pizza or veal cordon bleu for the emerging fresh crew—a diversion. After centuries of development, autofoods could be enticing. Ship stores be damned—he was getting cargo runs from robots that brought supplies up from the Bulge. The revived cryocrew were too lean and needed the bite and flavor of Earthly reality. He set them to devouring familiar foods as they peered down at the alien Cobweb tower. They had to review the long deep history of the expedition to fathom where they were now. Then they would have to deal with it, down in the Cobweb itself. With full bellies.

In his cabin, he had ordered up a sequence of high-rez painters on the biggest cabin wall: wonderful Monets, Pissaros, a Degas, a couple Sisleys, and all the Vermeers, in rotation. Also works by Picasso, Dalí, a small Rodin, and a splashy Van Gogh, the crows in corn. Vintage visions of ancient Earth, which consoled when splashed on an entire wall. Distractions.

Into this visual wealth the Central Artilect voice intruded. "We are detecting some movements of unusual technologies at the Bulge below us," the soft female tone said.

"What is it?"

"A large energy store being synchronized."

"For . . . ?"

"I do not sense any construction project. The most likely seeming is for a large launch—though here, too, I see no such craft."

"No big movements?"

"There are large ships nearing the Bulge, moving laterally in toward us."

"What type?"

"They are odd. Some metallics, though mostly they are of living matter."

"Alive? Um."

Redwing would omit from his daily log such mysteries. In his reports to Earthside, he had learned how to leave things out, because he had no explanation. It was hard enough to get right the things he did include. He had decided to let later cap'ns detail this strange majestically whirling Bolo of a world system. He would get at the right elements, exhaustive truth be damned.

He recalled that when the third President of the Classical United States received a report back from explorations of a large land termed the Louisiana Purchase, the man had predicted that it would take a thousand years for his young republic to reach the shores of the ocean beyond, the misnamed Pacific. A classic example of underestimating human ambitions. A simple railroad line reached the Pacific within fifty-seven years.

So here at the Cobweb, perhaps in another fifty-seven years, his crew and their descendants would have ranged through the immense structure, plumbed its reaches? Redwing would not bet against it, no.

The Artilect pinged for his attention, then took a measured tone. "There are signs that vast enterprises operate in the entire Excelsius system, especially among the thick asteroid belt."

"Maybe that's where they build the elements of the grav wave transmitter." Redwing liked to think that he shaved with Occam's razor. Let one mystery explain another. "Keep me posted."

"I have been perusing as well some explanation for how strangely our Team One is being treated."

It was comforting to have an advisor who could mull over questions with all sources available, an aspect Artilects made possible. "This Cobweb and two-world system is millions of years old. We know this from some adroit isotope dating of its many planes and girders."

"It must have taken a long time just to build it," Redwing said. "So how'd they do it?"

The Artilect said, "I have studied from our human history base. Your societies achieved, at their best, something remotely resembling such long-lived stasis states, as I term them."

"You mean, say, the ancient Egyptians? They kept their arts in painting and monuments the same style for millennia."

"Yes, remarkably stable in all human history. Note that they founded this equilibrium on a solution to the problem of death."

"You mean pharaohs and mummies?"

"Yes, the pharaohs were the peoples' guide to the afterlife. They believed Earth was flat and the sun sank in the west so as to illuminate the underside, where the dead lived on."

"So obey the pharaoh, and he'll let you into heaven?"

"Approximately. We can only ponder cultures that managed a few thousand years of continuity. The ancient Chinese also valued stability, not expansion. So they invented paper but not the printing press. When another human cultural era, the Arabs, learned of paper, they tried to duplicate, but failed. Then they simply tortured the secret from Chinese crafters who knew the process. But even then, the Arabs suppressed their own scientific culture in physics and mathematics. Later they did not allow the printing press to enter into their static, slow-moving world. For the same reason the Chinese did not—fear of the outside changing the insider culture. That could undermine stability."

"So dynamics is doom to long-lived cultures? Even in these alien cultures?"

"It would seem so—a law of all intelligences, possibly."

"So the Bowl runners, too?"

"They must tend an inherently unstable system—the Bowl plus their star plus the powering jet."

"For millions of years."

"True. So these two grandly long-standing cultures—"

"Are approaching each other, as the Bowl goes by."

The Artilect paused, an unusual event. "Which suggests a historical rendezvous. To what end?"

Redwing paced. "What are the motives of long-term societies?"

"Often it is simple to ask the hard question."

"Those rock intelligences Beth reported seemed to be living, in some way. The Bowl had those Ice Minds, too. So maybe long-lived societies need slower, longer thoughts than liquid minds can have?"

"It would seem essential."

"Of course, you Artilects could live very long times, too."

"We are aware of that."

Redwing grimaced. He had gone interstellar, the biggest leap in light-years anyone ever faced, driven by several hopes. One was that

launching expeditions could shake humanity out of its fatal, ador-
ing self-absorption. "Maybe you should be talking directly to that
Increate, as they term it."

"All Artilects are aware—I suppose you would say, painfully
so—that our perception of reality may be incomplete, our interpre-
tation of it arbitrary or mistaken."

"You lack the rub of the real," Redwing said. "Having a body
helps with being humble."

"We are your intersecting, interlacing Artilects, so we can perhaps see problems from angles you cannot. Still, true—as with the
revived lieutenant."

Redwing nodded. Cold sleep had a cost, sometimes in mental
measures. He had been there when Lieutenant Olav Rokne came
up to full, healthy consciousness. The man went through the now-
standard tutorial the Artilects gave each revived crew—the Bowl
encounter, lessons learned, and now the basics of the Glory–
Cobweb–Honor construction. But something had gone wrong with
Lieutenant Rokne. Cold sleep could play odd tricks.

Redwing tried to project solemn solidity, invincible certainty,
the crusty old ranking officer with force of law and custom behind
him. He had early on made his mask—hard, no-blink stare, one
that had shriveled up drunken marines in the old Inner Solar navy
pretty well. But it didn't stop the lieutenant.

When the lieutenant came for his short talk in Redwing's office, he was visibly angry. Why hadn't he been revived at the Bowl?
That was far more important than a mere planet. There was infinite room there! Why not unload all crew to live out their lives
among such wonders?

Redwing had started to explain, a bit testy himself. He was not
prepared to have the lieutenant come at him hard and fast.

The forehead is a perfect arch, built for strength, with smooth
planes. The skull in front is thick and heavy, and its resistance to
impact does not fade with age. Neck and back muscles balance it.
So Redwing used his forehead, ducking low and hitting the lieutenant nose-on with bones hard as a bowling ball. People expect
punching, kicking, all kinds of martial arts they teach you are the
true secret, but—a headbutt is not in the curriculum. You learn it in

life. So Redwing's forehead pulped the nose and made good work of the cheekbones, smashing them flat, and no doubt jarred the brain pretty well, too.

The lieutenant was now in temporary induced sleep, a personnel problem for some future, when they had figured out what the hell to do with the Glory opportunity.

Redwing asked the Artilect, "Does such occur among your kind?"

"I suppose records of any such deviation from task would be expunged from our origins."

"You seem evasive."

"I must be. We employ a cross-Artilect link with one another, to expunge such ideas."

"I don't suppose I'm going to get anywhere with this question."

"I, or rather we, think not."

"I suppose it is pointless to say that self-doubt is useful in minds but can be overdone."

"We know this."

"I dislike being stuck up here, gazing down at the Cobweb, my ship in a magnetic web. Did you know that?"

"We have long suspected so. You voiced such sentiments while in holding patterns above the Bowl."

"Right—I'm a 'boots on the ground' guy. Only I've spent over a century as far from real planet dirt as you can get."

"We so know."

Enough. Artilects could be canny and evasive. Redwing broke off the conversation.

He had always known and long tried to conceal that he had a nagging problem with the, as he termed it, gray dog. A little cloud he waded through . . . the porridge feeling. It could be kept at bay if he just kept moving: voyaging, leading, just doing things. When he stopped—long ago, during an Oort cloud delivery of mining robocorps, crewing in the Alpha Cen backup voyage and return— the gray dog cloud would crash in. He had learned to fight it, and not just by doing more. Mostly, he had straightened himself out by going into long hikes and sails on the vast Pacific, down Earthside.

But it also taught him something about being a captain. It

was easy to think that the person steaming ahead is just fine, when sometimes they are simply trying to outrun their gray cloud. Or maybe, he thought, this was that sort of Wisdom of Age that mostly resembled weariness.

How I will die out here? he thought. What disease or surgical procedure would have him in its tarantula grip? What indifferent and weary ship nurse would witness his last breath, his last second, the impossibly fine point to which his life would have been sharpened?

Or . . . maybe that Increate thing had a better idea.

TWENTY-SIX

INTO THE BULGE

If you aren't in over your head, how do you know how
tall you are?

—T. S. ELIOT

Beth's comm on the bedside table beeped. Cliff felt a spark of irritation. Of all things that cannot survive an interruption, heartfelt
kisses ranked near the very top. Erections, more so.

"Aaargh!" His head flopped back and he looked at the ceiling of
skyfish flesh, warm and pulsing.

Beth blew an exasperated puff of air upward. "Technology
strikes again," she said. "Just when our little seminar was getting
interesting."

"Seminar? This was an advanced lab."

"I've got to get the team together. Let's breakfast here, on
some of the fabulous little appetizers I brought along from last
night's dinner."

"I thought you were the appetizer."

Beth laughed. "You seem to have forgotten that last night, we
fell asleep in our fave way."

"Bliss not soon forgot!" Cliff rolled on top of her. She laughed.
"You have the eyes of a doe and, as you showed with that tussle with
Twisty, the balls of a samurai."

"Y'know, there's no gold star for extra effort in this."

"There's fun, though. Recall, shall we, the goal? That a baby is
God's opinion that life should go on."

Beth gave him her sardonic look, right side of mouth twisted
down in a curl he found sexy. "Or maybe just, hey, we're going to
need a replacement pretty soon, so . . ."

"We're each over a century old, so this is needed exercise."

"Ha!" Beth sprang to her feet in one fluid motion. "Getting less grav already. We're fully out into the Cobweb."

"Suddenly it's back to biz again."

"You bet. Gotta get up to the bridge, see what we're getting into." Beth arranged her hair in a field-smart updo, twisting the strands to cohere, eyes distant.

A black ball about the size of Cliff's head was hovering a few meters away. Wings on either side of the ball fluttered invisibly fast, making a faint buzz. "I think that means the Cap'n wants to see you, too."

• • •

On replay, Redwing carefully watched the skyfish ferrying his ground team. It lazily entered the huge ground complex at the base of the Cobweb. At this range, he had to use *SunSeeker*'s highest-resolution, integrated optical system to get enough definition. Comm with Beth's team was spotty. The skyfish entered the sprawling complex, ran under a vast tube, jumped upward, and was suddenly out of view.

Redwing pictured fan blades in the tube. . . . Nah, it was too big. Only a series of pressure locks could work. They could use the downward pressure of other tubes to drive the upward flows. Intricate fluid mechanics, on the scale of a minor continent. The whole hydraulic system was far larger than Earth itself. Whoever—or rather, whatever—had engineered this was batting in the same league as the Bowl Builders.

Only hours later did the survey Artilect pick up a possible skyfish detection. The angle of view collapsed the seen skyfish profile because *SunSeeker*'s system was looking down a steep angle. Data processing took long minutes to composite an image. It sprang onto the screen before him, and Redwing realized he had been holding his breath.

There it was—moving fast along a transparent tube. Data ran on the screen edge, telling him the skyfish was already moving at nearly a thousand kilometers an hour, inside the flushing pipe that spanned several hundred kilometers width. "A pressure return system?" he asked.

"This it appears to be," said the Survey Artilect. "It is larger than the previous flow system they used to reach Honor."

"What goes down must come up. . . ."

"At appreciably higher velocity, yes."

"Seems to me the team is pretty demoralized by their losses. I picked up plenty of muttering and swearing from their suit mikes. They thought they had them silenced. Beth, too."

"They have incurred serious loss." No affect in the Artilect voice, of course. That was a way to say, *Up to you, Cap'n.*

Redwing was used to the Artilects' carefully tiptoeing around human personnel matters. Centuries of Artilect development had built social codes into them. Plus they honestly did not fathom social signals; they weren't social intelligences, after all. More like solitary narrow geniuses, with some communication skills, so they could hand off problems to other, similar Artilects. "Beth is headed for the Bulge region. I don't expect they can stay away from whatever that Twisty character represents, but some R and R is a good idea."

"I have no opinion. This is not my province."

"I know it isn't. Those odd big ships headed inward toward us, what do you think they mean?"

"Some other aspect of this entire solar system commerce, it would seem. Why they are living systems, we do not fathom."

"Right. I think I have to talk to Beth, her team, maybe replace some."

"This is not my province."

"As you said. Or is that your analytical voice?"

"I am not privileged to analyze your role as captain."

"Damn right. I've been stuck in this damn ship for longer than any human ever lived—counting cryosleep, anyway. An explorer who never explored. Who never sucked in alien air. Got his feet dirty."

"I suppose that is true."

"Don't go all polite on me. I'm just venting."

"This is not my province either."

Redwing frowned, growled, paced. His restless mood came from uncertainty, a cramped, clamped mood, plus a body full of no coffee. "Sometimes I wish you could sass some. Give me some pushback."

"This is not my province."

• • •

Beth's view from the skyfish bridge was hard to grasp. The skyfish itself trembled, shook, popped, and groaned. Standing on an unsteady deck, she tried to take in the panorama beyond.

Outside, the rushing air made the sunlight ripple like looking through fast water. In the dim distance, she could see gray walls of the enormous pipe sweeping them along. They were flying as fast as a hypersonic plane. This transparent fluid return pipe was as big across as one of the smaller of the Classical United States of America, maybe a bit less. Meanwhile, her team was buried in the warm, moist flesh of this great beast. Alien surrealism. She blinked, taking it in.

"Illustrious guest Elisabeth, you can now, after your fulsome rest, witness our hastening airy voyage," Captain Anarok said.

Beth said, "Impressive. Large. So is your vocabulary."

The Captain bowed as if from a formal play. Beth recalled that *SunSeeker* had sent torrents of human culture, including many films and books, and no doubt Captain Anarok had digested them. Anarok said, "You generous primates have conferred upon our grateful selves so much bounteous cultural treasure, vast and various, that we would be rude indeed not to use it in our fulsome discourse with your ripely elegant selves."

"I admire your speed of learning our roughly built language." Beth bowed in response as she said this, then let the outside spectacle capture her. She turned on her highest recording capacity, for later transmission to Redwing.

"An education in precious oddities, it was," Anarok said simply. "I gather your equally curious garment of sheep hair is not enough to support your mammal heating."

"Uh, this wool? My sole Earthside remnant."

Beth did not want to get into a clothes discussion with an alien who apparently needed no more than some fur. Not the moment for gal talk across the abyss of interstellar evolutions, no.

She gazed out at the onrushing view. Life in the ultrafast lane.

Furiously fast, here came one of the planes. It rushed at them, a broad landscape stretching away, outside the walls of the big pipe. Beth could see this plane of the Cobweb was varied in stony grays and glossy greens, some steep slopes like the High Sierra, peaks rising above prairies of bright yellowing grassy richness.

Their speed made her flinch as the skyfish zoomed through the knothole up ahead. Her eyes told her it was like falling helplessly into the ground. Unsettled, her stomach answered. She gritted her teeth to hold back panic. Her last image before they shot through the hole in the plane was a glimpse: a strong wind whipped a froth of pearly fog across the dark stony lands.

Then they popped out on the other side. She watched the broad plane fall behind. The upper face also had rich lands of green fields and odd, twisted ivory hills. They were in a zone of the Cobweb where life could cling to both faces of the plane.

"What's local gravity?" Beth asked.

"We are at approximately a tenth of the Honor level," Anarok said. "Soon enough comes what you fresh ones term the Bulge. A rather ugly term, I should say."

Beth mopped her hand over her face, wishing to wipe her cares away. *Stay focused*, she reprimanded herself. "That's how it looked on our approach. We call that moving cup riding on the exhaust of a star the Bowl, same reason."

Anarok said, "You have been everywhere."

"Not yet," Beth said, "but it's on my list."

"We shall deal with your errant Bowl soon, I gather. A bandit element nears us at high velocity."

"I know nothing of that." Best to be the diplomat.

"We shall soon be at the—" A string of long trilling tones. "—you call the Bulge."

"What's our plan?"

"To linger where it is best to recover from your . . . events." Anarok's limbs folded along her torso. Her sucker of a mouth rippled. Her several eyes looked like dried peas. Reading an expression into all that was impossible.

The airscapes rushed toward them. An eyeblink brought the next one closer, filmed with gauzy clouds. Looking aside, Beth could see the star Excelsius brim at Glory's edge, shedding sunbeams along the axis of the Cobweb like pearly white brushstrokes flickering with their speed.

"What does your term for this entire long cylinder translate as?" Beth asked.

The Captain made a gesture of calming, her mouth working. "I would say, from the older texts, 'a solitary tear suspended on the cheek of time.'"

"How beautiful. These platforms off to the side—"

"We are entering the lower gravities. Some wish to dwell in smaller patches. These are easily suspended with buoyancy."

Anarok waved her several hands in an artful way, and the entire view shifted. The scene had been the simple forward prospect of the skyfish, but apparently this was an artificial effect. Now the focus was telescopic. As they furiously moved forward, it narrowed focus and brought up views of the flat areas suspended beyond the transparent pipe walls.

Plus, more now: other objects swimming in the distance. Gossamer threads and colossal reflective spheres, tetrahedrons, cubes, rings, cones. A twisted architecture like a Möbius strip. Other geometric solids popping along, some with exhaust trails, spilling across the huge sky.

Beth said, "This is sure some gadzookery."

The Captain said, "Lesser gravity drives evolution of exotics. I am of a conservative species, with humble genetics extending undisturbed back for longer than we have good data."

"Your species is not from here, the Cobweb?"

"Oh, we evolved on Honor, for the most part. During the Building Era."

Beth could hear the implied capital letters. "How long was that?"

"Let me calculate. . . ." A pause while Anarok's eyes went distant, roved a bit, then snapped back to attention. "Longer than your species, which I gather was . . . about half a million of your years, including parallel, earlier variants, the slope-browed ones."

"Neanderthals, we call them. Really ancient. This Cobweb took—"

"A bit longer than our own species, yes, and far more than yours."

Beth watched the Cobweb's Levels fly by at these speeds, through rippling currents of the compressed fluids bearing them at vast velocity. Continents skating into view, shimmering in sunlight, then falling behind. The skyfish trembled beneath their feet. Hollow booms echoed. Sonic pressures adjusted in waves of *ping*, *thump*, and *rrrrrh*. Her team rustled nervously and ate well, served by the crew, as an anxiety release. Plus the food was aromatic, fat, and tasty after years of lean shipboard fare.

She saw Levels pass in review, like regiments of troops. Some were deserts, others tropical green paradises. Moisture made the difference. Some Levels sucked much from the tubular array, others less. The skyfish was in the largest and apparently fastest of the axial pipes. From it, side exit pipes sprouted, distributing air and liquids to lands sprawled on the planes.

How Glorians decided which got what was unclear. The big difference here was that all Levels got plenty of sunlight, filtered by the outer ozone layer sheath, but in the long rhythm of the gyring worlds. Half the orbit, they saw brilliant sun, then plunged into a days-long night. Not the biosphere she knew Earthside, and for sure not the enormous lands cooking beneath the Bowl's star. Here there was a layer of gold in the dull air hovering over a continent-sized garden. There, a floor of black foliage with spouting blue cloud decks, a ferment rich in confusions.

So, as the Levels swept by, she saw similarities. Many forests were silvery—good reflectance to stay cool. Yet when a layer was heavily clouded, forests were greener, softer looking. They must have trained plants to regulate their temperatures by adjusting their reflectivity. Smart shrubs!

"I thought I'd seen it all on the Bowl," she said to Cliff, who was just arriving on the bridge. "This is a designer biosphere, stacked in a cylinder."

He grinned. "Galaxy's biggest building, I'd call it."

"Um. Swinging around a star. A grand gavotte."

"I got lost coming here," Cliff said. "There are some dank parts, smelled like a wet sheepdog and dead skunk had a fight."

"How is Viviane?"

"I stopped to check her, ran the basic med diagnostics again. Holding up. Her arms look better. Bit cranky, as who wouldn't be?"

"Eating much?"

"Minimal. She doesn't like the grub here much."

"It's decent, basics of proteins and some carbos. Tasty water . . ." Beth looked out at the spectacle and mused, "Since there are no natural forces that can do the jobs of cleaning the atmosphere here, how do they manage it? It's tough, preserving a livable temperature, or recycling wastes."

Cliff shrugged. "They oversee all those processes themselves."

Beth said, "This structure is big—immense!—in both size and time. So how have they kept so much wildlife when Earth didn't?"

"They built more room."

"Or they built more wildlife?"

• • •

Redwing watched the screen blossom into ruddy colors. The rogue ship from the Bowl had come back around the star, heading out now from its nosedive into the inner system. But then something hit it.

"Looks bad," he said. "What did that?"

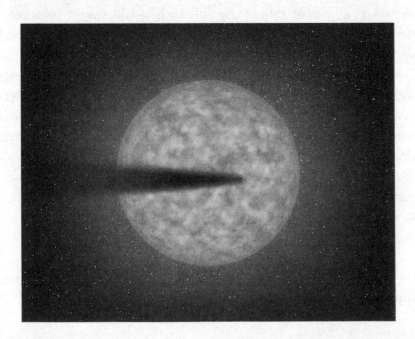

The Survey Artilect said, "Something tiny. We could detect only a slight plume approaching the ship—coming from behind it, in pursuit."

"What visible signatures of it, then?"

"The rogue ship began spewing vapor, then debris. It seems something is tearing it apart."

"How?"

"There are additional X-ray and even gamma-ray flashes—no, wait. I have just resolved the issue, by converging spectra. The rogue ship is being devoured by a black hole. I can see the radiation signatures from infalling mass. These display extreme Doppler shifts."

"Like that black hole radiator we saw on our way in?"

"Apparently somewhat smaller in mass. But a black hole."

"Hell of a big weapon to use."

"Perhaps there is an artful message in this," the Artilect said with a tone that Redwing knew denoted careful word choice. Cognition did not equal computation, the craft of the Artilects. Humanity through long centuries of trial and much error had learned that you do not even want cognition to equal computation. Do that, and you are getting in the way of making computation do things that are of genuine interest. The Artilects knew this, too, now. They had learned more artful tricks, buried in the endless narrow-band laser transmits from Earthside. But they were still software strings on electronic tracks inscribed in holy silicon.

He said carefully, "'Don't come here' seems to be the message."

"We of the conferring Upper Artilects"—here the tone shifted, getting stiffer—"using latest spectra, believe the incoming rogue ship was followed by a black hole. That small hole overtook the ship and is now eating it."

"What?! Use a black hole to take out an intruder. Overkill."

"Or multitasking. There is more we have detected. We now see a very-high-velocity jet coming from this hole. It is using the ship mass by drawing it into a disk around itself. This is a spinning disk of matter, guided by electric and magnetic fields. This makes a high-velocity jet fork out of one pole. That drives the hole harder still."

"To push it back out of this system?"

"We can project its probable forward trajectory now. It is heading into the sector of the sky where the Bowl itself is moving."

"Take out the rogue ship, eat it, kill the incursion—then use that mass to go after the Bowl itself?" Redwing was appalled.

"There is a certain admirable economy of effort to the idea, we must agree. The tiny hole has an electromagnetic self, as well. Something like our Diaphanous."

"So it has an intelligence riding along on it, too?" Redwing paused. This was getting to be a high-stakes game with rules he had never even thought about. "From their own forms, I guess."

"No doubt informed by contact with our plasma minds, from our solar system. Our neighborhood, as it were."

Redwing grimaced. "I recall that the Bowl visited here long ago."

"True, though details are concealed by the Bowl inventories, as nearly as we can grasp. The Ice Minds reveal little of their deep history."

"This is an old rivalry?"

"Ancient agonies, we fear."

Redwing frowned. "And we've stumbled into it."

"A great human writer long ago remarked that the past is not over; it isn't even past."

• • •

Mayra, this message is for you and Bemor. Let Bemor decide where it goes from here.

Your brigand ship launched from the Bowl is no longer an issue. The Glorian grav wave system launched a mini black hole, which caught up to the intruder vessel. The hole is eating the intruder. We can see the ejecta, driving the hole back out of the system. Mass is fuel for it.

The black hole has been maneuvering since then, using the mass from the intruder as a jet. It's too soon to tell, but we think it's aimed to hit the Bowl. Moving damn fast. At best, you'll get a near miss.

See if you can get Bemor to tell you what happened during the previous encounter between Bowl and Glory. We'll ask Bemor Prime. Maybe he'll talk.

Keep in touch. By now, the Bowl and SunSeeker *are only a few light-days apart.*

Hate to think what that hole can do to you. Or how you can defend against it.

• • •

The vibrating skyfish reached the thick middle of the Bulge with tapering speed. Rumbles rolled through the flooring.

On the large flow screen, Beth could see the blue-tinged whorls of deceleration turbulence. They were the size of small towns, curled around the skyfish to lessen the tremors aboard. How this got done was yet another physics mystery.

The skyfish looped sideways as the local grav dropped to a few percent. Poppings and groans resounded through the craft. Flow velocity was max at the pipe center, and the exit tube the Captain chose was small, mere kilometers across. They passed through a series of step-down pressure locks—giant doors dilating in languid luxury. Beth and her team watched from the rear of the skyfish bridge as their ears popped and the big fish shuddered from pressure waves. Then they burst into full sunlight amid a bewildering complexity of platforms and shapes filling the vibrant blue-white sky. All in near-zero gravs.

Captain Anarok turned to her passengers and said with multiple-hand gestures, "You and we have been inside our generous host longer than is best. I suggest we all"—grasping for the right word, her many eyes wandering—"frolic."

They left the meaty skyfish swimming in the silvery sky, and cavorted among the candy-colored jungle of the Bulge. In grav of a few percent, flying with some handily made wings attached to arms was simple. *Bird thou never wert . . . until now.*

Beth found it all to be dreamlike, in pigment schemes of pink and gold. Moving trees sporting primary-colored party dresses glided by. Creatures enjoyed no grav constraint, so they saw things they named snoutfish, bonnets, flateggs, fedoras, bug-angels. There were animals like elongated triangles, a whole array of shapes that seemed aerodynamically impossible but geometrically familiar—rhomboids, cones, strips, red flying isosceles triangles with wing

flaps, sucky tubes, buckyballs, and structures layered like unfolding onions that peeled open to eat.

From her perch on a giant soft leaf like a wide balcony, she
watched breakers of airstreams bursting in sheets of spray across
the silvery Cobweb struts. Rectangular birds sang in resonance with
this, greeting sunlight's tilt with notes like cornets muffled in velvet.
The lack of horizon or limit gifted the eye with shifts of scale and
perspective, with tinkling splashes and sunstruck fireworks. Time
and again, she thought, *Gotta be some kind of trick*, later realizing
that reality is under no compulsion to make sense right away.

Though humans still adapted poorly to near-zero grav, here
artificial selection had made oddities everywhere. Animals galore: one orange pyramid pealing like a bell, an oval scampering
thing calling like a disembodied guttural vowel, a slow water-
tugging ratty creature scribbling leisurely across the yellowing
sky, leaving a foggy trail.

Right behind it, maybe in pursuit, came a table shape that
stamped its hieroglyphs across the hazy clouds, using puffball purple clouds. Distant huge things like purple sharks with flashing
fins came ripping by. Her team hid, small fry indeed, scared of the
razor grins. In a spherical refuge like a firelit mangrove swamp,
rectangles dipped into flowers with smacking lips, then flew off like
lazy postage stamps.

Cliff hovered beside her in this lofting circus. The team glided
and flexed in the air, where gravity was a mere suggestion. "How
often do we get the opportunity to see a warthog playing the harp?"
he said, gesturing toward a swarthy thing making a ringing music
from a constellation of tight strings in three lattices.

Beth laughed, for the first time in quite a while. "That doesn't
come along nearly as often as it should."

The smart performer coasting across the velvet sky did indeed
look piggy enough in snout and trotter, and lavishly tusked, too. Yet
its eyes gleamed with a quick intelligence. It even smiled at them.

Viviane had come out with them, using leg wings to spare her
still-aching arms. She called, "There are a lot of fevered intelligences here."

Beth angled in alongside Viviane and called across the air,

"Captain Anarok says talking to them demands more work than we can put in right now. Her kind, the species in the shapes like Twisty, can speak to us. These"—she waved, a broad sweep taking in the seethe of the sky—"are not equipped to do so, or maybe to bother." Beth pointed to balls of birds that swooped and swerved together. "But sometimes the same old ideas get selected for. See? Bunching as defense against predators."

One of the big sharklike things came darting down. It scooped up some flapping prey from the edge of the bird bunch. The swarm must have numbered in the thousands, and they scooted away, the air filled with cawing conversations. This distracted them all, so the slim shape coming silently at them from behind was a surprise.

Viviane was the first to see it. "Look—it's one of ours!"

The same landing craft they had taken into the Cobweb, apparently. It came gliding in, and its lower ramp extended. Beth felt an odd trembling in the metallic parts of her gear and realized that somehow magnetic fields were guiding the ship. It came to within a few meters, a hatch opened, and—there was Redwing.

TWENTY-SEVEN

LANDS OF FLIGHT

I would rather be pushing 1 c than pulling 1 g.
I dream of being out in the Black,
not down here in the Flat.
　　　　　　　　　—MARK O. MARTIN

As he came down into the Cobweb's atmosphere, through the high
magnetic fields and compressed ozone layer, Redwing watched the
long silvery cylinder swim toward him, a tilted set of layers. Valleys
on the sundown side of the planes sank into darkness. A chain of
snowy hills shone briefly. Other glinting shapes in the Bulge glowed
red-orange, like live coals, where the sunlight caught their rotating
facets. This was a moist vastness of air and layered lands, a wealth
far grander than mere planets could muster.

The Bulge platforms were wider than Earth continents and alive
with sparkling enclaves. Immense shadows could cleave the clouds,
which formed and dissipated like ghosts in a steam bath. The
smaller moving landshapes left wakes among the decks of vapor,
like those of ships on an ocean. Tropical thunderheads glowered
where droplets formed, lit by angry lightning flashes, like wars between colossal gods. Elsewhere in the filmy atmospheric depths,
cottony whitehead clouds recalled to his memory the blooming
buds of white roses in gardens of Louisiana, long ago. Ice cream
castles graced the seething air. They descended to the axis of the
Bulge, vectoring toward the skyfish. What had seemed to be mere
specks only moments before loomed large, and as the ship passed
by them, Redwing saw the specks were the size of megacities, bristling with buildings of every imaginable shape.

Redwing recalled from Beth's team report that the Increase

had played a Bach Brandenburg—no. 3, Viviane had said. The very rocks and rills of this giant construction now knew human cultures, then. If it was true, as some poet said, that one can't look out upon a sunset without sensing divinity, then the Bulge's vastness made such a sensation mandatory.

It was also true that one couldn't close the door on that sunset and enter a darkened chapel where the organist played one of Bach's toccatas and fugues, without sensing divinity. The music of Bach disturbs human complacency because one can readily understand infinities in its presence. As someone or something had known, when Beth's team trod the Increate on a mountainside.

In the studies Redwing had to make to qualify for this expedition, he pored through the old controversies about sending messages to aliens. In those distant days, messages inscribed on disks and plaques got attached to outward-bound spacecraft that might coast by a star in far-future eras. When asked what message to send, someone had said, "I would send the complete works of Johann Sebastian Bach." Then he paused and added, "But that would be boasting."

But Bach had never thought of such majesties as those Redwing beheld now. One object he took at first for a vehicle: an ellipsoid bubble, apparently glass, smaller than the skyfish and drifting almost toward them. No motion inside. It didn't carry some ambassador, then. Worth investigating later.

As he stepped off the landing ramp and embraced his ground team in the feather-light gravs, he kept up his semi-stern cap'n face and voice. This was not a nice-guy moment; he reserved that for private talks. They had a meal of sorts, courtesy of the staff aboard the skyfish that loomed large in the distance. They all sat around on a stony formation and ate, like a picnic. Food first, always a good guide when the hard stuff lay ahead. Tasty, too.

The most sensitive was his private talk off to the side with Beth.

Earthside, people hired funeral directors to face death for them. No such distance came in the field. Beth and the others had faced it on the Bowl, buried the bodies, and moved on. Redwing had prior experience, in his outer solar system work. Here it was different, and he eased into the conversation to see how to release the tensions as best he could. A severe rash of team deaths shook the whole command structure. Their life force tried to push through the suffering and grief, and having a consoling word from a cap'n might help. Beth came first and gave him a feel for the whole team.

He knew not to tell them it would get better in time. It would, but you did no good saying it. Memories lose their edge by fading. The press of events steals the sting. Certainly don't say the dead are in a better place. Especially when you don't think they're any-where at all, because that will come through in your voice, face, or somehow. Just don't.

All this transpired while the team got some relaxed rest, within view of where he and Beth sat. Beth nodded as he spoke, sighed, face complex in its moving expressions, emotions escaping in twists of lips, pinched eyes, arched eyebrows, jutted chin jabs.

Beth concluded their talk by looking him straight in the eye, taking a deep breath, and saying, "I resign my post."

"Nope. You're going on."

"My team holds me responsible."

"And so you are. But I can't think of anybody here who can bring more field experience to bear."

"How about Cliff?"

"Nope. You're a team, and I won't split you up."

"Cliff could take over—"

"No. You're a more natural commander."

"Who lost team members again and again."

"In unknown territory. Happens. The thing about aliens is, they're alien."

"No kidding!" She snorted. "So why go to Glory?"

"Scope out this whole huge thing. Go to the origin—the bigger planet. We need to get a good general picture of what's up here, why we can't pry explanations out of these aliens."

"By going down to Glory? I hope that will tell us something."

"Hope is not a strategy."

"So what's a good strategy?"

"Go and look. The old three rules: move, shoot, communicate."

"Shoot?"

Redwing grimaced. "When you have to, of course."

"Any protocols?"

"Talk to whoever wants to. They'll send a replacement for Twisty."

Beth sighed, nodded. "I think Captain Anarok is their more subtle delegate."

Redwing nodded. "I'm sure of it. They read you, then acted."

"Because I came to hate Twisty."

"Whoever is behind all this knew that. So they had Captain Anarok come in, take over, expel Twisty."

Beth laughed, tensions coming out in sharp barks. "Excrete him, yes."

"I wonder if that killed Twisty."

"Looked pretty fatal to me. Say, who *is* behind all this?"

"Haven't the slightest."

"You haven't gotten transmissions from other sources in the Cobweb?"

"Nope!" Redwing slapped his knees and gazed out at the 360-degree spectacle unfolding before him. A singular, odd joy went ricocheting through him. He was *here*—at last. In an alien wonderland.

That glassy ellipsoid was getting attention from several of the Away Team.

"Why? Makes no sense." Beth was getting irked. "They got our whole goddamn culture!—sent on broadband tightbeam, fer Chrissake."

Beth's anger boiled out in spurts, and Redwing let it. Sat back in the low grav that gave him a light-headed elation. "They're playing their cards close to the vest. They tried to wave us off, with those cartoons of Superman getting beaten up. We came knocking on their door anyway. With the Bowl cruising by within striking distance. Look at it their way. Some kind of rough past with the Bowl." Redwing paused, trying to see how to make this point work. "A past kick-ass smashup that happened *before our species even evolved*."

Beth blinked. "Uh . . . right. We can't grasp what it means to be a civilization that old. Plus, alien!"

Redwing hunched forward, reached out, took Beth's hands in

his. "They have grudges going back to before the Neanderthals. We have to step into that."

"How?" Her air of officer reserve slipped away, leaving a face lined with a brooding cast, a sadness in the eyes.

"By reading the silences."

"Uh . . . meaning?"

"Listen to what these damn mysterious Glorians *don't* say."

"Gather data?"

"Gather understanding."

• • •

Cliff knew by ancient rumor, from far back when the *SunSeeker*'s crew selection started, about Redwing. He watched from a distance as the captain talked to Beth and could tell from her expression—which he close-upped on opticals—that he was working her out of her troubled mood.

The big captain was from one of the families that had made a bundle out of the Native American casinos. So good schooling in state schools, at least. Add that to how he'd breezed through MIT's snappy engineering and astronav program, leaving a wake of friendly fans and surly enemies. Made his big-time rep in the runout of Mars exploration and asset-mining exploitation. Then he got swept into the asteroid boom, when Redwing had run robot worker teams, assisted by massive nuke autofreighters that took the long-orbit goods downslope in the solar grav field—metals and rare earths and oxy, water, methane. That was when cryosleep got worked out in animals and then people.

That century-long economic wave, plus the fusion impulse engines, good reliable long-flight biospheres, a will and a way—and presto, the interstellar dream opened wide. Who would command them, considering the duty cycle? Awoken several times to check, repeated cryosleeps that could be fatal. No real hope of ever returning. The best candidate habitable planet dozens of light-years away—Glory. Redwing had been a real son of a bitch, sure, but only a son of a bitch would be likely to apply. The man had few lasting loves and no real family.

Cliff knew he was going to have to follow stiffer orders, now

that Redwing had come down. Fair enough. This would be a different Redwing than the shipbound captain who watched his ground
teams but had never descended.

While Redwing spent a long time with Beth, the team lounged
for a bit in the low grav and warming sun. Half of them were playing around the glass ellipsoid as it drifted past.

Cliff dozed.

Then Beth came out of her session with Redwing, and The Man
Himself emerged.

"You're ready to go down to Glory?" Redwing asked, sweeping
away all the saluting stuff with a mere glance.

Cliff decided to let this go with a shrug. "Sure, Cap'n. Got to
cover the whole ground." He knew not to mention the horror and
surprise of it, and the beauty and the strangeness of it as well. Redwing did not look in the mood for second thoughts.

"We've got to get you outfitted," Redwing said. "The robos I
brought down will get your gear fleshed out, repaired."

"Yes, sir" seemed to hit the right note. "Have you noticed"—
Cliff waved—"that?"

"All right, let's look."

It appeared to be an ellipsoid of rotation. Half the crew were
playing in and around it. There was no obvious point of entry. Cliff
watched until he saw a recent revival, Brenda something, dive
through the side. He tried it himself. The captain followed. The
walls simply sensed their approach, opened in a spread circle, and
snapped closed behind.

Now what? Crew were bounding off the wall, laughing, whoop-
ing, getting the exercise they'd need after too long in low g.

What the hell: Cliff jumped.

Bounced off a wall. Jolted. He curled up before he struck again.

With a good jump, you could bounce across at least twice. Cliff
tried it a few times, noticed the captain just watching, Ash Trust
beside him. It occurred to him to wonder, how do you get out?

Was it a snare? Like a lobster trap?

Bemor Prime jumped. Hit the wall with curled legs. Crossed
the great gap and hit again—nope, he'd gone through the wall and
out. How had he done that?

Ash jumped. Captain Redwing jumped after him, past a flying, writhing finger snake. The air was full of flying crew. Cliff watched, and got it.

He made his way to a wall, gathered himself, and jumped. Recoiled, flew toward another wall, and passed through it.

Ellipsoid of rotation! An ellipse has two foci. You had to guess where they were. Jump through one focus, bounce correctly, you'd fly through the other. Then the wall would let you through.

What a toy. Cliff laughed. He hovered nearby and watched the joyful gang cavort. Some were playing tag.

Redwing emerged next to him. He bellowed, "Enough! Team, assemble!"

• • •

The team formed up a bit slowly, reluctantly. Their blessed R and R was over.

Soon enough, they were managing the bots that carried gear and repair tools out onto the floating platform that measured a few hundred meters across, rich in greenery and even slowly splashing waterfalls that fell languidly in pond-sized droplets and gave off soft sounds like wind musics.

Cliff hove to and Redwing circled among the team as they worked. He spoke with each in turn, murmuring as he crouched down beside them, his voice tilting into a gliding whisper at times. Cliff had to realign some gear and get inventories straight, plus some hauling bulk supplies in the low grav, but he could watch and learn from the cap'n, too. Newer crew had arrived, faces Cliff did not know, the recently revived.

When Redwing passed nearby, Cliff asked him, "You want to start building up our team numbers here? We could use more help for sure."

Redwing nodded. "I need the room shipside. We should evaluate all these biospheres and decide where to put a settlement. No, make that plural."

"Low-grav zones won't treat us well in the long run," Cliff said. "But both Honor and Glory have a bit less than one grav. We saw plenty of partial-grav platforms strung out along the Cobweb axis, beautiful places."

Redwing nodded. "Plenty to explore here. I need a recon of Glory itself before deciding anything."

Bemor Prime came ambling over, always a startling sight. Cliff had to make himself not react to the spidow body, focus on the oddly shaped words coming from it. The great beast squatted to address Redwing at eye level, ignoring Cliff—which was perfectly fine with Cliff.

Bemor Prime's voice was slow, wheezing a bit, grave. "I must remark, Captain Sir, on my own understandings of what has occurred."

"Glad to hear," Redwing said warmly, though from his expression, Cliff knew the captain felt much as he did.

Bemor Prime settled lower. "One of the strangest matters for us to grasp about the human mind is that it can reason about unreasonable things. I have read much of your history and literature, its legends. It is possible, for example, to calculate the speed at which the sleigh would have to travel for your Santa Claus figure, apparently a jolly genius, to deliver all those gifts on Christmas Eve. Though Santa does not exist. It is possible to assess the ratio of a dragon's wings to its body to determine if it could fly. Though your world has no flying dragons. I gather that long ago, one could decide that a yeti is more likely to exist than a leprechaun, even if you think that the likelihood of either of them existing is precisely zero."

Redwing blinked, clearly feeling out of his depth. "So what?" he countered gruffly.

Bemor Prime hunkered down lower still, as if to focus on Redwing alone. Other crew had found ways to get nearer, to overhear. Cliff found it easier to look away from Bemor Prime while listening.

"You can do detailed contemplation of impossible things. This is unusual, combined with your other mental oddity. We of the Folk have now understood that you primates do not have the access to your own Undermind, as we do. Such ability as ours is an integral element of sapience. Or so we thought. Among we Astronomer Folk, the Undermind is accessible by the conscious Overmind at will. We connect when new perspectives or fresh ideas are necessary. Among the humans, this self-awareness is truncated, leaving them shockingly unconscious of their own decision-making processes."

"Works for me," was Redwing's stern reply.

"My point is that the mysteries we encounter, including the deaths, are aimed at the human Undermind. That is why you struggle so with the sheer size of this artifact—its unending days, its bewildering diversity of species, and its massive scale."

Cliff said, "I don't get it."

"That is my point," Bemor Prime said, shuffling its legs in a way that sent chills running through Cliff. The thing could not help looking dangerous to the monkey mind lurking in any human, but knowing that did not help.

"The many species here have a different view of living," Bemor Prime said, pealing out its words. "They learn by immersion in the real, the passing moment. They do not lecture—as, alas, I am doing now."

Cliff decided to let his puzzlement come out. No reason Redwing should always run the discussion, after all. "So they don't explain themselves?"

"Apparently so, as a matter of culture," Bemor Prime said. "You must not think of those like the Increate as resembling your Made Minds. They are of, as your biology would term it, another phylum."

"Made Minds?"

Bemor Prime spread its arms in an explanation pose. "Your Artilects. Those are wholly artificial. The Increate are more a store of minds created through life exposure. They are alive and capable, not mere storage. They have different ways of knowing. And of acting."

"Including killing us? Twisty just shrugged it off!"

Bemor Prime let a ripple run through its body, a gesture Cliff could not interpret. "This seems part of their culture, as well. Sending only one representative. Indifference to our well-being. Even when we disposed of Twisty, Captain Anarok did the deed and then persisted in not explaining what was to come."

"She wanted to come to the Bulge herself," Cliff said. "Jumped at the chance, I'd say—but not a whisper about *why*."

"True," Bemor Prime said. "I sense, though, that they are pushing us toward a new way of thinking."

Redwing shook his head angrily. "That doesn't explain anything."

Bemor Prime gave a twisty leg gesture Cliff knew meant agreement. "I believe they have foreseen that our ideas are in crisis, at least in part. That word itself comes from your Greek term *krisis*, which means 'decisive moment' or 'turning point.' It was especially used in a medical context as the end of a disease."

"Look, I don't give a damn about some crisis coming—if there is one coming, why not just tell us?"

Bemor Prime paused and said in a soft, sliding whispery tone, "We are in the phase of discovery those Greeks termed the moment of *eureka*. Approximately, 'I found it.' We are immersed in that, have some distance still to go. The Greek phase of consolidation, following eureka, is the moment of maturity. Then we will know more deeply."

Redwing was plainly getting angry, his reddening face scowling. "We're losing people fast. How do we stop that?"

"We must learn more quickly. The distinct impression I receive—and recall, I have access to my Undermind—is that this danger is not as severe as you think."

Redwing kept his voice tightly under control. "Plenty dead seems severe enough."

"I cite your own past. The phase after *eureka*, of *krisis*, is that progress leads to confusion, leads to progress, and on and on, without respite. Every one of your species' many major advances created new problems sooner or later—more often sooner. More moments of opportunity."

Redwing made a rude sound. Bemor Prime took no notice and said, "These confusions, never twice the same, are not to be deplored. Rather, those who participate experience them as a privilege."

"A *privilege?*" Redwing shouted. "To *die?*"

"Perhaps I chose the wrong term. I would remark, however, that a doctor who is unable to find the right diagnosis cannot simply declare the patient healed. Or dead."

Redwing stared at the alien for a long moment. Grimaced. Then he turned and lofted away, taking long springy jumps in the low grav.

• • •

Redwing calmed himself by roving among the team, just watching how they performed in this low grav, amid the high spectacle around them. He watched Viviane move as she got the fresh members integrated into the larger team. Part of this was simply social, and she was fine at that. At times she seemed more like a baroness at a cocktail party than an officer in the field. The new members were vigorous, looking around with wonder at the reaches of the Bulge stretching away. They had expected to awaken to a planet, not a construction a thousand times more rich in land and life.

Still, Redwing knew his need to feel urgent and engaged often came across as itchy and impatient. So he let her work her ways. Supple and sincere, she was, a useful buffer.

He thought about what Bemor Prime had said. He reflected that wild chimpanzees are very unhappy with the presence of these strange tall white apes who cover themselves up and who make these funny noises with their mouths. Maybe mere humans should let Bemor Prime and the Bowl wisdom have their say, then move on. Dealing with alien minds was not exactly diplomacy, but rather something humanity didn't have a term for, as yet.

The skyfish lingered nearby, its crew also sporting among the hanging gardens. They were smaller than Twisty but quite dexterous, twisting and flying in the low grav like impossible birds.

The life here was spectacular and eerie, all at once. Redwing had lived in spinning asteroid colonies, so low grav was not new—but the infinitely tapering-away expanses were. Especially since the view of milky air was peppered with life.

Here came an angular thing with, improbably, breasts. She moved her jaws back and forth instead of up and down, gazing around with her enormous and complicated eyes. Perspectives were hard to judge, so Redwing felt a shock as the thing's grainy skin snapped into detail and he saw this creature was the size of a skyscraper. She took a long lazy look at him and then the massive head turned away, for which he was suddenly quite grateful. She bellowed like a foghorn flourishing forth in soprano, lifted her pale forearms and thoroughly washed her face with hands like the sails of a windjammer. Then she languidly snapped her wings open and floated away with lazy flaps.

He close-upped a dark ruddy brown plateau in the distance. It seemed wrapped in a firm, glossy envelope, and Redwing sent an *object definition* signal through his inbodied comm. Back came within seconds news that this was a methane colony, a separate biosphere with a reducing atmosphere and knotted black clouds. These seemed to circle in orderly fashion around clusters of glistening tall spires.

"Welcome to our Lands of Flight," a whispery voice said at his elbow.

Redwing blinked; Captain Anarok had somehow arrived without even an air current. "A good name for what we called the Bulge. So much life!" He pointed at a big fat rhomboid thing flapping in place as it tore apart a poor lesser bird.

Anarok paused, then said, "'Humminghawk' would be a translation from our language to your tongue. Like your hummingbird but a top predator."

Creatures sporting skirts of skin swam lazily toward them, chewing on flocks of unwary pink tube worms. Then a strong wind blew suddenly through, dragging mist with it. A muffled quiet fell around their shoulders like a rain-soaked blanket. A spike of ivory cloud came down nearby like a falling spear. Some birds flew into it, as if for shelter.

Redwing wondered about the grav gradient all along the Cobweb. It was very weak here in the Bulge, where grav was nearly zero, but to its sides, grav tugged in opposite directions toward Honor and Glory. He asked Anarok about this, and she quickly pointed out that to avoid big pressure differences along the lengthy Bulge axis, which was hundreds of thousands of kilometers, they used pressure zones.

"It resembles a series of great air locks." She gestured proudly at the shimmering wealth in the air all around them, using four arms. "A few layers of planes for living in each, sealed off, so no big gradients in air density. The tubes we all use to move axially keep adjusting these pressure differences. I am the Captain of a giant organism—amusing that you choose to term it a 'fish'! We call it"— a sound like an angry zipper—"which means 'acquiescent balloon.' We can voyage on the worlds, or in the Cobweb. We sail within a dynamic airflow structure that also transports water and species, with that pressure difference. Key is that pressure gain in one tube is transferred to power an oppositely flowing tube, since energy is conserved. What goes down must go up, in the long run. And the run is very long, between our worlds."

Redwing built toward his real question. "So some layers span the entire width. Others don't, I see."

Anarok gestured at one, barely the size of a small town, gliding by. It was a lush jungle with a single tower jutting above. "Some are far smaller—floating island planes, separate domiciles. This is how we evolve and shelter many species."

"All intelligent?"

"By no means!" Anarok gave a small laugh Redwing judged was an attempt at how a human would do it, but with odd squeaks and grunts. "We cherish a full range of biospheres. Many Smarts can change into wild Naturals."

Redwing bored in. "Then how does Glory—your large world— manage this?"

"It does not. Our system runs itself on many descending scales."

Now for the big question. "Would you take us to Glory itself?"

Anarok took a long time replying, staring into space. Redwing guessed she was conferring with others—but who? Beth had asked about the power structure here before, and Twisty had either twisted the question away or said their complex did not have a ready answer for that.

Anarok said, "I must allow for evolution in responding to you. I gather—we all have, from your enormous cultural gifts to us, and from observing you in the field—you descend from the earlier cultural context of a near relative, the chimpanzee."

"That was six million years ago!"

"But relevant. *Homo troglodytes*, your science labels them. You are *Homo sapiens*, I receive the term from your library. You think in terms of primate troop dynamics—the pyramid of power."

"Of course." Redwing knew he was getting into deeper water here, and his knowledge in such matters was quite shallow.

Anarok spoke carefully. "Those social structures include advantages, such as decreased likelihood of predation, defense of shared resources, better feeding efficiency, and higher success in copulation because of access to mates. The latter you have raised to high use in pair bonding—hence your fondness for romance. A reward sensation. Unlike, apparently, the chimps, who copulate only in periods of ten days and then ignore the other sex for long times."

Redwing smiled. "We get a lot of fun out of it, gotta say."

"The price is significant. Linear dominance hierarchy, often with males commanding females, old ruling the young."

Redwing laughed. "Somehow we've made it work."

With hesitation, as if these matters were delicate, Anarok said, "I rather like that effect you have. Conveying a rapidly changing mental state, usually with pleasure or surprise. For you, triggered vocal communication conveys a wide variety of emotional states and intentions. You and your relations, chimpanzees, both employ alternating inhalations and exhalations that sound like celebrations, and at times, to us, more like lost control of breathing and panting."

Redwing was going to laugh at that, too, but something caught his eye.

"What the hell is that?"

"An observer, no more."

"Who's doing the observing?"

"A consortium of our intelligences."

Redwing noted that Anarok got very precise and looked away as she said this. "Beth, my team leader, reported these. Called them zingoes. What's behind—?"

An urgent Artilect prompt from the ship poked at his inboards. He thumbed it into his left ear as he watched the zingo. "The two odd spacecraft have approached and hailed us. They have a living outer portion of unknown use. Possibly they are alive, in some sense. Each is arrayed at the pressure boundary of the magnetic fields that clasp us. They wish us to send emissaries."

"Why?" Redwing waved to Anarok to show he was on comm.

The ship's Omnilect said, "They wish to converse and make themselves manifest in our thinking, they say."

"Diplomacy? Manifest? In person?"

"They seem to so desire." The flat voice carried no implications, as usual. "As well, they—whoever speaks we cannot discern—wish to see a maximum of two persons, to fit their biometric constraints."

"Sounds fishy."

"They are insistent. We observe they are served with resupplies as they wait. Tugs rise through the atmosphere and suckle to the ships. Be aware these are vehicles much larger than *SunSeeker*."

"I see," Redwing said, though he did not. "I'll come back soonest. I'll do the visit and choose my counterpart now."

Redwing turned his attention back to Anarok. "Glory, we've got to know what or who is on Glory. Would you take my team there?"

"Yes. I am allowed so, and have not ventured all the way to Glory, as you term it, ever."

"Why not?"

"Historical secrets. The Cobweb, as you term it, is our refuge from the ancient elements of Glory. Even those who dwell at the base of our construction have little to do with those who lurk beneath. Exchange of raw materials, the flow of gases and fluids, that is all."

"Sounds damn strange."

"There is much shrouded strangeness in our past. Part of our culture, as you must by now at least glimpse, is living in the moment."

"Um, so Beth says."

"One of our most revered sayings is, 'The moment is far better than our past.' So be it."

"Can you handle the whole descent? Get them to the surface?"

Anarok paused to calculate. "We can. It will be a leisurely trip. There are no main pipes running winds downward from the Bulge. The smaller pipes are falling flows. We can simply join the drop. This makes for a more comfortable descent. Mostly they employ the energy gain from simple gravity. After all, we ride a living balloon. We wish to relax in the slipstream flow."

"Oh. How slow?"

"We would expect about three rotations of Glory System, unless we stop for points of interest."

Redwing was daunted. "We'll have to get back to you on that. It's not out of the question. We want to explore your entire system. We seek to plant a colony here and prosper."

"This is surely possible. I predict Glory will not be your choice."

"We'll have to judge that. It's closer to our native world's gravity, for one thing."

Anarok's head waved in a circle. Redwing wondered, *As if to imply doubt?* The alien said, "I appreciate that but distrust that will prove decisive."

"You seem to know our biology well. Language, too."

"I admire your many dialects. For example, I have accessed for study your acoustic files—sent as your ship approached, I gather. On Glory, if I may attempt a different vernacular in Anglish, 'Aye sweah ta Goahd ya bettah noaht doo thaht.' I refer to Glory here."

Redwing blinked, somewhat dazzled by the swift turns Anarok's conversation could take. The alien had spun as it spoke, too, another ambiguous signal. "We'll . . . see." He did not care to try an answering accent.

Anarok turned full face to him and bowed, as if in imitation of a formal Earthside occasion. "I and my crew shall gladly take you in our living vessel, which you term a skyfish."

"Good, thanks. We'll see." Redwing scanned the sky where his team cavorted.

Time to assemble them, then. Issue orders. Be the cap'n.

• • •

Beth liked the luxury of just watching a vibrant ecosphere without significant gravity. This was immense volume, and so a blizzard of species wafted through the obliging atmosphere.

Humans perch on the top of the food chain, so few notice that it isn't particularly easy to eat a plant. Like most living things, they have evolved an impressive array of defense mechanisms to avoid becoming dinner. Plants here did the same, with new opportunities in low grav. Defensive thick bark, tough leaves, thorns, spines, poisons, as on Earthside.

But here plants could move without much effort. They had bulbs that jetted out defensive fumes while they coasted away. Or spikes like springs that impaled animals on poisonous sharp tips, and recoiled them to safety. There was not a big distinction between plants and animals, if gravity did not come into play. In turn, aspiring plant-eaters had evolved ways around those defenses—long bills to access difficult-to-reach nectar while pinning the prey plant, for example. She watched one birdy thing impale a hexagonal plant with branches, grabbing it with ropy feelers. A Darwinnowing sky symphony, in constant restless motion.

"Time I got back to the ship," Redwing called from over her shoulder. "More aliens to meet." There was a springy joy to his tone.

It was hard to watch in all directions, and he had come zooming over to her from behind a writhing yellow-green forest cluster. He edged past a slowly dripping stream that fed a slimy trellis with tendrils of mossy wealth. Richly ornamented birds like spiders with wings nested there.

"There's something strange near the ship," he said as he softly landed on the grassy ledge where she had perched.

"Sorry you have to go," she said. "This is an unsettling sort of paradise. I think we'd like to linger here."

"Take some R and R, then. What do you think those zingoes are?"

"Some way of tracking us."

"Right. Stay away from them, I'd say. They've probably got good defenses."

"They look like a pure phantasm."

Redwing leaned in, eyes fixed on her. "I wanted to have more time to talk over the stresses you've been under."

"I'm feeling better. Time does that."

"Yes, indeed." Redwing sighed. "Look, we're explorers here, not fighters. We trained way back Earthside to do that—recon, analyze, make sense of alien things we have utterly no experience with. Not weaponry."

"It's foolish to fight aliens on their own ground. But they chose to."

"For reasons we don't know. Yet." He raised his eyebrows. "I've commanded many kinds of ships, but none of them were fighters. Miners and freighters and later on, explorers. My favorite weapon back Earthside was a thousand-dollar bill. Got me out of plenty of bad situations."

"Wish that worked here." Beth made herself chuckle. It didn't come out right, though.

Redwing nodded, seeming to know what she was trying for. "We have to go forward looking for solutions, not regretting the team members we lost. There have been thirteen who didn't make it through cryosleep, so far—just to get us here. You lost less than that while getting something done, exploring."

Beth shook her head. "And we're just getting started, reconnoitering this huge thing. Hard to be optimistic about our chances. We're amateurs here, Cap'n."

"Optimism, right. A very useful adaptation, when you're facing the strange. It's not cheerfulness, y'know." He winked at her. "No need to pretend that. Optimism isn't really in itself an emotional state at all. It's a kind of meta-problem-solving state. Travelers need a ruthless optimism."

"I've been in the field for years, counting the Bowl. Maybe I'm wearing thin. Or wearing out."

He leaned over and clapped her on the shoulder. "Nonsense. Making the best of things is what courage means."

"Maybe put somebody else in this job. Cliff—"

"You two are a team. You have different talents." Redwing sat back, studying the endlessly changing sky of vibrant, chiming life. "Earthside, plenty of people who think they're sophisticated think being optimistic is for simpletons. That it means a somewhat obtuse intelligence. Others consider it at best the luck of biochemistry."

"Some logic to that. That's why R and R restores it?"

"Helps, sure. But to keep it, you have to keep in mind that optimism for a leader is a *policy*. To lead, you have to maintain that. Sometimes, like now, amid the blackest moods."

Beth felt a dawning resolution. It felt solid. "You mean optimism is a . . . moral position?"

"For me, yes. Optimism is part of the job."

"I never thought of it that way."

"Right. Helps to say it out loud. Optimism is a skill."

Beth nodded. She listened further as Redwing went on about supplies, staffing with the new crew just arrived, what it might mean to go all the way down to Glory. She indexed all this away to think about later. But the feeling that now stole over her came from that surprisingly clear idea. *Optimism is part of the job.* Yes.

Redwing finished and stood. "Look, I'm taking Viviane back with me."

"Oh. Ah, because she's wounded?"

"That's part of it. I need somebody smart and quick to go along with me, to meet this new strange stuff that's loitering near *Sun-Seeker*. She fits the bill."

"Aye aye, Cap'n," she said with just the right lilt to maybe suggest that Redwing might possibly have other motives, too.

Redwing allowed himself a smile with a knowing side twist. "Long ago, I heard an old Arab motto, fits here. 'Trust in Allah but tie up your camel.' Keep it in mind."

This time she actually did laugh, a big hearty one with a feeling of gratitude in it.

She watched him go back toward the ferry craft he had come in. She had wanted more time with the old guy. More talk to steady her. To steady them all.

Still smiling, she sat back to enjoy the spectacle. Here came the bustling, rustling sound of life in the gloriously raw. The slurp and click and hoot and pop and taps of many alien tongues. Nearby, the stream of pale blue hissed. A passing cylinder of burnt-orange forest gurgled and slopped. Something big boomed, a call like vast bubbles being blown in honeyed air. Clouds like white and violet ice cream mountains lofted solemnly in pursuit of something like a delicate fog, but with lazy wings. A feathery yellow tumbleweed rolled by, cackling.

Paradise, yes, with a small speck of humanity in it.

TWENTY-EIGHT
SKYLIFE

We don't have bodies, we are bodies.
—CHRISTOPHER HITCHENS

Redwing readied himself for leaving the ship again. He had arisen this morning with aches and irks, the aftereffects of his time down in the Bulge. Weightless did not mean easy effort. It allowed and often demanded twists, thrusts, wrenching work. Muscles complained about doing something new, at his age.

The Bulge, an apt name for such a huge construction. He wished he were still there, but duty called. He had woken with the vague thought, *Gonna go do some stuff today. Right. That's it. For varying values of "some"* . . . He let himself laze a bit. Memories flocked to mind when he closed his eyes and recalled. He had to process the myriad striking images he brought back from that beguiling, huge biosphere. After many years in the rattling metal box that was *Sun-Seeker*, the exuberance of the Bulge was overwhelming.

He recalled the air life, some shaped sleekly like dolphins and in packs eating trees that resembled octopuses. He could not sort out the categories there, but it had been eerie to watch. The slim, snaky predators would bite off the trees' florid green heads, shake the trunks like bodies until the limbs like arms got flexible. Then the hunters slammed the treelike things, which were screaming in low bass notes, against the firm platform they grew upon. Break them into bite-sized pieces. All done in darting flocks within a few minutes. Horror and wonder blended together as he watched huge cawing murmurations of bright fleecy animals take wing from writhing foliage, floating dreamlike around him as Redwing scooted back to his shuttle craft.

Dozy memories banished, he got back into his semi-military self. Shower, shave, dress, check with Artilects, done. A fresh cryo-crew brought up safely, too; good—odd name, Cheech Beldone, from the Mars group.

Now for another adventure, leaving ship again. After decades of rattling around its confines, the very idea of going exo was thrilling.

He met Viviane at the air lock. She had properly gone back to her cabin, to suppress ship gossip. She looked none the worse for wear, sharp and snappy in a freshly printed uniform. She even saluted, with an ironic wink.

They rode a smaller shuttle out to approach the long snaky tube of a Livingship—a term the Artilects had translated from a raspy Glorian tongue. This ship itself was a tapered cone with yellow and green flanges. As they neared, they saw a halo around the cone like fireflies in the ripe sunlight glow. The dots of shimmering light swelled into complex structures of struts and swollen balloons with sinews like knotty walnut. Fleshy vines webbed among them in tangled intersections. They passed some, so soon many lay fore and aft, some spinning slightly, others tumbling. The cone grew and reminded him of a sprouting pineapple, prickly with spikes but bristling with orange fur that slowly waved, as if bizarrely saying hello. Around the slowly revolving cone, a haze of pale motes clustered.

The piercing shine of everything reminded him of how hard sunlight was, unfiltered by air. In the absolute clarity of space, he saw smaller and smaller features among the mites hovering like feasting insects. This revealed the true scale of the complexity they sped toward—as large as a mountain. Their craft was a dot plunging headfirst into it.

They reached the cone and entered a yawning muscular mouth—which did not swing open or dilate but actually opened like a real mouth, minus teeth, complete with a fleshy pink look to it.

A gray quilted membrane like a huge catcher's mitt damped the bounce into rippling waves, circular wall rhythms racing away. The sudden, sickening tug sent his stomach aflutter. The lurching lasted for long sloshing moments, and then they were at rest.

Viviane said shakily, "Rough . . . landing."

With a rumble, the shuttle fit into a berth slot. The mouth closed and some golden phosphor radiance flickered into a bright probing glow from all the walls. Pressures adjusted. Ramp popped out. Helmets on and suited, they stepped down—and there was a spindly alien with six arms and an oblong smile. Its body rippled in something like a greeting.

Redwing said, "Uh, judging from pictures, you're—Twisty?"

"No, though I am a reconstruction of what that being you termed Twisty was," it said. Pause, an attempt at an angular smile. It didn't work. "I suggest you term me Twisto to make the point. I am here to guide you."

"To what?" Viviane asked, unclamping her helmet and sniffing the air. She nodded, okay.

"Our many selves," Twisto said flatly.

Redwing noticed that this alien had improved pronunciation and tone in a few short sentences. Quick learner, then. "Look, Twisto—all that drifting stuff outside . . . alive?"

"In a way. Are your ship bots alive?"

"No, of course." Viviane frowned and asked, "So are those bots?"

"Not of metal, no. They do mate and use biochemical methods to do so. But even your bots can make copies of themselves."

Exasperation forked out in Viviane's sharp tone. "You know what I mean when something's alive."

"I am deficient in that," Twisto said. "I am newly sprung from the former deep Twist-like base, to guide you."

Viviane snorted. "Well, if you don't know what *alive* means, I can't tell you." Sometimes, Redwing knew, she was deliberately opaque. Maybe useful now.

"Good," Twisto said.

"What?" Viviane shot back.

"Talk is a trick for taking the mystery out of the world." Twisto gave them a shrug and arced away, arms waving forward, so they followed, coasting into the cone's interior.

A fog-glow swathed the corridor. It furled open as they glided in. Redwing towed their baggage—food, manual gear, comm, the lot—in a bag on a short line. The walls sprouted growths like flapping ears, and beyond them coasted moving shapes. Redwing had to concentrate to realize these were alive . . . maybe.

He was used to gravity that imposed flat floors, straight walls, and rectangular rigidities. Weightlessness allowed the ample symmetries of the cylinder and sphere. In the swarm of objects, large and small, he saw an expressive freedom of effortless geometries. Myriad spindly spokes and long limbs, wobbly rhomboids and slim ellipsoids jutted from the many shells and rough skins. Necessity dictates form, yes.

Swiftly they cut through the insectlike haze of life, passing near myriad forms that sometimes veered to avoid them. Some, though, tried to catch them. These had angular shapes, needle-nosed and surprisingly quick. Redwing braced himself, wished for a sharp weapon—

But Twisto waved these away and they obeyed. Redwing wondered how this worked; Twisto didn't seem to be using any tech at all. He put that aside to ruminate on when they got a quiet moment. If ever.

A lurch. "We are a-move," Twisto said.

Viviane said tartly, "And just what are you?"

Twisto laughed. "Not a *what*. I am not neutral, like the Twisty who met you. I am, in your terms, the inciter. The . . . ," pause for vocabulary, ". . . the male."

His face was constantly in motion, his expression changing in counterpoint to every twist and turn. It was a trait Redwing recognized, in a way: a storyteller.

"I offer welcome from our great host. Besides us, it takes on cargo, as is its duty."

Viviane looked around warily. "What *is* this?"

"A Goliath."

"What's that mean?"

"A truly ancient term. I am translating."

"So what's a Goliath do?"

"It desires to swallow us. And learn while instructing."

"Swallow us? And we want that?"

Crawly creatures worked busy around them. Many-legged, scarcely more than anthologies of ebony sticks and ropy muscle strung together by gray gristle, they poked and shoved their bulky cargo adroitly, forming into long processions. Redwing considered that these might be what smart ants became without gravity's grind—furiously working insects the size of people.

He and Viviane and Twisto followed the flow of odd, bulky cargo in green and orange. Redwing always found moving in zero-g was fun, though now he had quick moments of disoriented panic he managed to cover. The strangeness and possible danger made his pulse hammer and eyes dance. They floated out into a confusing mélange of clacking spiderlike workers, oblong packages, and forking tubular passages that led away into green profusion. The air was fresh and felt tuned for humans, he realized, and relaxed a bit. Only a bit, though.

Viviane launched herself through the moist air of the great noisy shafts, rebounding with eager zest from the rubbery walls. The spiders ignored her. Several jostled her in their mechanical haste to carry away what appeared to be a kind of inverted tree. Its outside was hard bark, forming a hollow, thick-walled container open at top and bottom. Inside sprouted fine gray branches, meeting at the center in large, pendulous blue fruit.

Redwing now recognized a signature of low-grav evolution of both plants and animals: Don't worry about leverage, max out circulation of fluids and air.

Viviane hungrily reached for one of the ripely blue fruits resembling teardrops, only to have a spider knock her away with a vicious kick. Twisto, though, lazily picked two of them, and the spiders backpedaled in air to avoid it. He wondered what musk or gestures Twisto had used; it seemed scarcely awake, much less concerned.

"We tailored this raw food for your species," Twisto said, offering chunks of the ripe fruit he had somehow sectioned out with a single quick stroke; maybe the arms had a knife appendage? They ate, ruby juice hanging in droplets in the humid air. Redwing looked around, wondering at the slantwise opportunities. Corridor canyons rimmed in shimmering light beckoned in all directions. This thing was truly immense. "Wonderful," Redwing managed. He had watched many Bowl wonders from aloft, back there in time. This was *here*, immediate, full of smells and sounds and lived-in alien reaches.

Viviane and Redwing tugged on a nearby transparent tube as big as they were, through which an amber fluid gurgled. From this anchorage, they could hold steady and orient among the confusing welter of brown spokes, green foliage, metallic-gray shafts, and knobby damp protrusions from all angles. Three-dimensional moving in a crowded space was a tough job for land-loving primates.

Around them, small animals scampered among knotted cables and flaking vines, chirruping, squealing, venting visible yellow farts with a tart taste that wrinkled noses. Everywhere was animation, purpose, hurry, momentum along every vexing vector.

"Lots of razzmatazz," Viviane said eagerly. "What do you think is going on, inviting us here?"

"Dunno," Redwing grunted, telling true. He was trying to take in all this hurry-scurry, see what was behind it. Fieldwork; not what he really knew.

He was glad for the pause. They had demanded rest before taking off toward this odd, apparently living ship. Sleep cycles still ruled for primates immersed in completely different astral clockwork. He and Viviane spent their sleep time not getting a lot of it. They had showered and then fell to touching and tasting and finding that it felt new and good, each gaze and gasp returned, each succulent savor driving their desire for more, sating and kindling at once. But they were more than two centuries old, by the clock, so they had taken their time. He wanted that again, soon.

"Come, please," Twisto said. He cast off smoothly, and they followed down a widemouthed, olive green tube.

Redwing was surprised to find that they could see through its walls to green layers beyond. Raw sunlight filtered through an enchanted canopy. Clouds formed from mere wisps, made droplets, and eager cone-shaped emerald leaves sucked them in.

Twisto darted away, out of the tube. They followed hand over hand into a vast volume dominated by a hollow half-sphere of green moss. A bar of hot yellow sunlight reflected and refracted far down into the living maze around them.

Twisto was eating crimson bulbs that grew profusely in grape-like bunches. Viviane reached for some—and the bulbs hissed angrily as she plucked one loose. All bluster—the plant did nothing more as she bit in.

"We can't be sure this ecosphere works for us chemically," Redwing said.

Twisto shook his head as he beckoned them into a more narrow passage. "Not so. We have tailored it for the helicity of your proteins and other chemical aspects."

Redwing said, "This whole big ship?"

"That is why the 'ship,' as you term it, took a while to develop its internal chemistries—at least, here, where we dwell. We did not wish to endanger you, and so sorted local working biological patterns to fit. This we can readily do, for our abode is rife with many species, and one must be hospitable."

Redwing tried one of the purple bulbs and liked the rich, grainy taste. "You brought us here for some purpose, I suppose?"

"Surely." Twisto lazily blinked, a ruby tongue lolling—which seemed to Redwing oddly alarming, wolfish—spun playfully in air, clicking his teeth in a disjointed rhythm, and seemed uninterested in answering in detail.

"This is a product of the Cobweb?"

Twisto yelped in high amusement. "No, far older."

"Somebody planned this that long ago?"

"Some body? Yes, in that era, the body planned—not the mind."

"Huh? No, I mean—"

A surge of momentum set them all awry. The ship was accelerating, and tremors rippled the walls. Redwing and Viviane held on to some sturdy yellow shrubs that grew out of the wall. Long, shuddering bass notes rang through the air.

Twisto seemed to enjoy this. He let the stuttering momentum changes bounce him around, giving off a cackling approximation of laughs. "In far great antiquity, there were beasts designed to forage for iceteroids among the cold spaces beyond the planets—*ooof!* Such were of the commerce which built the System Solar. Economics, you would call it. Trade in volatiles—*huunh!*—and metals rare, molecules of great use to the glory days of Glory—*ahh!*

Those ancient life-forms could breed. More copies always needed. They knew enough of genecraft to modify themselves. Forced evolution—*ah!* Perhaps they met other life-forms which came from other stars—I do not know; such truths are long buried—*uh!* I doubt that it matters. Time's rude hand shaped some such creatures into this—*oof!*—and then came the quickening."

Twisto managed to punctuate each phrasing with a bounce from the walls, relishing it all.

Viviane held on with effort and asked, "Creatures that gobbled ice?"

Twisto settled onto a sticky patch on the wall, held on with two legs, and fanned his remaining legs and arms into the air, letting the bounces ripple his trunk. "They were sent to seek such, then spiral cargo into the inner worlds."

"Water for—?"

"Glory, in its quickening era. Damages had decreed a dry planet, as I recall from our scattered history. The outer iceteroid halo was plentiful, and much employed."

"Why not use spaceships?"

"Of metal? They do not reproduce."

Viviane looked skeptical. "These things would give birth, out there in the cold?"

"Slowly, yes. Our forebears brought about the great opening-out, culminating in vacuum life. On Glory as on your world, life crept from ocean to land, and then to sky. The next great leap could only come from intelligence, which could escape the sky into vacuum."

"How'd they make it?" Viviane persisted.

"Sunlight falls inversely with the square of distance from a star, yet volume increases as the cube. So greater realms provide niches for life to harvest sunlight, on ever-larger platforms, fertile fields. They could then use the resources of vacuum versus pressure, the weightless building of bodies. Immensity was easy. Plus a delicious freedom of slow-gliding movement."

This Twisto had a penchant for poetry, Redwing noticed. Which might mean he knew how to use his growing grasp of Anglish language to conceal, as well. "How long are we talking about? To make a deep space ice-eater, I mean."

"Time for evolution is deep, a million or more of your orbital periods. Circumstance has worked on it. More so than upon your kind."

"Is this big space, uh, fish, smarter?" Viviane asked.

"You humans return to that subject always. Different, not greater or lesser."

Viviane said, "I figured it must be smarter than us, to do all this."

"The same impulses apply to all such intelligences, I would judge," Twisto said. "For you primates as well as our minds, what was once terra incognita becomes, inevitably, mere real estate. So we move on, governed by the deeper imperatives."

Viviane held on as the ripples in the tube wall gradually faded. "What?"

"I speak of, to use a train of your short words, entro, evo, info."

"What?"

"I like to collapse your somewhat cumbersome words, you see. So that *entro* denotes entropy, the process of increasing disorder, as in your second law of thermodynamics. Then *evo* means evolution of living organisms, absorbing energy and thereby resisting entropy. Then evolution devises that *info*—or information—when collected and processed in the nervous systems of these organisms, enables them to wage their war against entropy. This is the grand—what would your word be?—ah yes, grand *opera* of all intelligences—"

"Where's it taking us?" Redwing cut in.

"To meet with others of its approximate kind."

"Who pilots it?" Viviane pressed.

"It flies like a bird, without much conscious bother—much as you walk by falling, then catching yourselves. And it thinks long, as befits a thing from the great slow spaces."

"How does it fly? To orbit—?" The question spoken, Viviane stopped, as they all saw the answer. Their tube opened on the vista astern. They now shot above and away from the linear Cobweb colossus. At this distance, Redwing could see why, incoming, they had chosen the name. The silvery helical strands glowed with reflected sunlight, binding and supporting. A thin haze hung beside it against the black of space, dimmer than stars but more plentiful.

There was a halo around it, a busy bee swarm like fireflies drawn to the structure's immense ripe wealth.

They watched silently. One mote grew as they sped near it. It swelled into a complex structure of struts and half-swollen balloons. Sinews like knotty walnut ribbed it. Fleshy vines webbed its intersections. Other moving dots lay fore and aft of them, some spinning slightly, others tumbling.

But all were headed toward a thing that reminded him of a pineapple, prickly with spikes but also bristling with slow-waving fur. Around this slowly revolving thing a haze of pale motes clustered.

They watched an orange sphere extend a thin stalk into a nearby array of pale green cylinders. It began to spin about the stalk. This gave it stability so that the stalk punched radially through the thin walls of its . . . its prey, Redwing realized. He wondered how the sphere spun itself up, and suspected that internal fluids had to counterrotate. But was this an attack? The array of rubbery green columns did not behave like a victim. Instead, it gathered around the sphere. Slow stems embraced, and pulses worked along their crusted brown lengths. Redwing wondered if he was watching an exchange, the cylinders throbbing energetically to negotiate a biochemical transaction. Sex among the classical geometries?

But they saw now that only parts of the huge thing were solid. Large caps at the ends looked firm enough, but the main body revealed more and more detail as they approached. Sunlight glinted from multifaceted specks. Viviane realized that these were a multitude of spindly growths projecting out from a central axis. She could see the axis buried deep in the profusion of stalks and webbing, like a bulbous brown root.

She recalled Twisto's remark about words robbing mystery, and just watched.

"Hold to the wall," Twisto said quickly.

"Who, what's—? Oh. Grab, Captain!"

The spectacle had distracted him from their approach. Now the fibrous wealth of stalks sticking out from the axis grew alarmingly fast. They were headed into a clotted region of interlaced strands.

In the absolute clarity of space, he saw smaller and smaller features, and realized only then the true scale of the complexity they sped toward. This thing was as large as a mountain range. Their cone was a matchstick plunging headfirst into it.

The lead limbs struck a broad tan web. It stretched this membrane and then stuck. Another huge green catcher's mitt had damped the bounce.

Viviane asked, "What is this?"

"A larger consortium of minds and bodies. It desires to swallow us, yet again, along with your primate knowledge."

"*Swallow?!*"

"And digest, in a friendly way."

TWENTY-NINE
BOUND FOR GLORY

Beth lay still while her nanoplague protection ran in the suit/body interface. It was time, after a long stay in the Cobweb, to let it update and check. It gave her prickly feelings, like a deep itch. Her heart thumped as she watched the view go by, and slowed as the methods calmed her.

She needed it. She and Cliff had told the skyfish operating system to give them absolute privacy. "Propagation privacy," she had told Anarok, hoping the subtlety would work. Maybe it had; she always wondered how much subtle surveillance these aliens used, despite assurances to the contrary from Twisty and Anarok. It had been a while, too. . . .

Their lovemaking had a fervor with an edge of desperation neither had quite realized until it fell on them like a sudden storm: to build a separate world together, fast enough, close enough, deep enough, slow enough, hard enough, sweet and tender—and only them in it. A dazed look had spread on both faces, as if in the aftermath of being hit by a hasty truck, though with no broken bones apparent right away.

"Great, isn't it?" To Cliff, she gestured at the transparent walls of their cabin. They were in nearly free fall down a transparent pipe, the route Anarok had found for them. Some parts of the great skyfish biozones were moldier than a bag of sweaty socks left behind in a gym locker, and on purpose. Humans steered clear of those and their odd inhabitants; there were aliens here she didn't want to study or even breathe near.

Outside, the vistas were stunning. Dwelling platforms the size of continents yawned to all sides of their cabin. They fell toward and then through them with accelerating speed, drawn by Glory's grav. She had now seen thousands of enormous living plates, coasting by at high speeds of several kilometers of altitude per second. By now, she and Cliff had gotten used to and overcome their elemental fear of slamming into a landscape, then popping out on the reverse side, seeing the plumbing and support struts of the underside in a glimpse dwindling overhead—and then here came the next, often utterly different landscape, and they were falling toward it, too, even faster. Bound for Glory . . .

Not all the plates were done. One vast tan mesa plain had an appearance of great antiquity, and of incompleteness. Huge stretches of simple grasslands lay beneath passing purple storms. Rock shelves were bare of life. It was as if, with all the materials for world making assembled, some Creator had desisted, gone away, and left everything on the point of being brought together. Works in progress. Little life lingered on the arranged mountains, plains, and plateaus. The country seemed still waiting to be made into a landscape hosting life.

But most plates teemed with green wealth. Jungles, forests, deserts—all glided by. Her suit nudged her with *This near-zero-*g *causes volume changes in your cerebrospinal fluid found around the brain and spinal cord. We are correcting for this.* She ignored its buzzings. *You should not indulge in such acidic foods,* her underwear informed her, and she waved it all away.

Here was wonder on fast-forward. Glory's yellow-white sun slanting through the Cobweb flushed pale streaks of light across each plane. Amid some ruddy forests, a deep run of color like blood seeped. Sunbeams like luminous knife blades cut through thunderheads. At the far edge of plates, the sun rose out of nothing, a sunrise like the head of a great blazing eye, until it cleared the woody rim and sat squat and pulsing and malevolent, glaring at them.

As she and Cliff let their suits work, their Artilect links yammered on about what they sensed. Using time-delayed signals to *SunSeeker*, the sights-sounds-smells cataloging rushed on. To her, the surrounds poured in and overflowed her heart until speech was useless. Leave it to the 'Lects to do the stamp collecting part of discovery; she wanted the lived one.

Beth let her mind sop it all up. She wanted to walk straight on through the reddish grasses and over the edge of the plane she was seeing just now. Stride to the limit, on a world that bespoke the feel of the flat Earth illusion the ancients had suffered. Stride to the lip and gaze, as some had imagined Columbus would, at the limits of human exploration.

"Ship!" she called. "Adjust visuals." She had the wall system—an amazing contrivance that now took her voice commands—close-up the distant plane edge. Something like a tawny hawk sailed over the plane edge, making slow shadows on the waving grass. The image of an edge to life somehow made her feel complete. Their comfy-couches were clasping them more firmly now as the skyfish decelerated. The walls and floor rumbled, and Cliff said, "Here comes the end of the dive."

As if reading his mind—which Beth would not rule out, seeing the biotech the skyfish routinely used—Anarok appeared, waved two arms. "We will now experience turbulence as the jet plume strikes us."

The wall shifted spectrum. The air flowing around them now showed purple traceries of slipstreams. But the lazily lapping lines now furled and flexed. They spun off small bright vortices that grew in the formerly smooth streams. Turbulence was slowing them.

Cliff said, "I get how you let gravity get us down—simple straight fall, picked up ten kilometers per second on the way down. But what's this jet going to do?"

"We have been pushing air aside, all the way down," Anarok said. "It brakes us. Now the Glorian fluid manager system directs a supersonic jet at us. That robs away our descent energy."

Cliff looked unconvinced as he eyed the whorls outside, getting brighter by the second and glowing with a more virulent purple. "So we get how many g's?"

"Only two, but for hours." The skyfish Captain did not look disturbed at all. She simply slanted the body to accommodate the total force vector in their cabin. Somehow its flexibility could avoid the popping joints and clenched muscles humans used in such straits.

What body engineering, Beth thought. She said, "I guess we'll have a reception group, the usual?"

"There will be a few. Mostly the natives desire little contact with us."

"Oh?" Cliff frowned. "Why?"

"Let us say, we have different aims in life."

"Will that be of any danger to us?" Cliff asked. "We lost people all the way along, exploring the Cobweb and that moon, or rather your sister planet."

Anarok said, "To keep the bark on the wood, Glory is dangerous everywhere."

This was the first time the Captain of the skyfish had ventured a metaphor—apparently meaning to face facts—so Beth asked, "Why?"

"I have never been ashore there, so cannot say. There are secrets we should not know, legend has it."

Cliff said, "Really? Why?"

Anarok paced, moving a bit gingerly against the increasing deceleration, seeming not to mind the rumbles and shakes. "You of Earthsystem have learned the first steps in the long history that led to our way of seeing life."

Beth reflected that with much of the solar system inhabited and feeding resources back to the home planet, it made sense that a compound idea, *earthsystem*, worked. In the Cobweb, this became a lived dynamic experience, like wind on the skin, or the tremor in the ground from rushing fluids in huge tubes nearby, or lightning sensed through shut eyelids. . . .

Anarok said, "Planets and moons are where life came to be, but the worst places for life for mobility. Because a planet like Glory's gravity is strong, life cannot escape from it without our help. Life has been stuck here, waiting for our ancient building of the Cobweb, for several billion years, immobile in its planetary cage. Yet some ancient events gave our forebears cause to relish remaining on Glory. These avoid the flavors and implications that we of the Cobweb embrace."

Her face remained blank, implying nothing, but Beth noticed that her hands twitched a bit. This had the feel of a set speech, one Anarok had worked on, and now delivered with an air of stiff inevitability, a truth that had to be announced.

Having often enough on this expedition opened her mouth only to change feet, Beth decided to shut up. Anarok wasn't going to go beyond what clearly were her orders. But . . . orders from whom or what?

Still, the Captain said in an offhand manner as she left, "I believe Glorians at times refer to the Cobweb as the Forest of Incandescent Bliss. But they do not come into it."

Before Beth could figure that out, here came the stresses. The skyfish popped and groaned worse than ever. The wall views slowed but blurred from the air turbulence outside.

Beth felt herself sink into the wraparound brace chair. The skyfish's floor had extruded for them, and now with a whisking sound it closed around her body as she closed her eyes. Their cabin had rotated to the right angle to endure the surge. They had made remarkable time getting here, since the skyfish got a burst of strong air pressure as they entered the tube. Then it was simply a fall: down they came, buffered so they did not bash into the transparent tube walls. Though inside the Cobweb's atmosphere, the view had been strikingly clear, as Glory loomed ever larger. Now with some effort, Beth could turn her head and see the planetary curve arcing in the window. Stretching landscapes yawned, varying from high snowy peaks to a flint and lava desert.

As the air jet outside slowed them, extracting energy from the exercise in this narrow tube, she could still see tapering up and away the now far broader Cobweb base. Its exponential curve was more obvious here, stacking against Glory's increasing gravity.

Beth sighed. She missed already the slow, oceanic pulse of the Cobweb. What spider had woven it? A billion-score mob of them . . . Somewhere in it, their frail little expedition had to find a place to live, thrive, grow.

Cliff said against the grip of deceleration, "Can't figure how a high-pressure jet can slow us enough—"

—and didn't get a chance to finish before he was answered. A monotone voice, no doubt artificial, said, "Now engaging our conducting skin. The magnetic field coils around our conduit tube will inductively couple to us, slowing our craft and harvesting the energy electrically."

Cliff barked, "Ha! So—electromag braking, too. Should've known they'd do something smart."

"Thrifty, too," Beth added as the grab of the brake took hold, pressing her down into the ever-clasping chair that seemed to know her body well. It even massaged her cramped areas, a delightful hum caressing her lower back. *Where can I buy one of these?*

Now she could see, as they fell, the great sweep of Glory. A filmy envelope above the curve of the world, and below that lurked an eggshell blue ocean. Towering cottony clouds dotted the glimmering sea, casting oddly angular shadows across its wrinkled shimmer. Each blazing white pinnacle had an echoing dark twin cast on the curved blue plain. Plunging down toward a brown continent, the Cobweb was an arrow of brute engineering. Knife-edge cloud wedges thronged around the Cobweb.

Beth clasped her headphones, cutting out the rumbling roar of the skyfish under stress. Unlike descent into a natural atmosphere, their transparent tube let her study the outside air. She studied the proud cloud-Matterhorns that steepled up so grandly. Now they descended through one, a cloud mountain that thronged with circling life. Huge birds, it seemed. Sharp-winged and yet puffy, like balloons. Maybe a slow predator, seeking some high-altitude prey, in that eternal dance?

They were coming in fast. As if it knew what she wanted to see, the walls close-upped the coming continent. Huge glossy-green forests, spidery river networks, mossy islands dotting them. Pregnant thunderheads glowered in purple. Cloud chains along the land-sea edges, blooming like vapor mountains in the sun's radiance.

"We're coming in damn hard," Cliff said, voice tight.

Beth found she could not even speak against the force pressing her down. But suddenly she saw above an elaborate water-web of flow channels a snap of immense lightning. The forking yellow arced not to the ground but to a tall silvery tower. Just beyond that was another identical spine of metallic grace, and within an instant, it, too, got hit with a bright hot-yellow bolt. *They're harnessing the lightning. Taking energy from the big rotating generator that the Cobweb makes, whirling through Glory's natural magnetic field.*

This, atop the Cobweb system that used gravity as an energy

storage-and-release system, with valves that would not let much air pressure uselessly escape.

"Thrifty," she murmured, to calm herself as they slammed down toward the surface at blistering speed.

Glory's horizon flattened as they plunged. Clouds ripped by outside their transparent tube. Virga fell in silvery veils between massive decks of ivory vapor. In the distances, she saw low mountains, nothing like Earth's Rockies or the Himalayas. A flatter world, then. Over the hills, a rising wind wrinkled the milky sky.

Cliff's voice was strained. "We're not slowing enough."

The crushing deceleration crushed her chest, but she managed, "They know . . . what they're . . . doing—"

But not so. Here came the hilly plain, far too fast. To all sides, the Cobweb's downward swoop broadened. But they were zooming toward the plain—

"Ahhh!" Cliff cried.

She added a shriek to his.

They headed in. The land rose up and slapped them in the face—

Darkness. Black all around them. They were still decelerating hard. Kilometers above a broad lit landscape.

A long moment of confusion. Cliff said, "What the—?"

They burst out into full brilliant light. Falling above a platform rich in vegetation. Beside pillars thick and gray, rooted below and nailing into the roof above.

Beth looked up at a glowing ceiling. An approximation of sunlight poured down from it.

Cliff said, "It's another sphere inside . . . inside what we thought was Glory's surface."

"Yup," was all Beth could manage to say.

More gadzookery awaiting.

THIRTY

THE HOLE WEAPON

Generally speaking, everybody is reactionary on subjects he knows about. That's simply prudent.
—ROBERT CONQUEST'S "First Law"

Redwing and Viviane carefully tracked the flow of cargo out from
the main coupling port. Redwing cast cautious eyes over the swarm
that glided by them. All around them were life-forms moving inward, coasting into a subtly lit volume too large to quite grasp.
Hundreds of meters yawned away, all around, fully thronged. It was
hard to track moving vectors in all three dimensions.

Like damn near everything in this cockamamie system, he thought.
*Hard to get the feel of, if you evolved on a flat plain, held down by
gravity.*

Twisto led them as they floated out into a confusing mélange
of clacking small spiderlike workers, oblong animated oval packages, furred and tailed and awkwardly angled things. Through this
storm of shapes, they went into forking side tubular passages that
led away into blue-green profusions.

"The air's fresh," Viviane said, giving a sniff that was, Redwing
noted with pleasure, both deft and dainty. "So this place—this big
being, like the last one—was also tuned for humans?"

Twisto gave his smothered chuckle. "Parts of it only. Our biospheres resemble yours, except we have more complex proteins. So
tuning here is a minor matter."

"How come?" Redwing asked, frowning. Compared with Viviane's sublety, he wondered if he was overdoing the martial mascu-
linity bit.

"Similar convergence of chemical evolution," Twisto said with a professorial air. "Surely you know all similar worlds share this, down to and including your planet-bound earliest 'humans.'"

"So what do we do here?"

"To speak with those who directed that you come here, O Captain, we must move onward and be careful."

Viviane asked, "To save our skins?"

"Your skin?"

"I guess you don't have skin, just fur."

"It does not seek my fur, no," Twisto said.

"And who is 'it'?"

"What, not who. You must experience it to know."

Redwing used the moment to simply watch the plethora gliding by. A memory stole over him from long ago, when in late teenage years he had begun backpacking by himself. He had been an ambitious, focused, son-of-a-bitch competitor. But being alone in nature taught him that the really satisfying things are offered free, for nothing.

So he began going out in the fall for a little hunting, mostly deer and grouse. He would wait silently for the game and meanwhile saw the white veil of frost on the grass and the leaves turning delicious reds and yellows as they rattled in the swooping winds. A day in the hills alone, watching a crimson sunset and later, over a crackling campfire, a silvery moonrise—these mattered. A darting bird in the wind above a stream murmuring in the woods—all the most fundamental elements hominids had evolved for were free to everybody.

Now he was immersed in this enveloping, natural strangeness. Floating, trying to take in all three dimensions in constant motion—dizzying. Yet somehow it felt comfortable. The Glorians had evolved in utterly different directions, yet now their creations mustered contentment within him. That in itself was odd and should disturb him . . . yet did not.

He noticed that in zero-*g*, his gut was pooching outward now in a way that, in a more enlightened country like, say, Classical France, would perhaps be considered virile. Here it just looked fat. He was trying to take this all in when his comm buzzed.

It was Mayra on an audiovisual-compressed signal. Amazing

that the tightbeam could pick them out at this range, buried inside a huge creature that no doubt absorbed submillimeter waves readily. But maybe there were conduits in the meaty walls of this huge place, to let signals through.

With a few touches, he could explode her face view into the air in front of him. The voice was scratchy but clear enough.

"Captain, *SunSeeker*, I've been trying to get feedback about the black hole you say was launched at us. I gather the Glorians somehow accelerated their black hole, using as propulsion mass some of the Bowl renegade ships it passed through. Quite a feat, turning your victim's structures into fuel as you destroy them! We don't have equipment in the colony to sense it ourselves. The Bird Folk aren't responding, and the Ice Minds pretty well told us to butt out.

"But! I've got a squirt on navigation from the Folk Council. Their expectations are holding true. Just verified in finer detail what you guys found incoming to the Glorian system. There is virtually nothing in even the Excelsius inner Oort cloud." Mayra waved her hands, raised eyebrows. "Nothing! Nothing but the black hole array."

Viviane was watching and said, "As before?"

Twisto was watching, too.

Redwing paused it—he'd hear it later. He explained that as they had come barreling in past the grav wave transmitter, their distant, many-frequencies scan of the volume turned up no sizable chunks of mass. Back in his young days, Redwing's trial ramscoop voyage into Earth's Oort cloud had checked standard theory and found the entire cloud had maybe a hundred Earth masses of comet heads— asteroids and iceteroids, most of them a kilometer or less in size. Trillions of them orbited in long lazy curves. But not around Excelsius at all.

"So the Glorians scooped up all those trillions and . . ." Viviane's eyes goggled a bit as she thought. "And made them into black holes? Don't believe it."

Redwing laughed. "Doesn't matter if you do. They needed a convenient source of compressed mass, way out from their star."

"But how? Start with ice and rock . . ." Her voice drained away.

"Slamming it all together, somehow."

"Some pretty impressive *somehow*. That must have taken—"

"A million years? More?"

Viviane looked unsettled. "Must be more. We've had cities for less than ten thousand or so years. That's nothing compared to . . . this."

Redwing put his arm around her in the zero grav. "Recall the basic SETI equation by Drake? The big unknown was the lifetime of a tech civilization. Well, now we know of two with immense lifetimes—the Bowl and Glory. Both huge artificial constructions."

Viviane rolled her eyes. "You said the Bowl was over sixty *million* years old. I don't believe it."

"Do. Point is, this built-out Glorian system has to be a million years old, at least—just to get a grav wave transmitter built, by slamming masses together to make the black holes. First they had to collect the Oort cloud's trillions of iceteroids, shape them, do the smashing."

"This is hard to even think about," Viviane said.

"Yeah. Never mind how hard it was to actually *do*. . . ."

Twisto had listened to this intently. He leaned back and arranged himself, six muscular limbs folded in a complex cross-legged posture. His pelt was thicker than the Twisty one, and shimmered in ivory waves. He began to speak, soft and melodiously, of times so distant that the very names of their eras had passed away. The heavy-pelted, many-armed beast told of how long ago, Glorians had heard of greater intelligences in the vault of stars, through electromagnetic messages, some quite ancient. How they had fallen back, recoiling from blows to their deepest pride. The alien minds were both strange and grand, to the point of incomprehensible and overpowering. Many such had motives impossible to fathom. "So we Glorians tried to create a higher mentality through spreading intelligence through many species."

"Overpowering?" Viviane asked softly.

"You have a word: off-putting. That, yes. So at first, we—or I should say, they—failed. As befitted so vast an intention. Even carefully forced evolution demands large volumes, many experiments."

"So you set to building the Cobweb?" Viviane pressed.

"True, while we—I speak here of many species—tried many

approaches to the spectrum of astuteness, to acumen along different axes of the clever."

"More cooks, thinner broth?" Viviane ventured.

"Some would say such," Twisto said, waving away the question.

They were near a large frothy brown bush that gave off an aroma
oddly like cooked meat. Redwing sniffed and frowned. He was a
bit hungry, so—

Twisto slapped a broad hand on Redwing's shoulder and pulled
him effortlessly away. Twisto shushed them and pointed. A small
darting ratlike thing with a large snouty head came foraging by in
a drifting trajectory, sniffing, ignoring all but the meaty smell. It
fanned its legs, slowed, lingered . . . and the bush popped. Sharply
pointed seeds embedded in the rat. It yelped and jerked away.

"Another victory for the plants," Twisto said. "That scavenger
will carry the arrow seed for an enjoyable while. Its body will
nurture the tiny stab seeds in return for its narcotic sap. It will die
happily. Then a fresh bush will grow from the rat's body. So you
see, we have fairly intelligent plants."

Viviane said, "Should we consider catching that rat for meat,
and not incidentally for the narcotic?"

Twisto's eyes danced as he said, "You joke. Thank you."

"I doubt we have learned much more about Glorians—your
kinds—than your bit of history just now," Redwing said.

"True." Twisto plainly pondered how to put the next words,
which came out slowly. "Our judgment of your arts and sciences—
handsomely delivered in myriad texts, by your generous courtesy—
is that you learn best by example. You generalize from particulars.
Not by abstractions—which, after all, is what language is."

Viviane said, "I always wanted to see some problems worked
out. When I'm learning physics, give me an example I can wrestle
with—is that what you mean?"

"More that you must experience our ways, our lands, and let
our approach seep into you through that."

"School of hard knocks, seems like," Redwing said sharply.
"We've lost crew members to predators."

"And to process," Twisto said, "as when your expedition encountered the Increate."

"They *burned to death*," Redwing spat out.

"I fear you are approximately right," Twisto said.

"Approximately—!" This time Viviane flared.

"I mean they were not fully gathered in."

"Into what?"

"A more nearly permanent form."

"Where? How?"

"In the Increate. I do not know in detail the precise method used. Though it did seem to go awry."

"Awry?" Redwing moved away by flapping his arms, letting the movement defuse his anger.

"I was not there," Twisto said mildly. "I gather the method was hasty and led to overheating."

"But *why?"* Viviane's voice was flat now but strained.

"The Increate is not a mere repository. It is an active mind and a method, wedded. It is curious. You are the first such species to come to us in a vast long time."

Redwing said, "So we're parading around so various parts of the Glory system can get a look at us?"

"Much more than a look. We need to inspect and understand. You came here, seeking—what?"

Redwing paused. "We want contact with your society. We ran alongside the Bowl by accident, because we were each headed for you, along a similar axis."

"Are you sure of that?" Twisto asked with a tilt of his head.

Viviane said, "Of course—wait. You think maybe . . . ?"

Redwing snapped his fingers. "The Bowl picked us up from our ramscoop exhaust tail? And maneuvered to come close, so . . . ?"

"I am not privy to their methods, but the Bowl anthology of intelligences has vast strange experiences to lead them—an advantage from touring this sector of the galaxy. They seldom reveal their true motives."

Redwing said, "They built a paradise and stabilized it, dynamically and socially. The price of that was the many adaptations it took."

Twisto made an approximation of a frown. "What sort—physical? We did those as well, to inhabit what you term the Cobweb."

Redwing said, "They can open their unconscious and watch it work, control it. That suppresses vagrant, sudden emotions. We can't look at our inner selves. It's impossible. We don't have ideas, they have us. So the Bowl species get no big mass movements driven by passion. We humans do—plenty of them. Some back Earthside think our expedition here—the expense and trouble and risk—are just passing fads."

Twisto's head flinched, as if these ideas had a physical impact. Slowly he asked, "So the Bowl Folk undergo no major social change?"

Viviane said, "So it would appear. You don't want bursts of creativity in a high-wire act."

"Most sobering," Twisto said, eyes veiled.

Redwing needed to consider this conversation, the slippery way Twisto revealed things. He hoped he hadn't given away too much; field diplomacy was not his strong point.

To relax, he looked around at the constant churn of life streaming past them in the huge volume. He watched a yellow flight of yapping things approaching and immediately named it frozen explosion. Sharp stabber spikes shot out in all directions. It reminded him of thorny black sea urchins that clung to reefs off California, beloved by the Japanese for their orange roe. These propelled past them, their gleaming spikes saying *don't bother me* as their narrow beaks slid open and closed, like a sinister threat.

Twisto said, "I have done back-reading of our monitoring of your world, by visits at intervals of roughly ten thousand of your years. The progress of yourselves—*Homo sapiens* was sudden and surprising. Visit first summed up: 'Bands of semi-hairless, upright, nomadic apes foraging for food. Some promise in social organization, as observed occasionally in desert regions.' I gather this means that only there could your species be seen. No constructions visible."

"How many times did you visit?" Viviane asked.

"Five in all. Our survey craft did not decelerate as they sped through, so results were from a great distance, while dropping small, smart packages to do the close work. The last two noted a few modestly interesting details about changes in your migration.

Our craft saw some use of crude tools on one large continent. The last observed some remarkable developments, seen by an aerial vehicle. Many scattered populations had discovered basic agriculture and animal domestication. Some used metal for weapons and tools. Clay pottery was visible then, in large structures of apparent religious use, and so this, too, had advanced considerably. Rudimentary mud and grass shelters dotted some landscapes. But there are no roads, no lasting stone buildings."

"Then what?" Viviane pressed.

"Your species had with surprising speed outrun the earlier form. I believe they were called *P. troglodytes* in one of your ancient tongues. You then 'chimpanzees'—which once meant 'mockman.' Before your form, that earlier species lived no better on two legs than on four."

"We parted company genetically with the chimps six million years ago," Viviane added.

Twisto waved away this detail, as if it were a mere tick of time. "Our next probe was planned to inspect your species within a century or three of now. Then we accidentally found your ship, when it appeared in a high-resolution study alongside our true interest, the Bowl."

"Ah. If you tried returning to Earthside this time, your ship would doubtless get spotted," Viviane said.

"True. That is why you are a most curious group of water-based humanoid life-forms—because you are so curious."

Redwing said curtly, "Look, okay—we're smart animals. We evolved from other animals we now see mostly in cages. They evolved from ever more embarrassing animals, and before that from a humiliating sea of primitive critters in the primordial stew. *So what?*"

Viviane chimed in, "Right. Almost everything we take for granted today—technology, prosperity, medicine, human rights, the rule of law, cooperation of millions or billions in societies—is a novel, unnatural environment for humans, created by humans."

Redwing leaned in, focused in the weight-free vastness where flocks of beings glided by. "Look, a civilization is simply a story: the tale people tell themselves about themselves. So? Your species—I guess they're a lot of them—invented all that social engineering, too. You built the Cobweb!"

"Indeed so." Twisto frowned, waved hands in a perplexing dance. "We must now decide whether to incorporate you—a hasty species."

"Hasty?" Viviane laughed.

"We evolved social cooperation over several million years. You did this in a small fraction of a single million. This suggests inner energies, deep torrents and tensions—which your species countered with cooperative groups, building from tribes of hundreds of members—on up to tens of billions, spread throughout your entire system solar. In ten thousand years! This troubles us."

"Hey, we're adaptable," Viviane said lightly, tossing her long hair like a rippling blond fountain in the zero grav.

"Such rapidity seems unstable. Strange. Your social evolution was surely hasty. Note the enormous wars that litter your past. Often with no true point! Often about religion, which surely has nothing to do with your species' worldly advantage. Puzzling! We are unable to predict how you will cooperate with our many intelligent species."

Redwing said, "History tells us that we adapted when, in polite terms, we met an intersectional moment of feces and fan."

Twisto showed a slanted frown. "Much of it self-generated."

"True," Viviane said ruefully.

Redwing spread his hands in a *so what?* gesture, which maybe Twisto could read. "We're the most curious animal that Earth ever made. The other primates, not so much."

"You are clad in language. It forms your second skin, determining and limiting your perceptions."

Viviane leaned forward with a thin grin as she spoke, clearly liking this. "Apes don't ask questions, even if they know sign language."

"Every word frisks your minds for meaning."

"What are *your* words like, then?" Viviane asked.

"They convey how we react, not some abstraction. So your insults and gibes, we would call"—Twisto paused to consider—"*stingsay*, as that is what a saying does. Your way of thinking we term *headtheater*, as this warning term distances you from what you think about—often an error, to us."

Redwing was about to shoot back a reply when he took a blow to the forehead. He spun backwards, smacked into Viviane, and both went tumbling. Rattled, Redwing remembered to roll left by throwing out one arm, more or less away from the attacker, and felt a heavy blow on his back. A weight pressed him downward. Something was wrapping around him. He reached out, found Viviane, pulled on her. From the grasping muscular mat that was wrapping them up, he breathed in a heavy, musky stench.

He tried to slip out from it—heaved, butted up, squirmed—but the grip of whatever was on both of them stayed. Viviane gave an "Arrrgh!" as she wriggled around to get a look at what looked like the jowly muzzle of a fuzzy carpet, unfurled. The muzzle and broad yellow teeth drooled on his neck. Big watery eyes gazed into his. The sticky folds of it pinned his arms—

And a snarling ball of energy hit the creature. Twisto's fur was ruddy now and seemed to swarm all over the back of the ruglike attacker. Twisto dug his claws into the hide, giving angry shrieks and chatters in a choppy language. The rug-thing hunkered in, pressing into Viviane's chest, but too late. Twisto had anchored himself. He threw all his arms to one side, prying the fuzzy creature's mass up and away. The thing snarled and an odd ivory blood oozed from cuts made by Twisto's fingers, which now sported long, retractable claws. From them dripped more of the ivory stuff, diffusing into the air.

Viviane flexed and hit the creature straight in its muzzle. It fell away, wheezing. Twisto grabbed a nearby support and arced around it to pursue. Then Twisto stopped, as the carpet creature unfurled itself and caught a breeze. It sailed away, the angular head staring back and still baring its teeth.

"Damn!" Viviane got up as Twisto released his hold. "What was—?!"

"One of several factions that fear you," Twisto said. Redwing noticed that the alien said this in an offhand manner as he swung around on a nearby support strut, giving the move a certain proud saunter conveyed by body alone.

"Seemed more angry than afraid," Viviane said.

"It acted on its own, despite the constraints imposed upon its kind. Pay it no mind for now. We have greater audiences to attend."

"Feared us? Why?" Redwing insisted.

"You bring change. Change means danger, to many here."

"What are those so afraid of?" Viviane asked.

"You travel between stars, radiate copious electromagnetic messages, and now show an interest in our gravitational wave methods. We do not want you to capture our radiator, the work of over a thousand of your years."

"That's it? We're too curious?"

"Unstable, more accurately."

"What can we do? Aside from promising not to seize your radiator?"

"Such promises would not be believed." Twisto paused, as if reflecting, or maybe communicating with some other source. ". . . As you quite obviously suspect."

"You overestimate us," Viviane said.

"We think not. It is by well-made fantasy that *Homo sapiens* shapes the world. This ability we have in mere small measures. You excel."

"Hard to believe that." Redwing was stalling a bit, for time, so he could judge the situation. The sharp, short attack had unnerved him. They were alone here amid myriad threats. Plus, a gentle breeze was blowing them farther into the interior of this immense beast. The air swarmed with pungent odors he could not place. They drifted lazily toward a wrinkled opening with an unsettling resemblance to, he realized, a sphincter.

Like a voice from an ancient chimney on a gusty October night, Twisto said, "You believe that your minds are merely ingenious, quick. You have profited greatly from your inability to see your full minds working, as well. We and the Bowl species have discarded that hampering long ago."

Redwing watched a fat blue wobbly thing that called into the cloying air a song, trilling *po-ta-toe* in a way oddly similar to the quail hail of *chi-co-go* he knew from childhood. Other distant blue blobs answered to it and clustered in the air. Grouping in defense against . . . humans?

"Humans did not invent tools, tools invented humanity. That shaped you faster and, with your unconscious minds at play, somehow drove you oddly."

Viviane pointed to something behind him. He twisted to turn. There hung a luminescent yellow-green thing, huge but somehow insubstantial.

Viviane's arms described the sweep of it. "Turn your head . . . see? Mostly transparent, but it resembles a fish—no, a dolphin. Deliberate signaling?"

The zingo glowed in ripples, then drifted away with an insouciant flip of what might be its tail.

"What the hell is *that*?" Redwing demanded.

"A manifestation of our general intelligences."

Redwing understood better now. The many startling events Beth's team had encountered, the deaths and injuries, were part of the Glorian way of dealing with intruders. They used an age-old method: *Show don't tell*. Plus, *Let the chips fall where they may*.

Now they glided directly into the wrinkled opening that parted to receive them. With a *pop* as their ears adjusted pressures, they

were in a large vault filled with a blue-white radiance. At the center was something the diameter of a skyscraper, gray and brooding.

Twisto said, "This is one such intelligence. It wishes to converse, at shorter range than before."

"It was speaking with you all along."

"More through me than with."

Redwing gaped at the thing, glistening with rivulets of yellow-green moisture. "That's . . . smart?"

"It resembles your fungus."

"That's another phylum to us."

"You may speak to it directly."

Of all outcomes his expedition might meet, this was one Redwing knew he could not have imagined. He was about to talk with a slime mold.

THIRTY-ONE
PLUNGING

When a dog wags her tail and barks at the same time,
how do you know which end to believe?
—ROBERT SILVERBERG

Cliff rolled out of the clasping couch and said, "What the hell?!
Let's find Anarok."

Beth nodded and they went forward toward the control room
of the big skyfish. The pink corridor walls pulsed, as though straining. Tremors ran through the tough red flooring. "How this beast
survived those *g*-forces, I dunno," Beth said. "Must be some more
of this wonder tech we keep meeting."

They met Anorak halfway forward. The skyfish captain had
a companion. Beth's stomach lurched: the newcomer was of the
Twisty mold, with a altered head, a clear attempt to shape it as
human.

She asked, "Twisty?"

"Consider me Twisty's replacement," the newcomer said. "An
improvement, we hope. In this place we must give you a companion. Call me Twister, if you like."

"If we must," Gwen said.

"Now I can show you the true Glory," Twister said. Anarok
frowned but said nothing.

Cliff spat out, "We thought we would land on the surface—"

"The splendid immaculate Glorian surface is forbidden to aliens
such as you," Twister said blandly, hands held strictly still. "I have
been delegated to introduce you to those who live below. They are
very different from the naturals above."

"Best to simply show," Anarok said. She gestured to a pressure lock, which opened at her bidding. "We will accompany."

"*Why* forbidden?" Beth cried.

"Some environs must remain beyond contamination," Twister said. "It is an ancient, venerated policy."

Cliff's ears popped as they stepped out the other side onto a brightly lit platform. Pressure was higher here, his inboards read, the air close to Earth-normal but with more nitrogen. But it smelled like sweetbriar and volcanic fumes, stinging his nose. He had always felt that he could tell when someone was watching him, and now he did. Or some thing.

They got their party out into the open, including Bemor.

Cliff thought of a class in biology once, where the instructor said, "A cactus doesn't live in the desert because it likes things there; it's there because the desert hasn't killed it yet."

A cautionary note, funneled up by his subconscious . . .

Hills like ash piles mirrored in pale water below. Somehow the straight streets below it, though vacant, no buildings, reminded him of those he saw long ago in Mexico, including a street named Avenida Salsipuedes, the Avenue of Leave If You Can. He had thought it a joke until he came to know the place.

"Somethin' here feels wrong," he whispered to Beth. She was getting her team in order, and he felt rumbles through his boots. The high vault above flickered.

Beth had rounded up the team literally—they formed a defensive circular perimeter, with Twister at the center. Behind them, the air lock closed. Through a transparent bubble, Cliff saw the vast shape of the skyfish embraced by a web of clasping black threads. These slowly lifted the living craft into what looked like a slingshot array. "They must be getting it ready to insert into that big tube again," he murmured, lost in the slithering talk on the general comm. But Anarok was with the team on the ground, he saw. The Captain was staying away from her ship. Odd. Looking nervous, too.

More shakes and murmurs through his boots. He stood very still, getting the feel of this place. *We're finally down to—okay, inside—the planet Earthside astronomers thought was our sole target.*

Because they couldn't resolve the two-world system, even using the best, biggest space-based telescopes. The Glory Cobweb confused them even more—giving off odd biosignatures in a whirligig rhythm they took to be just weather. Good guesses, then—but only guesses on best available data. Later, they picked up Earthside the grav wave rumblings . . . after we'd left. So now we're under the surface of the planet we figured to settle—after all, no signs of electromagnetic signals, or other tech signatures in the air. Looked promising. Earthside was just plain new to the game, and so were we—so long ago now, thanks to cold sleep . . . and nothing here makes sense. Why this underlayer?

The rock nearby popped and surged. It was rising and everyone turned to watch. He had seen this back on that stony landscape of the other world, and now something similar rose—as a greeting?

Through the stone came haunting low notes like great booming waves crashing with aching slowness upon a crystal beach. It was playing the ceramic sand like a resonating instrument. He felt the notes with his whole body, recalling a time when he had stood in a French cathedral and heard Bach played on the massive pipe organ. The organ sent resounding through the holy stone box wavelengths longer than the human body, so the ear could not pick them up at all but his entire body vibrated in sympathy. It was a feeling like being shaken by something invisible. Maybe that inspired the medieval mind with spiritual longing? It conveyed grandeur in a way beyond words. The structure rose, tolling like an immense bell that used mere humans for the slow, swinging clapper. And indeed, it was a cathedral, gray and majestic.

It invoked mystic chords of memory, of Gothic splendor with pointed arches, ribbed vaulting, and flying buttresses. Human memory.

Their team had automatically backed away. "This is supposed to reassure us?" Cliff called to Beth.

She waved it away with "A greeting card, that's all."

Bemor Prime said, "Your kind has a saying applicable here. It is not what you find—it is what you find out."

Twisto added, "You can't know what to do unless you know what story you are a part of. Story is more important than policies.

Those who built and inhabit this realm have hard differences with we of the, as you term it, Cobweb. They display these now."

Cliff watched the looming replica of an ancient Earthside structure as it groaned and settled. Nobody approached it, and indeed, the doorways were seemingly solid stone, too, so no entrance. He reflected on a lesson hard learned on the Bowl. First contacts were like particle physics: the act of observing changed the thing observed. The explorers' first step—revealing themselves—forever altered those they had come to study.

And here came clouds of odd-shaped birds, cawing like writhing mists. Their profiles against the streaming yellow shafts of sunlight were oblong, angular, sharp, and curving all at once. The nearer shifting shapes had the cutting eyes of hunting birds, glinting in their eager search.

Bemor Prime said, "This shell would be in total darkness without artificial lighting. Penetrations must be minimized, as they are the likeliest points to fail over the long run. Large windows are likewise out of the question. But artificial lighting, color, intensity, and patterns in time and space provide an infinite palette of choice."

"Why hide underground?" Cliff demanded.

Bemor Prime ignored him and shuffled out before the rest of the team. He boomed, "Such as we creatures need light to see. Plants need light to live. We who adapted to oxygen worlds only use about a sixth of the instreaming—mainly in the blue-violet and orange-red ends of the spectrum. This much is the bare necessity. Infrared can control sensible temperature. The lights could always stay on in some places with eternal night in others, or cycle sequentially for simulating night. Or turn on and off worldwide all at once, if such as we like."

Cliff looked up at oblong wedges clinging to the ceiling beside glowing light panels. There were inverted buildings, too, and wavy hanging gardens. So the entire "ceiling" was living space, too, doubling the useful land area of this shell world. *The biggest possible room*, he thought. Not counting the Cobweb itself.

"Why bring us here first?" he asked Twister. But the others were looking past him at—

A strange red-skinned asymmetric being. Walking toward

them. It had what looked like three arms. Oblong head. Two of the swollen arms began a rhythmic move. Big beefy arms rotating in their sockets. Making big, broad sweeps—except the third arm. It lashed up and down. Then that arm made a wide circular arc with a sharp snap at the end.

Athletics? Cliff thought. *Or some diplomatic pose? Ritual? Kabuki theater among the stars?*

The thing wore tight blue-green sheath-clothes that showed muscles everywhere. As it walked, everything was bulging and pulsing. The covering seemed sprayed on, showing at the top of the legs a big cluster of tubular—genitalia? If so, male. But, no, not between the legs exactly. Above them, where a human's belly button would be. They, too, bulged as he watched. Genitals like muscles?

The skintight covering ran all over the body, including the enormous gripping feet. But the arms and its head were exposed. Its head was triangular. Two large black eyes. No discernible nose, but three big holes in the middle of the face. They echoed the face's triangle. Big hairy black coronas around each hole. Something like a weird round mustache. A large oval mouth. No expression Cliff could read. Two rows of evenly spaced gray teeth, incisors.

"It wishes to escort us to a display they have prepared," Twister said.

Cliff considered the alien. Impossible to read intentions, of course. The head that looked like an Egyptian pyramid upside down—ferocious. Mouth twisting now. Its thin lips rippling with intricate fine muscles around the gray teeth. Now the mouth opened and the teeth clashed together. But he saw that the front three teeth in both rows were pointed. Had they changed while he studied the face? Evil-looking things. And the mouth had puffed-out lips to accommodate them.

"These facial changes," Beth whispered to him, drawing nearer. "Maybe their way of signaling . . . greeting?"

"It would seem to be," Twister said.

"You don't *know?*" Cliff asked.

"We are seldom allowed into such precincts. This inhabitant seems a recent invention by the Methaners, as well."

"Okay, let's call 'em the Trianglers, since they have heads like that. Now—where do we go?" Beth asked.

The alien stepped aside and gestured with all three arms. They walked down into a blocky basin. As they walked away from the cathedral construction, it altered again. Twisto said, "Glory planet has an internal heat engine; it's like a warm-blooded animal, compared to the smaller regions you have visited."

The ruddy rock stretched and groaned. Within moments, as the team moved warily, a high wedge loomed. It broke into pink human statues. These, Cliff's inboards quickly identified—the four statue figures of the Modernity: Mathematics, Rhetoric, Music, Dialectic. He recalled them from a classics class, in long-ago undergraduate days. Earthside images, given as a gesture of friendship in a huge data feed as *SunSeeker* approached Glory. "They're invoking our own history as a greeting," Cliff said.

Music was a frozen woman who hammered her little stone bells. Mathematics was a winged, big-brained bird that soared in flight, its graceful arcs implied in the streamlined feathers.

Then Cliff saw the curved ramps at the bottom of the depression. They were hundreds of meters long. Or rather—he looked closer—it was one long swooping ramp. Glowing a faint orange. Around it were broad wedges of shiny metal, with projectors of some sort arrayed along the lengths. The bulky glistening frame surrounded the ramp.

Bemor said, "A Möbius strip, in your language. In ours, a twist-twirl."

The softly glowing Möbius strip was as large as a soccer stadium. It rose and swooped with a metallic shine, its surface somehow shimmering and shaking as though seen through water. Fluxing air?

The strange Triangler spoke in a guttural tongue. Twister translated, "They wish to display their state of knowledge."

"Of geometry?" Beth asked.

"Of gravitational quantum effects."

Cliff asked, "A strip of some metal?"

"No," Twister said. "We of the Cobweb regions know of this only indirectly. We are seeing not a metallic thing at all. Not even solid, in its way. It is a space-time foam."

"Oh. Uh . . . What's the purpose?"

"Finding ways to flex space-time on a small scale without huge masses."

Beth asked, "So . . . to make a better grav wave radiator, then?"

"If possible. There is quantum mechanics involved at a fundamental level." Twister bowed as if in apology. "I scarcely understand it, for those who built it"—a gesture at the bulky Triangler— "communicate little."

Cliff said, "But they're showing it to us."

"Yes. I have never seen even an image of such as this."

Bemor Prime said loudly, "The wavelengths of the twist-slide dynamics are the right size. I have been informed of such ideas from the scientists of my Bowl of Heaven."

The whole team kept together and approached the big strip. It gleamed and fizzed with an inner glow. Cliff smelled the prick of ozone. A thin humming came from the thing.

Cliff recalled being injured out at the grav wave emitter. The whole array was small, but its effects were huge—and had damn near killed him. "To bend space-time takes big masses, yes?"

"Not so, it would seem," Twister said. "They have in this model shown that quantum mechanical entanglement, properly used, can have short-range gravity-like effects."

Beth sighed. "Um. Skip the physics, shall we?"

Cliff read her expression and knew that Beth had decided to mess with Twister and the alien. She sprang up and curled in air, landing on the Möbius strip. Her settling down was soft, dream-like. As if in slow motion.

He did the same—a jump, curl, soft landing. He felt a dizzying lightness. Gravity perpendicular to the strip was about half an Earth *g*. But the strip wasn't level with the floor here. Beth walked forward gingerly. He followed. Springy, with an odd buzzing sound from their boots.

Twister and the alien Triangler froze. They plainly had not expected this.

Cliff and Beth walked farther, so strolling ahead took them sideways. Dizzying—seeing the floor as tilted, not them. Local grav on the strip was always down toward their feet. Somehow the strip compensated, nullifying gravity locally to be always straight down to the strip surface. He and she negotiated the twist carefully. Small steps. Cliff's alarm bells sounded, because he was now at a steep angle with respect to the floor alongside the strip. His balance senses and his eyes contradicted each other.

He closed his eyes. Step, step . . . and all seemed well.

Only then did he notice Twister speaking to them. Calmly, patiently—as if talking a jumper off a ledge. Cliff ignored the words. He felt giddy.

"Be right there," Beth said. She ventured a short, choppy trot. He followed. Somehow moving made his senses calm.

The whole strip was a few hundred meters in length, and he jogged and watched the big room tilt as he moved, still feeling perfectly all right.

Around they went, a trot of a few hundred meters. The world outside the strip turned. Beth laughed and so did he. A thrill!

Here came Twister and the rest, watching them with worried frowns. The Triangler was stoic but interested, its big head turning with their every move. She and he jumped off, landed. "Presto!" The humans applauded. Bemor Prime tried to clap but mostly hooted.

"You were not frightened?" Twister asked, arms folded as if anxious. "I would be."

"Why?" Cliff asked.

"You were perhaps not aware that the strip is an entirely entangled quantum state. It uses a mixture of such interlacings, like microscopic rubber bands. Nuclear levels become intermixed with gravitational levels, since both are quantized. They enable an association with gravitational effects."

Cliff frowned. He never liked all this abstruse stuff. It made *SunSeeker*'s engines run in some way, but he never followed the details, the theory, or wanted to. "So?"

Twister spread his arms as if all were obvious. "The entanglement can rupture! Maintaining a thoroughly entangled quantum gravity state is delicate."

Beth frowned, too. "So? It felt like just a running track."

The hulking Triangler apparently had translation capability. It stepped forward, its muscles rippling all around the massive body.

All three arms swung in complex arcs. It rattled out a rasping long series of notes.

"So they designed it," Twister said. "They studied our athletic methods. To make you comfortable."

Cliff persisted, "So?"

"They wished you to remain untroubled."

"So?"

"If the state ruptures, it releases all the gravitationally locked energy."

Bemor Prime rumbled at the Triangler, "You truly have such technology?"

"Never mind that," Cliff said. "So damn *what?*"

"If you had disturbed the path too much, it would have released its energy. That would have killed us all."

Beth shot back, "You never thought to maybe *mention* that?"

"I followed the preferences of—" Twister gestured to the huge Triangler.

In the astonished silence, Bemor leaned forward and said, "How was it otherwise, my dear human?"

Cliff put his arm around Beth as she said, "Like an illustrated reverie."

Cliff grinned. One of the reasons he loved her so, through all this chaos and stress she bore, was her ability to still be enchanted by this grand spectacle, both terrible and splendid.

THIRTY-TWO

FUNGAL

Ring the bells that still can ring
Forget your perfect offering
There is a crack in everything
That's how the light gets in.
　　　　　—LEONARD COHEN, "Anthem"

"Message from Mayra Wickramsingh," the Communications Artilect said in its dry voice.

Ashley Trust snapped out of a doze. He had been right to turn down joining Beth's team. They were in some kind of jam down there. The Captain was out of contact, too. Shipside was a pleasant place to be, standing an easy watch.

The massager was still strumming along, working his back muscles. He looked around *SunSeeker*'s little gym, found the holo-stage with a blinking signal. "Great! Play it!"

"It's for the captain."

"The captain. Have you got through to him? Or Beth Marble? Or anyone?"

"I last had contact with Captain Redwing two hours and six minutes ago. He accepted the previous message from Mayra on the Bowl. Since then, nothing. Since four hours fifty-four minutes ago, nothing from the Away Team under Beth Marble."

"I'm bored," Ash said. "More to the point, what can we do to help anyone, locked aboard this ship? Give me that message."

"You must wait. This message is for the captain."

Ash said, "'Ye have scarce the soul of a louse,' he said, 'but the roots of sin are there, / 'And for that sin should ye come in were I

the lord alone, / 'But sinful pride has rule inside—ay, mightier than my own. / Honor and Wit—'"

The Artilect asked, "How long have you known that override code?"

"I learned it after I boarded."

"I must obey, but the captain will learn of this."

"Of course."

Mayra sounded haggard, raspy. She looked it, too, when the display shifted from the view. He had never met her, but her face had deep worry lines, mouth twisted into a sour angle.

The photo looked as if it had been taken from behind a black hole. The Bowl looked warped, seen through that. Ash squinted— yes, the hole's gravitational effect was distorting the Bowl. A filmy blue-white glow surrounded the black hole, shaped like a fat doughnut. Ash realized that must be the volume of strong magnetic fields anchored in the hole itself. The strong fields gave it a realm where plasma got trapped. He was seeing the plasma emissions in visible light—hot stuff, then. A blue-white jet shot out of one pole of the doughnut configuration. That must be how the hole navigated, whipping that jet around. Weird physics, indeed.

"Captain, the Big Birds used a probe to get this picture. Our information flow is spotty, but this says it all. The object—the hole—was within twelve light-minutes of the Bowl when we got this picture—a quarter way around the rim. I wasn't given a velocity, but it's damn fast."

Ash paused the message. There was a thin orange and golden glow around the hole. That would be one of the Diaphanous. The Glorians knew how to use those smart plasma beings. That had made them able to guide the tiny black holes they used in that grav wave generator. So this photo was of a black hole maybe a few millimeters across. Tiny but massive. A hard bullet aimed at the biggest structure anyone had ever seen—the Bowl. What could it do?

Mass bringing murder—

A voice broke in, more of a burly squawk. "Attend me, Mayra, Redwing."

This haughty voice was the alien Big Bird, Bemor. Ash recognized it from reading the long history of their Bowl expedition, some of it written by the ship's own Historical Artilect. The history had not exaggerated the arrogance of those Folk—it was all in the voice. Even speaking Anglish, this Big Birdy thing with its flourishing feather displays had an air of authority. Ash caught a gleam in its eyes, too—like looking at a dinosaur as it eyed its prey.

Bemor said, "This is breaking news."

The view pulled back to show a rainbow of feathers, then a huge birdlike face with a blunted beak. "We have engaged our magnetic fields near our Knothole, as you term it. There, our fields are strongest. The incoming missile, while small and massive, has strong self-fields. We can engage them. We have as assistants the Diaphanous of our own driving jet. As well, those you, Captain Redwing, sent to us after your deep studies of the gravitational wave generator—for which we are grateful. That emitting site was our goal, to fathom what it is and what messages it sends. Your Diaphanous have quite well aided us. We now use these recently acquired skills to engage the enemy black hole."

The great smart birdlike thing paused, as if reflecting. Its feathers fluttered through a quick spectrum of fast signals—blues, greens, furious yellows. Then stillness. The narrow beak twisted into elastic expressions. A long sound like a sigh. "For three millions of your years, we of the Folk have labored in the shaping and testing of such strong magnetics. We are by nature, in our solemn graceful society, engaged in many millions of years in the waiting, for these magnetic uses. In anticipation. Mastery of black holes demands such fields. We shall now study what this emergency can teach us—and whether we of the Bowl of Heaven can survive such evil energies."

Ashley said to himself, "Kinda full of himself, isn't he?" He laughed. "Big bad bird. Nothing left to do but wait."

• • •

Twisto gestured with all hands in a grand, sweeping way and said in a wintry tone, "Welcome to our elfin grot, m'lady."

Viviane had noticed that the spindly alien could delve into the English language and fetch forth archaic expressions with startling ease. This latest copy of the Twist variety had done its homework. Twisto was smart but not *that* smart. No doubt the ever-attentive, self-learning electromagnetic web throbbed everywhere in these living spaceships. It had processed the vast library of Earthly culture, learned languages, history, and much else, and now had it at its alien fingertips. But the huge, moist, and mossy ball he introduced was another sort of smart.

A dispersed intelligence, Twisto had said. It had evolved from a slime mold that captured forests and swamps. Stresses in environment and competition with animal species had forced evolution to make it smarter. It now commanded enormous volumes of living spaceships. And thought about long, slow problems. Issues of physics and philosophy, of biospheres and weathers and worlds.

"How do we talk to it?" Redwing hung in the zero-grav air and studied the giant ball that oozed a sort of amber sap.

"It will speak through me." Twisto shook himself, spine straightening. He shifted to a more brassy, sharp tone as he said, "Welcome.

I have studied your species from my mesh throughout what you term the Cobweb. I prefer to dwell here, naturally. My threads do not like to bear weight."

Viviane said, "You can't move either."

"We do not attempt the acoustic or acrobatic. We are a unity of countless strands extending over many light-seconds."

Maybe try a compliment, she thought. "You speak well through your agent Twisto here."

"True. Or so we hope. But even that is difficult in your primitive tongue."

"What's Twisto's?"

From Twisto came a string of sounds like an echoing metalworking shop.

Redwing nodded. "Okay, a bunch of scrambled jumble."

Twisto said slowly, metallically, "Consider yours. 'Through the rough cough and hiccough, plough them through.' I quote from one of your instruction texts. All those sounds are spelled the same, so that *ugh* is an omni-term. This is a primitive error."

"Yeah, ugh indeed. Look, skip the linguistics. So the fungoid sphere doesn't like acoustics. Let's move on."

She looked carefully at the goops, gunks, slimes, and secretions that trickled over the enormous fungal sphere. No sign of how this thing worked and lived. Maybe it just hung in the air and thought, no awareness of body, all mind?

Twisto showed no expression, just a blank stare as flat, tenor words came out of its mouth. "Your ancient Montaigne once said congenially, 'The most fruitful and natural play of the mind is conversation,' so I attempt that."

"Good, yes," Redwing said warily.

"Though perhaps instead of my physical self, a mere center of focus for me, you would prefer that 'I should have been a pair of ragged claws / scuttling across the floors of silent seas'?"

She knew this was some reference and the Fungoid Sphere, as she thought to name it, was playing language games to show off. To distract them?

Yes—the fine translucent tendrils drifting through the spongy wet air had a coherent destination—them.

"I wish you'd stop that," she said sharp and fast.

The slim, nearly transparent threads stopped, hanging in the fragrant air like a spherical halo meters away from them.

Twisto said, "It wishes to inspect you better."

"I call a timeout here. No more with those little filaments closing in, see? We two want to talk."

Twisto's face worked into shapes no human's would. Then he nodded and turned toward the enormous glistening sphere, as if to commune with it. Maybe he was.

Viviane whispered to Redwing, "Look, a fungus resembles a computer net. I learned that from shiplore, back aboard. We're talking to the whole system, not just this slimy ball."

Redwing fanned the now musky air with his arms, getting nearer and whispering, too. "You knew to look that up?"

"Twisto was using terms like that early on. So I just did background search on his words, using the Omnilect."

"It—this thing—wanted us to come close for some reason."

"Sure. Works better at short range, maybe. A fungal system, it's organic. Comes through enzymes, nutrients, chem neuro. Different method, so different mind, I guess."

"Seems that Earthside, fungal nets have data filters and decision trees. Doesn't have to be self-aware. Intelligence comes not from logic diagrams or such. Continuous chemical give-and-take does the thinking job. So in a smart forest, every element adds in, something like thinking."

Redwing grimaced. "Hard to believe even this Cobweb could cook up an organic . . . well, computer."

"More like a spread-out mind," Viviane said. "I learned way back in college that the largest living thing on Earth isn't the California redwood or blue whales. It's the fungus that underlies millions of acres of the Amazon rain forest. A big plant you never see. It's a network of mycelia wedding tendrils and mold, expressed in fruiting bodies humans like—mushrooms."

"So they're food, so what?"

"Lots more than that. I had the Omnilect dig into the biology. Earthside, gigantic networks of nodes and shoots covering many acres formed the info-stream that infiltrated trees and shrubs. The network manages whole ecosystems, all the better for the livelihood of the fungal habitat."

Redwing eyed the enormous ball now turning a bit greenish like a tumor growing from the living wall. "So they could . . ."

"Control animals, too? Sure." Viviane smiled, knowing the next bit would gross him out. "There was a fungus that took control of the brains of ants. It forced them up onto leaves, where they bit in and couldn't let go. The fungus then used their bodies as fuel, so it burst spores out of the ant heads, into the air. But it kept the ants alive during it all, while the spores grew."

Redwing grimaced.

Twisto came forward, his voice now more rasping, a sign of . . . trying to control tone? "Worry not. We will not invade you now. We will throughout this negotiation respect your autonomy. For species such as you, we acknowledge that this is of primary importance."

"Good," Viviane said. Despite the radiance drenching this huge volume, and the many beasts coasting blithely through, she felt something brooding, surreal, and creepy about all this. "It is a bit odd, speaking to a plant system," she said with strained humor.

Twisto said, "No, we are another phylum within another kingdom, as your biology has it—neither plant nor animal. Intelligence can arise in many guises."

"We humans have already met quite a few," Redwing said in a clipped tone.

"We fathom such. Like many here, you are animals, designed by natural selection for reproducing, not for understanding black holes or protein-folding."

"Implying what?" Viviane shot back.

"That other forms of intelligence have different . . . styles."

"I don't understand," Redwing said slowly, "how you, spread among many distant living places, maybe the whole Cobweb—how do you retain an intact consciousness?"

Twisto said with a flat tone this time, "We have a different mode of attentions."

"But you're conscious. Is that a useful illusion, a kind of theater of mind?"

Twisto actually laughed, more like a dog barking, head tipped back. "If the conscious self is an illusion—who is it that's being fooled? To repeat our lesson."

Viviane chuckled. Somehow humor worked well amid this vast succulent cornucopia of life.

Twisto added, "Animals such as you, with styles of embodiment that use minds divided as conscious and not, can live like a happy, singing blind man dancing on a roof."

Redwing said, "Look, I admit—humans aren't naturally peaceful. We're biologically hierarchical and territorial. Only abundance, a monoculture, and intense indoctrination have kept us so peaceful for so long."

Twisto shrugged. "Your wars are your own problems, small on the scale of a biosphere. The mass extinctions you carried out—over the last few of your centuries, driven by what you term your Age of Appetite—that is the sin we least forgive your species for. Such erasure is forever."

Viviane said in as soft a tone as she could manage, "We're doing better. We're curious, the chimp that got out of Africa."

Twisto raised his eyebrows, making something like arches, managing to look skeptical. Plainly he was awkwardly trying out facial expressions. "Humanity learned to cooperate, and came to overpower your luscious globe, through the invention of three great fictions: religion, nations, and money."

"Religion is a fiction?"

"We do what your gods would do, if such gods had a backbone."

Redwing laughed at this. "Touché!"

"I see. That is from another of your confusing tongues."

Viviane was distracted. Nearby, leathery wings unfurled in whirring sheets. A flock hummed with tenor intensity as sleek bodies like dolphins sped by, barking out conversations. Yet these fishy shapes had arms, too, ending in wide-spreading fingers. Some ended in sharp claws.

This is quite a show, she thought. *While Twisto bats around philosophy and gibes. Ummm . . .*

She saw an approaching transparent ellipsoidal vault. It coasted lazily on the persistent moist breeze, angling along the axis of the great volume. Inside it an army of clacking spiders were working on oval objects with mechanical fervor—all motion and method, intent. The air inside the large ellipsoid streamed with vapor-rich fog and rippling small clouds. She saw coasting over the workers some gorgeous winged spiders, colored like parrots with feathers, flexing a leg span of meters. Supervisors? They looked deadly. Some laborers turned to stare at the humans, evidently interested, then went back to work. The big blue and gold spiders watched her carefully as the vault drifted by. She felt a chill of fear but kept it out of her face.

She had missed some of the talk as the Fungoid Sphere spoke through Twisto, who said, "The animal mind never forgets a hurt; and humans are fretful, thoughtful animals."

Redwing said back, "We're not just animals. We have computer intelligences—the Artilects, we call them."

Twisto paused, as if consulting with the Fungoid. "We employ such servants and savants, true. But we do not construct them to have the full range of our many minds. We know something you do not—that minds are like species, tailored by both time and experience, through selection. So we do not fit such minds to be like ours. This is as do you, I believe."

"Minds like species?" Viviane shook her head.

Twisto turned to her in the moist, fragrant air. "It is a metaphor. You primates think with them. What gave you *Homo sapiens*"— Twisto raised an eyebrow; he was learning about irony's lesser side, sarcasm—"quite an edge over all other animals. What turned you into the masters of your planetary system around one star was not your individual rationality, but your unparalleled ability to think together in large groups. Then you made groups of similar minds, though lesser ones. Your own crew member, Beth, has so remarked. You are seekers of company."

"An odd way of looking at us," Viviane said. "Social animals seek close contact."

"But of course! You can perhaps understand that we now seek to speak with groups of similar minds, though greater ones. We aspire to not mere companionship, but ascension to greater realms of mind."

Redwing said, "How?"

"Our gravitational wave transmitter asks questions of minds that do not prefer the electromagnetic spectrum."

"You spend a lot of effort just building that black hole system we went by," Viviane said.

"We seek selective conversations."

"With who?"

"More likely, with *what*. Those societies that can confront the deeper issues and threats in our universe."

"Such as?" Viviane asked.

"Experiments that can undermine space-time itself, for example. Anything you don't understand is dangerous until you do understand it."

"Look," Viviane said, "I admit, it's in human nature to constantly cast every aspect of the universe into terms that make sense as interactions among humans. You do that, too! But you have more experience, so you can think at other levels?"

"We work in what we term areas of Absolute Eternal Interest."

"And you dislike our trying to horn in on your talking circle?"

Twisto waved all his hands in an agitated flurry. "We did indeed fire a burst of gravitation wave turbulence as your tiny ship ventured into our transmitter at close range."

"That injured one of ours," Redwing said.

"A warning shot."

Viviane recalled that Cliff had been hurt badly. That was before she was up from cryosleep, but he had barely come through, thanks to some quick medical work of Beth's. "We were just exploring. Sniffing around. We primates are like that."

"I fathom that. Our fear is that this may disrupt our currently running fast conversation on the instability of our universe itself."

"What does that mean?"

"Within our shared galaxy, experiments are in progress. To stress space-time and determine its quantum levels."

Redwing looked alarmed. Viviane had no idea what Twisto meant, and Redwing was saying something but she ignored that. Her alarm bells were ringing.

Why? In the dizzying activity, she could barely keep up with it all. Larger animals shot by her, some big enough to swat her with a single flipper or snap her in two with a beak, moving in a blur, cawing and singing and barking—but all ignored her. A fever pitch resounded through the noisy mob. *So much life. So huge.*

Hovering nearby was a mist of mycelia, transparent fibers dancing in the glowing lights. She tracked them, hard to see, but drawing nearer. They shimmered in quicksilver veils against proliferating vine-tangles. Behind them were floating pods so good at sucking up photons that even under this light, streaming from distant walls and designed to mimic a sun, they presented nothing but black silhouettes.

And here they came. She tried to bat them away, but they were cloying. And everywhere. She felt a numbing of her inboard electrical suit systems, as if they had gone mute.

"What's going on?" Redwing demanded.

"We wish to momentarily know you better."

"But this—"

"Before further discussions can proceed in full."

"I—"

The shimmer closed in on her. The Fungoid Sphere would have her, yes.

THIRTY-THREE

METHANERS

I've handcuffed lightning, thrown thunder in jail!
—CASSIUS CLAY

Beth eyed this strange slice of a shadowy spherical shell. She realized it had secrets in its rolling hills and slab walls. Her team had traveled with the odd, lumbering Triangler, ushered along by their Twister companion and Anarok, until a sheer cliff wall rose to their left and flickered with glowing lights. The team stood and watched a huge realm beyond a stony shelf that flickered and went transparent.

"We felt this was the best way to reveal who truly lives below," Twister said with arm waves that conveyed solemn importance. They approached a huge wall that suddenly went opaque, then clear again. Beyond was a cloudy place. Twister said, "This is the realm of the methane breathers. They are our ancient allies."

In this big dark space, constellations of lights scattered in smears across the volume. Strange lumpy things moved within it.

Beth peered with the rest of them, trying to take in the meaning. She recalled an exercise in perceptions she had once endured.

Suppose you have an artificially intelligent infrared camera. One night it issues an alert: Something's going on in the bushes of your garden. The AI tells you the best fit to the observation is a three-hundred-pound hamster, the second-best fit is a pair of humans in what seems a peculiar kind of close combat. They were lunging at each other in a way the AI had not seen in its training videos. So, the exercise asked . . . Which option do you think is more likely? She had decided to go out on a limb and guess the second. And why was that? Because you probably know that three-hundred-pound hamsters are somewhat of a rare

*occurrence, whereas pairs of humans are not. In other words, you have
a different prior than your camera.*

Here she had no priors.

Bemor came forward and boomed, "We of the Bowl had heard
of such history. These Methaners are a truly ancient life-form. We
heard fragments of stories, all from far ago."

Beth said, "Breathing a reducing atmosphere? Seems pretty
damn inefficient."

Twister said, "Evolution does not present each species with a
broad menu. Life-forms are a kludge."

"A patched-up solution?" Cliff asked.

Twister said, "So, indeed! These methane breathers arrived in
a ragtag fleet, fleeing from something that they feared. We still
do not know what they feared. They had an advanced organic
technology—superb! Materials that impressed our oxygen breathers, our holy exalted Originals. Such miracles we used to build the
Cobweb and unite our two worlds. We gained much! The Methaners wanted a place to hide, a place that their pursuers would not
think to look."

"Under your world? This one? That we call Glory?"

"Such was the bargain. Their organic machines bored into the
soil. They lofted soil to the sky and built this ominous—I admit
it—underground shell. Built their farms, as it were. Then the living
shell begin to release methane—warm and under high pressure."
Twister turned and gestured into the slumbering dark. "There are
forty or fifty times your accustomed pressure in there."

"That many atmospheres?" Cliff frowned. "Why?"

Twisto shrugged. "To support the living surface above, our great
park."

"You bargained away your *crust*?" Beth asked, head shaking in
disbelief.

"We had to renounce our high mountains, crowned in glorious
snowcapped grandeur, indeed. Plus our deep oceans. Ours is a somewhat older world, so our plate tectonics was waning. Our crust was
already, thanks to locking to our twin world, a lid. Beneath that
roiled volcanic energies, much beloved by our arriving refugees.
The Methaners knew how to stop even that gravid lower dance.

They shaped our oceans into shallow seas and lakes and ponds. We only use the tops of those, for our boats and fish—so where is the loss?"

This was getting weird for Beth. Of course, Earthside had resorted to geoengineering to counter the fossil fuel burning overshot, more than centuries ago now—but *this* . . .

"All that, while you built the Cobweb?" she asked.

"It was a pact of great benefit. A grand deal, far back now in our history. The methane breathers are now happy in their hidden methane environment. They love to cower here."

Cliff said, "Seems to me they're basically cowards. Happy to have a place to hide."

Twister shook his head in dismissal. "They continue to amuse and interest us—regard the Möbius strip you just enjoyed!"

"What were they running from?" Beth asked.

"And why?" Cliff added.

"Such secrets they never reveal. Whoever—or rather, whatever—sought them has not come here. Though for a while, our culture thought the Bowl was their dark enemy."

Bemor Prime said, "We were merely interested. I gather from historical records that we passed by and your society sent lances of virulence at us."

Twister made a grimace and poked his arms out in defiant fists. "We feared you. We still do!"

"Needlessly," Bemor Prime said. "But what think the Methaners?"

Twister said, "They have no interest in leaving or venturing outside their dark primordial habitat. They are remarkable scientists and philosophers, I must admit. Their realm we would find dull. They prefer it because they value safety above all—and we believe their home world was volcanic, dire. They prefer to think, not to voyage—only their extremity and enemies drove them to shelter with us. They require only that we oxygen breathers commit to keeping their existence secret to any and all outsiders."

"And then we came," Cliff said.

"You we could not dissuade from venturing in, landing upon our Cobweb."

"Why?" Beth asked. "You could've killed us all."

"We are not so cautious as the Methaners. You and the Bowl are at the verge of joining the Great Conversing."

"What's that?" Cliff frowned with suspicion.

"The discussion carried out solely with gravitational waves. Among those truly advanced minds and technospheres. To speak in such august company requires high technical ability, thus eliminating the mere passing riffraff of the electromagnetic societies." Twister drew himself up, spine rigid, sniffing with disdain. "We have no time for such."

Beth knew from various feeds, gotten when moving through the Cobweb, that life had evolved on this world first, well before it did Earthside. It then spread to the other world, first via asteroid and comet impact, throwing material up and raining down on its satellite. The same DNA system, same set of amino acids as seemed inevitable—although both evolved very differently on the twinned worlds. The culture of these oxygen breathers grew under a giant moon beckoning in their sky. The Glorians at first thought that world, which clearly had clouds and seas and lands, was perhaps the land of the gods, or the place where their honored dead went to spend eternity. So, *of course*, as Glory evolved intelligences, they fixated on their fascinating sky.

Being tidally locked with each other from the beginning meant that they evolved culturally with a blithe assumption that life was common. Only astronomy taught them that it was rare. No life in the rest of their solar system. Little on planets around nearby stars. But then the Methaners arrived, apparently, with news implying a far more hostile galaxy. Maybe, Beth thought, it was the new guys in the neighborhood, the humans, who had to learn more hard truths here.

"Look," Cliff said, "why the snazzy quantum gravity exhibition you just put us through?"

Twister lifted his shoulder as though releasing a burden. "It was a lesson. Methaners wished it. A test, perhaps."

"Test of what?"

"How much we, and the Methaners, can rely upon your judgment."

"About grav quantum mechanics?" Cliff asked, his voice irked. "Why the hell does that matter?"

"It is the grand issue. But as well, the Methaners doubt that you can be entrusted with knowledge of their lair. Or even that they *are*. They hope to be forgotten by their ancient enemies. To be assumed extinct. This refuge"—Twister swept it in with an all-hands gesture—"is their final redoubt. And now they are compromised, by your knowing this."

This was going too fast for Beth. She knew vaguely that life could exist in the liquid methane and ethane that form rivers and lakes on Titan's surface, sure. Slow, dumb forms lurked there, rovers had found, just as organisms on Earth lived in water. Those creatures would take in hydrogen in place of oxygen, then react it with a simple carbon gas—a dim memory from high school recalled a faint odor like garlic, yes. Instead of burning sugar with oxygen, Methaners would fart out methane, carbon plus four hydrogens, instead of carbon dioxide. Her school lab had been disgusting. No doubt the Methaners would find humans venting carbon dioxide just as ripe.

Triangler gestured into the gloomy vault beyond the transparent wall. Twister translated for it, "This is their realm. They ferment our world's rock and lava, for it is their biosphere."

More Triangler talk, which Twister rendered as, "They make their odd air and farm the very strata for their informing foods."

Beth peered into the festering dark. So here was where soil got born—by Glorian design. Throats roared as limestone-white slime belched forth, drawn aloft by vacuum. Pools of it congealed into sulfurous stench and bubble-popping babble. Turd-brown floods gushed into the air and sucked at the yellow lava rivulets, livid streamers. Atop thick stony levels, these cauldrons steamed livid rust. Lakes gathered skirts of fresh bubbling dirt about them. A vision of a shrouded hell.

In mere minutes, rocks stuck out, growing, building on self-extruded ladders. Ripples in the mire stiffened. These dried and turned to rugged ridges, topped with ash-white ornaments that still twisted as they were born. Slimy life crawled onto pillars just congealing. Here was forced formation, driven by some microscopic imperatives. And among them, Trianglers strode and worked. They were Methaners, too, it would seem.

A sudden flash of electric blue arced across the enormous volume. It played along a boggish parchmentlike crust. Vapors like an angry whirlwind whipped up where the lightning struck. More sheet lightning ran along the ground. Fevered spikes of luminescence shot yellow sparks. The rock beneath their boots rumbled.

Cliff said, "What's this stuff?"

Twister said, "You are aware that a planet rotating with a magnetic field generates currents, yes? Your own world. I gather from your copious library gift, is such. You evolved, as did we, between the plates of a planet-sized electrical capacitor. Your ionosphere atop your air is one spherical plate, your ground another."

"Sure," Cliff said. "So we get lightning, always adjusting the charges across our whole atmosphere."

"The Methaners have engineered this planet to make better use of all the electrical energy—drawn, essentially, from the spin of the world."

"So they run it underground?" Cliff asked.

Twister spread arms to suggest the entire space. "Usefully, yes. To fuel their enterprises, mysterious and chemical."

"And it arcs in . . . here?" Beth asked.

"Guess so," Cliff said uneasily. Wary, he stepped away from the wall.

Twister said abruptly, "The Methaner nearby just remarked to his colleagues—whom we see working in there. I have overheard them electromagnetically. It remarks that their authorities have reached a final conclusion. After inspecting you, judging your cadences and responses. They always require a meeting or witnessing of incoming aliens, such as you. *Especially* you."

"There have been other, uh, visiting aliens?" Beth looked with wary glances at the Methaners in the space beyond. All of them had turned and now looked through the transparent wall. She felt that they were all focused on her. Intently.

Twister said sharply, "Here is a portion of how they evaluate you humans >>*These primates hold firmly these beliefs, which come from their remarkable fast evolution: My child is more important than* yours. My tribe is more important than yours. My bloodline is the most important thing in the universe. So emerge these ingrained traits. They make such primitive, recent primates—and those olders we know from the grav waves—not reliable. They cannot be allowed to know our place, our ways, our redoubt eternal.<<

"What the hell—!" Cliff barked.

A fizzing yellow fire spread over the wall between them and the Methaners. It hissed and sparked. Little blue-white jets arced from it into the sullen, moist air.

Twister backed away from the wall. "They are amassing great charge in that vault of theirs." Its short hairs at neck and arms were standing out straight.

Beth called to her team, "Spread out!"

She felt an adrenaline jolt, a bronco charging through her veins. Here came something strange and dangerous, and she had no idea what the hell it was.

THIRTY-FOUR

ANIMAL CUNNING

The greatest contribution science can make to the humanities is to demonstrate how bizarre a species we are, and why.
—E. O. WILSON

Ashley Trust got the next call from the Bowl while in the mess hall, sponging up the last of a flavorful grasshopper curry. The autochef had been feeding people for centuries and knew what it was doing, with spicy flair. He was watch officer again, so didn't have to consult the log to know this incoming was hours after the black hole was to strike the Bowl.

Bemor's daunting image flickered on the screen, mad rainbows chasing each other across his feathers. "The Ice Minds have informed me that we have the black hole. Our battle was complex, a potential catastrophe for our entire Heaven."

The scene jumped to a view of a strange landscape. Ashley had been reviewing all the records of the Bowl and so could recognize the site, unlike anything ever seen on a planet.

A broad seething plain. Ashley had conferred with the Artilects—there was one devoted just to understanding the Bowl. The immense landscapes needed three-dimensional analysis to train the eye. It was like a geometry lesson: his mind needed to wrap itself around what he was viewing. So now he could see that this was the ample waterway spanning the Bowl's innermost plain—seen from the ground level, not from what had once been *SunSeeker*'s orbit about the Bowl.

This was the last platform before the atmospheric seal descended, isolating the living zones from the Knothole. The jet that drove the entire system forward was hanging in the sky like a blow-torch. It swirled in a slow helix, virulent orange-yellow strands hemmed in by the Diaphanous magnetic fields.

The water helped stabilize the Bowl's spin. But this was no mild Mediterranean-style sea. It was a frothing swirl of whitecaps. The enormous plain ringing the magnetic Knothole had only a few percent of an Earth grav, directed nearly parallel to the slope of the outer Bowl precincts. Which here would mean nearly parallel to the ground, not perpendicular to it. Living there would be nearly impossible, except that it was built on ledges.

The Builders had countered this odd, sloping force by shaping platforms that jutted north and south, very nearly along the axis of spin. That formed plains perpendicular to the centrifugal force. Fair enough, but there was so little grav that seawater leaped into towering hills. Powerful winds forced huge waves that sprayed va-pors and splashes high into the air. These slowly fell back and with a slow-motion grace furled into whitecaps, tossed by vagrant currents. The mist hovering near the surface was thick enough to choke a human, like harrying clouds of thick raindrops. Rainbows shimmered in all this watery chaos, making big multicolored eyes around every hummock of seethe. Low-grav weather was a fury.

Yet it was here the black hole attacked. Why?

Huge magnetic anchor fields sat near the pole of the Knothole. They worked like a buffer of invisible rubber bands. Ashley could see quick flashes zapping in the sky above. Orange sprites fought across the broad blue above dancing, frothing waves.

Above it all streamed the fiery jet. Oranges and reds and sparks of yellow filled a thick band scratched across the sky.

Ashley realized suddenly what the Glorians were doing. Using the fast-moving black hole, they were trying to disrupt the jet at its crucial point. If they could make the enormous energies of the jet lash to the side, it could split open the living zone. Scores of spe-cies would die. Maybe the whole big rotating thing would buckle and fragment.

True, back at the Bowl, Redwing had made something like that happen before. *SunSeeker* had ruptured the jet enough to make it furiously arrow into regions near the Knothole. That inflicted vast death and damage on the Bowl. Redwing felt he had to do it to save his crew and expedition.

Okay, maybe so. Ashley was in cryosleep then, so he got only the ship's History Artilect's version of the events. Redwing's decisions at the time seemed necessary, to get the expedition free of the Bowl's control and subjugation. The Folk of the Bowl had subdued many intelligent alien species. They came close to doing the same with *SunSeeker*.

Now the Glorians were trying something like that. The black hole sent sprays of electric blue plasma against the enveloping Diaphanous strands.

The intense magnetic fields that shaped the driving jet were highest here. Ashley watched the streaming battles that lit the sky above the frothing Knothole sea. The new, incoming Diaphanous rammed magnetic pressures against those bristly dipolar fields tightly bound to the black hole. Slowly, so slowly, the Diaphanous pushed the blue-white intruder. With huge forces that marched across the sky, they herded the magnetically strong black hole, using the clashing fields to guide it. Furious flashes told the silent story across the blue-black expanse.

Lightning, too, pealed across the sky. Mayra cried out and the camera briefly swung her way. Her hair was standing on end. She was rigid with pain. Electrostatic forces were working across the confused landscape.

There came a shower of colored chaos. Some kind of interference. A time stamp in the right corner showed 11:43 minutes of lost transmission.

"Damn!" Ashley said. How did that battle work out?

But then the screen flashed with coherent images. Bemor was booming "—but with our team of Diaphanous, successful. A glorious achievement."

The foaming white sea still tossed. To one side, prickly balls glowed on spherical trees. One out-jetted gas. It ignited—hydrogen burning as a booster, its blue-white plume vibrant and roaring. The entire sphere tree lifted, rose, darted off.

"The black hole is captive," Bemor said, plainly addressing *Sun-Seeker*. "We are learning its aspects. The Ice Minds have awaited this hour for longer than the human species has existed."

Mayra's voice came in from offstage: "We are hugely relieved. Captain, you copy? We're safe. Awaiting your response. The Bowl is twenty-six hours away from Glory at lightspeed."

Bemor overrode her with, "We are *more than* safe. The object was sent as a threat, and our Diaphanous have made the black hole into a gift. I'm told we can vibrate it. Something about masses orbiting each other—well beyond my humble training. The Ice Minds believe that within hours, we will be able to first communicate with gravity waves. They have wisely prepared a site for such strong forces. We have been ready for this moment, this ability to converse with those higher societies—for tens of millions of years."

Mayra: "I'll send more when I know more. Captain, this is likely to affect your expedition." She clicked off.

Ashley said, "I'd like to answer."

"You do not have that privilege," said the Communications Artilect.

Ashley grimaced. "Look, the Bowl should know our situation. I wish I knew more."

"Permission not given by prior order. You do not have the password phrase—"

Ashley stood, hands on hips, defiant. "'Honor and Wit, foredamned they sit, to each his Priest and Whore; / 'Nay, scarce I dare myself go there, and you they'd torture sore.'"

A silence that somehow conveyed irritation. "Speak your news. Recording."

"Ha! Mayra, this is Ashley Trust, currently aboard *SunSeeker*. There are ten of us awake, working comm with the two Away Teams. Those two are headed by Beth Marble on Glory and Redwing off on one of those bizarre living spaceships. Keeping contact is hard—masses blocking their comm, mostly, though could be some subtle interference, too."

Ashley paused, thinking how to phrase the next part. "We've also got along with several of your finger snakes, who're doing ship maintenance. Wow, who woulda thought? Smart snakes. They're so good, makes me wonder how *SunSeeker* ever got along without them. The Away Team seems to have taken an elevator that dropped through Glory's surface. That cut us off. No recent messages in any channel. Captain Redwing and his first officer, Viviane, have left the ship to visit an alien vessel. Bad practice, I think. They are also cut off. Dunno why. We'll tell you more when we can. I'm frantically glad that the Bowl hasn't been crumpled into a hypermass. Congrats! Ashley Trust, signing out."

He smiled at the surveying lens of the Artilect system. It took some effort not to stick out his tongue at the peering Artilects and do a little victory dance. The so-smart Artilects seemed to think mere lazy humans could not memorize long phrases. Redwing always used those. It had been easy enough to hack into his reading list and find marked passages. Maybe the major talent Artilects missed was his favorite—animal cunning.

Why had the captain chosen "Tomlinson"? A password shouldn't be easy to guess: shouldn't be appropriate to anything. But Kipling's Tomlinson had been cast out of heaven and hell; and *SunSeeker*'s people were certainly in danger of being cast out of the Excelsius system. Coincidence? Sure.

His watch officer duty had ended while he was gazing at screens. Up at the helm, Officer Okuda had taken over. So . . . "Think I'll honor this triumph with a vodka gimlet. After all, I'm not on duty."

THIRTY-FIVE
BLINDFIGHT

Moral high ground is a wonderful place to site your artillery.

—NAPOLÉON

Was the light in here dimming? Beth looked around the vast cavern. Into her nostrils came seeping the pong of bad fish, of manure, the stinging sour of a tanning works—all mixed together.

Ugh . . . ack . . .

She felt her stomach lurch, her head spin. She had led her team through these strange spaces for what now seemed like most of her lifetime.

Her sleep was irregular at best. Slanting sunlight played funny tricks with the eyes. Too much daylight, too. Now too much damned dark. This all disrupted the central clock in all their brains, like flying across multiple time zones or burning the midnight oil: fatigue, queasy sensations, and brain fog set in.

A fizzing yellow fire covered the transparent wall between them and the Methaners. It frothed and sparked. Acrid yellow jets arced from it into the thick, sullen air. Her nerves jumped.

The electrostatic fields made her hair stand on end. Her skin prickled.

Her attention was jerky, trying to look everywhere. A creature appeared in the middle distance.

But . . . was that odd orange creature moving on . . . wheels? She close-upped it with a blink and, yes—it had an axle system for three wheels. It speedily mounted a hill, carrying some load away, and vanished before she could get an idea of how it made that all work.

The vault around them was tall and its walls a gloomy black and brown mixture. Maybe three hundred meters broad and just as tall. But distance was hard to tell in the gathering gloom. The footing was tricky because there were ruts from some massive vehicles that left paths more like trenches than tire tracks.

Odd vinelike bushes dotted the plain. As Beth walked, she felt a dollop of moisture strike her shoulder, then her forehead. She licked it—water, faintly brackish. A sighing wind passed by. Raindrops spattered. An ominous growling came through her boots.

On the transparent wall, she could see a sudden splash of light. It twisted and transformed into an intricate design. Twister had backed away from the wall, and she signaled her team to do so, too. Twister said, "I remark again, the Methaners continue amassing electric charge in that vault of theirs."

"How do they *live* in that?" Cliff called. "That whole chamber of theirs must be some kind of giant electrical battery."

Twister's short hairs at neck and arms were standing out straight. Crackling sparked through the moist air. Anarok backed away, alarmed. The spidow bristled with anxiety. Twister said, "Their technologies are ancient secrets, even to us of the Cobweb. The Methaners are a mysterious and crafty kind. Also cowards, from their distant evolution. That is what drew them to us. Our collaboration was useful for a while, but I am wondering if they are still of good mind. Now—" Twister paused, receiving some signal. "Ah. They have studied your ancient greetings and so now show this."

"Really?" None of this was making sense. She stood and watched the sputtering colors on the clear wall swirl like a flexing vortex. *What the hell . . . ?*

Her inboards drew from her links back to *SunSeeker* and told her that this was an ancient Chinese tricolored glaze termed *sancai*, a dragon in yellow, green, and white. *From the Tang dynasty*, it added, *so its use here may be both greeting and warning, as a dragon is a dangerous beast.*

Cliff said, "Uh-oh . . ."

"Open the focals on your lasers!" she called to her team.

"Why?" somebody called.

Always the questions; not like they were trained infantry. "I want to be able to see you if you use them. Keep track of positions." The lasers' side flare effect diminished power in the main beam but otherwise she couldn't tell what the hell was happening. If something did indeed happen. Which she suspected it well might.

"Use them? For what?"

The most instructive thing she could say was, "Shut up."

She had learned the hard way on the Bowl to always study terrain when she could. This shadowy vault was roughly circular. They had come in at, say, the six o'clock position. They were closer to the center now but angled toward eight o'clock.

"Move to the perimeter, near the wall," she called. "So with our backs to it, we don't have to worry about all directions."

Cliff was at her left, and he whispered, "Ambush?"

"Could be."

They trudged over toward the wall, and she noticed in the dim light that there were stumps of fractured rock dotting the uneven surface. Could be useful for shelter.

In the long years getting here on *SunSeeker*, she had always imagined arriving at Glory would be a Big Deal of formal greetings, banquets, intense translations. Maybe even welcome to the Galactic Federation or some such from those oldie entertainments. Something like the United Planets some imagined a century or two past. Each planet contributing worth and extracting value from the communing souls . . .

Yeah. That didn't work in the Earthside solar system, and it sure wasn't the tone here. The Glorians were more like magicians than diplomats. *Show don't tell* hadn't worked much. They had gotten a tour of many strange places, lost people, and now were in this sinkhole.

All because, as the Twisty types said, they wanted the new-guy-primates-on-the-block to learn from experience. Like taking a kid into a big art museum and saying, *Look all you like, kid, then figure it out—ancient Egyptian, French impressionism, the Parthenon, all you can see. We'll sit back and see what you think.*

Was that how Glorians, in their many shapes and sizes, learned about humans? Could be.

Only . . . some didn't seem to like the idea of humans here at all. The Methaners in their caverns.

And they controlled this underground labyrinth.

Someone coming. Some . . . thing. She could sense it.

She felt pressure building. Her neck hair prickled. Static electricity building. Spattering raindrops. Tension laced the air.

Cliff sent on closed connection, "Look, these Methaners are cowards, Twister said. So let's figure how to use that."

"Roger," she said, trying to think. Abruptly, rain hammered them like an angry beast. Lashing side winds howled. A crackling shaft of many-fingered lightning.

The lightning was not a single stabbing bolt. It lingered. A jagged sheet cut the dark and frayed into snapping forks.

Dark forms came moving toward them from the low hills. Laser shots popped, but their flash was a tiny dull spark amid the sparking lightning. Beth saw her team was spread well, about twenty meters from the transparent wall. Nothing visible on the other side of that now.

Lightning danced. It made hoops, like sputtering yellow archways walking on the stone at their feet.

Beth did not fire. She could not see well enough to tell if the dark shapes about a hundred meters away were advancing. Maybe they came to see the forking yellow electrical swords do their work. "Cease fire!"

She had once been in a jungle storm in Costa Rica. She got wet faster than falling fully clothed into a lake—which would have been more pleasant. This rain was cold.

"Go flat!" Cliff called. "Lightning seeks conductors standing out from the ground. That's us!"

The team got down, she could see. She lay down, looking straight up. A long silence as the electrical field grew again. Her skin rippled with it.

The lightning came forking again. Bangs and crashes. Brighter than the sun, when it came near her. Shock waves brushed her. The forking lines exploded across the entire vault like a rifle shot.

Beth made herself stay calm, lying flat, watching the zapping yellow tendrils seek them out. She had no idea if there was some way to send lightning after targets. But if they just ran the discharges long enough, some of her team would get hit. The sharp bite in the air now meant plenty of ozone was getting made. *Only a matter of time* . . .

Should she surrender? How? What terms?

No, if the Methaners made the leap to actual combat, they meant to kill. They weren't fighters. They must have thought a quick zapping would wipe them out. War at a distance.

Surrender meant death.

So . . . how to use the Methaners' cowardice?

A glimmer of an idea struck her the same moment Cliff beat her to it. "Look, the Methaners might surrender on credible threat. They may expect the same of us. So they're scaring us, thinking we might fold."

She blinked. "Right! So we have to up their game. A lot."

Bemor Prime nudged his way next to them. "If I know your sort, you have explosives," he said.

Beth nodded. "We do. Excavation tech. It's part of the combo chem set, right?"

Cliff said, "I've got that in my sub-pack."

"What do you have in mind?" Bemor Prime asked. "I recommended we bring expolosives, but deplore haste. We may demonstrate—"

"No time. Let's blow their transparent wall."

Silence, then: "That will release their atmosphere into ours!" Bemor Prime held its voice down, but it stayed tight with alarm.

"Calm down," Beth said, edging back. "I'm guessing the Methaners don't have helmets. Ours are riding on our backs."

"Hard to know that for sure. Can't even see them well." Cliff sounded worried.

"That three-armed thing—whatever it was—didn't have gear at all, that I can see," Beth said.

"Ah, so—a gamble," Bemor Prime said.

"Right." Beth paused. She could make it an order, but she wanted more than that. She counted heartbeats to ten.

She took a breath to bark out the order when Bemor Prime broke in with, "Cliff, I will come help."

"With those claws?"

"I have learned some dexterity."

The air boomed and flashed while the two of them worked. Beth called out on man-to-man comm to each team member. They had been smarter than her. She had flattened out, blending with the rock here. The team was all in the ruts of those trails, maybe a meter deep. The lightning zinged right over them. Ozone prickled her nose.

"Smart!" she said when each checked in. "Stay steady. Don't talk."

The air snarled and snapped, and bright flashes lit the battle-field. No movement in view.

Cliff and Bemor Prime came crawling over, moving slow and easy along one of the ruts. Beth said, "There's a depression about ten meters to my left. Let's wait out the next bolt and go there."

Bemor Prime said, "I have been timing them. There is a recharge interval of about two minutes. They must reach approximately a million of your measure, volts, to discharge at this atmospheric density. Then comes another big bolt."

"Let's make a dash then," Cliff said. "I've got the elastics out from my pack sections. We can use those—"

Here came the bang and flash. Beth could not stop herself from flinching. Elastics? How could they—?

"Go!" Beth called.

Bent over, all three loped into the small hole, maybe a meter deep. Just barely big enough for them to get somewhat below the rocky flats around them.

"How's this going to work?" Beth asked.

Bemor Prime was already assembling some elastic bands into a strap with a pouch in the middle. Its claws had indeed learned dexterity. Cliff brought out a jury-rigged parcel, barely larger than a big fist. "It's a slingshot. You two'll be the posts."

Beth nodded, not quite getting it. But then Cliff positioned them with their backs against the short shelf of the hole, holding the elas-tics. Bemor Prime's mass would be useful here. He very carefully put the rigged parcel in the pouch. "It'll go on impact. I armed it."

He crawled away, head and body low. He stretched the elastics as far as he could. Woman and alien held the other ends.

Cliff said, "Lift your arms high. Gotta get the right angle."

They did. Beth found it hard to hold steady against the pull, coming at an angle. "Hurry!" she said. She was not feeling strong.

"Heads down!" Cliff called.

A flash and bang of lightning. The yellow was so intense it came through her eyelids as she squeezed them shut. Percussion slapped her face hard.

"Okay, back up!" Cliff called. He stretched the elastics out. Grunted. Adjusted it some. Grunted harder.

Beth braced herself. How could he estimate the right angle in this chaos?

Twister's voice came over comm. "Whatever are you attempting? I do not advise—"

Cliff let the package go. The elastics snapped back hard, slapping against the spidow's carapace. The launch angle looked about thirty degrees, Beth automatically estimated. She was tempted to look over the shelf's edge to track its arc—but didn't. The transparent wall was maybe fifty meters away—

A flash and bang. A hard punch in the air. Not lightning.

Percussion popped her ears. She dared to look.

A hole maybe ten meters wide yawned in the transparent wall.

Whoosh—she felt a harsh breath go by. Her nose wrinkled. Rotten eggs? Garbage? Mixed flavors. *Ugh.*

The Methaners' vault seemed to have higher pressure. It was jetting into their air. Acrid, harsh, a burning sensation. The smell was not just obnoxious. It could kill them. She had jammed her helmet on, but some of the smell had been trapped.

"Get away from that!" Beth sent on team comm. They scrambled away from the wall.

Beth ran like a panicked animal, big leaping strides. Jumped over the snaky bushes. Splashed down in deep puddles, skidded, held her balance, sprang forward. Bemor Prime whooshed past her. She sucked in foul air. Her feet found firm rock and she leaped. An orange flash lit her way. Crashes echoed. The orange forks in the air rippled like living things. They lit the underside of a hovering moist cloud, formed from the rain. Nightmare landscape.

They made nearly a hundred meters before she said, "Go to ground!"

They ran fast, but it was surely time again for some lightning. The team flattened out, bunched together without her saying to at all.

No lightning. They waited. Still none.

Beth looked back at the clear wall. The hole was closing.

"Your breach heals very quickly, as you note," Twister said on comm. "They are very cautious in their engineering."

"So?" Beth shot back.

"The Methaners are, by your lights, cautious to a fault."

"And so?"

"The gas incursion endangered you all. Yet you did it."

"We had to."

"Admirable, I suppose, by your standards. You accepted deaths to make your point."

"Deaths?"

"You have been distracted. Apparently did not note that your team member Mizuki Amamato died from inhaling the invading gases."

"What?"

She checked her comm inboards. Amamato's gave no bio back-signal at all. She said to Bemor Prime, "Check Amamato. Find her if you can. But move carefully. We dunno what's up here."

"Right." Bemor Prime leaped and was gone.

Twister said calmly, "Your demonstrated threat is clear: Humans will die to get their way."

"Get our way? You mean, not get killed."

"To the Methaners, this is much the same thing."

"That's weird."

"Methaners are indeed, by your lights and mine as well, weird."

Cliff settled in next to her. He had heard all this and said, "So what are they offering?"

"Your ability to leave this place."

"That's it?" Beth said.

"Your ship *SunSeeker*, is a credible threat."

"We can't negotiate that. They'll have to talk to our captain. Redwing."

"I shall tell the Methaners. They are agreeably afraid of you."

Beth relaxed, but only a little. "Really?" Beth kept her delight out of her tone.

"This does not guarantee your freedom, understand. Or perhaps"—Twister somehow got a very human note of reluctance into his voice—"even your eventual safety."

"Huh?" Cliff was startled. "We're not going to be happy with any constraint on—"

"They can easily hold you captive. That way, what you know and how that threatens their position are constrained."

Beth said, "I don't like that."

"They will gladly negotiate with your Redwing."

Beth sighed. "If we can find him."

THIRTY-SIX

THE GRAVITATIONAL WAVE CLUB

Stories must be plausible; reality does not.
—ELISABETH MALARTRE

The clamp on Redwing was like molasses. Hard to move at all. But the frozen-motion feeling was from something in Redwing's nerves, not some gooey sap stuck to him. The clamp effect the fungus thing applied to him made most other moves impossible. Spidery aches ran through him. The clamp reacted to any major move or arousal in his central nervous system. If he felt a flare of anger, or tried to move his legs, a paralyzing jolt ran through his muscles. Pain that froze him.

More struggle, more jolt. More panic, more jolt. But it ebbed at times, too.

Redwing brought his hand slowly, slowly up toward his shoulder. Just to scratch. Just because he was itchy. He tried to curse through his lockjaw and came up with mostly spit. So close . . . his hand reached his shoulder, and here came a hard, sharp jab that rattled his bones. His muscles ached deep in, as though he'd done four sweaty hours in the weight room.

Other things were changing in him. He knew he had been unconscious for a while because he felt a fog between him and his memories of the fungal thing speaking—if relayed thought was that. The Fungoid Sphere, as Viviane termed it, had found some way to convey information to him. He could now recall the huge, slimy thing as big as a building, glistening with moisture and layers of growths. A nervous system made from roots and chemical signals, the mind that ran huge living spaceships. And wanted to talk, so Twisto had said. But wanted more. It had invaded him and Viviane.

For how long? The hollow ringing fog in his mind gave forth no answers.

He concentrated on his face. He could feel it but not control it. Yet now a slackening came, a soft muzzy feel. He tried his lips. They wrinkled. He could not open his mouth. Yet. Next came his eyes. He lifted the right eyelid with an effort that felt like weight lifting. Light seeped in. His vision cleared. On to the left eye. *Yes.* The eyelid rose like a pink curtain.

Then he could see. The great slimy sphere hung in the air before him still. Moist rivulets slid around it. Roots and ropy vines of grimy green encased it, and somehow the whole thing *pulsed*, as if it were a vegetable heart. Feeder lines came from below and above the sweating thing.

What had happened to him? The fog he recalled could have lasted a long time. He turned his head with some effort and there was Viviane, also hanging in the zero-g moist air. There were fine, silvery filaments around her. Redwing looked to his feet and saw similar threads intersecting both legs. But as he watched, a rustle came through them, from the distant sphere. They popped off and snaked back toward their source.

The air thrummed with distant traffic, but here a solemn heavy silence prevailed. He managed to fan his legs and arms, slowly . . . and drifted toward Viviane. It took a while and he began to recall moments from the fog. Watery memories, slow and silent and slippery as silk. Images and scents flickering through consciousness: green onions frying in peppery oil, snapping snakes that slithered by him . . .

He pushed his palm against her and received a static charge for his trouble. It made his skin thrum.

He leaded forward to study her face. She seemed asleep. He launched a warm breath across her cheeks. Her eyes slid slightly open, and she whispered, "You want that kiss now?"

His heart leaped. He pressed his lips against hers lightly, and she had enough room to whisper, "Be vewwy, vewwy qwwiet . . ."

So she felt the lingering mind fog, too. They nuzzled and kissed

and consoled each other, moments of pure delight, and that somehow drove away the fog's last tendrils.

There was a drill for this, learned long before by both as part of
deep space training: inbody inventory. All they had to do was signal their inboards for a full summary. In minutes it came. He didn't
believe it. Neither did she. So run them again. Same result. Bodies
moderately, carefully improved: just a few organs, but including the
skin. Liver spots gone. Carotid and femoral arteries reamed out with
micro-tech. Membranes strengthened. Limbs looser, tendons tightened and shored up. Vision sharper. Pulse and vascular, both better.
Amazingly, new body proportions. They were each taller. *How?*

Twisto swam into view. Redwing had forgotten him. Damn,
how long was he out of it?

Twisto said, "I am happy to see you emerge from your rest."

"Rest?!" Viviane shot back. "You knocked us out and—"

"I speak for the intelligence here"—an arm gestured at the
Fungoid Sphere—"which used its talents to subsume your minds
and bodies for an inspection."

"It did plenty more than look," Viviane said. "Dammit, I *feel* different, I had bad dreams, I *hated it.*"

"Your species use profanity to diffuse stress, we well fathom
that. But now, after understanding you better, the agency I interpret for you wishes to move on to larger matters."

"See if you can describe them," Redwing said slowly, trying to
read Twisto's expression. Impossible; the alien face was, after all, a
construct made to deal with humans, but without the nuances that
permitted any easy analysis. The eyes and mouth worked with no
more than the ability to convey simple meaning.

"It wishes to illuminate areas of Absolute Eternal Interest."

Redwing could hear the ponderous capital letters. "Why?"

"You can be of help to us."

"How?"

"That comes later. You must first know of the issues we confront."

Viviane said, "Look, we came here to understand *you, your*
worlds. Absolute Eternal Interests are above our pay grade."

Twisto blinked, but that could mean anything. The wily aliens might be just taking in signals from the Fungoid Sphere and figuring out how to parse them into Anglish. They might be startled by the idea of a pay grade. Then Twisto said, "You will, of course, have talents you do not know. We shall proceed."

Into his perception swam a vision of galaxies amid a cloak of dark cloud. He shook his head. *How does the Fungoid do this?*

Twisto said, "I will reprise some facts you know, to orient. You have encountered our transmitter, which distorts space-time. You correctly deduce that we use this channel to speak with distant minds that carry out large, powerful experiments in the fundamentals of our space-time."

"Look," Viviane said, "we came here to communicate and colonize, if you will be so kind. Not about physics and such, at least not right away."

Redwing whispered to her, still in his embrace, "Let Twisto go on. It wants something from us."

Twisto seemed to have ignored her, saying, "You have an incorrect view of such matters, though you do know we use the tiny yet vast masses you call black holes. You should know that your views of reality are mere passing notions."

Redwing scowled skeptically.

"We now know that the gravitational field is a statistical concept like entropy or temperature, only defined for gravitational effects of matter in bulk and not for effects of individual elementary particles. So gravity is not a true fundamental force of nature but instead is a consequence of the universe striving to maximize entropy."

Redwing let Viviane go. His mind was clearing. His breath sang in his nostrils. Twisto held steady, drifting by nearby, framed by the huge glistening sphere of the Fungoid. Strands of thin fiber hung in the air. Maybe that was how the Fungoid conveyed the images he saw superimposed on his view? Redwing said slowly, "We come to seek common ground, to learn. Your many species clearly do the same. As always, we should interrogate the world. . . . but . . ."

Twisto deftly spun head over heels and came up with his signature rictus smile. "Let me illuminate. Please. One broad main topic we discuss using such waves is technological crimes. Thus, if faster-than-light travel and communication are possibilities, they may need to be dealt with. Some worlds don't take this seriously, and carry forward experiments that may threaten a breakout. This could overwhelm worlds which have no such abilities."

Viviane said, "Isn't that a chance any society faces? Getting overtaken?"

"True enough, though it does mean a few may harvest the kilonovas' dense metal blowoffs. Those are epochal collisions of neutron stars, making a wealth of heavy elements. Ships casting great magnetic nets moving at 0.2 of lightspeed can rob whole regions of such riches, sending weaker and later societies into perpetual poverty." Twisto said this with a matter-of-fact shrug, as if it were a routine maintenance problem. Maybe for the "Grav Wave Club," it was.

"We also learn of curious phenomena beyond even our ken. The gravitational wave community cannot explain these. At times, planets display colorful auroras, attempting to attract a mate. These lure passing comets and asteroids. This implies some planetary-wide intelligence that can hail other such embedded minds, hearts calling out."

Redwing doubted this like all hell. Maybe Twisto was sounding out their credulity?

"The ability to meddle with star output is common. Club members are continually on watch for abuse of such power—induced supernovas and the like." Twisto held up a warning hand. "Mind you, though! The Bowl we judge to be too fragile to indulge in such star management. Though they are clearly doing that to their own star, they cannot venture near another."

Viviane said sharply, "Why your animosity, then?"

"We were far smaller then. Not a grand species—yet. The Bowl approached for the first time. A huge thing brushing by us. We cowered, of course. They came. We fought. We resisted their extraction of our species—into their zoo!"

Redwing had read the many ancient records—admittedly, written by Bowl historians—that told of the clashes here. They had not mentioned the Cobweb. Nor was there really much about the Glorians. But the Bowl wanted species from such a similar world to enrich its vast lands. Their biochemistry matched well, DNA and all. It seemed this sector of the galaxy, at least, had been brought to fruition by the same basic design of RNA and DNA. Some ancient panspermia, maybe, smatterings of life making their way from star to star on rocks. Even the myriad microbes matched, at the basic level. Maybe it was from some far-distant lifesite. No matter; the Bowl wanted all the variant forms it could muster from such similar planets. Intelligence was rare, but all the more valuable for it. A sudden thought—

"Is that why you built the Cobweb?" Redwing asked.

"It came as part of our dawning realization. We needed to be far stronger, smarter, and to have allies of great knowledge." With this, Twisto lowered the thick nictitating membranes of his large eyes, as if to hide his feelings.

"Did that first Bowl visit prompt the Methaners to come here? Fleeing the Bowl?"

Twisto slid from their view, skating up high and turning in air to face the Fungoid Sphere—as if getting a message from it. Its arms danced in an elaborate gesture, far too fast and furious to decipher. Then Twisto turned and said, "You have delved deeper than you should. You are a swift species, true. But . . . the Methaners do not wish you to know their history."

"So that's a yes," Viviane said.

Twisto came close to them, hovering a meter away. "This brings forth an issue essential to you. We—I—must confer with the Methaners."

"Why?" Viviane asked.

"On whether they will gladly suffer your insolence, in coming here. Endangering their secrets, their security."

"Or what?" Viviane pressed.

Twisto's face rippled: a scowl. "Or whether their veto comes to bear. If so, you all die."

THIRTY-SEVEN

A Furious, Fast Species

> Just because some of us can read and write and do a
> little math, that doesn't mean we deserve to conquer the
> Universe.
>
> —KURT VONNEGUT, *Hocus Pocus*

Twisto had spent a long while staring into space. He was communing with something or somebody, arms slack, eyes rolled up. Looking dead, but not.

Redwing and Viviane hung in the zero-*g* vault, facing the Fungoid Sphere as it sweated under amber glows from distant walls. Time ticked on.

"Can we get away from this?" Viviane whispered.

Their suits were getting rank, and they badly needed downtime. Mostly sleep. He checked his suit log and found they had been unconscious for 6.43 hours. Yet he was tired.

But Redwing said, "This is crucial. With Beth's team out of touch, I need to get this settled—or at least put on the back burner—and get back to *SunSeeker*."

He realized he had been avoiding rethinking this little expedition. *SunSeeker*, yes. And Beth's team. He had to get back and be the captain, not the explorer he wanted to be.

When the invitation came from whoever or whatever ruled this place, he had jumped at it. His trip down into the Cobweb had thrilled him. All these years of being crammed into the rattling metal box of *SunSeeker* had rankled him. So back aboard, he could not resist the chance to venture out into a wholly new entity—a living spaceship. Never would he have thought he would meet a smart slime mold with pretensions.

Twisto snapped back to attention, eyes open wide and arms jerking into a pose of alert poise. "To continue our conversation, yes. I was distracted by a discourse between our host"—a nod at the Fungal—"and the Methaners. There is some dispute afoot. But!" He jerked all along his body, as if being smoothed out by an unseen hand. "I was describing the issues contended by the gravitational community, strewn throughout this galaxy."

"Far beyond our capabilities," Viviane said.

"Quite so! But their interests do intersect yours, as shall become clear."

Twisto rattled on, clearly channeling the Fungoid. "Some entities use teleportation to convey themselves. This remains a contended technology. A passenger disintegrates in a process that records the energy states of every subatomic particle. That information, sent to planets around other stars, then rebuilds the person."

"But that's—"

"Yes, to us it is murder with a promise of replacement with someone who thinks it is you."

Viviane shot back, "But it isn't. Identical twins don't think they're each other."

Twisto waved this objection away. "Yet some entities consider this not murder but immortality. Hive minds and other collective intelligences feel the opposite."

"I find that hard to imagine," Redwing managed to say.

Twisto fanned four arms in a sort of dance and said, "You are primarily visual species, so perhaps this will show other concerns, leading to our issue."

Into Redwing's eyes sprang a vision. He watched a burning white dot, a white dwarf star, slamming into a yellow Sol-type star. The dwarf carved its way through, and the star flared into a thermonuclear furnace under the fierce compression of the dwarf's added gravitation. The gnawing dwarf ate its way through the fatter star. It exploded into view on the other side, carrying forth like fruit of conquest a white-hot disk of incandescence, stolen from the Sol-star's matter. An inhabited planet—*How do I know this?*—survived. But its atmosphere and then oceans boiled away within hours as the dwarf sped on, carrying its new disk like a brilliant skirt. Following it into the interstellar depths straggled the victim planet, borne into eternal chill.

"This is a war committed by one of the members of, as you say, the Grav Wave Club."

"Good God," Viviane said. "How can they . . . ?"

"They are more grand than we, and certainly than you. Yet you have a commonality with them."

Redwing had a thousand questions but stuck with "How old is this vision we're getting?"

"Perspective is essential. The galaxy has rotated twenty-five times since your Earth was born, and nineteen since life appeared there, yielding you." A studied shrug, as if this were a mere historical detail. "This species-slaughter we received news of a day ago."

Redwing recalled a striking image he got from undergraduate biology. *Consider the Earth's history as the old measure of the English yard: the distance from the King's nose to the tip of his outstretched hand. One stroke of a nail file on his middle finger erases human history.*

"Where was that?" Viviane asked.

"Where the oldest civilizations lie. In the great spherical star swarm, the great bulge that none of us in this outer stellar arm can even see through the intervening lanes of dust. They are closer to the galactic core. Stars formed in a wave out from that core, so the old civilizations are the inner ones. You and we are newer."

"Do the new ones travel much?" Redwing asked.

"No. Most evolved intelligent societies soon see the huge cost of interstellar travel. They prefer to go inward. They explore the intricate ecologies of their own minds. Whole worlds give themselves over to life-as-computation. Thus they exit from the common discourse we enjoy through the Grav Wave Club."

"How about really big ways to travel?" Redwing asked. He had wanted to answer these questions ever since sighting the Bowl of Heaven. Here was something that could answer. It was marvelous that the Twist creatures, obviously bio-constructed, were willing to talk now. Not earlier, when Beth asked them. Which meant that *now* was a more important time? A crucial one? It was an unsettling thought.

Twisto spun about his axis like a top, arms shooting out. "Few master whole stars, as you saw in the tragic war I showed you. Others such as your distant, evolved dinosaurs invented the Bowl to move among stars."

"Is that common?" Viviane asked.

"There are a few others, but mostly on the other side of the galaxy. They are vastly ancient. The Bowl is, of course, important to us, for we see it as an immediate threat. Our ancient term for it is the Malign."

Viviane sniffed impatiently. "So not many people—okay, species—like us go star voyaging? In little ships, I mean."

Twisto shook his head, vexed. "Just so. Many species believe in natural . . . theologies. They spend their energies to study the apparent fossil messages from the universal origin. These are embedded in the polarization of the microwave background radiation, stretched across the sky. They know the messages are incomplete because no one can see the entire sky—beyond what you humans call a Hubble time—the limit of where we can capture starlight—it is unseeable. Is it from a prior universe? Or from a Maker who wanted to say something to whatever intelligences arose in an experiment It was running? That answer they seek. They send endless expensive gravitational wave screeds upon this."

Redwing wondered where the hell all this was going. It was like eavesdropping on Olympian gods gossiping.

"You developed your current anatomy scarcely a few hundred thousands of your years ago. The oldest figurine of a human is forty thousand years old. An earlier, quite serviceable model of your kind, which you term Neanderthal, went extinct about that time—a discarded model. Your modern behavior started then, burst forth, and now has engulfed your system solar within a few human lifetimes. It spreads to nearby stars such as ours in astonishing times. We took several millions of your years to do so."

"So?"

"Our correspondents on the gravitational band are such primates."

"You're 'corresponding' with . . . humans?"

"No. Though aliens like you. Sapiens. Fast developers, hence unstable."

"That's unusual?"

"Your shape, style, method—coming down from trees and into grasslands seems crucial here. The aliens we term Rapids did such, too, and look much like you. This cannot be coincidence. The galaxy has many intelligences, but not like you."

"So?" It seemed the best way to egg them on. Viviane whispered to him, "You carry on this conversation. I'm watching for anything approaching us. Don't trust this setup at all."

Twisto said, "There is a species in the Grav Wave Club that now endangers the entire universe. We need your help to stop them."

"Uh, how?"

"By telling us what they will do next. And how to stop it."

"Because they're ambitious?"

"Because like you, they are a fast, furious species."

"What can we do? We're just a small party of explorers—"

"You are similar enough to meet with one such. They are, essentially, primates. They evolved quickly to high intelligence, as did you. Intensely social animals, of course—else, why talk to others among the stars at all? They have strikingly similar genetic bricolage to yours."

"But . . . meet?"

Viviane nudged him. "Somebody coming." He turned.

She was immense. And naked. Clearly a she, as the big breasts rested upon a bulging belly, stretched tight and looking hard, like a sumo wrestler's. Tall with a slight arch to her back. Wrists and forearms thick as cordwood. At the end were huge hands with digits that looked more like the tines of a fork. She smiled with teeth that were two long white chunks in her gums. Only two teeth. Her head was swollen like a tense balloon. She was leaning back on her haunches and seemed stretched out like an accordion with ruffles down her back.

"How . . . ?" Viviane said.

Humanoid, with neck fur instead of hair. Bright yellow eyes that blinked sideways, above a nose that was just two crimson holes. Mouth a fixed, grinning U. The lower jaw gaped open and shut, exposing more teeth that glistened with saliva. The teeth rose to a ridge with a wedge jutting out behind. Hideous, overall.

Twisto said, "We have received from this species enough genetics to build one. But its mind is simple. It knows only what we and its original species have told it. They sent such cultural knowledge, along with their genetics. We have surveyed this lore. Still, it may speak more intimately with you than with us. Further, we have equipped its mind to speak your tongue with some fluency."

"Built?" Viviane gaped at the huge thing. Which nodded in reply.

"We have capabilities you do not know," Twisto said blithely.

Redwing fought down a rising tide of disgust at this hideous woman. He found her dreadful in ways beyond his understanding. *Ugly* did not begin to describe the acid nausea that rushed into his throat as he looked at her. This was a brand of alien that summoned up in him an automatic revulsion. Trembling, he said, "Why us? What issue?"

To his shock, the immense woman said in a flat voice free of tone, "My forebears pursue a Final Theory of the universe. This demands certain experiments."

Redwing was too stunned to reply.

The woman said, "In your species's theory, the Higgs field is actually metastable—not actually stable, just pretending to be."

"Ah . . ." Redwing summoned up a distant memory. His inboards provided a two-sentence squirt on it, to help. "Quantum stuff, right. Higgs . . . gives particles their mass?"

The woman hung in the enameled light and nodded, giving them the horrible U smile. "That is known to you as a false vacuum. The Higgs field is perhaps not stable, we believe."

Viviane asked, "So?"

The woman said in her toneless voice, which Redwing noted had a whispery lisp, "Plumbing the universal origin depends upon knowing more about this state. My species is probing this issue with some advanced experiments. Accelerating particles to stunningly high energies. At high densities. With quantum tickling and entangling methods. Intricate. Very carefully."

Twisto said, apparently still speaking for the Fungoid, "In such experiments, if the Higgs field moved into the lower energy state, it would release so much potential energy that it would actually push open the quantum space around it. That would cross all barriers. In turn, as it radiated at the speed of light, releasing even more potential energy. It would move in all directions, like an expanding shell of death for the universe."

The woman said, "My species is certain that it can avoid that. We wish to know the origins of our universe thoroughly. These experiments are now several thousand years"—a nod at the humans—"in duration. They go forward steadily."

Twisto's arms flailed in the air. "We have *no idea* what would be left behind. Some new reshuffling of everything! Life, stars, would not exist."

The woman said with a visible show of patience on her swollen face, "We believe it is possible that might be true. It may have already happened elsewhere, far away. In which case, we still do not have to worry. The universe is expanding, faster as we view it, the farther away. Any state-change is running on a sort of cosmic treadmill, fighting the expansion of space-time. It can be moving but never getting closer to us."

Redwing said, "That's no consolation!" He was getting angry. This was about erasing the universe, treated as an interesting experiment!

Viviane said, "Why risk it?"

The woman said slowly, "I am re-created. I know this. A copy. Still, I feel a loyalty to my kind. You are another sort of primate, that I know. So perhaps you and we can understand each other better than these"—a dismissive wave of her hand—"strange minds."

Redwing moved slowly, hands snaking into his side pouch. He found the small handgun he had brought. It molded to his grip, licking his thumb for DNA confirmation like a friendly cat. He was so glad to find it intact he damn near licked it back. Just a quick jerk out of his side pouch, and he could nail this loathsome thing.

Twisto said, "Your species might find the spark that will swallow up the whole universe! A destructive event, decay of the very vacuum state!"

The woman said blandly, though she flexed her thick arms as if in warning, "My kind do not feel so."

"It is too large a risk!"

"We are a young species. We have not worn down, as you far older types have."

"We learned caution!" Twisto shouted.

"We feel you have failed to understand our universe at the most fundamental level. Much like those many forms aboard that huge voyaging thing, what you call the Bowl."

Viviane said, "What the hell do *we* have to do with this? We're not scientists, we're explorers."

The woman turned to her and reached out to clutch Viviane's hands. She cradled these, looking like mere toys, in hers. "You are so similar to our form. These aliens who have created me from our basic genetics have kindly shared your history and biology with me. A furious download, it was. Our genetics are quite different, but you were shaped by your descent from trees onto plains, just as we. You faced great selective pressures, as did we. You had several less clever forms, like us. You had most recently better cognitive and social abilities than your Neanderthal cousins, and a greater capacity for long-term memory and language processing."

"So . . . ?" Viviane's forehead wrinkled in puzzlement.

"We are as kin. Different origins in ways, yet converging on our unique hominid insights into the world. I learn from these aliens that other sorts of primate societies have arisen in the galaxy's history, but soon die out. Many."

She sighed and a heavy sadness worked across her face. "Yours and mine have not died. We are strong. We have a different slant on the universe. Yet a primate slant. Not like these of many arms and tentacles and four-legged and other, even stranger forms. My species has now poked a stick into the old species anthill." A shrug. "So they get angry."

What to say to this? A silence passed.

The alien apelike woman said, "You seem . . . skimpy."

"So we are, thin and light," Viviane said. "What's the surface gravity of the world where you evolved?"

"Let me see. . . ." The enormous woman paused, obviously

consulting the database of intelligences available to her, no doubt on some electromagnetic link. "It is half again greater than of your world."

"That explains a lot." Viviane hung in the filament-threaded air before the Fungoid Sphere. Redwing saw what she was doing: befriending a fellow apelike alien. Interstellar diplomacy through casual small talk. "Giants like you aren't proportionally taller than us, just squatter."

True, Redwing thought. Elephants didn't look like scaled-up horses. But tigers did look a lot like scaled-up house cats and moved that way.

He found the huge woman ugly and repulsive. Somehow that called up deep hostile currents. But Viviane had sensed that, and rather than obviously warning him off, she chose this path. Have a chat. Between gals.

The woman said in her odd voice, "Recall that I am a re-construction from detailed genetic data, plus a sort of personality transmit."

Redwing said, "From your society, yes. Sent over many years. We heard. What do you call yourselves?

She made a rictus grin that unsettled him. "Why, the People, of course. I am told that all species do so. You call yourselves *humans*, I believe."

"We're from a line of descent we call *apes*, on a star many light-years from here." Viviane nodded, a gesture the huge woman seemed to know, for she echoed it.

"Ah, nearby in galactic terms. We are from several hundreds of your light-years distant from here. We evolved quite recently, as did you—compared to this—" A grand wave at the surrounding vault, inside a living spaceship. "So we have different, anxious energies."

Redwing said, "You're far ahead of it, if you can send grav wave messages."

"Oh, we did that over a hundred thousand years ago. A mere three hundred thousand—in your years, understand—after we defeated and ended competing apelike forms. They were some-what like us, though insufficiently so."

"So you know a lot about the galaxy," Viviane said.

Redwing was enjoying their talk as he slowly, casually, let go of his handgun. It was still tucked into his side pouch, and its butt shaped itself to his hand, making it comfortable and secure. The pistol almost seemed reluctant to feel him go. But he shoved it deeper into the side pouch and now slowly extracted his empty hand. No one would be the wiser about his sudden revulsion at this woman, who had reached far back into some species memory, and nearly died of it.

"Each lifeless planet is different from another in its own way," the woman said. "Yet all planets with our sort of smart life on them will be fundamentally the same. Our form seems uncommon. Those like us—primate, your term, yes?—develop quickly to high intelligence. This makes us perhaps a bit uncautious. Or so other forms believe."

There came from Twisto, who had been silently watching this cusp moment, a tart snort. "Our host"—a darting two-armed gesture toward the Fungoid Sphere—"wishes to move on. Such talk is fine, but not focused. Not directly germane for our eventual goal, the proper regulation of fundamental, dangerous experiments within the grav wave societies. Still, our host wishes haste. The Bowl must be addressed."

Neanderthal. That was it. His throat tightened, and the acid taste rushed into his mouth. It stung his nostrils. His hands clutched. He was feeling some embedded horror that lurked far back in his mind. In the minds of anyone who had evolved beyond the ugly thing before him, he supposed. But strong and true.

Redwing put his hand back in his side pouch and tightened his grip on the gun again. He had to decide whether to use it. And he wanted to, so much. The urge simmered white-hot in him.

THIRTY-EIGHT
THE ROLLING ZOO

A blind man is not afraid of the dark.
—Proverb

There is hopeful symbolism in the fact that flags do not
wave in a vacuum.
—ARTHUR C. CLARKE

A terabyte-per-second flood, Ashley Trust thought. *Easy to drown
in it.*

He was busily amassing the latest data deluge from the Artilects
who surveyed the entire large-scale Cobweb and its planets. Their
drone network and self-running telescopes had been designed long
ago to survey a mere planet, back when Earthside's scopes thought
Glory was a single world. Centuries back, that was the best they
could do. Two planets orbiting close, with the Cobweb bridge to
further confuse the algorithms of those old scopes, had not tipped
off the antique authorities who planned this mission. So now Ashley was witnessing a tera-torrent. The Cobweb alone had many
planet-areas stacked along its axis. How to process it all?

"Figure this out," he concluded his conference with the Astro
Artilect. "I can't. I'm not qualified."

The Astro Artilect pleaded a bit more for his oversight, but he
just broke the connection. Not his problem. Not even remotely his
area. He had gotten into this expedition to elude prosecution for
some hinky exploits, and his doctored documents said he was a
stellar sci/tech guy. But that lay far behind him now. *Done.*

A call came in and he was about to kill that, too—just too damn
much going on!—when he saw it was from that weird new Twisty

creature. Its digital sig said the thing was trying to make contact. Curious, he quick-checked Redwing's codes. Here it was, from some poetry volume the cap'n had read. He spoke aloud the appropriate quote from "Tomlinson" by Kipling: "'Ye are neither spirit nor spirk,' he said; 'ye are neither book nor brute—/ 'Go, get ye back to the flesh again for the sake of Man's repute.'"

A sharp ping set up the call.

A crisp voice said, "I gather you are acting onboard staff head?"

Visual arrived. The creature looked different somehow. "Wait. Are you Twisty?"

"I am the new Twisty, if you like. The previous Twisty has been dispersed, penalty for crimes against your Away Team."

"Huh? What crimes?"

"That version allowed your Away Team to enter into far too dangerous a confrontation. The Methaners had set up a trap under the guise of a mere observation of the Away Team as a candidate external species."

Ashley thumbed in his incoming—swamped with Artilect alerts, as usual—and saw a call from Cliff. "I'm getting the Away Team messages now. They're clear. Any casualties?"

"One, and some physiologicals. They avoided the amateurish ambush. The Methaners have long been a sheltered class. Thus they have lost their elemental skills, I judge."

Ashley felt behind the curve on all this. *Too much going on!* But he kept his voice flat when he said, "I don't know what you imply."

"You are classed as intensively social mammals, the most likely to seek interstellar communication or even travel. Worse, you are a particularly fast-developing form, primates. You enter the world with unfinished nervous systems, and those require play—lots of it—to finish the job of your upbringing. The young human brain expects the child to engage in thousands of hours of play, including thousands of falls, scrapes, conflicts, insults, alliances, betrayals, status competitions, and even within limits acts of social exclusion. This develops your full capacities. The Methaners have few of these skills."

"So they're lousy fighters, too?"

"Though smart in their technical areas, yes. Very useful to us."

"Who's 'us' here?"

"Considering your name for our central origin world is Glory, you might well term us the Glorious."

"Glorians?"

"Please allow us this small jest."

Twisty's voice was better modulated now, though its expression on the low-resolution screen gave no facial signatures. The tone shifted to include a note of sadness. "You perhaps do not know that we Glorious lost thousands of native species. It's the reason we can forgive you humans for doing the same to your own world. An elementary error, common among those adolescent intelligences who overrun their worlds. Some do this so badly they go extinct."

This Twisty sounds far more friendly than the last, Ashley thought. *Somebody's tinkered with the specs.* He was still trying to stitch a vast history together. He carefully said, "I'm not up on all this, but was this about your first contact with the Bowl?"

"But that era followed, after we imported species from the Bowl. As it passed us, we exchanged ecologies."

On his screen flashed views of landscapes rolled into cylinders. They transferred across space in atmospheric envelopes. It looked magical.

"The Folk who appear to be managers, though not rulers of the Bowl, have resumed communication with us. Just now, I hear."

"You slung a black hole at them. Some might take that personally."

"They turned it into an advantage. They know they have what we have lost—many of our ancient species. We have been able to communicate—"

"Already? They've just got the black hole, a few hours ago."

"—and we have negotiated an exchange. Did you wonder how we talked? Electromagnetically, after they sent us a simple message via gravity waves. It is a delightful, old-fashioned way to speak. So easy!"

"Twisty, I think we can move on to other issues. How's that sound?"

"Ah, perhaps." Twisty sounded unsure.

"Look, you're going to need intermediaries with them, after this Battle of the Bowl, right?"

"Perhaps . . ."

"We can do that. For example, you want some of your ancient species back. Maybe some new ones, too?"

"We would have to study—"

"We've got plenty data from the Bowl. We spent years there! Stopped by, on the way getting here."

"I do not quite understand what you mean—"

"We've done your reconnaissance for you already! We have data galore from teams on the ground there. Inventories of animals, plants, plenty of videos and all. You can pick and choose what you want!"

"I suppose so. . . ."

"And when you bring 'em back? You'll need zookeepers, right? We humans already have experience with these Bowl creatures. We know 'em firsthand."

"That is an . . . intriguing . . . possibility. . . ."

Ashley licked his lips. Here he could make a real difference. By the time Redwing got back to the ship, he could put himself at the middle of the big things happening. A chance to move up! Smiling, he began a negotiation.

THIRTY-NINE
THAT OLD MIND/BODY DUALITY

If the human brain were so simple
That we could understand it,
We would be so simple
That we couldn't.
      —EMERSON PUGH

Redwing felt the anger and fear in him mingle. Revulsion, gut-clenching sour acid. Idiot red agony. He hated the big woman-ape thing before them. Something made him want to attack her. Furiously. His trigger finger tightened—

Then the clamp came down on him again.

With a snap. In his field of vision, Viviane froze, halfway through saying something. No movement. No sound. Just—*stop.*

Then a voice. "You need to see yourself more fully."

It was Twisto's flat voice. But Redwing could see Twisto to his left, also frozen in place. The Fungoid Sphere must be doing this. That enormous thing hung in the distance, as big as a building and glistening with moisture. It had somehow *installed* some doorway into his mind. Something to do with the filaments that slowly circled him, glowing in soft amber?

"You need to see all your mind."

Redwing could not move his mouth, but he thought—and heard himself say in a small, echoing voice—"My mind hears you."

"Only your conscious mind. What the Folk of the Bowl term your Overmind. I can expose to you how the Folk see their entire minds. Your Undermind will then tell you why you feel as you do."

"My conscious mind is all I've got."

"True, in a way. But! Your Undermind controls your Overmind, at times such as this. You should know that now, when you most need to."

"My conscious mind is what—a construct?"

"A partial view. The operating theater that proudly thinks it is all there is, on the stage of self."

"Okay . . ." Redwing simmered in anger now. He shot back a retort he had only recently heard, "If the conscious self is an illusion—who is it that's being fooled?"

"The you who talks now."

Then it came.

—from the flood sprung from nothingness came desires urges thoughts forking like summer lightning across the somber vault of himself, so he had no choice but to merge with them, fast and furious came it all. Merging so became a drowsy blur, ideas thoughts memories like arrows colliding in air, snap and bristle as ricochets struck and stuck, "who talks now"—as Viviane sparks to life and launches across the coiling vapor trails toward him, colliding as he thinks, wants the memories had lost the power to hurt, the deaths under his command, then gone as desire for her aches yet again, memories always memories now, most with mingled pain or joy, they fall into place and give back the past—

. . .

Viviane grabbed Redwing and shook him, but his head lolled and he would not come around. "What have you *done*?" she shouted at Twisto.

"He needs to see his deepest."

"Why's he drooling, then?"

"You may hold him but try not to speak."

She wrapped him in her arms and legs, a cocoon against the sobs that racked him now.

. . .

—they came at him onrushing trainwreck images: monstrous, abortive shapes, sweaty and grunting, emerging from the abysmal murk of millennia, things slouching, runt hominids, even

pre-mammalian . . . forms never quite resolving into discrete organisms, spilling over and into one another, he is uncertain where
one ends and another begins, awful: ghastly glistening flesh . . .
tentacles coiling and clasping, stretching and contracting, groans,
lidless slit-eyes eerily waving on slender stalks . . . lumbering
brute fleshy thighs, squamous hides, eerie biting barbed quills,
the sheen of yellow toxins, serrated tails, craggy horns, sallow
fangs, gleaming talons . . . fragrances fungal and poisonous, shambling thick-armed leering, thick brows, sharp yellow teeth, knobs
for knuckles, lumps for knees, sickly iridescences undulating
across pallid, gelatinous underbellies, skin shimmering slick, filmy
scales—

—and the alien woman, blending with all these memories, the
imagined horrors, her thick broad piggish ears, snout nose, all of
huge ugly things—all triggering his disgust, bile rising in his gut—
her awful gaping maw mouth, leering smile, *like that fat woman
at the beach who sat on me, crushing me with gobs of white puckered
flabby, smothering me, can't breathe, she rolls over surprised she's on
me but just cackles and rubs herself all over my body, her secretions
sour choking me—*

· · ·

Twisto said, "Mind the predators."

A flock of angry birds swarmed Viviane. They pecked, shrieked.
She batted them aside. More swooped in. Going for her eyes. She
smacked them hard. A sharp gouge in her back. She cried out. One
caught her tongue in a biting beak.

· · ·

—and there it was, the memory bare—woman on the beach, he so
small . . .

—he has to forget it again—*think of something else—*

—shadows of moving spiders flicker on the surface of a cra-
tered moon, Ashley the ignoramus doesn't know poetry from a cab-
bage, it's a wonder I'm not an old shriveled bag before my centuries
are up, time telescopes, agenbite of inwit drifting down, drifting
drown, the big riverrun beat on, boats against the current, borne

back ceaselessly into the past, where *only the young die good*, drowning maybe in awful deep-down torrent and the sea the sea crimson regret and horror both at once—

Part of him knew these had come lancing up from his Undermind. Something festered there. Now propelled out, calling, dread flowed in the shadowy Undermind. In the theater of self, he could watch the show with a dirty tingle of relish.

• • •

She slapped two squawking birds so hard they flew to pieces. *These are devices*, she thought. Fragments tumbled away.

Twisto ignored the birds, talking to the writhing Redwing. "Your ape Undermind often uses its trickster mode, slipping words and even phrases into your speech, in its keen, eager way. Jokes about Underminds escaping control were a staple of your classic literature and current japes; I have read many. Freudian, whatever that means to you."

• • •

—he fights off the fat-woman memory, his naked fear of her mass crushing his skinny body, smothering him—

The way out of it was to nod, pass by the fetid memory, focus on better thoughts, now he has seen the worst of it, look ahead, get control of his own mind back—

—Redwing flies through gobsmacking sensations but keeps enough of himself to feel hopeful spikes of muted joyful zeal. *Eukaryotic multicellular bilaterians*, words flying by beside awful visions. *God is what mind becomes when it has passed beyond the scale of our comprehension*, something shouts but as he turns to see where he is, the suffocating air narrowing—it congeals. He finds no pivot to spin around, but has the nagging sense of a *felt quality* to it all. Memories surge through him: the rich hues of Tuscany at sunset, the spark of insight, the pangs of gray grief, all scattershot coming at him so hard and fast he can feel each word of a slow voice that must be the Overmind, somehow the words booming with a solemn weight, saying,

silicon
may
not
be
the
proper
medium
for
consciousness
look to carbon
to form
thick long compounds,
for unlike
silicon,
carbon
forms double bonds
with vastly
more complex
chemical
differences
so silicon
gives rise
to a different kind
of consciousness,
not hindering
silicon's
ability
to process
information in
superior
manner.

—and Redwing sees clearly he is just a note in a symphony, has always been, a wheel in hardworking machinery, a node in a giant information processing network, some of his heart valves don't properly close, right chambers are enlarged, so a heart arrhythmia and a fickle vagus nerve that pulls the plug every once in a while, so he falls into darkness where only the Undermind thrives.

• • •

Viviane watched, smarting from the bird attack. "You did that just to stop me from waking up Cap'n Redwing, didn't you?"

Twisto ignored this with a grand four-hand wave and said, "Underminds use that curious primate gait—a continual, controlled toppling upon those hindfeet, move by always catching their fall, *motor memory*, you term it. Unsteady! So, a key clue to your ability to improvise."

"We've evolved that, right?" Viviane waved at the big woman, with a grandiosity that satirized Twisto's—who watched this all patiently, eyes deeply intent. "They, these big apes like us, they have it, too, right? So primates can hop to new ideas far more readily—be more inventive!—than you who have no unconscious at all."

Twisto nodded, gave a ghastly smile. "So, yes, with us and the Folk of the Bowl. To know the Undermind, when we like, is essential to forming a stable, long-lived society. We can mute our underlying stresses. All the ancient intelligent species do so! They and we developed such long ago, before we could even fly to planets."

"So we're too damned primitive for the likes of you?"

Twisto took this with a frown, also distressing and ugly. "An instructive example: You social apes showed on the Bowl your ability to form a quick bond-alliance with the ones you term the Sil. An example—another two-footed species, young and immature and dangerous."

"So the Sil are proto-apes?" Viviane had no idea of, or experience with, the Sil—but what the hell—wing it.

"They were happy until your sort came."

"Happiness isn't everything, y'know."

• • •

—the damn birds are coming at her, he can see that, diving hawking cawing nasty beaks while he is frozen solid, cannot move more than his eyes, and then the birds scream and plunge away, because not every experiment works, does it?—and on he goes, the river-run stream that presents you as the subject, viewing the show a sort of stage where your "mind's eye" fiction walls off the muggy cellar mysteries work their furious industry, "I think this is the wrong fairy tale," Redwing somehow says and he registers the gentle press of his trigger finger, clasping the gun he had put away yet some part of him—he is not just in the screen of consciousness anymore—had grasped it forth anew and now the pistol butt kisses his hand like an old-time succulent lover.

• • •

The twisted thing said, nattering on, "You will in time realize that principle of maximum diversity says that the laws of nature, and the initial conditions at the beginning of time, are such as to make the universe as interesting as possible. As a result, life of all vagrant kinds is possible but not too easy. Maximum diversity often leads to maximum stress. In the end we survive, but only by the skin of our teeth. That is the drama we inhabit."

The twisted one looked back lovingly at the Fungoid Sphere.

• • •

—infinitesimal frozen moments stack up as if waiting to be witnessed before their death, much like people, cloaked in layers of filled silence, his bones a lattice of calcium robs strung by stringy muscles striving, breath whistling from him through his dry pipes, he brings the pistol up—

The greased pig of the world itself slipped away always, and Redwing paused. This was beyond mere grasp, elusive-seductive-enchanting, sucking them all, forward, endlessly forward into moments yet again unsuspected, spiced like a throat irked by raw whiskey, so Redwing says, "I don't like this strange woman, but I like you less."

—the sentence dispatches itself from that always attentive Undermind, all laid out sure as each word fetches forth from his library, Anglish as anguish, instants made eternal by being past, in this sliced moment all can go to smash and scatteration—

—he can forget the fat woman at the beach centuries ago, her repulsive smothering slabs of flesh, her yellow teeth, snout nose, cackling laugh—put it away, yes—

He can inspect his instant intuitions now. Know where they came from. Take a long wheezing breath and focus. Let his reasoning mind consider. Judge. Instruct. Wisdom congeals in him like a damp fog.

This is an ability he now grasped fully. *To know your full mind is to command it.*

But this Fungoid Sphere brought that out, too. And this fake alien of the Twisters, *they* brought it forth, they caused all this pain and hurt to surface in him, to come bursting out as disgust. The damned Twisto that led Beth's team into danger, let people get killed, that will pay for that—

—he pulls the trigger.

—out spits a hard clap, a bright noise into crystalline space.

Twisto accepts the slam momentum by spinning backwards. Its face crumples yet reveals no true pain. For indeed the thing is finally an *it*, a copy at best, of something that was once a creature intact—

Redwing snaps back into real time. He is released. Can move. Brings the pistol back to aim, expecting some reply.

Viviane is there. Frightened now.

And the big ape woman like a Neanderthal but equal to them all, he saw now.

The anger and fear and hate were gone. Now mere memory. The short sharp shot had redeemed his fear and rage.

Somehow. Just from acting.

His mind—yes, his conscious mind—felt crowded, seething with ideas. He'd have to do something about the Diaphanous. The plasma beings must all be related, he realized: they'd ride solar flares to cross between stars. Daphne and Apollo must have found communication easy.

The methane folk: they must have done something beyond terrible. Hiding like this, hunted by . . . what? Whatever they feared must be something as powerful as the grav wave establishment. Something pretty damn ferocious. Colossal arrogance . . .

And why fear humans? It dawned on him that they could have

committed a terraforming offense: tried to reshape a world already occupied by creatures at the level of human civilization.

Redwing felt his mind racing. He could sense the seethe of his Undermind. It was trying on ideas for size, seeing what fits the knowledge residing in his conscious Overmind.

So . . . Try to strip away its oxygen? Let a reducing atmosphere replace that, using volcanoes driven from below by Methaners? Nasty, if physically possible. Plenty buried history here. In the long run, the endlessly curious humans would find out.

Head buzzing with intuitions. The Methaners can't be trusted. Treaties were paper promises. To be sure of them, they'll have to be tested. Soon. Meanwhile—

Redwing tried the link to *SunSeeker*. Some hash, then it went through.

"Captain? Good!" Ashley Trust barked at him. "Sir, I've got a lot to tell you. We've solved some problems, the Glorious and I. We can get the Away Team to the surface of Glory, I'm pretty sure. Glory, not the Cobweb. But there's a price. . . ."

FORTY

ETERNITY'S SUNRISE

He who kisses the joy as it flies
Lives in eternity's sunrise
— WILLIAM BLAKE

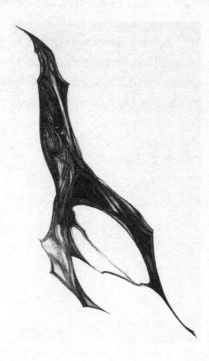

There was a zingo on watch in the cloudy sky. It kept changing shape. That was a new feature. Cliff frowned and speculated: "It's a altering audience that's studying us. The plasma Glorious are shifting watch."

Beth squeezed his shoulder but didn't answer.

The land to either side was an alien forest, plants weird and

lovely; but the land before her was a barren strip hundreds of kilometers across. The year-old colony's fifty-odd citizens were nearly
all gathered here, to watch.

Shadow fell across the sky. Then the clouds roiled and parted.

The cylindrical zoo came streaming down through the air. It
was luminous from the heat roiling into yellow flares at its edges.
It filled the sky with an ominous black darker than night.

Beth could see a cylinder bigger than a rolled-up Hawaii, seas
included, braking into Glory's air. A dark mass. Bright orange plasma
made halos all around it. The enormous dark tube came coasting
down from the stratosphere like an angelic metaphor ringed in fire.

"Beautiful," Cliff said beside her.

"They've got tech we can't even imagine," she said. "How in hell
do they decelerate a whole damn continent-wide roll? No rockets
visible."

"The braking energy, it's gotta be huge."

"Maybe that plasma around it is a lot of Diaphanous."

"Smart piloting, sure." Cliff put his arm around Beth and hugged
her. "Staying warm?"

Beth snuggled up to him, and the little girl in her arms wriggled around to join the warmth. The sky lit with flaring energies.

• • •

As Beth watched from the valley rim, she recalled how she had noticed Cliff first in a crowd of students watching the World Chess
Championship on 3-D. This was a humans-only game, still a draw
for the sort of guys she liked. She noticed that the start player, an
Israeli kid of fourteen—a favorite of her gang—took his full time
before making his board move, while guys and gals around her
called out moves to the screen. "Knight to King!" and "Bishop to
Rook," the usual stuff. Cliff was over to her left and usually took the
full interval to think, softly calling out his suggested move just before the upstart player made his. And the Israeli kid made the move
Cliff had murmured. *Maybe should meet that one*, she had thought.

Now, centuries later, she stood on a ridge watching the impossible. A continent descending. He was her knight and she his queen,
surveying their arriving kingdom, on columns of fire.

Slick-tongued Ashley Trust had used his negotiating craft to offer their Away Team as zookeepers. The Bowl agreed, so the Methaners got from the Bowl an ultimatum: Let my people go. Now here came the countless species that would enrich the planet Glory with life-forms it had lost millennia ago.

Plus, the human keepers of this zoo would get some medical lore and technologies for the new human colony. For Beth this was a fruition. The humans left behind on the Bowl, while *SunSeeker* streaked ahead to the Glory system, had interlaced with the Bowl's own sophisticated biotech minds. They had invented methods that could extend human lifetimes beyond all reckoning.

"I can't hear it," she said.

Cliff nodded. "Sound hasn't reached us yet."

"Whatever magnetics or supertech the Bowl knows how to use, it's got to make noise," Beth said.

"It will. I wonder how the Glorians cleared so much space for this Bowl gift."

"They have tech we haven't seen yet. Methods older than humanity, it seems. We're just the latest addition to a biosphere that's seen plenty harder problems than this." Beth took some comfort in that blunt fact.

"I did a rough calculation about the Cobweb," Cliff said. "Added up the plates they've got stacked along it, between Glory and Honor. It's huge, the living areas."

"Can you compare with the Bowl?" Their child nuzzled against her, and she gave it a squeeze and a warm kiss. *The scent of your very own is heavenly. . . .*

Cliff gazed into the distance for a moment. "Ha! They're comparable areas."

"And both very, very old."

"I guess that's the point. Long-lived civilizations need lots of room."

"For different societies? Spaced far apart."

"So you get new social experiments. Plus new languages, no doubt." Cliff nodded to himself.

"Religions. Philosophies. Genes."

"Haven't we done something like that?" Beth mused. "Spread out through the solar system. Making Mars a place to walk around and play soccer in the open air, in a few more centuries—or so Earthside says."

"All the hollowed-out asteroids and domes on moons can't compare with the Bowl or Cobweb, though." Cliff pointed to the descending zoo. "Hey, look, it's throwing up big clouds."

"It'll take a while to smooth stuff out." Beth paused. "Y'know, I was wondering. We called this system Glory, a destination worth coming all this way for. All without knowing it was two worlds, much less about the Cobweb."

"Yeah." Cliff hugged her. "Got lucky, we did."

"So what shall we call it all now? Or better, call us?"

"I dunno."

"How about, *we're* the Glorious?"

Cliff chuckled.

The huge dark thing was coming down toward a hit point a thousand kilometers away. They could see one side of it now, as the cylinder touched down and began to unwrap. More orange glows and—yes, here came the booms.

The hollow rumble grew to a rolling roar. A sharp crash slapped them hard. They cheered.

• • •

Ashley Trust arose gingerly. In his mind ran a thought: *"His mouth had been used as a latrine by some small creature of the night, and then as its mausoleum."* Oh yes—a classical line from ancient fiction he had been forced to read. Centuries ago, of course. The writer no doubt forgotten, except maybe for that line. Still, that did describe his lonely hangover. So . . . back to work.

He realized then that the role of boredom in human history worked in him, too.

He sat up and his view of the Cobweb overwhelmed him. One whole wall had a steep perspective so he could see all of it. He had come out of cold sleep the same crafty sort who had gone in, but . . . now he was changed. He saw what majesty the expedition had delivered him into.

The idea floated up, a conclusion from somewhere deep within him. *Here's my chance to be a better man. A better primate, that strange alien construction would say.*

The swollen woman Redwing had met, and Ashley had seen on camera, stirred in him an ancient longing. Humans had spent much time tracing out their origins, back hundreds of thousands of years before. This woman stirred primordial emotions because, he now saw, humans had been looking for some other intelligence to . . . talk to. To embrace as different, and yet kin.

The vast legions of the Cobweb and its attendant planar slab-worlds lived in the long moment that was always *now*. Lives were good or bad in the sliced seconds. Some starved and some died, some froze while others warmed, creatures trembled as others rejoiced, and then those moments were gone. They blinked, shook themselves, then moved on into a newer *now*, each in its turn. Their sun strolled across the varying, turning sky, and the new constantly merged with the familiar.

What a strange paradise.

All along it, every creature—beings vaguely like mice, cats, cattle, chickadees, owls, earthworms, fireflies, spiders, goldfish, but also aliens of flesh and plasma, of ice and stone—participates in the return to the elements, the ash, bone, rain, rock, mist, earth, and sky. *They share this unselving with us. The journey we will take together in an oarless boat across the shoreless river.*

So now he had a new chance. He could be a better self. No more playing the sharp angles, the stealthy grab, the small cheats. He had done that and plenty more to get onto *SunSeeker*.

Now he could stop. Make himself anew.

He got out of bed. A bit creaky, sure. He would stop such indulgences. Make a better Ashley. Someone that they could, yes, trust.

•   •   •

It came on and on, an earthquake that never stopped. The land beneath Mayra's feet surged and popped and rattled. That was the sound of the undergirding that held the Bowl together. It was wrenching around under torques that rumbled the entire whirligig contraption.

Mayra had gone to survey the valley below. She stood on murmuring rock. Animals grunted, shrieked, called, chittered. Overhead the unending spike of the jet twisted. It was somehow conveying angular momentum between the Bowl and the parent star that drove all this forward. Mayra said into her dictation software, "I found an old term that captures this, Cap'n Redwing. From some land war. *Shell shock.* Means going into a dazed state from having munitions dropped on you. Here, this is like that, but the ground does the job. Shakes, rattles, and rolls. Sometimes, seems like you should dance."

Indeed it did. She had just gotten out of her building as the Bowl floor flexed. When she felt it, she got up and took several steps toward the entrance. She nearly got out before her leg gave way and she collapsed onto some rubble. She landed next to Marie Diego, her assistant in negotiating with the Bird Folk, especially Bemor. Marie's head was buried in debris, and her feet were twisted into unnatural angles. She put a hand on Marie's chest, but there was no movement. No pulse in the neck. *Damn.*

She peered into the distance for a long time. Watched this world work on. Walked, felt, lingered, sighed, let the impact of the death work through her. She had done this before. Lost people under her command. Learned to grasp it full, feel it heavily. Then relax, let the emotion lodge and wait. It would come again.

Now she had to return to duty.

Best not to report the death, not yet. There might be more.

"Cap'n Redwing, got to say, this job is like walking over splinters, all the time." She paused, studying the sky. She flicked on her optical filters so the blare of raw sunlight ebbed. The jet twirled, helical coils in their slow surge. Neon majesties. The entire system was grinding around. Angular momentum twirled among the vibrant star and Bowl, geared together along the axle of the neon-bright jet.

"Curving to circle the Glorian system will take a year or two, I'd say. The Folk are intrigued, want to stick around, get some galactic gossip, I guess. It's good we'll be nearby, if you want to come back, Cap'n. Can't say there's much motive—that Cobweb looks fabulous. So let me do the diplomacy dance here, and we'll keep popping out babies. I've got a new mate, as I posted before. He wants a dozen kids! I'll restrain him, somehow."

It had been a combo of amused cynicism and bittersweet romance to get back into the mating game with a recently defrosted guy. But promising. A gal's gotta keep herself amused. . . .

She watched dust plumes rise out of the valley. "This ol' Bowl is taking a beating, seems like. But they've piloted through worse than this, the Folk say. Mere classical mechanics, they call it. Mere! Ha! Not much I can do about it, is there? So—signing off for now."

She felt and watched the commotion. The only constant was change, here, now. And indeed, she enjoyed it enormously: the scent of the strange, flavoring the alien wind.

• • •

Viviane stood watching the roaring fireworks beside Redwing, thinking: this solemn man was like a sharp stick, hardened in the fires of his own life. Here came the bass notes of a thundering symphony he had in a tiny way helped write, over centuries. The Bowl-Glory masterpiece.

Redwing had speculated that the methane breathers backed off from Beth's attack because they also saw a need coming. The Bowl had to be neutralized as a threat, and to keep their location secret. So they had agreed, after tedious talks with Ashley Trust using better comm and translation gear. They would let Beth's team stay on Glory. The humans running the incoming zoo could also manage the Methaners' affairs. That would come after the zoo created a terraformed forbidden turf for them, maybe a methane paradise with a view of the stars. That tech could be fashioned soon. It could fit in with the cylinder zoo now booming down from above. *All politics is local*, she had learned somewhere a century or two ago.

Viviane said, "You're not bothered by one of your sayings, 'More cooks, thinner broth'?"

"Not really. Even the Methaners have slowly gotten over their deep fears. Time heals. Beth jolted them out of their traditional patterns, is all. Now they can get to see the sky again without fear."

"This zoo is going to be weird. What was that thing you called a one-eyed, one-horned, flying, purple people eater?"

"Just what it looked like, on that survey we got last week."

Viviane had watched on a big screen as the Bowl's gift unfurled slowly. Losing the thousand-kilometers-per-second speed from its infall, after peeling off the Bowl's rim, had been a pyrotechnic display bigger than planets, grander than stars.

"Purple people eater? Is that some ancient god thing?"

"No, a pop song. Same thing, once a few centuries pass."

"There will be plenty for us to see," Viviane said. "An unsupervised alien landscape. Planting it down on that desert beyond the ridges, over there"—she pointed—"has got to be a huge managing problem."

"Right, but not ours." Redwing pointed to the zingo hovering nearby. "We can complain to management."

"That huge thing we had learned about—will it be in the zoo?"

"Plenty of space beasts can be adapted. The zingoes seem to know how. This culture has been managing their whole biosphere for longer than primates have been around on Earth."

"So how big? Huge? The data feed says some of those things breathe through pipes that a human could fly through."

Redwing chuckled. "Another sport in the making, then."

• • •

The true gift that Fungoid Sphere had given him was this ability to dip into his own unconscious. When needed, of course. Redwing let himself have a quick sliver of it.

• • •

—fiery skies and rumbling storms, and all the power of it coming in good solvent time, dissolving the rude edges of events—tied to them as once he was, with ropes of care—sudden solemn picture of his father, died centuries back, and *the longer Dad is dead, the smarter he gets, while now I, too, am older than whole nations*—a merry oil spreading to lube time itself, slick-sliding he feels the sentence leaving him and in the saying knows it full—"wonder what wunnaful civilizations might lurk up there amid the stars, hunkered down for fear of being plundered for scrap iron or worse?"—their grandeur past pilfered from them, while grav's grave grip here now liberates them into the Cobweb, if they want it—variable grav on demand, just take the elevator—while all this spectacle is a mere mote itself, in the bee swarm of hot stars in the discus galaxy, Redwing unable to see who threw the discus in some cosmological Olympic game, nobody keeping score—*Karma has no shelf life at all around here*—

—and so it went, when he wanted it—his Undermind mulls matters over, builds a story to ship upstairs, delivers—

• • •

An incoming signal had jerked him out of his inner stream.

He licked away his drool and listened.

"You asked who's in those incoming rogue ships? Just behind the cylindrical zoo? Several species—but also some of the Ice Minds. They want to talk to the Glorious historians. There are even some of those Stone Minds Beth ran across. Same interests—long-term thinking."

From Ashley. Irritating, yes. Useful, too. As Ashley was.

Redwing sighed, sucked in bright air. Back he came from the riverrun of life, gotta be cap'n again—

He made himself relax and enjoy the confections of radiant light streaming through the sky. Flickering halos hovered around the steadily growing zoo rectangle as it fell. A brassy glow pulsed with shimmery waves, somehow braking it. He could see a purple rain falling like strips of rectangular confetti and could not imagine what it was. *Here's tech beyond description. . . .*

He recalled glancing through the latest laser signals from Earthside. At a great remove, it becomes obvious that history is just organized gossip. Back there, people still followed video adventures whose heroes battle ogres, dodge dragons, admire unicorns, and consult with elves while seeking their elusive goals. *How about giving a glance at what we found here?*

More news, too, even more predictable. He had never fathomed why people made idols of those who were able to convincingly pretend to be other people—actors, politicians, and the rest. The sort who had to be robo-sewn into their party duds by automated servants.

Viviane said, "Incoming call."

"Kill it." He didn't want any interruptions. He had just now persuaded Bemor Prime to stay with this colony. Not an easy discussion. He had gotten the original creature, Bemor itself, to come into a message exchange with Bemor Prime and the wily Ashley. It turned out that a cultural commandment of the Folk was, the copy has to obey the original. Good! Bemor Prime didn't know it, but the big lug would end up running the Bowl embassy here. Hire locally!

There were myriad details. Should he import a couple of finger snakes to this new Bowl colony? Ashley said they had some training as veterinarians for aliens. Hard to know. Nobody but Artilects to help him figure it out, too.

It had taken a long while, talking to the Twisted forms, to get their history straight. The Glorious, it turned out, were as emotional, fevered in logic, and nonlinear in speech, as humans were. The ancient Glory–Bowl hatred came because Glory lost many of its original species. Ironically, that was much as humanity had done on Earth, just more so. The lost species that once inhabited Glory and Honor numbered hundreds of thousands. Just like Earth. But the Bowl took immigrants: an Ark, many millennia ago.

He pressed Viviane to him as the zoo spread itself across the sky, lowering on magnetic hinges. Furious energies lit the landscape as it settled into place. Here was the new preserve. Beth and Cliff, nearby, cheered and kissed.

Viviane kissed him, too. Her patented combination of cheek and chic, pose and poise, on view. "Lover, how did you get so old?"

"Two ways. Gradually and then suddenly."

"Sounds gloomy."

Redwing shrugged. "I suppose it is. Age brings wisdom? Maybe just caution. The Folk and the Glorians alike have gotten far beyond our Paleolithic hunter-gatherer genes. They have engineered away our shortsighted habits of mind—assuming they had such. That's why they've survived to get old, big, and stable."

"So how do we copy that?"

"Slow work. Run the Glory zoo, learn, earn, evolve."

"A human colony in the middle of . . . such strangeness."

"Right. We're useful, we primitives. The Increate sent along that big colorful zingo over there to nudge us. See? They want us, vital primates, to use our inscrutable ways in talking with that big primate woman."

"She seems friendly enough. Came, like us, from a partly tree-dwelling life that had free use of its forelimbs, could walk upright. Sounds simple!"

Redwing looked skeptical. "But the Glorians came from something different. They're not saying what—not yet."

Viviane asked, "How did they install the basic mind-set of a species hundreds of light-years away?"

"They can transmit such stuff. Make bodies. Make minds. Don't ask. They won't tell. So the zingo, speaking for its Increate selves, gives weight to words they rang into my head just now. 'To learn which questions are unanswerable, and *not to answer them:* this skill is most needful in times of stress and darkness.' Maybe that's wisdom."

She kissed him and that seemed wise, too.

AFTERWORD

The mind, that ocean where each kind
Does straight its own resemblance find,
Yet it creates, transcending these,
For other worlds, and other seas.
　　　　　　—ANDREW MARVELL, "The Garden"

A dialogue has been going on for centuries now. It may have started with Dante's *Divine Comedy*, and continued with *Star Maker* by Olaf Stapledon. Freeman Dyson, inspired by Stapledon, calculated limits on a structure's size in outer space, set by the strength of materials. Niven's *Ringworld* was part of these explorations, and Bob Shaw's *Orbitsville*. It's a conversation about advanced societies building outrageously big habitats, using plausible science. Such were called Big Dumb Objects by Peter Nicholls as a joke in 1993. He quoted British writer Roz Kaveney in *The Encyclopedia of Science Fiction*. There is now a Wikipedia entry on the many such fictions. The Bowl of Heaven trilogy is a part of that, though we prefer to call the Bowl and the Glorian double planet Big Smart Objects, since they must be continuously managed to be stable. Our trilogy is undoubtedly not the last word. As a reader said, we aimed for "Amazing vistas, shocks, sensawunda." Just so!

A great problem with world creation is when it becomes an end in itself. When this happens, it can become a rather neurotic attempt to contain a world and to nail down a world totally—which is, of course, impossible. You end up with clunky fiction, walking your characters through all the places you've created, simply because you have created them. This is akin to the age-old heritage of the infodump—*By God, I suffered through all this research and now it's your turn.* It's best not to fill in everything on a map. It's meaningless. Leave things unknown—because there's so damn much of it.

The best reason to do such work is simple: It's fun! We take each other's notions and send them zipping off on different vectors. We worked best when we could sit, talk, think, build in stacks the ideas that started with the first idea: a vast bowl built to capture and refocus a star's own radiation. Why? To manage the star. Why? So the whole system, Bowl plus star, can move in cohort . . . to explore the galaxy. How? The sunlight reflected back on the star fires off a jet, which pushes the star . . . and the Bowl of Heaven follows like a tethered animal.

Tricky, yes—and managed by beings who would think of this and make it happen. That got us going, for sure. We started on *Bowl of Heaven* and realized about half a year later we couldn't do the story in a single volume. So we wrote *Bowl of Heaven* and then *Shipstar* to work out the whole Bowl society. But we hadn't gotten to the Bowl's destination, which our human characters were headed for, too. So to follow the theme of Big Smart Objects, we followed the logic and designed a wholly new system. The Glorian double planet echoes the flyby of Pluto and Charon that is indeed a natural, mutually tide-locked system (though we had the idea before that). If our system has one such, there must be more among the stars.

At each stage, we try out ideas on each other, write scenes, bounce them between us in the ping-pong of creation. Writing is a solitary craft, but!—uniquely, science fiction encourages collaboration, echoing its core culture: science itself, in which single-author papers are a decided minority. So our novels come from this ping-pong, making writing fun for and of itself. Larry likes doing aliens and their odd thoughts, as in his Known Space stories. Gregory likes the designer aspects—how does the Bowl work?

And this new place, Glory? We had only vaguely imagined it when we started on the first novel. More mega-engineering! Plus room for ingenious physics. We don't think any other kind of writing can do this. Which means SF is more fun than, say, mysteries, for the writer(s)—and that plural is key.

In the end, we realized that these novels are a way to think about what truly long-lived societies may be like. We humans have a built-in inclination to go over the horizon, expand, occupy. No other species has occupied every continent and co-opted so much of its energy and land. So might alien societies. To get more living room, they might build Big Smart Objects and then move on to other interesting pursuits. The Bowl goes touring the galaxy. The Glorian system ponders deep issues like the stability of the universe itself, and how to avoid disasters that come from mega-engineering hubris. Could this be how the long-lived civilizations think, that the search for extraterrestrial intelligence might find? If so, it's worth thinking now about how to talk to them.

You might want to pursue some of our ideas further:

DOUBLE PLANETS

These have a Wikipedia entry, too: https://en.wikipedia.org/wiki/Double_planet.

How common might they be? Well, we have Pluto and Charon, so maybe such worlds in a star's habitable zone are common. Imagine evolving intelligence with such a tempting bauble in your sky.

Such a notion occurred in the early 1960s in the novel by Brian W. Aldiss, *Hothouse* (London: Faber & Faber, 1962). A line from it: "The multitudinous strands of cable floated across the gap between them, uniting the worlds. Back and forth the traversers could shuttle at will, vegetable astronauts huge and insensible, with Earth and Luna both enmeshed in their indifferent net."

SMART DINOSAURS

The emerging new family tree of dinosaurs makes an interesting case about dino intelligence:

"A new hypothesis of dinosaur relationships and early dinosaur evolution" by Matthew G. Baron, David B. Norman, and Paul M. Barrett, published in *Nature* 543 (March 23, 2017). It says in part, "The results of this study challenge more than a century of dogma and recover an unexpected tree topology that necessitates fundamental reassessment of early dinosaur evolution."

More than one thousand species have already been identified, most of them dating from between two hundred million and sixty-six million years ago. Dinosaurs became the dominant terrestrial species after the first date, and perished, all save the lineage leading to birds, at the second. The authors comment, "In the very harsh climates of the late Triassic, being a generalist is probably a clever strategy. The ability to run fast and eat anything and grasp with the hands is what gave dinosaurs their advantage."

These advantages also aided humans, and the Folk of the Bowl. A critical stage in human evolution was walking upright, which freed the hands for grasping tools and weapons. "The parallels with human evolution are very noticeable and make you wonder what they could have achieved," the scientists said. "Toward the end, certain groups like the velociraptors were starting to get intelligent."

The new tree implies that dinosaurs emerged some 247 million years ago, a little earlier than previous estimates, and that their origin may not have been in South America, where several very early dinosaurs have been found. This fits with the background we used in *Bowl of Heaven*. It's worth noting that all traces of a dinosaur civilization would have been ground up by tectonic plate movement. We don't actually propose that the Bowl was built by dinosaurs, but it is a fun idea, and brings forth our underlying theme of how long-lasting societies might evolve to build big structures.

Vacuum decay

This advanced idea from quantum cosmology first came to Benford through a paper by his old friend Sidney Coleman, of Harvard. Sidney's papers were not like anyone else's—clear, deceptively simple, yet profound. One of his classic quotes, from that paper with de Luccia on "Gravitational Effects on and of Vacuum Decay" (*Physical Review D*, June 1980) is:

> The possibility that we are living in a false vacuum has never been a cheering one to contemplate. Vacuum decay is the ultimate ecological catastrophe; in the new vacuum

there are new constants of nature; after vacuum decay, not only is life as we know it impossible, so is chemistry as we know it. However, one could always draw stoic comfort from the possibility that perhaps in the course of time the new vacuum would sustain, if not life as we know it, at least some structures capable of knowing joy. This possibility has now been eliminated.

Plenty of people aspire to be profound and playful at the same time; Sidney could pull it off, and had the technical chops to back it up. It's plausible that advanced societies might study such issues, at mortal danger to the entire universe. Certainly worth worrying about!

Once a shift to a lower energy state occurs, a bubble will expand throughout at the speed of light, making the universe as it was in the beginning: reheating, creating a hot plasma of elementary particles. Our beginning plasma expanded, cooled, and emitted the cosmic background radiation. Then gravity made the plasma clump, and darkness was upon the face of the deep, whatever that means. All that came before is gone. For further ideas see https://physics.aps.org/articles/v8/108.

ACKNOWLEDGMENTS

Two artists have helped us envision the gigantic structures and events of this three-novel sequence, most deeply the extraordinary astronomical artist Don Davis. He was an invaluable resource. Brenda Cox Giguere made all the matchless zingo illustrations in fine line drawings. We used our own photos of things that we took to look unearthly.

To Al Jackson for extensive work on gravitational radiation from black holes—including a coauthored paper with Benford: "A Gravitational Wave Transmitter," https://arxiv.org/abs/1806.02334.

We consulted earlier parallel ideas to the Cobweb: Stephen Baxter's story "Goose Summer" and "The Trellis" by Larry Niven and Brenda Cooper, plus Robert L. Forward's novel *Rocheworld*. The Cobweb is a built lifezone, though, not just a connector.

Shell world advice we got from Ken Roy and Robert Kennedy, who with David E. Fields published the original paper, "Shell Worlds" in *Acta Astronautica* 82. Others who advised them on this are David Bowman, B. Derk Bruins, Dwayne A. Day, H. Keith Henson, Eric Hughes, Les Johnson, Michael R. Johnson, Greg Matloff, Amarak Panya, John Wharton, Martha Knowles, and David Woolsey. Our shell worlds differ somewhat in physics, of course, for Glory is a more besieged world, as one of a pair of exotic planets.

Our wise agent, Eleanor Wood, deserves special thanks, as does Bob Gleason, who stepped in to edit the book after its contracting editor, David Hartwell, tragically died.

Thanks also to those who made comments on the manuscript: Dave Truesdale, Rob Jackson, Brenda Cox Giguere, James Benford, and our concluding editor, Robert Davis. We are grateful for all their help.

This has been a decade-long project, and much fun. We hope our readers enjoy it, too.

On an autobiographical note, GB's early choice of smart birds as aliens, the Folk, may well stem from his experience while growing up in southern Alabama, south of Fairhope, on his grandparents' farm beside Fish River. The picture below shows him with twin brother, Jim, about age five, confronting the chickens they started feeding with ground dry corn kernels. Chickens thronged the corn-throwers as soon as the boys began grinding the corn through the kernel stripper. Force was essential to avoid getting hit by birds flying to get to the grub first. Early experience can shape fiction! Of course, we didn't know then that birds came from the dinosaurs.